Superstars Trilogy
Book Two
Vasallus

HEATHER,
THANK YOU
FOR ALL YOUR
SUPPORT!
ENJOY!

Errol Barr

DEDICATION

To Lyric, my beautiful granddaughter, whose distance keeps
apart for far too long, is always in my heart and thoughts.

ACKNOWLEDGMENTS

My editor, Barb Green of Articulate Professional Writers is incredible. Anyone who considers themselves a writer can only do so if they have someone as good as Barb working with them.

As in Book One, Evil Rises, Allie Brown's proofreading and insight on Vasallus was amazing.

Josh Daignault, a talented graphic artist whose vision created the book cover for Vasallus.

My biggest supporter, of course, is Kellie. Her love, support and commitment is beautiful and as a writer and a man, I am truly blessed.

Chapter 1

Patrick Benning, now fifteen years old, looked much older than that. A lot of that could be attributed to how mature he was and how he carried himself amongst his classmates. He exuded self-confidence; it swirled around him like a jet stream. He had become the most popular kid in his school. His physical development was way beyond the other kids of his age, and instead of looking like he should be in grade ten with a fuzzy chin, bad hair and pimples, Patrick was tall, muscular and chiseled, with lots of body hair. He grew his hair long to his shoulders; his dark wavy curls had naturally lighter strands running through them, giving him Hollywood good looks. His musical talents on the drums and bass guitar were well known among the other students, further fuelling his popularity. Guys from all grades wanted to hang-out with Patrick, or be seen with him. The fortunate ones in his inner circle got chicks just because they were friends with him. The only ones who didn't like him were the jocks. They despised him. He could care less, because he hated sports and he hated jocks.

The girls in his grade knew they never stood a chance to date him, so instead, they idolized him. They gathered in groups in the hallways, gymnasium or outside on the school grounds to stare and ogle him. The more developed grade eleven and grade twelve girls fought for Patrick's attention like a pack of wolves in heat. Some of the girls pushed the envelope of the school's dress code, revealing enough cleavage to get them hauled into the Vice Principal's office to be scolded or reprimanded. They didn't care; they just wanted Patrick to notice them. He did notice them. He noticed all of them. He didn't want them; even though he knew he could screw anyone of them in the blink of an eye. In his mind, they were all just pathetic sluts trying to be the one who could brag that she slept with the famous Patrick Benning. Some of them even tried to spread lies that they had slept with him, but they were quickly dismissed by their peers as wishful thinkers. He was no angel, however, and did, on occasion, succumb to his sexual urges. He only chose the obvious virgins because he knew that they would be so ashamed about what they had done; that they wouldn't walk around the school bragging about it afterwards. There was one girl who caught his attention. She was a senior, blonde and beautiful with large breasts and a killer ass. She was also smart and popular, and she paid absolutely no attention to him. He approached her in the hallway, outside of her locker, one day to engage in small talk. He hoped to finish the conversation with a trip to the school supply room for sex. She told him to: "go jerk off in the boy's bathroom with all of the other nerds".

The storage room was closed at 3:30 p.m., but it was never locked during the night. The large room that housed the school's paper supplies, including forms, textbooks, teaching aides and other miscellaneous stuff, was the perfect place to fornicate. The only problem with it was that it was so popular that many of the other students used it to have sex. Each of them ran the risk of being discovered by other students coming in to use the room. Patrick didn't care about being discovered, but the chicks were always paranoid about it. That and the fear of losing their virginity made them almost want to change their minds at the last second, especially when they'd seen how physically endowed he was. The combination of fear, Patrick's charm and his magnificent body always broke them eventually.

Cynthia Saunders, the blonde, was a different story all together. She was the only girl in Arcadia High School who didn't wilt when he was nearby. This intrigued Patrick immensely and he wanted her, badly. The fact that she was so damned hot only added to his desire to take her to the storage room. It was Friday afternoon and the school was emptying early as it was game day. The school football team, the Apaches, had a home game against their arch rivals, The Pasadena Bulldogs. The school always let the students out at 2:00 p.m. on game days, so that the school could prepare for the onslaught of students, parents, family and fans from both schools that would descend on the school playing field for the 6:00 p.m. start time. The Apaches were in first place and looking to stay there.

When the horn sounded at 2:00 p.m., Patrick made a beeline from his science class to catch Cynthia by her locker before she disappeared into the sea of students exiting the school. Brushing off the girls along the stairs calling out to him, he sped past them in search of the hot Cynthia Saunders. He saw her in front of her locker, loading books into her backpack. Pushing through the students trying to make their way out of the school, he felt like a salmon swimming upstream during spawning season. He reached Cynthia just as she was snapping the lock closed on her locker. Patrick leaned in.

"Hey Cynthia, have you got a minute?"

Looking disdainfully at Patrick as if he was her annoying little brother, she said, "What do you want Benning? Getting bored of those sluts standing in line for you, so you need a bigger challenge? Excuse me, but my boyfriend is waiting for me in the parking lot."

He felt his face burn slightly at her brush-off. "Its okay", he thought, "he expected this". He blocked her path as he replied to her nasty rebuttal, "Just wanted to see if you needed a ride to the game tonight. I was thinking of going and thought if you were planning on going, maybe we could hook up and go together."

Pushing past him, she joined the exodus, forcing Patrick to keep up. She stopped in the middle of the fleeing students to look him in the eye and, with a stern voice, hissed at him, "The only thing worse in my mind than a girl whoring herself to the likes of you is a male slut like you trying to whore themselves to someone like me. Now get lost Benning, I'm not interested. Believe it or not, my boyfriend is bigger than you and will kick the shit right out of you if I tell him you were coming on to me."

"Holy shit" he thought, "she is one nasty little bitch". He could feel his crotch hardening, warming from the anticipation. As he quickly glanced behind him, he noticed the flow of students was thinning. Most of the teachers would have bolted just as fast. In a few minutes, they would be alone in the hallway. The door to the storage room was the second last one to the left, before the main exit doors. He needed to slow her down for another minute, then, when the hallway was completely clear, he could drag her into the storage room.

He reached out and held Cynthia by the elbow to slow her down. The look in her eye was pure venom. "She really does hate me," he thought. "Fuck her; he was going to do her," her attitude just added to the fun. "Hey Cindy, come on, I just want to talk. Why are you tripping so badly?"

When she spoke it was a controlled shout, "Listen dickwad, my name is Cynthia. Now let go of me before I yell out for school security or worse, my boyfriend."

Turning to keep up with the fleeing blonde bomber, Patrick looked over his shoulder one last time to make sure that there was no one left in the hallway. There wasn't, the school had turned into a ghost town as fast as if a fire alarm had been pulled and a real fire was raging. Waiting out in the parking lot was her pussy boyfriend, trying to look cool driving his Daddy's car, he thought. As she reached out to push through the double doors, he made his move.

He reached around her shoulder, almost clothes-lining her to the ground before clamping onto her neck. Then, he shoved her, hard, against the door to the storage room, and he could hear the hardware on the door almost snap. The look on her face had changed from 'go fuck yourself' to one of pure fear, "Please Patrick leave me alone. I'm s-s-sorry for talking that way to you. Please."

Reaching behind her, he grabbed the door handle to the storage room with his right hand while his left hand was squeezing her neck. Throwing the door open, he pushed Cynthia inside so hard that she flew against the storage desk, then catapulted over top of it and onto the floor, crashing head first into the wall. He snapped the lock on the door in place as he turned towards the desk and Cynthia, crumpled on the floor.

****

Cynthia was stunned and her head was throbbing from the impact. She looked up to see Patrick leap over the desk and land beside her, his face wild with anticipation. His eyes? They were burning a bright crimson red! Her throat felt so tiny, her tongue so thick from the fear that she couldn't even muster a scream. His eyes looked monstrous. Her fear went from thinking he would sexually assault her to realizing that he would likely be doing grave harm to her. Her fear was much worse. He would kill her. "Oh my God, what is happening to me?" a tiny voice inside her cried.

****

The dark power surged through Patrick's brain. He knew it was now in full control of his mind. Reaching down to the recoiling and sobbing Cynthia Saunders, he picked her up by her throat and slammed her down onto her back on the desk. The phone and a pile of papers stacked on the desk went flying. Taking his hand off of her throat, he used both of his hands to grab the top of her buttoned blouse, tearing it away like tissue paper. Her exposed breasts were enormous. Her fear was so palpable that it caused her nipples to rise, as if she was aroused. Her dark mascara was smudged and wet around her fear-widened eyes.

He reached down and held her mountainous breasts in his hands for a brief second, enjoying the softness and enormity but then, he heard a bang on the door. What the fuck? He looked down at her, letting his red glowing eyes silence her, while he stood perfectly still, waiting for the locked door to open. It never did. Probably some student walking by knowing some couple is screwing, so thought he might scare them. Nice try.

He leaned down over top of Cynthia and licked her neck, rolling his tongue all over her, enjoying her scent on his tongue. Her body was almost vibrating with fear, and soft sobs were escaping from her throat. Suddenly, there was a noise and then the door to the storage room burst open, scaring the shit out of him. Some jock stood at the entrance to the storage room. On his face was a look of shock that quickly turned to pure rage. Right behind him was the school Vice Principal, Mr.

Barlow, a set of keys dangling from his hand. Patrick knew the jock would rush him in another split second. He leaned down to Cynthia before the jock jumped him and said, "You say anything other than this was consensual, that you came onto me, and I will kill you."

The charging jock plowed into him, his shoulder hitting him square in the side of the rib cage and causing the air in his lungs to escape in a rush. As he bounced off of the storage room wall, he instinctively rolled to his right, gasping to get some air into his lungs. He braced for the next assault from the jock. He was big, muscular and pissed. He knew he could snap his neck in a heartbeat and silence the prick for good, but he needed to get out of this situation, so he took the blows that would come. They didn't come as he looked up to see Mr. Barlow pin the jock against the wall, yelling at him to calm down. Then he heard Cynthia cry out, "Jeremy stop! It's not his fault! It was mine. I brought him in here. I wanted him Jeremy. I am so sorry! I'm sorry!"

Patrick stood up and watched the drama unfold. It was sweet to watch Jeremy grapple with the realization that his girlfriend had just cheated on him. He looked at the jock and smiled from ear to ear and said, "Come on, Jeremy, don't be so selfish. Those big tits need to be shared. It's just not right you having them all to yourself and your former girlfriend obviously agrees."

Then Mr. Barlow yelled out, "Okay that is enough. Benning, you and Jeremy are coming with me to my office right now." Looking at Cynthia like she was a total slut, he continued, "You get yourself together and get the hell home. What is it with you girls?"

Back in the office, he and Jeremy were put into separate rooms while they waited for Mr. Barlow to come in and rag on them some more. The school was deserted except for them. He flirted with the idea of killing the two of them right then, but he fought back the urges. He had caught a break with hot little Cynthia's fine acting, so there was no need to turn his own school into a murder investigation. He could hear Mr. Barlow's muffled voice coming through the wall as he chewed out Jeremy, telling him to stay away from the game tonight and to stay away from Cynthia, otherwise, he would suspend him. "Poor kid" thought Patrick, "getting himself into a situation he didn't deserve. Nah scratch that, I hate jocks and they deserve everything they get," he laughed to himself.

The door opened and Mr. Barlow walked in, closing the door behind him. He walked around his desk and sat staring at Patrick for a moment before he spoke, "I called your mother. She is on her way here now to take you home. You ar…" his words were cutoff as Patrick interrupted.

"You called my mother? Why the fuck would you do that? That stupid bitch came onto me like a whore desperate for a trick. My mother has been through enough in her life. She doesn't need this."

Cutting him off, the Vice Principal's eyes burrowed into his before he spoke, "Shut the hell up Benning. You assaulted that girl and were minutes away from raping her. I don't know what you threatened her with, but that story she told of her coming onto you is bullshit. Cynthia Saunders wouldn't be caught dead with the likes of you. You're fucking lucky this time. Your mother is coming down to get you because I am suspending you from school for two weeks. I don't want to see your face around this school for the next two weeks. Do you hear me? In two weeks, you will come back into this office and convince me you will never do anything like this again before I reinstate you. Do I make myself clear?"

He could hear his mother ring the desk bell in reception while he stared back at Mr. Barlow. The rage was boiling inside of him. He desperately wanted to kill this man before his mother walked in. It would have to wait. He would kill him alright, just not now. All he could think of to say was, "Yes sir."

****

Watching Chelsea Benning escort her son out of his office and out of the school, he couldn't shake the cold fear he felt while sitting alone in his office with Benning. That kid was dangerous, very dangerous. He could sense it with every nerve in his body. He could feel that Patrick was seconds away from leaping over his desk to wrap his hands around his neck. But that's not what scared him the most. What sent chills down his spine were those eyes of his. They were flashing a bright crimson red just before his mother opened the door. He wasn't one hundred percent sure that was exactly what he had seen. It was just for a split second, but it freaked him out. He would watch Benning like a hawk when he returned in two weeks. She was a strong woman, that Chelsea Benning. She had to be after what she had been through with the death of her detective husband and this crazy and wild son of hers. One little screw-up by that kid and he would make sure he was done in this school for good.

****

On the way home they were both silent as the late afternoon traffic of a Friday was starting to build. Their home was only ten minutes away but when traffic was congested, they might as well have lived in another county. Chelsea broke the silence, wanting to hear Patrick's side before she tore into him. "Want to tell me what happened?"

Staring straight ahead into the windshield, his long wavy

15

locks of hair sticking out from his hoodie pulled over his head, he mumbled, "I don't want to talk about it, Mom."

She looked over at her son, then reached over and pulled the hoodie down off his head and in a stern voice said, "Oh yes you will. You have some explaining to do. According to Mr. Barlow, if that Saunders girl had told the truth, you would be sitting in a jail cell right now. What the hell were you thinking Patrick?"

She watched as Patrick turned his head towards her, his eyes stitched in sadness when he spoke, "Mom, you have no idea what goes on at that school. The girls go crazy over me all of the time. They follow me everywhere, trying to get in my pants. Sorry, mom, but it's the truth. Cynthia Saunders has been after me for weeks, relentless. When school was let out at two o'clock I was making my way out of the school and when I passed by the storage room, Cynthia grabbed my arm and pulled me into the room and just started kissing me and groping me. She was crazy. Next thing I know she rips open her blouse, exposing herself and pulls me down on top of her on the desk. It was insane. Then the door burst open and her jealous boyfriend comes after me and assaults me. I am telling you the truth, Mom. The girls in that school won't leave me alone. I don't want to go back there Mom. I won't go back there. This will happen again, I know it."

The truth was clear now to Chelsea. She believed her son. She knew he was very popular in school. His incredible good looks and talent had made him a target, she just didn't realize to what extent. Now she knew. She would get Patrick out of that school and into a better one. That pathetic Barlow was targeting Patrick, because even he was jealous of him. It was sickening. Maybe she should consider bringing charges against the Saunders girl for sexual assault, sue the school for its inability to properly provide security and safety to its students, and in particular her son. That would teach them.

She reached over with her hand, tussled her son's thick wavy hair and said, "How about you and I swing over to the Showenstein's, and grab Seb for a sleep over? You guys can go pick out a few Xbox games at the video store and I will pop some popcorn. What do you say?"

His signature smile stretching across his face, he looked at his mother and said, "You are the best Mom anyone could ever have. I love you."

Chapter 2

It had been three years since the horrific carnage that took place at the home of Kathy and Richard Ovens. The brutal slaughter of the Ovens by the demonic beast, disguised as Robert Best, also left Ann Lockwood clinging to life. It seemed like a lifetime ago to her now. Long healed from the vicious blows she received from the attack, Ann swore an oath to herself that she would end this evilness that had stalked her family the past fifteen years. Satan had murdered her husband, mother, her friends, and raped her, resulting in the birth of Michael, her son, the son she shared with the devil.

During the past three years, she had devoted her entire life to the rising musical career of her son Michael and to his well being. Even though she knew Michael was the spawn of Satan, she loved him fiercely. He was still her flesh and blood and she would protect him, no matter what, including her own life. There was a plan for him and for her, she knew, and she clung to the hope that her beloved God would intervene and save the soul of her son. She didn't care if she died soon but she wanted to live long enough to see God's grace work a miracle on Michael and save him. She would spend hours immersing herself in the teachings of the Lord written in the Bible. Ann believed with all her heart that it was Him who saved her that terrible night at the Ovens, and it was Him that spoke to her as she lay dying on the floor. She believed God wanted her to rise up, be courageous and fight the evil that stalked her and her son. She wanted God's armor wrapped around her, no, she needed God's armor, His protection, from the beast that stalked her every move and thought.

Ann had not encountered Best or the beast since that fateful night at the Ovens' three years ago. She would give him no reason to return to finish her off once and for all. Best needed her to keep Michael safe and continue growing his incredible talent. Michael was a musical genius, a prodigy, so incredibly talented; it was hard for her not to think that Michael's talent could not have come from the devil himself. She had no idea why, but she knew that music was the key. Why would Satan father a child with her that would grow to create beautiful music that would inspire thousands of people? Ann also suspected that once Michael was old enough, she would no longer be needed in the beast's plans and she would surely die. When would that be? When Michael turned sixteen next year, or seventeen, or maybe eighteen? It didn't matter, because she was going to die; she was sure of it. She needed to save Michael from the darkness that lived within him. She needed to set his soul free. She would do everything she could till the monster came for her.

Ann needed help; she could not do this alone. She was confident that God was with her, guiding her, beside her, but she needed to make a plan. A plan that would disguise her movements, shield her intent from the beast, and keep him confused. She knew what to do, and she had known for awhile now. She had a plan. She just hoped that she would survive long enough to see it through.

****

Father Thomas O'Sullivan was now seventy-three years old, but physically, he was hanging in there. He had his health, and he thanked God every day for it. He was busy meeting with the contractor in charge of the renovation and addition to his beloved parish, St. Colmcille's Parish Church in Swords County, Ireland. When he was thirty-one, Thomas had left his previous posting to come to St. Colmcille's. He had been under the tutelage of Father O'Malley at the Church of the Immaculate Conception & St. Patrick in the Diocese of Cork and Ross. This was in the south part of Ireland, in the township of Bandon.

St. Colmcille's was long overdue for some much needed upkeep repairs to the entire building, including running new electrical wiring throughout, upgrading the plumbing, replacing old cabinets in the kitchen and to the delight of all the parishioners of St. Colmcille's, brand new comfy pews. Gone were the original oak benches that tested the backs of young and old. The new pews would include forgiving contoured benches and cushioned backs. Thomas would joke with the congregation that the new benches were to prepare them for his new policy of longer sermons, laced with long excerpts from scripture. However, the biggest change was the addition of a new, 2,000 sq. ft. wing being built onto the south side of the parish. This would house Thomas's dream of three children's activity centers. Currently, the preschooler's packed into the small basement of the parish, where church volunteers tried in vain to keep them occupied in the cramped space. The new addition would include three rooms: one for the preschoolers, another for middle grade children and finally, a teen/young adult room. Programs and activities could be implemented to enrich their lives as never before and more importantly, to attract or retain more young families to St. Colmcille's.

Church leaders wanted St. Colmcille's demolished and a new, bigger, more modern facility built, but Thomas fought hard to keep St. Colmcille's intact, and worked his contacts within the church hierarchy to prevent the demolition. The church leaders were not happy with the decision but as construction was coming to an end and the new activity rooms were almost complete, they agreed that saving St. Colmcille's was the right decision. The generations that had passed through this church, Thomas felt, would be lost if a new building was built and the savings to the church through the preservation were significant, so the decision was made to renovate.

While he was engaged in talks with the contractor just beyond the front steps of the church entrance, Thomas was interrupted by the church administrator informing him of an important phone call from London. Looking up at the doorway, he nodded to Mrs. Beckeridge that he would be right up. Informing the construction supervisor that he would catch up with him later to continue their discussion, Thomas bounded into the church to take the call. Who would be calling him from London? Father Beckstead, maybe? They weren't scheduled for a SOSL meeting for another six weeks. Taking the call in his office, he spoke into the receiver, his voice thick in Irish brogue, old-school in tone compared to the confident and airy tones of the young Irish, "Hello, this is Father Thomas O'Sullivan, how may I help you?"

A male voice he did not recognize spoke, "Father O'Sullivan, my name is Peter Highfield. I am the personal assistant to Mrs. Ann Lockwood, from London. I hope I am not bothering you Father, but have you got a minute to talk?"

Thomas searched his memory for the name of Ann Lockwood. He knew the name, but couldn't pin it down exactly, so he replied, "Yes, go ahead Mr. Highfield. I do not recognize the name, but what can an old priest from Ireland do for Mrs. Lockwood?"

"Mrs. Lockwood is the daughter of Sherman Oakley, of Oakley Steel, a company you might or might not be familiar with and she is also the widow of Dalton Lockwood, of the Lockwood Business Furniture empire" he explained.

Now the name was familiar to Thomas. Ann had been very active in charitable work in England with various foundations before her husband Dalton's terrible death. Dalton, he remembered, was viscously murdered by a gang of thugs in a home invasion many years ago. Ann had also been brutally assaulted, almost dying herself and the papers, if he remembers, had reported that she had slipped into isolation and privacy to recover and raise the child of her murdered husband. It had been a terrible tragedy. Thomas stated, "I do remember Mrs. Lockwood and her terrible circumstances Mr. Highfield. How are she and her son? I hear that he is quite an accomplished musician?" Thomas asked.

"He is indeed Father, and that is the reason for my call. Ann's son, Michael Lockwood, is performing in Dublin next month with the RFÉ National Symphony Orchestra and it is the wish of Mrs. Lockwood, that Chloë, would join Michael onstage, for a duet performance."

"This is very unexpected, Mr. Highfield. I will need to speak with Chloë's caregiver and, of course, her school administrator. I don't see that as a problem, however, Mr. Highfield. Give me a few days and I will get back to you."

"Just one more thing, Father. Mrs. Lockwood is insistent that you personally attend the concert and Chloë's participation and performance be kept a complete secret."

Thomas found this request a little unusual and replied, "Why all the cloak and dagger Mr. Highfield? I am sure the Dublin press would greatly enjoy promoting this event."

His reply did not enlighten: "I cannot answer that, Father, as Mrs. Lockwood gave me no details, but she is adamant that it be kept totally quiet until the night of the concert. Not even Chloë should be told until that night, and neither should her school, nor her caregiver."

Thomas began to feel that all too familiar dread building in his stomach. He had begun to accept the feeling as a pre-warning system that something bad was about to happen. He asked, "This is very unusual Mr. Highfield. You're asking me to keep quiet and not tell anyone that Chloë McClosky will be performing with the RFÉ? Not even Chloë? It doesn't make any sense. I would like to speak with Mrs. Lockwood personally, if I may, in regards to this engagement."

Mr. Highfield's response was like a punch to the gut. "Father O'Sullivan, it is imperative that you attend the concert. I am not privy to the reasons, but Ann did ask me to mention this to you, in the hope that it would convince you, not only to attend, but also to keep the engagement with the RFÉ completely secret until the very last minute. Does Chloë have a birthmark that resembles three musical notes on her right thigh or anywhere else on her body?"

Thomas struggled to recover from this revelation. He felt the room begin to shrink until it was just him and the phone, while everything else retreated into a distant fog. Terror began to take over his body. Satan was crafting his plan of destruction and he somehow was a part of it. At first, the demonic circumstances surrounding the birth of Chloë, and now, fifteen years later, a direct connection to another child. This was madness. The fact anyone else was aware of Chloë's birthmark was impossible. The only people on this earth that knew of the mark were himself, Sister McGarrigle and his late friend, Cardinal Zorn.

Gathering his composure, Thomas replied, "Please tell Mrs. Lockwood that I would be delighted to join her at the concert."

"Thank you, Father, and don't you worry about anything, Mrs. Lockwood will be taking care of all of the details. Chloë will be performing a song that she will be very familiar with."

Thomas ended the call a few minutes later, leaned back in his office chair and looked up at the ceiling and closed his eyes. He prayed for God's protection and for the strength and courage that his aging body would need in the spiritual battle that loomed on the horizon. The dread, crashing like waves, washing up against the shoreline boulders, was his internal compass and it pointed straight at the direction of danger.

****

Ann finished up with her assistant, Peter, who had just filled her in on his telephone conversation with Father O'Sullivan. She was feeling confident that she would have the opportunity to speak with Father O'Sullivan at the concert in Dublin in a few weeks. She could not risk a phone call to Father O'Sullivan with a request, 'Hi my name is Ann Lockwood. My son's father is Satan and I was hoping to get together with you to discuss the girl Chloë McClosky, who is under your care. I think she is also the child of the devil. What time would be good for you?' She knew that there was a very good chance that the beast would appear at any moment in front of her, reading her mind from whatever depths he arose, his claw-like-talons poised to slice off her head. Even with that fear hanging over her like a storm cloud ready to drop a tornado funnel, something felt different now. She couldn't explain it, but she felt *safe* somehow.

She would use the opportunity of the concert to speak to Father O'Sullivan about her suspicions of Chloë McClosky's birth and the circumstances surrounding it. According to the research which Peter had gathered for her on the McClosky girl, as well as information she had obtained from Detective Jeremy Cookston of Scotland Yard before his tragic death three years ago, the births of Michael and Chloë were eerily similar. Her instructions to Peter to reveal the knowledge of the birthmark to Father O'Sullivan and his reaction convinced Ann that she was right. Chloë McClosky was the child of Satan! She whispered to herself, and the realization was of cold comfort.

****

It was Wednesday morning in London and Ann took a moment to savor a cup of coffee after seeing Michael off to his school, The Richmond School of Music for the musically gifted or in Michael's case, musical prodigies. Her assistant usually drove Michael in the mornings and then she would pick him up after school. Sometimes, they would switch and at other times, Peter would do all the driving. It didn't matter to Michael. He looked forward to every single day of going to school and studying music. His regular class work included his core subjects of Math, English and Science. He breezed through these, scoring high marks in everything, but it was always the music that was the fuel that drove his engine. At the age of fifteen, Michael, had become one of the most celebrated students ever to attend Richmond. His ability to play all instruments, combined with his hauntingly beautiful voice and his striking good looks gave him celebrity status in London. Three years ago, when he was only twelve, he played a concert with the London Symphony Orchestra that blew the roof off the concert hall, and his popularity after that had skyrocketed. Michael had become a target of the massive British tabloids, the cute little twelve year old music prodigy who also happened to be the son of Ann and Dalton Lockwood. Michael's popularity was a conduit for the press into her past and the sensational, brutal murder of her husband Dalton, who had been killed by a gang of thugs while Ann was left for dead. After her recovery and the birth of Michael, she went into seclusion, surfacing only briefly when her mother was also violently murdered. She came out of seclusion completely when Michael's musical abilities became evident. It was stressful and chaotic, dealing with the press from the moment she walked out of her house until she came home again. Ann had the financial resources to disappear completely in another country and to raise Michael in a more normal environment, but she knew that was impossible. She was destined for this duty to continue to nurture Michael in his musical abilities by the most horrible and frightening entity in this world, God's arch enemy, Satan himself.

Ann finished cleaning up the kitchen from Michael's breakfast, then went to her bedroom to shower and get dressed for the day. The concert in Dublin was only three days away and all of her suspicions about the McClosky girl would come to bear. If there was any chance that the demon would be there, it would be to see the latest performance by Michael. The invitation by the RFÉ NSO in Dublin was garnering huge press both in England and in Ireland. A British musician performing with the Irish symphony was unheard of and the surrounding controversy was building. When young Chloë McClosky made her surprise appearance alongside Michael, it would create a furor in both countries. During the concert, she would take the opportunity to communicate with Father O'Sullivan about her suspicions. Either Father O'Sullivan would think she was crazy or he would believe her because he already knew it to be true about Chloë. Even if he believed her, what could he do? What could they do? They must become allies of God, and fight the evilness that plagued Michael and Chloë. That was all they could do.

****

It was Saturday morning, on the day of the Dublin concert. At the London City Airport, the Embraer Phenom 300 executive jet was fuelled and awaiting its passengers. The jet was one of many owned by Oakley Steel. This one was used primarily by Ann, especially in the last year, as Michael's burgeoning music career took him all over Europe for guest appearances and concerts.

The jet was the only connection Ann had anymore with her father and his companies. They hadn't spoken to each other in years, although her father occasionally made contact with his grandson. Ann would let Michael attend large Oakley family events, but she never did. She decided that she would not block Michael from knowing his grandfather, his four uncles and the Oakley family. Ann noticed that Michael was sort of indifferent to his grandfather. He didn't say much after his visits other than that he enjoyed himself, but he never elaborated and she never pushed him. Dalton's side of the family never made contact with Ann, and that included Michael. They did not exist in their eyes. Michael never asked her about his father. There would come a time when Ann would tell her son what a wonderful father he had, how much he wanted a child of his own and how he would have loved Michael.

Michael showed little interest in anything outside of music; for him, it was all about becoming a better musician and extending his vocal capabilities. She knew this was why he had been born in the first place, so she never tried very diligently to get him interested in anything else.

Peter pulled the Mercedes S600 onto the tarmac, next to the Phenom jet. He quickly got out and opened her door, allowing Ann and Michael to slide out. As Michael climbed the steps into the plane, she took a minute to talk to Peter.

"Goodbye Ann, you and Michael be safe. I'm not sure what this is all about, but I have a bad feeling that you are in some sort of danger. I never should have allowed you to talk me out of accompanying you," a worried look spread across his face.

She studied Peter's face for a moment before answering. His face was ruggedly handsome, with short, black hair, laced with strings of gray, and a two inch, light-colored, thin scar running from his left ear towards the middle of his face. The two day stubble he always wore could not cover it up. He was an ex British Special Forces officer, recommended to her by her late friend, Detective Cookston. He was loyal, professional and in another lifetime, Ann could easily fall for the ex-soldier. She shook those thoughts from her mind as if they had no business being in her head in the first place.

"Thank you, Peter. There is nothing for you to be worried about, we will be fine. I will call you after the concert, when we are on our way to the airport, so you can meet us here. We will talk soon," Ann reassured him with a smile and a slight squeeze of his forearm before she turned and headed up the stairs and into the plane.

****

His eyes followed Ann until she was safely on the plane and the cabin door was pulled closed and latched. Only then did he turn back towards the car and then drove back home to the Lockwood estate in downtown London, just minutes away.

While he was driving the short distance home, he thought of Ann and how much he respected her. The woman had been through so much tragedy, a normal person would have crumbled many times over, but not her. She was one of the bravest and fearless women he had ever known. She handled the crushing media with class and patience, and the demands of Michael's musical career like a seasoned pro. He wondered if she ever thought about the possibility of another relationship, if her heart could ever be open to romance again. What was he thinking anyway? He was just the hired gun, paid to keep her and Michael safe. He could be a chaperone, assistant or whatever she needed, he would get it done. She is a very special woman and he would protect her with his life.

Chapter 3

The fall weather in Los Angeles was still very warm even though other parts of the country had begun to cool down in preparation for the onslaught of winter. The consistent balmy weather and always present sunshine soothed the soul and made each new day something to look forward to. That's how Bentley Paxton approached each day when she awoke in her trendy and colorful apartment in the Silver Lake neighborhood of Los Angeles. For the past six years, she had been the senior writer for *Music Talks* magazine, the country's leading music publication. During that time, she covered the west coast music scene and she lived in the hip borough of Silver Lake. She had moved there from Berkeley, where she'd obtained her Master's degree in Journalism.

Her parents were horrified when they first came to visit her in Silver Lake. They wondered why such a highly educated and professional person as their daughter chose to live in a neighborhood that was full of misfits and wannabes. The neighborhood had such a special vibe, it was intoxicating. Hipsters roamed the streets, the fashion-conscious walked their dogs and the entertainment executives bragged about their next big projects. One minute you would see a tattoo covered mother pushing her baby stroller, a man in a leather jacket playing air drums on the sidewalk or an elderly lady reading a book on a sidewalk bench. This was the essence of Silver Lake – all walks of life embracing a neighborhood filled with art, part-time jobs and an easy life. She loved it all including the smells of home cooked meals, and espresso burning, permeating the air with its distinctive scents. After about the third visit, Bentley's parents grew to love Silver Lake as well. They were excited to get out onto the sidewalks to soak up the atmosphere and the splendid foods that were hidden in hole-in-the-wall cafés like well placed secrets.

This weekend it was her 40th birthday and not even her parents would be here to celebrate her milestone. It was not like she was looking forward to another year gone by. She was turning forty, still single and no kids. "It's getting too late for that anyway," she thought. She was happy anyway to be alone on her birthday. It was kind of shocking that she had no friends here in L.A. that would take her out. The only person besides her parents who even knew it was her birthday was her boss, Jonathon Green. All of the other people she knew were just professional acquaintances. All, that is, except one. There was one man out there who still made her heart flutter when she allowed her thoughts drift to him. After all these years, their careers kept them connecting from time to time, but those same careers kept them apart and killed any chance for a meaningful relationship. Bentley wondered if Avery Johnson would remember her birthday and touch base. "He had never called her on her birthday before, so why would he now?" she wondered. "Does he even know when my birthday is? Why would he? This is crazy thinking about him all of a sudden", she scolded herself.

She shrugged those thoughts from her mind as she entered her bedroom to get out of her clothes and into her ratty old denim shorts and her alma mater t-shirt from when she was at the University of Missouri, where she got her undergraduate degree in Journalism. She had just decided to run a hot bath before she changed into her comfy clothes, when she heard her Blackberry ringing back out in the living room, where she left it on the coffee table. She was in no particular hurry to get it, knowing that it would be her mother, wondering who was taking her out for her birthday this weekend. She missed the call, as it stopped ringing when she reached down for her phone. She checked the missed calls and was shocked at first, then mad that she didn't move quicker to answer the call. It wasn't her mother that had tried to call, it was Avery. She thought about hitting the send button to call him right back, but she hesitated. If she called right back, then he would think she was vulnerable. If she didn't, then he might think that she was ignoring him and didn't think it important enough to call him back. She was about to hit the send button when the phone lit up and began ringing again. He was calling her back. Suddenly nervous, and feeling like a teenager, she answered the phone after the third ring.

"Hi, Bentley Paxton speaking."

The confident husky voice of Avery Johnson came barreling through the earpiece, "Bentley how are you? It's great to hear your voice again!"

She was not sure if he was calling her about her birthday, but she didn't care, she was just happy to hear from him again. Keeping her voice low and controlled, she replied, "Avery so nice to hear from you. How have you been? To what do I owe the pleasure?"

"Are you kidding me? Happy birthday, Bentley! What is it now, twenty nine?" Avery asked, playfully.

Her stomach began to warm; he had such an effect on her it was crazy: "I wish, but thank you anyway. Its official now. I am getting old. Its forty, so I now have to start accepting dates from sixty year olds. How old did you say you were?"

His laugh was genuine and hearty when he replied, "I don't think so my dear, you could steal a Miss Universe title away from a twenty year old, so don't even go there."

"Thank you Avery for that and for thinking of me but my birthday isn't till Saturday so you jumped the gun a little bit".

"I know it's on Saturday. That's why I am calling you tonight. Have you made any plans yet for Saturday? If you haven't, I would like to take you to dinner and maybe out to dance if that's okay with you".

She hoped Avery would call, but she didn't expect a date. She wanted to go out with him so badly, but she could feel herself moving towards saying no to him. Why, she did not know, maybe it was because she had been single her whole life with no really serious relationships. If she said yes to Avery, she knew she would be unable to resist, not only his charm, but her feelings towards him. Maybe she just felt that deep inside; she was incapable of having a serious relationship with anyone. Taking the easy way out, she lied and said, "Avery I am so sorry. My parents are in this weekend and had plans for me. Can we meet at another time, maybe?"

"Perfect. The more the merrier, I always say. I have never met your parents and I would love to, so how about if the four of us go out for dinner then? What do you say?"

If her parents actually were coming to town, it would be a wonderful date. Instead, her stupid lie gave her no choice but to say no. "I'm sorry Avery, not this time. I believe they are taking me out of town. Flights have been booked, so next time we will plan this better."

The disappointment in Avery's voice was obvious and Bentley felt terrible that she had lied to him. The one thing she wanted the most was the one thing she rejected. "It must be Time to see a shrink," she thought.

"Okay Bentley. That's too bad; it would have been fun with or without your parents. You take care of yourself and I will hold you to it on the 'next time'".

She made a beeline back to the bathroom to run the bath. The lie to avoid Avery made her feel dirty and she was furious at herself. The hot water and suds felt wonderful; she could feel her tension begin to loosen its grip. She closed her eyes and thought of Avery. His eyes, she remembered, were like pools of the bluest ocean water. They were so mesmerizing that it was dangerous to gaze at them for too long because she was fearful that she would fall under some sort of spell. He called her on her birthday to take her out and she lied to him to avoid him. Why? What was she so afraid of? Was it the fear of commitment? Whatever it was, she just blew it and would likely never see him again. Maybe she should just pick up the phone, call him back, and say that her parents cancelled, so she was free after all. That was another lie. No, she wouldn't do that again. She'd think of something.

On the Saturday two days later, she headed down to the streets of her neighborhood, hoping that the atmosphere would enliven her spirits.. She decided to hit Millie's Coffee House for some of the best pancakes on the West Coast and great coffee to match. Fortunately, it was just around the corner from her apartment, on Sunset Boulevard. It was ten in the morning and the place was buzzing. Mostly locals came here, but on the weekends, the odd tourist would somehow stumble upon this place, love the food, and then go home and tell everyone about it. "I guess that's how these places become legendary," she thought. Like most shops in Silver Lake, Millie's was shanty-like, old and badly in need of some upgrades, but full of charm and character, which resulted in great atmosphere. The smell of the pancakes and sausages permeated the air, and the locals argued over the President's policies, or another non-playoff year for the Dodgers, served by the colorful waitresses who had been a fixture in the restaurant for as long as the wall paper. They could take orders of food from parties of twelve and not write down a thing to remember them, then serve the food and coffee exactly to the person who ordered it. The stories they carried in their heads from all the different people who had come and gone over the years would be a best seller, if they ever decided to write a book. Bentley loved this place and she loved Silver Lake. It was home. Maybe that is why she feared commitment. It just might take her away from this place.

****

She spent the rest of her day walking the district, milling about the shops, talking with the shop owners and generally keeping her mind off of the fact that it was her fortieth birthday and she would be spending it alone, as per usual. She did however get a call from Jonathon Green, her boss from *Music Talks,* wishing her a happy birthday. She wished she had just let the call go to voicemail. Her mood just wasn't up to his sarcastic barbs.

"Good afternoon my beautiful, but still single journalist".

"Good afternoon Jonathon. It's Saturday and I'm not working today, so why are you calling me?"

Suddenly her ear was invaded with the most awful sound as Jonathon broke into a happy birthday serenade. It kind of sounded like a very, very poor rendition of the Marilyn Monroe singing to the President version.. When he finally ran out of words to the simple jingle, she interrupted him.

"My God, that was awful Jonathon. How can someone who makes his career in the music industry sound so bad?"

"Hey it's the thought that counts, so get over it. Happy

birthday, Bentley. Tell me, what does the most beautiful and most eligible woman in L.A. have planned for her fortieth?"

"Thank you Jonathon, that was awful but very sweet. This boring journalist is staying home tonight with no plans. I'll probably watch Netflix, I'm sure I can find a movie that will remind me what a dull life I lead."

"Excuse me girl? Why the 'pity me' all of a sudden? You are drop dead gorgeous, have a dream job and it's your birthday today. Be happy for Christ's sakes will you? Do you want me to fly out there tonight and take you out? I can do that. You know there are flights leaving every hour out of New York for L.A. I can make you feel like a real woman, just ask me."

"I'll pass, but thank you anyway. I don't need your little kids growing up only to track me down to accuse me of ruining their childhood when their father left their mother for a pathetically sad employee."

"Okay but you know I'm right. You need to stop feeling sorry for yourself and get out there. You have the pick of the litter for men in L.A. I don't get it. What about that music producer, Johnson. You had the hots for him at one time. Give him a call. I'm sure he can find room for you in his social calendar."

"Oh wow, I thought for a second there you were actually being thoughtful, Jonathon. You should be grateful I'm not in a relationship anyway. It means I'm just that much more available for the magazine, doesn't it? No maternity leave issues to deal with and no long vacations away with the family to schedule around. I am at your beck and call twenty four hours a day, isn't that right Jonathon? Well maybe I should start using up some of the holiday time I have accumulated over the years and never taken. Or maybe even start taking a closer look at all the opportunities to move into television that keep coming my way. What do you think?"

"I think you need to chill out, baby. What you really need is to get laid. How long has it been anyway? Probably been years, hasn't it? I'm being serious now Bentley. Taking some time off is a good idea. Take a few weeks off and go to Mexico or South America and screw your brains out. Huh? Why not, Bentley? In fact I know a great place in Puerto Vallarta that is relaxing, fun and full of single, good looking professional guys looking to get laid. Sounds like paradise, right? What do you say?"

"I say no to Puerto Vallarta, but thanks anyway. Listen Jonathon, maybe I do need a break. Let me think about it and I'll get back to you".

****

As the day began to wind down, Bentley contemplated ordering some Thai food for delivery. It seemed as if she no longer had the energy to go out again. While searching for the number of the restaurant on a menu she kept in the junk drawer of her kitchen, she was startled when the apartment doorbell rang. "Who the heck could that be" she wondered. She made her way to the door, calling out as she did so that she was coming. She peaked through the peep hole, but whoever it was had moved out of the line of sight, as if knowing the person opening the door would do that. She opened the deadbolt, but left the safety chain intact and opened the door the three inches. Still seeing no one, she called out, asking if anyone was there. She was about to close the door when she heard a voice that was familiar, but she couldn't believe she was hearing it. It was a voice she had just heard two days ago on the phone. Her heart began to race and she instantly began to feel paranoid, knowing that she had no makeup on, her hair was a mess and she was still wearing a tank top and shorts.

"Do I have to stand out here all night?"

Bentley nervously pulled the safety chain from the door and swung it open. Avery Johnson was standing there with a grin on his face, and looking like a complete clone of Gerard Butler. In his hands, he was holding a bouquet of pink roses and a wrapped gift box. When she was finally able to work up the spit to unlock her tongue from inside of her mouth, she replied, "Great to see you, Avery. What a surprise you being here. I thought I told you my parents were taking me out."

"I know, but I thought I could muscle in on the party like a wedding crasher well more of a birthday crasher, I guess," laughed Avery, as he stood waiting for Bentley to invite him in.

She just stood there for a few seconds, not quite believing Avery was standing in her doorway. Her stupor was interrupted when he thrust the bouquet of pink roses towards her and said, "Hey are you going to let a guy in who shows up to surprise you on your birthday AND brings roses, pink ones I might add?"

"I'm such an idiot Avery, please come in. I am just so surprised to see you here is all."

He handed her the flowers and said, "I apologize for just showing up, Bentley, but I really did want to see you and wish you a happy birthday. So, happy birthday, beautiful!"

She reached up and gave him a big hug, "Thank you Avery, it is kind of you to surprise me. The flowers are beautiful. Come and sit down while I get them into some water. What can I get you to drink? A beer or some wine maybe?"

"Red wine would be great Bentley, thank you. Where are your parents? Are you sure I'm not interrupting anything?"

Oh boy, now she had to lie again to cover up the first lie. No, she couldn't do that anymore. Better to tell the truth even if it meant him turning and heading right back out the door he just came through. "Hang onto to that thought while I get your wine. I'll be right back."

"Why don't we talk over dinner Bentley? I took the liberty and have made reservations for the four of us at Cliff's Edge, not far from here. I thought you might be familiar with it and it's close. What do you say?"

"I'm not dressed or ready to go out for dinner Avery. I honestly thought I would be staying right here tonight. I would need at least an hour to get ready."

"Well if you get me that wine, I can wait or tell me where it is and I will help myself so you can get started getting ready."

"Deal. Come and follow me I will show you where the wine and the glasses are." She led Avery into her tiny kitchen, pulled out a bottle of Cabernet, a couple of Bordeaux glasses and a corkscrew and handed it to Avery. "I'll let you get started on the wine while I go get ready."

As she turned to head into her bedroom, she felt Avery's hand reach around her waist and turn her towards him and before she could even react, he had pulled her in close to him and his moist lips were on hers. It was so unexpected; it came as a complete surprise, but she leaned into his kiss like it was her first. The fire beginning to flame inside her stomach was warming her She wanted this, and she needed it. His beard stubble cut into her cheek as they explored each other's mouths and his hand found its way up the backside of her top and then made its way to the front of her and up to her breasts. He squeezed her through her bra, soft moans emanating from the both of them. She knew this wasn't going to stop and she didn't want it to. The wine could wait. She pulled away from his mouth and whispered in short gasps, "Take me Avery, now. In my bedroom."

Pulling each other's clothes off as they made their way to her bedroom, they fell onto the bed naked, the heat palpable between them. The long overdue desire came to the surface as they explored each other's bodies. They made love, the passion overwhelming and the physical pleasure was beautiful between them. She often thought how it might be between the two of them but she didn't expect anything this good. Physically, he was beautiful and there was so much more to him than his beauty that she could sense and feel as they held each other. This moment was something she had wanted for a very long time. They should have done this years ago. She felt him roll onto his back, take a deep breath then propped up some pillows angainst the headboard. He then reached down and pulled her up until she was comfortably snuggled against him.

He stroked her hair, the two of them quiet for what seemed an eternity, but was only a few minutes, when he whispered to her, "That was amazing Bentley, you have no idea how I've longed for this moment. You are such a beautiful and amazing woman. I am so happy to be here with you right now."

She pulled her head back to look up at him and into his eyes and spoke, "I'm so sorry that I lied to you Avery. It will never happen again, I promise."

Looking into her eyes with a look of confusion, he replied, "I don't understand. How did you lie to me?"

"When you called me the other day to ask me out, I panicked for some crazy reason and I lied to you that my parents would be in town and I would be unavailable to go out. My parents are not here, and they never were coming this weekend. I lied to you because I was afraid that this might happen and it wouldn't be beautiful. Does that make any sense?"

"Yeah, I guess in a weird kind of way. Was it beautiful Bentley? Was it what you expected?"

"I didn't expect it to go down the way it did so quickly, but I'm glad it did. It was beautiful Avery, it really was," she replied as she ran her fingers down his taught stomach, watching them dip down and up over his abs.

"What about those dinner reservations? Are you up to it?"

"Let's just stay right here in bed, Avery. I couldn't ask for a better birthday than that. We'll order delivery. Do you mind?"

He reached for her, pulling her chin towards him where their mouths met again, their tongues exploring, the heat returning, desire taking over. Sometime later they rolled off of each other, covered in sweat, her body warm with satisfaction as she sat up on her elbows beside him and looked into his sparkling blue eyes. "It's getting late to order food but I don't care, I'm starved. I am going to jump into the shower and why don't you order us some food? Surprise me, just not Thai, okay? I don't want bad breath to ruin all the kissing we're going to be doing all night, so choose wisely, Mr. Johnson," she laughed as she rolled off him and headed towards the shower.

She looked back at him before she entered her bathroom and asked, "I'm curious, Avery. How did you know where I lived?"

"Your boss Jonathon Green called me right after he had spoken with you earlier. He told me you were spending your birthday alone in your apartment and asked me to surprise you for dinner. He said if I didn't do it he would make sure that none of my clients would ever be mentioned again in *Music*

Talks! Now that was a threat I could never ignore!"

She laughed at the thought of Jonathon calling Avery. As she turned the hot water on in the shower and climbed in, she couldn't help but think that this was the best birthday she had ever had.

Chapter 4

Radio Station KJAY 950's afternoon DJ and radio host, Nathan Steck, was prepping Connor Asker before the producer gave the on-air sign in thirty seconds, "Just remember, Connor, that you are the star, not me. I am the one asking you the questions. Just relax and have some fun with it okay?"

"The poor kid", thought Nathan, "so young and being pushed in a million different directions", he couldn't blame him for being nervous. His manager, this Best dude, was an asshole. The control he exerted over Connor was way over the top and unnecessary.. As a professional radio host and one of the most renowned in the US, he had been handpicked by Best to conduct this interview. The interview was to announce the debut album release for Connor Asker, the music phenomenon that was taking the world by storm. His success on 'America's Got Talent' three years ago was the launching pad for this very talented young man. As much as he disliked his manager, he couldn't help but admire him for how he had slowly and deliberately brought Connor along in the music business. "How many times", Nathan thought, "had he seen young singing sensations come and go in a matter of months because of poor management trying to capitalize on the popularity of the moment? The scrap heap could reach to the clouds. Connor's manager was in no hurry, it seemed, choosing to school young Connor on becoming an accomplished musician and singer before he threw him to the wolves of the media and fans after his early success on 'AGT'". While thinking that, Nathan realized that he was impressed by the manager's methods.

There had been rumors floating around for the past few months that Asker was getting set to release this album, so the announcement would not be a shock, but Nathan knew it would likely set off a media frenzy and pubescent young fans would go crazy if the album was any good. The first single "Follow Me Follow You", a teenage anthem song about breaking free, was good. No, it was very good. The kid could sing, his melody was spot on and the writing and production was top notch. At the conclusion of the interview, KJAY would be the first radio station in the land to play "Follow Me Follow You". Nathan watched his producer in the adjacent booth as he used his hand to signal the countdown to "on air": 5-4-3-2-1, and then he pointed, meaning, Go "As promised to KJAY 950 listeners, as well as to the listeners from our syndicated network around the United States, joining me live in studio is a young singing sensation whom all of you should remember. He was the winner of 'America's Got Talent' three years ago. Please help me welcome Connor Asker. Thanks Connor, for coming in."

Whatever nervousness, stage fright or fear Connor had shown earlier was gone like he had thrown a switch. This showed the work that his manager had accomplished in preparing his client for this moment.

"Thank you for having me, Mr. Steck; it's an honor and a pleasure."

"Please, you can call me Nathan. Only my lawyer and my agent call me Mr. Steck. Let me ask you right off the top Connor, what took you so long to release this album?"

"That's an easy one. I wasn't ready. When you release an album, you have to be prepared to tour to support it. I was only twelve years old when I won 'America's Got Talent'. I was singing cover songs on the show. I had no original material then and, not surprisingly, no one was knocking down my door offering up their original music for me to sing, so it took awhile. Thankfully, Mr. Best took me under his wing and not only taught me how to sing even better by learning how to harness the power of my voice, but also to be patient."

"You have certainly been that. You mentioned your manager Robert Best. Tell me more about him. I know he is with you here in studio and I will give him an opportunity to join us in a minute, but tell me Connor, what has he done for you and your career over the last three years."

"In a nutshell, everything. In the beginning I just wanted to hit the gas, capture the moment and ride the popularity train as far as it would take me. I wanted it all, but Mr. Best kept me grounded. He taught me that good things take time and not to take my success for granted. He found songs that fit my voice and my style and, most importantly, that I wanted to sing. I owe him everything."

"Your parents, Connor, how are they with all the success you have had and with the release of your new album. What do they think of all this?"

"I have the best parents a child could ever have. I mean that, I really do. They have been so supportive in everything I do, not just singing. They trust Mr. Best and the decisions he makes on behalf of my career so I am very lucky."

"Are your parents with you here in New York?"

"No unfortunately not. My dad is a park warden at Mt. Rushmore National Park and he has to work and my mom is a school teacher and since the school year recently began, she is very busy."

Nathan detected a hint of sadness in Connor's voice when he talked about his parents. He had to remind himself he was still only fifteen so missing his parents would be only natural, but there was something else there. He just couldn't put his finger on it. Nathan knew that Connor's birth parents had been killed while he was still in his mother's womb, a subject he had been instructed by Best not to discuss with Connor or he would end the interview immediately. Nathan finished up about Connor's parents by saying, "Well I guess you will have to get used to being away from home from here on in."

Nathan continued, "We are being joined now by Robert Best of Blackstar Studios, Connor's manager, and one of the top producers in the business. Robert, how do you explain the maturity and talent of Connor, considering he is only fifteen years old? It is very rare in this business, for someone so young. Is this something that you take credit for, or his parents, or a combination of the two?"

Nathan's assessment that Best was an asshole was based upon a gut feeling and years of interviewing celebrities. There was something just not right with this man, yet he was unable to pinpoint it. Maybe he would be able to identify what that was by the end of the interview. Best's response to his question affirmed his gut feeling that he was an asshole: "Connor is a very special young man, his talents are endless and it took someone of experience and vision to realize these special talents at such a young age."

"Tell me about his parents from South Dakota. How supportive are they of Connor's success? Is there any concern about his age from them? That maybe he should wait a few more years before he jumps into the cauldron of the music business?"

With this question about Connor's parents, Nathan detected a change in Best's facial expression. He flashed anger and for a split second Nathan thought he noticed his eyes turn color. "What is that all about?", he thought. Best's voice reflected his displeasure at talking about Connor's parents. This subject was supposed to be off limits. It was one of the conditions presented by Best before the start of the interview and something that Nathan would not agree to, but he was over ruled by his producer. Best, his voice almost spitting replied, "Listen Nate, as Connor earlier commented, his parents are in full support of his success and his chosen career. I would think your listeners would be more interested in hearing about Connor's new album and the first single "Follow Me Follow You" than what his parents think about his career."

Best referring to him as 'Nate' was a direct shot and a signal to back off, as the anger seething from this prick was filling the small studio. Nathan succumbed to the hand signals frantically being flashed by his producer on the other side of the glass wall to move on. He hated being dictated to regarding what he could discuss with his interview subjects and he would let his producer know it later. "Fair enough, Mr. Best. Tell me about the album. Who wrote the songs? Did you have any collaborators helping you to produce this album?"

Best's face loosened slightly as the topic moved on to the music and replied, "I produced every track on the album with no outside collaboration. You seem to forget, Nate that I am a multiple Grammy Award winning producer and I do not require input from anyone else. I might add that Connor is such an accomplished musician and singer that producing this album was one of the easiest projects I have ever done and yet will likely be my most successful. The songs were written by another client of Blackstar Studios, an extremely talented young musician and songwriter by the name of Patrick Benning. Remember that name Nate; you will want me back in the not too distant future to discuss his career."

"Okay I will try to remember that. By the way, Mr. Best, did I tell you my name is Nathan and not Nate? Moving along, tell me about "Follow Me Follow You", the first single of the new album. It is about a young man breaking free from the constraints in life that have held him back, either his parents maybe or school. Is there a little bit of Connor in the words of this song?"

Best's face narrowed as he looked at him from behind the microphone dangling in his face and replied, "It's hardly that, in fact the song encourages fans to follow Connor, to follow the example he has set, to be free. Have you even listened to the song Nate?"

Nathan suddenly felt a sense of impending doom like something terrible was about to happen. It was weird as he has never felt this before. Staring back at Best, their eyes locked for a brief second and Nathan could have sworn he'd seen Best's eyes turn the color of a deep red. It was just for a millisecond but he definitely saw it. It was no reflection from any of the studio equipment. This fucking Best was crazier than a loon. It was time to end the interview with Best, and get Connor back on microphone. "Actually, I have listened to the song, Best, and though the song doesn't specifically target youth to revolt from their current situation and follow Connor for whatever reason, the song sounds like it is. It's only my opinion and who cares anyway, right? I hate social constraints as much as the next guy, but they are a necessary evil, wouldn't you agree?"

Best glared at him and again the sensation of doom entered the pit of his stomach. The longer Best glared at him the worse it got. It felt like his eyes were burrowing a hole right through him. "Well we'll see how our listeners like the new track "Follow Me Follow You" as we are going to play that song right now. I'll be joined once again by Connor Asker after the song to take your calls. You're listening to the drive home show on KJAY 960 radio."

Nathan immediately dropped his headphones on the table and got out of his chair and left the sound proof room of the on-air booth to go to the restroom. His producer could deal with Best. He needed some water and fresh air. Making a beeline for the bathroom, Nathan was going to be sick. He was shocked to see Best standing beside the sink. How the fuck did that happen? Best was still sitting in his chair when he left and there was only one hallway leading from the sound booth to the men's room and Best certainly didn't pass him on the way. This dude was one creepy asshole. Searching for an empty stall, he ignored Best and when he opened the last stall to empty the contents of lunch, he was jolted when Best crowded into the stall before him.

"What the fuck is the matter with you Best? If you're trying to creep me out, you are, okay? How the hell did you get in this bathroom ahead of me and then into this stall? You know what? Forget about it; just get the fuck out of my way before I fill your shoes."

Nathan saw a blur as he suddenly found himself pinned against the wall of the bathroom stall with Best's hand locked onto his throat, choking him so completely that his air supply was cut off. This maniac was killing him! Looking down for leverage to brace a foot to try and roll out from under his grip, he noticed Best was holding him several feet in the air, his strength incredible. Nathan knew he only had seconds to live and desperately tried to kick himself free. He looked down into Best's eyes and was horrified at what he saw. They were glowing a deep crimson red, on fire, with the hatred from them burning into him. Then he spoke and the fear turned his blood to ice.

Best's voice was guttural, like nothing Nathan had ever heard before. It was pure evil and he knew he was about to be killed by something not human, "How dare you mock me you worthless piece of garbage. I could kill you and everyone in here as easy as swatting a fly. I'm letting you live only because you're going to go back in that sound room and tell everyone listening how great Connor Asker is and how great I am, is that clear? Then from this day forward you will promote this album and play the songs off of this record every hour. Is that also clear? I can't hear you, Nate!"

His eyes bulged and were about to launch from his skull when Best loosened the grip on his throat ever so slightly to allow some air to pass through, into his starving lungs. He gasped for air, causing him to wretch as his lungs screamed for more. He nodded his head to Best to let him know that he understood. Best suddenly squeezed his throat once again, and this time Nathan could feel the tendons in his throat begin to separate. The bathroom began to shrink as the blackness filled the corner of his eyes and, looking down into those hideous eyes once again, he could only moan as Best's face had transformed into something as evil as his voice. Deep cracks had opened up on his face, and his teeth had grown long and wider with black spaces in between them. His face seemed to move independently of his skull and his grotesque, oversized tongue thrashed over his decaying lips as he screamed up at him, "I will tear you apart and flush your meat down the toilet if you don't do exactly what I just instructed you to do. I will torture your kids and your wife for hours before I kill them and then send their souls to a special place for eternal pain and suffering. Do you hear me Nate? Now get out there and finish the interview."

Nathan dropped to the floor with a thud, his throat burning like a raging fire as he desperately sucked air into his lungs. He rolled onto his elbows and vomited all over the bathroom stall floor, gagged and then puked some more. With his head almost level with the floor, he could see Best's shoes going out through the door and, to top off his terrifying encounter with this monster, he could hear him laughing as he walked out.

****

When KJAY 950 played Connor's 'Follow Me Follow You' it created an instaneous buzz, with the radio station's lines being jammed with callers wondering when the cd would be released for sale or for download on iTunes. The hip hop song with the intro rap by J Tick Tock Dbl J followed by the melodic chorus by Connor was a monumental hit. The lyrics to "Follow Me Follow You" were quickly streamed onto You Tube with millions of hits in just a few days as word spread quickly of the song that played on KJAY. Within just a few days of the interview with Nathan Steck, the single was available for download on iTunes. It set a record for the most downloads ever on the first day of release.

After his afternoon drive home show finished up at 5:00 p.m., Nathan Steck told his producer that he was staying late to get caught up on some research for an upcoming interview so he would be in his office and did not want to be disturbed. At his desk with the door closed, he took out the printed lyrics for "Follow Me Follow You". The attack by Best a few days ago was still fresh in his mind; the soreness and bruising around his neck were a constant reminder of how close he came to dying in that bathroom stall. He was convinced that Best was a monster, but he was completely baffled by his interest in the Asker kid. The journalist in him was driven to find some answers. He decided to begin with the lyrics to the song. Staring at the words to the song, he looked for meaning.

"Follow Me Follow You"

Do you see what I see
I see what you see
A world hungry for me
A world that needs me
I will be what you see
When your world collapses
Chorus…
Follow Me to see what I am
Follow You to show you what I am
Follow Me to see what I believe
Follow You to show you what I believe
Reach down and take my hand
And see where I live and breathe
A world like no other you've seen
A place with only one master you see
Be with me yes be with me you will see
Come and embrace what I am
Chorus…
Follow Me to see what I am
Follow You to show you what I am
Follow Me to see what I believe
Follow You to show you what I believe
The world will belong to me you will see
Oh how I want us to be together forever
Look down and see this is where you want to be
Be with me for all eternity you and me
Give your soul to me trust me I will lead

Reach down and come to me you will see
Chorus…
Follow Me to see what I am
Follow You to show you what I am
Follow Me to see what I believe
Follow You to show you what I believe
Repeat…
Follow Me to see what I am
Follow You to show you what I am
Follow Me to see what I believe
Follow You to show you what I believe

Nathan placed his glasses down on the desk and buried his face in his hands. He knew what this song meant and what it would do if Connor turned it into a hit and the youth of this world embraced it. It would be a hit, he had no doubt: he knew a hit song when he heard one. He had encountered the devil in that bathroom. He was convinced of it and the chills cascading down his spine caused him to slightly spasm in his chair. Then he heard a voice call out from the shadows of his office and the chills turned to ice in his veins.

Robert Best stepped away from the cover of shadow in the far corner of the office and spoke in a voice so evil that Nathan froze in his chair: "What do you think of the song, Nate? You think it will be a hit?"

"How the fuck did you get in here you crazy freak? I'm calling the poli..," Nathan's voice seized as he watched Best transform right in front of him. He thought to himself: "Oh my God what is happening! Sweet Jesus, he is turning into some sort of creature."

What used to be Robert Best, the music producer, was now transformed into a hideous beast with massive arms covered in slime and claw-like talons for hands. His upper body was a combination of grayish slimy skin on huge muscles and scaly plates like he was half reptile. Nathan was horrified when he looked up into those red glowing eyes that were encased in an oversized, monstrous head covered in sores and scars. His purplish and bleeding tongue poked through a mouth full of oversized teeth and fangs. Nathan knew that was about to die and there was nothing he could do, not even scream. The monster tilted its ugly head toward the ceiling of his office and screamed a guttural roar that finally snapped Nathan out of his trance. He pushed his chair back and made a run for the door, knowing full well it was useless.

He reached the door and was about to rip it open when his wrist was caught by one of the beast's enormous claws. He was thrown into the adjacent wall with a force so hard that it almost punched him into the next office. The beast grabbed him by the throat, pulled him from the demolished wall and held him straight up in the air. The strength of this beast was incredible. Nathan's air supply was cut off by the claw and he looked into the crimson red death eyes of the beast and willed it to finish him off. Suddenly, he felt a pressure in his chest and, from the corner of his eye, he could see the talon of the beast's other claw impale him. The pain from being choked muted the pain of the impalement, so he felt nothing but he could hear his entrails hit the floor as the beast gutted him.

He was already dead when the beast snapped his brutal claw in one quick motion, severing the head and dropping the ravaged body of Nathan Steck to the floor. The beast stepped back, its burning red eyes taking in the carnage like a proud warrior. Then it transformed back into the human form Robert Best.

As Best left the tenth floor offices of KJAY 950 he laughed out loud, thinking of the shock investigators would feel when they arrived at the scene and found dead bodies torn to pieces all over the place. He even considered going into the sound room and making an announcement to the live audience. He realized that they must have been wondering why the radio station was just transmitting static noise, and he wanted to tell them to get out there and buy the new Connor Asker CD. Nah, he better not, but it would have been fun.

Chapter 5

Bentley and Avery ended up spending the rest of the weekend in bed with neither of them wanting to leave each other for a minute. It was like they were making up for all the lost time they could have had together over the past fifteen years. Avery confessed that it was love at first sight for him when she walked into his studio all those years ago for the interview with *Music Talks*. Bentley tried, but failed to control the tears that leapt from her eyes as she heard those words.

"Why didn't you tell me Avery? It would have been nice to have known that. I cared about you the minute I met you. Isn't that crazy? We both liked each other but never pursued it"

It was 9:30 a.m. Monday morning and neither of them were in a big hurry to use work as an excuse to end what they had both wanted for so many years. Avery adjusted the pillows behind his back so he could look straight into her eyes when he spoke, "Lets choose to be thankful that we found each other now rather than not at all. You are an amazingly beautiful and smart woman Bentley and I am crazy about you."

She reached her arm around him and nestled her head against his chest and whispered, "Avery I am crazy for you too."

After more whispers and kisses, both of them fell asleep, exhausted from hours of lovemaking and talking. As Bentley dozed off, she couldn't remember a time where she was as happy as she was right now. It was almost noon when Bentley was jarred awake by the Beyonce ringtone of her Blackberry, perched on the dresser on the other side of the bedroom. In no rush to answer it, she slowly and quietly peeled herself off of Avery as he continued to be fast asleep. While Bentley was tip toeing across the bedroom carpet, she heard Avery stir, then say: "Did I tell you yet how beautiful you are?"

'Yes you have, but just remember to never stop telling me that, buster," she giggled as she grabbed her phone off the dresser and entered the bathroom. She checked the missed call and saw that it was her boss, Jonathon Green, and he had left a voicemail. Jonathon's message stated that he was flying into L.A. tomorrow and had some important news to share with her over lunch. He said he was due to land at 11:00 a.m. and, if she could pick him at the airport, they would go straight to lunch as he had a 4:00 p.m. return flight.

She turned the shower on and climbed in, thinking that Avery had likely dozed off again. "Poor guy", she thought, as she had probably made up for a lack of sex over the years in the last two days. Embracing the hot water enjoying the energy returning to her body, she suddenly felt a hand grab her around her waist and turn her around. Wrapping her arms around Avery's neck, she kissed him as his hands moved up and down her back and buttocks. She could feel that the energy had returned to him as well.

****

The next day, Bentley awoke refreshed, but immediately missing Avery not lying beside her. They had said their goodbyes after a wonderful dinner at the Cliff's Edge last night, where he had originally planned to take her on the Saturday night of her birthday. It was a beautiful three days with him and she was already looking forward to their next date this weekend. He was cooking dinner for them Friday night at his condo in West Hollywood.

Her thoughts turned to her boss, Jonathon, and why he was flying all the way to L.A. from New York to take her out for lunch in order to discuss something important. What could possibly be so important that he couldn't tell her over the phone? She finished getting dressed and was ready to head off on the thirty minute drive to LAX. She arrived at the airport and waited in the cell phone pickup area till Jonathon called to tell her that he had landed. While she was sitting and waiting for Jonathon, her cell chimed with an incoming text message. She looked at her phone, expecting Jonathon to have arrived, but it was Avery. She felt her heart skip a beat as she opened his message and read: "Hi darling, just hoping you are having a spectacular day! Talk soon!" She read the message again and her heart warmed. It had only been a few days with Avery, but it seemed a lifetime because of the feelings she had held for him for so many years. She thought for a second, then text right back, "My day is spectacular because of you. Thank you."

She was lost in space, thinking of him, when her phone chirped again. Quickly checking to see what Avery had texted her back, she was almost disappointed to see that it was Jonathon, he had arrived, and was on his way out of the terminal to look for her at passenger pickup.

****

They arrived in plenty of time for their noon reservation at the exquisite Campanile on Le Brea Avenue. Jonathon ordered a bottle of white wine and a plate of mussels and, with her permission, took the liberty of ordering her the restaurant's signature entrée, the sautéed trenne with beef Bolognese, kale and parmesan. Jonathon ordered the pan roasted pork chop with sautéed Blue Lake green beans, bacon lardons, garlic, pearl onions and a shallot crème fraiche. It was way too much food for this early in the day, but Jonathon loved Campanile's and he insisted.

With a straight face he asked: "So Bentley, tell me, how was your weekend? "

"Oh please, save it Green. Next time you plan on setting me up on a date, can you ask me first? I was dressed in shorts and a tank top, ready to call it a night and get ready for an evening on my couch with a bag of popcorn when Avery Johnson showed up at my door with pink roses."

Jonathon tried to appear occupied opening up his mussels and not listening but it was all an act and she had seen it many times before. Soon, he dropped his fork on the plate, wiped his mouth with the napkin, looked at her and said: "You need someone in your life Bentley, you're forty damn years old. What about a family?"

Here he goes, trying to play Dad again. He does it all the time; it's cute, but it drives her crazy. "Tell me, Jonathon, even if I had a husband, how I would have time to raise a child? You seem to forget that this is an 'all in' job."

The small talk went back and forth for a few minutes more until eventually, she was saved when one waiter offered more wine and then another waiter brought plates of food. As she enjoyed the trenne, she was about to ask Jonathon about his wife and kids, when he placed his napkin on the table, joined his hands underneath his chin and took on a serious tone: "Did you hear about the murder of Nathan Speck last night?"

"Oh my God Jonathon, no I didn't, what happened? That is awful."

"Torn to pieces in his office by some crazed killer or killers, is more like it. Everyone in the office was killed. Seven people in total. It was a massacre."

"Oh no, that is terrible, Jonathon. I can't believe it. Nathan was your friend, Jonathon, I'm sorry.

"Thanks for that Bentley. Nathan was one of the few good guys. Didn't buy into the industry bullshit you know, spoke the truth always, a real straight shooter."

"His family, Jonathon, how are they doing? Do the police have any leads?"

"I think it's still too early for that but the cops aren't saying anything. Denise and I were with his wife last night before her family could get there. She is a mess, as you would imagine. The cops interviewed me, asking if I knew anyone in the industry who might have a beef with the radio station. Of course I don't, but they did ask me if I knew the music producer, Robert Best. The interview the day before the murders with the Asker kid and Best didn't go so well, according to a co-worker who wasn't working at the time of the murders, but was working when Nathan interviewed Asker and Best. According to the co-worker, when Nathan came back to the interview after a bathroom break, he was visibly shaken and upset. He finished up the interview quickly and immediately left the sound room and went into his office."

The mention of Best in this terrible news took her breath away. Best was trouble with a capital T. "This is unbelievable Jonathon. I listened to that interview on the radio and the new single by Connor, "Follow Me Follow You". It's going to be a huge hit, but the cops don't suspect Best, do they? I mean, I hate the guy, but I don't think he's capable of that kind of violence."

"I agree Bentley, but they are covering all their bases for now and will be interviewing everyone who has any connection to the radio station."

"I just can't believe it. Who could do that sort of thing?"

"Listen let's change the subject, okay, enough talk of that. The reason for this lunch, Bentley, is that I have an offer for you."

Glad to be done talking about the murder of Nathan Steck, she placed both of her elbows on the table, cupped her chin in her hands and asked, "An offer, Jonathon? Really, now what could that possibly be?"

"I'm being serious Bentley, and you're looking at me like I am about to sell you shares in Fannie Mae."

She sat up and folded her hands in front of her, taking on a more serious face, but underneath holding back impending laughter: "I'm sorry, Jonathon. What is it you would like to offer me?"

"That's better, Paxton. When someone tells you they have an offer, don't smirk okay, that's rude. Anyway I am offering you Vice President of Business Development and Licensing for *Music Talks*. The board of directors have agreed to allow you run the position from here in L.A., with a requirement of two to three trips to New York a month. It's a senior position with the largest music publication in the industry, Bentley and one of the biggest publications period. You will be responsible for the company's growth, including our online website publication plus our music charts. The salary is enormous Bentley, in fact, it is ridiculous. It is bordering on seven figures."

"A million dollar salary?" she thought, "that really is ridiculous." "Jonathon, I am extremely flattered that the board is considering me for this position."

"The board is not considering you, Bentley; they have considered and made their decision. They want you for the job."

"I am a journalist, Jonathon, not a desk jockey. I'm not sure. I need time to think about this. This is such a surprise. Will you give me a few days?"

"You have till tomorrow, so go home and call up your new boyfriend so he can tell you himself what a fool you would be to turn this opportunity down. You're forty now remember, so you need to start thinking more long term rather than the next gig you will be covering, okay?"

"Alright, I will let you know by tomorrow. I doubt if I will bother Avery on such a trivial matter as this, but I will consult my cat, I promise."

"Ha ha that's funny, Paxton. How many people get offered a million dollar job today in this country? Please don't be stupid and do the right thing. I am staying the night at the LAX Hilton because I knew you wouldn't say yes without thinking about it. I have a contract in my briefcase and the board wants your signature on it when I land tomorrow, okay sweetheart? Call me if you have any questions or concerns about the position. I have to run now to another meeting, so I will catch a cab. Order some dessert, take your time. I will pay the bill on the way out." Jonathon stood up from his chair and went around and bent over and gave Bentley a kiss on the cheek. "Just think, you won't have to put up with me anymore as your boss, now isn't that a decision maker for you right there?"

****

Jonathon left the Campanile in a taxi which had been parked in front of the restaurant. He instructed the driver to take him to his hotel at LAX, and then he checked his iPhone for messages. There were a lot of them. One email caught his attention. It was from Robert Best, of all people, and he was interested in meeting with him in L.A. before he returned to

New York in the morning. How the hell could he have known his itinerary? Very strange. He checked the time and it was 1:30 p.m. L.A. time, so the office would be open for another thirty minutes. He dialed his secretary's direct line, by-passing the main switchboard, and Diana picked up on the second ring.

"Good afternoon, Jonathon Green's office, how may I help you?"

"Diana, it's Jonathon. Have you taken any calls today from a Robert Best or anyone calling on his behalf?"

"I haven't Jonathon. I have been here all day and the phones have been light. No one called asking where you were or even how to get a hold of you. Why, what's up?"

"What about Angie at switchboard? Can you check with her to see if she received any calls from anyone asking for me or anyone pressing for information on where I was?"

"Jonathon, all calls, regarding editorial matters or any of the journalists in the field come to me, without question."

"I know that Diana, but please check with Angie for me anyway. It's important."

"If you insist, Jonathon. Hold on the line and I will dial Angie's extension."

Jonathon waited but it wasn't very long before Diana was back on the line: "Jonathon, she did have a call from someone insisting to speak with you, and, apparently, I was away from my desk, likely in the restroom, so she told the caller you were away in L.A. on business and that you would not be back till tomorrow afternoon. The caller would not leave a message or a name for you to call back when you returned; he simply hung up."

Jonathon thought: "It had to have been Best. So he knew he was in L.A., but how did he know I was staying the night and flying home in the morning?" "Thanks Diana, I have to run, talk to you tomorrow."

He emailed Best back, letting him know that he had a very tight schedule for the rest of the night and an early flight home, so he would have to catch up with him another time. He also let him know he could call his office in New York and make an appointment to see him. "That should make the pompous ass happy", he chuckled. He wasn't scheduled to leave until 11:00 a.m., but he needed Bentley's signature before he left and he was in no mood to meet the arrogant Best tonight. There was a very small circle of people in the music business that could by-pass his office and email or call him directly. Best certainly wasn't one of them.

He spent the rest of the drive to the hotel returning emails, a text from his wife and then he saw a new email arrive from an unknown address. He was about to delete without opening it, when he glimpsed the subject line, "Have you seen Nathan Steck?" "What the fuck?", he thought. He opened the email and he wished he hadn't. The gruesome corpse of Nathan's headless body with his guts spread across his office floor was clearly displayed on the iPhone's high resolution screen. The caption below the photo read, SEE YOU SOON! Jonathon felt lunch making its way up his throat, so he instructed the taxi driver to pull over. The taxi pulled to the curb and Jonathon whipped the door open and emptied his roasted pork chop all over the pavement, drawing honking horns from passing motorists. His thoughts tumbled, one over the next, "Who is the sick fuck that would have sent that photo? Was it the killer? How did he know my email address and why would he send me that photo?" The cold sweat working its way down his back in the air conditioned cab was not from the outside heat. Jonathon was afraid, in fact he was terrified. He would get to his room, shower, then call the cops.

He would show them the photo sent to his email inbox. They would have the means to trace the sender. "Jesus", he thought, "I might be able to solve a major murder investigation." He told the driver of the taxi to hurry.

****

He slid the room key into the card reader of his room door and entered. Jonathon dropped his briefcase on the chair and flopped on the couch beside it. He dialed Bentley's number.

"Jonathon, you gave me till the morning, remember? I just barely made it home from the Campanile, so I haven't had a real chance to think about it yet."

The tone of Jonathon's voice frightened her, "Bentley, listen to me. I think Nathan's killer is after me too. I don't have the slightest clue as to why, but he is."

"Jonathon, you're scaring me. Why the hell would the killer be after you? What are you talking about?"

"Maybe it's some crazed religious freak murdering people in the music industry, thinking today's music is evil and he needs to kill the people responsible for putting it out there for listeners to hear it. I just received a photo, sent to my inbox from an unknown sender, with a picture attached of Nathans's headless corpse. It's fucking sick, Bentley. Be careful please. I will talk with you tomorrow about the job and I will courier the docs for your signature when I get back. WHAT THE FUCK ARE YOU DOI…"

The phone call abruptly ended. "Why was he yelling at me, asking what I'm doing here?", Bentley thought. "Shit, he wasn't talking to me, he must have been talking to someone else. Someone in his room?" Jonathon was in danger. She dialed 911.

Still holding the phone to his ear, hearing Bentley yelling

his name, all Jonathon could do was stare at Robert Best walking out of his hotel room bathroom towards him. As he did, he was changing. By the time he reached him at the couch, he could only stare at the monster that had transformed out of Best's body. Two massive sinewy and grayish arms, dripping in slime with two claw-like talons on the end of them reached for his throat.

Ten minutes later, an army of police officers stormed into the room and discovered the mutilated corpse of Jonathon Green, torn into pieces and spread around the room like discarded pizza after a college food fight.

Forty-five minutes after that discovery, Homicide Detective Sam Showenstein of the LAPD knocked on the door of Bentley Paxton.

Chapter 6

It seemed that the world was going through a youth movement in the music industry. First, there was the huge success of twelve year old Connor Asker three years ago, when he won 'America's Got Talent' in such dramatic fashion, shocking the TV audience with his raw talent. At the age of fifteen, Connor had just released his debut album and its first single, "Follow You Follow Me", which was rising up the charts rapidly. The winner, three years ago, of Latin America's version of 'America's Got Talent' was Juan Jimenez, also twelve years old. His success had continued and he was still playing in front of packed houses in concerts all over South America. During a recent concert in Buenos Aeries in which Juan opened for Enrique Iglesias, the 90,000 fans demanded an encore that delayed Iglesias' entrance by thirty minutes. They made it abundantly clear that the majority of the young teenage audience members were attending the show to see Juan, and not the headliner. The buzz out of Ireland was about fifteen year old Chloë McClosky, who had the voice of an angel. There was a young girl out of Montreal, Elizabeth Leroux, who was all the talk of Canada, guest performing with the top orchestras in the country.

In the U.S., water cooler discussions centered around fifteen year old Brittany Campbell. She was singing her way to the top on the talent show called X Factor. After Brittany's quarter final performance, the show's creator and one of the

judges, Simon Cowell, told the TV audience that he'd just seen:
"The single best performance he has ever witnessed". That
was after Brittany absolutely killed the Amy Lee song 'You', by
performing a hauntingly beautiful piano solo while also making
a stunning vocal performance. The story of her amazing
childhood talent included a performance on the piano with the
Boston Pops when she was merely twelve years old. It simply
enraptured the TV audience. 'X Factor' rode the Brittany
Campbell band wagon to the top as the most watched show on
television. There would be no stopping Brittany Campbell in
her victory at 'X Factor' and the five million dollar recording
contract that came with it. Even some of the top female artists
were weighing in on Brittany's talent. Katy Perry recently told
Music Talks journalist Bentley Paxton that she was blown away
by her talent; that she had never heard anyone so good, at so
young. She went on to say that Brittany's biggest challenges to
her continued growth as an artist would be to stay grounded,
choose her music wisely. Furthermore, she would need a very
good management team to help her make the choices not only
in music, but her career as a whole. If she was not careful, the
music business could swallow a talent like her and spit her out
just as quickly.

Brittany's mother, Nancy, was one of the leading
environmental researchers in the United States. It caused her
to be away frequently on research projects, speaking
engagements or consulting work. However, she did make it to
see Brittany's quarter final appearance live, along with
Brittany's live-in nanny, Leanne Reston. Without Leanne,
Brittany never would have had the opportunities that had
come her way in music. It would have been impossible for
Nancy to manage Brittany's affairs and her own. As a former
high school teacher, Leanne could assist Nancy in tutoring

Brittany when she needed it. She could also accompany Brittany on all of her trips for concert engagements and 'X Factor' tapings. It also helped that Leanne and Brittany were like sisters, best friends in fact, even though Leanne was twelve years older than Brittany. Nancy was fortunate to have Leanne in her life and in Brittany's life. She also paid her so generously that money could never be an issue between them.

Preparing for her semifinal performance in the coming week was all consuming for Brittany. Nancy felt that she had better get back to doing some work and let her and Leanne do their thing. On Thursday morning, after giving her daughter and Leanne big hugs and letting them know she would be back in L.A. on Sunday night to be with them leading up to the Wednesday night performance, Nancy caught a taxi to the airport and flew back home to Providence. She wouldn't be home long. She just needed to grab a fresh set of clothes, spend a few hours finishing up a paper, and then set off to D.C. on Friday afternoon for a presentation. The science of taking recycling another step further to benefit the planet seemed to be sucking up all of the research funding on Capitol Hill these days and Nancy fervently hoped that trend would continue.

She made her way to the airport security and was happy to see that the line-ups were minimal. Getting through security in less than ten minutes at LAX was an impossible feat, but she just did it, so maybe that was an indication of more good things to come today. She had some time before they would call her flight for boarding so she thought she would grab some breakfast. She found an airport diner specializing in breakfast. Almost succumbing to the smell of the greasy bacon, she settled for an egg and cheese croissant with a side of fresh fruit and cottage cheese. Finding an empty booth that looked out over a section of a terminal, she dug in and discovered she was starving, not just hungry. She took a sip of her coffee and watched as a well dressed business man approached her table and asked: "Excuse me ma'am, I apologize for interrupting your breakfast, but are you Nancy Campbell?"

Still a very attractive woman in her early forties, Nancy often had men approach her for conversation with the intent of hopefully securing her telephone number. She was used to it and was an old pro in deflecting this type of come-on. "Well, I guess that depends on who wants to know?"

The man smiled, revealing a perfect set of even white teeth, "My name is Robert Best. I am a music producer and I noticed you in line getting your breakfast and I just had to say hello. I am a huge fan of your daughter Brittany, an amazingly talented young girl, so it's such a coincidence to bump into her mother at the airport."

The name Robert Best was instantly recognizable to her. He was one of the most influential people in the music industry today. "Mr. Best, I am honored. Nice to meet you and thank you for those kind words about Brittany. She really has come a long way. Please sit down and join me. I have some time before I need to be at my gate."

"Thank you, Nancy, I will join you. Like I said earlier, this is such a coincidence, as I wanted to talk to you about your daughter and her musical career. I was hoping to catch you at the studio this week during the semi-final performances. Have you thought about Brittany's future in the music business?"

"Honestly we have never spoken about it, it is my hope she will go on to university and get a degree. With all her success on the show, I guess it's pretty apparent that we need to start talking about it. But why, would you, the biggest name in music, be interested in Brittany?"

"Nancy, your daughter is a truly gifted musician and she has been since she was a very young girl. Only now is she starting to reach her potential and 'X Factor' has given her the stage to show the world her talent. With her voice and her beauty, she will be a major star in pop music, Nancy. It's absolutely critical, however, that she gets the very best management, or otherwise it could turn into a disaster. Both for her professionally and emotionally. She is extremely talented and beautiful, Nancy, but she is also very young and the music industry can be awfully hard and cruel to kids like her and once the industry has wringed her dry for everything she has, they'll cast her aside like yesterday's news."

The thought of Brittany being emotionally destroyed was a risk that Nancy would not take so she replied, "I will not expose Brittany to those kinds of risks, she's too young and impressionable and she has her whole life ahead of her to pursue her music career."

"This is what I wanted to talk to you about. I would like to represent her, Nancy, both as a manager and as a producer. I am the very best in what I do and I will ensure that she is safe, that she continues her education, including college, and I'll give her every opportunity to be successful in the music industry. The right way. As you know I am currently managing the career of Connor Asker, who is also fifteen years old, and the winner of a TV talent show. I know talent when I see and hear it and Brittany has that. Now is the time to start her career, Nancy, and I believe a career in music is what she wants."

There was a ring of truth in what he was saying as Brittany could ride this popularity she had garnered from the show into a career. Best did seem genuine and he was currently managing the Asker kid. He was a real heavyweight in the business and was well respected. "I will talk with Brittany after the competition and see what she wants to do. If she wants to pursue a career now, I will arrange for the three of us to get together and discuss it further. Now if you will excuse me Robert, I must hurry along before I miss my flight."

****

Best watched Nancy Campbell hurry off towards her departure gate. Within a few days he would have Brittany in his stable, along with Connor and Patrick. Then soon after, he would have the remaining kids as well. His plan was moving along exactly as he knew it would. During the next few years, he would mold their individual careers, making them all superstars. He had waited over seventeen hundred years for this moment and he was getting so close to destroying mankind once and for all that he could barely contain himself. In fact he wouldn't. LAX was a massive airport, one of the largest in the country. Surely, somewhere nearby waiting for a flight, there had to be an unsuspecting man of the cloth that he could shred to pieces. His power churned in his soul like the diesel engine of a Caterpillar. He was ready for battle and when the time came he would rule the universe; it was that simple. "It's a good time for a walk", he laughed to himself, as he got up from the table and flashed his crimson red eyes at a kid who had been staring at him from the next table over and who now grabbed onto his mother like he had seen a ghost.

****

The three remaining contestants didn't stand a chance against Brittany in the semi-finals of the inaugural show of 'X Factor'. It was a race to see who would finish second, because not only did the contestants know they wouldn't beat Brittany, the entire nation knew it was a foregone conclusion. Choosing to sing opera with the Sara Brightman classic, "Time To Say

Goodbye", to showcase her vocal range, Brittany was taking a risk. She had built her audience on pop songs and the detour to classical at this stage, even for her, might be a mistake. It was not. Standing at the front of the stage, away from her piano, she looked absolutely stunning in her gown and the vocal performance was through the roof. The audience and the four judges leapt from their seats in unison to cheer an incredible performance. Fans across America voted for her and she was swept into the finals along with another female singer, much older and very talented, but no match for Brittany Campbell.

Nancy chose to stay the entire week with Brittany and Leanne, setting up office in her hotel suite so that she could be close to her daughter during what could be the defining moment of her young life. She arranged her schedule so she could stay in L.A. She hardly saw Brittany or Leanne the entire week as the show's producers kept them very busy with photo shoots, interviews and more importantly, rehearsing. Leanne kept a watchful eye on Brittany the whole time, making sure she was properly fed and her school work was completed. When the two of them got back to the hotel suite at night, they were so exhausted that other than a few words describing their crazy day, they were fast asleep.

Nancy attended the final rehearsals leading up to the finale and she was blown away by the amount of work that went on behind the scenes of a major live show such as this. The choreography, the props, lighting and the two remaining contestants rehearsing for hours backstage was a lesson in organized chaos. Brittany had chosen to sing John Lennon's "Imagine" and play her piano with no other instruments or backup singers. Listening to her daughter in rehearsal brought tears to her eyes and a moment of wonder at just how bloody good she was. Oh, how she wished James was here with her now to enjoy this moment. Brittany was born to sing and play an instrument. As soon as she thought that, she had a flashback to the day Brittany was born. How she had filled the delivery room with beautiful sounds, like angels singing. It was a miracle from God and that miracle was still giving to this very day. She was so overwhelmed with emotion while watching her sing such a hauntingly beautiful song, that she didn't even hear Brittany finish and walk over to her seat near the stage and wrap her arms around her.

"Mother what is the matter? I've never seen you cry like this before."

Nancy looked up at her daughter and tried to reel in her tears, "I'm sorry baby, sitting here listening to you sing brought back so many memories for me all in a rush, it was overwhelming."

"Were you thinking of Dad, Mom?"

"I was sweetie, he would have been so proud of you right now. If only he could have known his daughter."

"Will you ever be able to let him go, mom? It's just that it's hard to see you when you get like this and, well, it has been fifteen years."

"I know, baby, you're right. I am getting better about it though, seeing you perform just now hit a memory button in my brain. I'm sorry, Brittany, you had to see me cry like this. It will be the last time, I promise."

"Oh Mom, I'm sorry too. I didn't mean to sound so selfish. I know you loved my father very much. I don't ever want to take away those memories from you, but I would like to see my Mom make some new memories. Will that ever be possible, do you think? I am fifteen now, Mom, and soon you will be by yourself. Don't you think it's time you met someone? Maybe you and I can go out somewhere and I'll set you up with someone. Wouldn't that be great?"

Hearing her daughter laugh at the prospect of setting up her mother on a date made her laugh and soon the two of them were giggling and laughing like school girls. Hugging her daughter then taking her hands in hers she said, "Oh honey, you have grown so much, you're no longer my little girl with all that talent but a strong young lady with all the talent in the world and a whole life ahead of you. Listening to you just now playing that beautiful song, I realized that you were born to sing and play. This is who you are and what you are meant to do. When this is all over tomorrow night what do you want to do? Where do you want to go from here sweetheart?"

Brittany looked her mom in the eyes, tears brimming to the surface and said: "This is what I want to do Mom, I want to sing and make music for the rest of my life. When I am up on that stage, I feel like it's just me and my piano and no one else. I feel free, like I have wings and I can fly. It's weird isn't it, but it's true. I love to sing Mom and it's because of you that I am here right now with this tremendous opportunity."

"Nonsense, Brittany, you are here because you are extremely talented."

"Mom, do you remember when I was seven years old and you gave my music teacher Mr. Hallworth permission to allow me to perform solo at the school spring concert, even though I wasn't in music class with the rest of the students? You unlocked my dreams Mom, you really did. I will never forget the support and love you have given me while I pursued music over the years and it is you to whom I owe my success.. I love you so much."

The two of them held each other and bawled some more. The stagehands thought they were crazy. They didn't care. It was a defining moment between mother and daughter.

****

The first season of the 'X Factor' started slowly and struggled to find an audience, but the emergence of Brittany Campbell changed all that and the show was #1 on TV and the finale would likely set records for a live show. Millions tuned in to see Brittany's performances, capped off with her spectacular version of John Lennon's "Imagine". The studio audience was deadly silent; you could have heard a pin drop when Brittany began to perform the song. Her hauntingly beautiful voice rang through the perfectly acoustically tuned concert hall like a splendid harp song. It was a magical performance and when she was done, you could almost feel the thunderous applause of the millions of fans who were standing in their living rooms across America, applauding a young woman on the cusp of superstardom.

The next night, Brittany was crowned the winner and America felt they were witnesses to a superstar being born in front of their eyes. Backstage, after the taping of the show ended and the celebrations began, not only all of the participants in the competition took part in congratulating Brittany, celebrities took time to say their congratulations and best wishes on her career. The show's producers and all of the dancers, stagehands and workers celebrated a long hard journey and took the opportunity to glow a little bit in Brittany's spotlight.

While the chaos swirled all around Brittany, Nancy and Leanne, they were motioned by the show's executive producer to follow him to a VIP lounge area to escape. Once inside, they were able to catch their breath and get some much needed refreshments. Then a familiar voice to Nancy spoke: "Congratulations, Brittany, on an amazing performance tonight and all season. You deserve this, you are truly a very talented young lady."

It was the music producer Robert Best with his hand extended to her and then to Brittany. "I'm not sure where Leanne went, she was here a second ago", she thought. She must have slipped off to the restroom. "Thank you, Mr. Best, it's good to see you again and thank you for those kind words about my daughter. Brittany, may I introduce Robert Best of Blackstar Studios, one of the biggest music producers in America."

Best smiled back at her, a slight blush taking over his face, then took Brittany's hand and said, "Your mother is very generous with her words, Brittany, but I must say she is right." He smiled even more, his perfect smile exuding mega-watt charm.

Brittany took his hand and replied, "Thank you, Mr. Best, for those kind words. And I am very glad you liked my performance."

"Liked is an understatement, my dear. I loved it and so did America. Have you and your mother thought about your career and where you would like to go from here?"

Nancy cut in before Brittany could say anything and took Brittany's hand in hers, looked her in the eye and then turned to Best as she stated: "Yes, we have talked. Music is what she was born to do and this is what she wants to do in her life. All we need now is someone to manage her career and she deserves to be managed by the top producer in the business. So what do you say, Robert, can you work with Brittany?"

Chapter 7

Peter Highfield, personal assistant and security guard for Ann and Michael Lockwood, guided the Mercedes Benz through traffic for the short ride back to Ann's downtown estate. Pulling the sleek sedan into the underground parking complex below the massive condo, Peter made his way up to his office quarters, which was part of the 7500 square foot residence. He had work to do that he wanted to complete before going back to the airport to pick up Ann and Michael. She had instructed him to use his contacts to do a complete work-up on the American music superstar, Connor Asker. She wanted to know everything about him, including his age, where he was born, where he was raised, and a full intel package. Peter felt like he was planning the assassination protocol for a foreign dignitary. What was all the interest in these young music stars anyway? Last week, she had had him research Chloë McClosky from Ireland.

Finding any information on McClosky proved more difficult than he had anticipated, but through his contacts in the Garda, he was able to dig up some interesting facts. He learned that Chloë's birth parents had been viciously murdered and that the baby had been placed in the care of the Roman Catholic Church. A Father Thomas O'Sullivan had overseen her care through Sister Beatrice McGarrigle, who was assigned by Father O'Sullivan to raise Chloë. The girl was now fifteen years old, a very accomplished singer and very well known in her native country. Outside of Ireland, she was relatively unknown.

He entered the massive condo through his own private entrance, which led directly into his living area and office. Entering his office, he threw his jacket and keys on the coat rack as he made his way to his desk and the work he needed to get done. To obtain the information he needed on Asker, he would reach out to a contact in the U.S. Secret Service whom he had met almost seven years ago, when he was stationed in the British MI5. Assigned to the Prime Minister's security detail at the G8 Summit in the United States, Peter was briefed by the Secret Service agent regarding all aspects of the security measures in place for the Summit site in the State of Georgia. A friendship had developed between the two of them that had lasted ever since. It had been awhile since they last spoke, but he hoped he hadn't yet retired. He picked up the phone and was about to dial, when a voice behind him almost made him jump out of his skin.

"Good afternoon, Mr. Highfield, you look like you were about to start working on something important."

Years of training in highly stressful conditions hardly prepares you for a completely unsuspecting surprise shock. Training does, however, give you the tools to recover in mere seconds with a clear mind to react to that shock. Peter already had his Glock 9mm pistol shoulder high and aimed at the stranger dressed in a business suit sitting casually on the couch at the far end of his office. "You have ten seconds to tell me who the fuck you are and what you are doing in my office."

Rising from the couch, and straightening his suit, Robert Best replied, "No need for an overreaction soldier boy, just looking for some information that's all."

"Then I suggest you stay right where you are and not take

another step, or I promise you it will be your last. I want you to put your hands, fingers interlocked, behind your neck and turn around slowly. You so much as cough and I will blow a hole through the back of your head."

Peter watched as the intruder did as he was told. Once his hands were behind his head, he moved in and wrenched one wrist downward, twisting it at a painful angle as he snapped a handcuff on the wrist. He then reached up to pull the other wrist down, when the stranger, with a speed that caught Peter off guard, slammed his elbow down into his cheek. He followed it up with a blow to his wrist that caused the pistol to fly from his hand and clatter across the room. The lightning bolt of pain forced him down onto one knee, but his training kicked in. He responded to the stranger's blows with a hard and vicious kick to the man's ankle, causing it to break and send him crashing to the floor. Peter followed up the leg kick with two more hard leg kicks to the stomach and chest area, forcing the man to roll over in the fetal position to protect against further blows. Peter reached down and wrapped his arm around the stranger's neck, cutting off his air supply, and then screamed into his face, "Who are you and what are you doing here? You have one chance to answer me; otherwise your neck will be broken in five seconds."

Before Peter could react, the stranger had somersaulted backwards up and over Peter's head, freeing himself from the arm lock. In one motion, he drove his fist into the middle of Peter's back with pinpoint precision and incredible power. The devastating blow was from a trained assassin out to kill him and Peter had no idea why. One minute he was entering his office to do some research and the next he was sprawled on the floor with a broken back and quite likely paralyzed from the waist down. Immobilized on the floor, he searched with his eyes for the pistol to kill this maniac. Peter searched his memory banks, trying to think of an enemy from his past that could give him a clue as to why this man was trying to kill him. He drew only a blank. Suddenly, he noticed the pistol against the far wall. Too far away to be any good. He was unable to move, his gun useless; he was a dead man. He wished he was as he watched what unfolded in front of him.

This well dressed killer was now transforming into some kind of monstrous beast. The swelling body of this changing creature split open the fabric of the man's clothes till they fell to the floor. Massive grey and purple muscles rose from the slender man's arms and legs. Long fingers curled into talons tipped by razor sharp claws. The man's head became gigantic, its ears disappearing, only to be replaced by disproportionately tiny pointed flaps. Its face erupted in cracks and fissures leaking puss. The horror of what he was seeing finally revealed itself.

"I am the Prince of Death, of Darkness, the Anti-Christ who will kill not only you tonight, but your beloved Ann and her son. Tell me where they are, you pathetic, washed up fool. Tell me and your death will be swift, or you can choose to be tortured ten times more brutally than the poor and helpless Afghanistani boy you murdered by that same means, years ago. You didn't forget about that now did you? I bet that little episode didn't appear on your resume when Ms. Lockwood interviewed you for the job, now did it?"

Peter knew he was staring into the fiery red eyes of the devil himself and not some maniac mercenary bent on revenge. No one knew about the murder of that child. No one knew because he was alone in the desert when he cut the kid till he bled out. The kid knew where Bin Laden was hiding out; the intelligence was clear. The nine year old boy was the son of one of Bin Laden's mistresses, living in his compound. He never told a soul in all these years and now Satan was about to burn the incident into his mind like a scarlet letter that he could take with him into his next life in hell.

"You are the devil, of that I have no doubt, but if you think I will willingly tell you the whereabouts of the Lockwoods, you are more stupid than even the history books state. I will not repeat the mistakes I made in that desert, I promise you. Now go ahead and kill me quickly, slowly, and painfully. I don't care."

The last word out of his mouth had barely escaped when the beast had wrapped a claw like talon around his throat, squeezing the air and the life out of him. Its eyes were blazing red, its menacing mouth hissed as the thing spoke, "I know she's in Dublin for Michael's performance you fool, do you think I wouldn't have a look-see at your calendar when it is sitting in plain view, on your desk?"

The words were barely audible as Peter struggled to speak against the blackness closing in all around him, "Why does the devil need to look in a calendar to find someone? Just look in your crystal ball. What do you want with them?"

Now Peter understood why the demon did not know the whereabouts of Ann and Michael. They were cloaked in God's grace and protection and could no longer be seen or felt by this evilness.

The last sentence enraged the beast and it opened its mouth wide, it's hideous tongue probed the air in front of him before it screamed, "Your soul will forever be encased in the coffin of the nine year old boy you murdered, soldier. Now die."

Peter Highfield, former British Special Forces, MI5 and killer of a child, felt the razor sharp claws of the beast rip into his chest, piercing his rib cage and wrapping its talons around his heart, his brain function sending one final signal to his dying conscious. His heart had been torn from his body.

****

In Dublin, Ann and Michael had made their way through the VIP entrance of the National Concert Hall after having been picked up by limo, when Ann suddenly gasped and bent over in obvious pain. Michael stopped and looked back at his mother when he heard her gasp, "Mom, what is the matter? Are you okay?"

Ann caught her breath, not sure what she had just experienced, but it was a sudden and sharp pain in her stomach, like an unexpected, hard punch. The feeling of doom and dread was overwhelming. She has felt this before, she knew. The demon was here tonight. She could feel it's presence. Looking up at her son, she replied, "I am fine Michael, I think the turbulence on the way over didn't like the lunch I ate."

She knew her rendezvous with Father O'Sullivan was now in jeopardy. She would not stop now, she couldn't. If he hadn't killed her yet, it was likely that he would soon enough. Michael would be safe and so would Chloë. She was still alive, which meant they still had time.

Their escort from the limo brought them to the symphony's producer, Adam O'Reilly, who led them into a dressing room to relax and prepare for the performance in two hours. O'Reilly informed Michael that there would be a rehearsal in twenty minutes. Before he left, Ann asked, "Mr. O'Reilly, would you happen to know if a Father O'Sullivan and Chloë McClosky have arrived yet?"

"I do not believe so, Ms. Lockwood, but they should be arriving in any minute. I will notify you upon their arrival."

****

Father O'Sullivan and Chloë arrived late to the National Concert Hall in Thomas's old, but reliable, Peugeot. Thomas hustled Chloë into the Hall and into the hands of the NCH producer, Adam O'Reilly. "This is going to be an unusual night", he thought, considering the unscheduled duet with the talk of London, young Michael Lockwood. The horror of another child carrying the same mark of the beast as Chloë frightened him and he struggled with the knowledge that this might be a trap and they would be killed. He never worried about his own life, only Chloë's. He would protect her at all costs. He seriously considered pulling Chloë out and taking her back to the safety of St. Patrick's Academy. He knew that the beast would not harm Chloë, even if he didn't understand why he knew that. There was a bigger picture that involved her and eventually, he would find out what master plan the beast was hatching.

He sat alone in the comfy VIP lounge of the Hall, waiting for Adam to escort him to his seat. Ann Lockwood was in great danger and he needed to warn her tonight. Then he heard the lounge door open and he turned, expecting to get the thumbs up from Adam, signaling that it was time to take his seat in the Concert Hall. Instead, it was someone else, a person whom he did not recognize and who didn't say anything to him as he crossed the room towards the refrigerator. Before reaching the other side of the room, the well dressed stranger turned and, in a flash, pounced on him, driving his knee into his chest. Horrified, Thomas looked up at the stranger's face and his eyes were ablaze like fire, glowing crimson red. The realization of who he was shocked him, even though he half expected him to be here tonight. "What do you want, demon? Come to kill another old and fragile priest like you did Cardinal

Zorn?"

Thomas watched as the demon's face transformed from a demented and horrible disguise to that of a normal man, and then back to a demented face, like an apparition floating in and out of reality. Then, out of nowhere, a powerful and thundering fist slammed into Thomas' cheek. The intense pain was quickly followed by a light show inside of his brain. "Go ahead and kill me, but that won't change the fact that your death is near. God's mercy will not last much longer and His judgment upon you will be brutal."

The man towered over Thomas, his eyes burning red hot, as if the heat of his immense hatred could not be contained. It grabbed him by his suit jacket, lifting him up in the air so that his feet dangled freely below him. It screamed into Thomas's face, with breath so vile that he thought he would pass out from the choking stench of it and not from the hand clutched around his throat: "Silence, you old fool. You priests think that the white clerical collar protects you from evil? You are all such misguided and stupid people, following a myth and thinking you will be saved for all eternity because of a few measly vows." The beast flung Thomas over the chair, where he landed hard on the floor. Dazed and in pain, Thomas struggled to get up but then he felt the familiar grip around his throat, lifting him up into the air, choking him again.

Coughing out the words through the iron grip of the devil's hand, Thomas looked the beast in the eyes and spoke: "I know what you're trying to do, demon. You are using these children to carry out whatever plan you have to inflict your wickedness upon us. It won't work. I will stop you."

The beast roared at him like a lion protecting its territory and then it screamed, "You're going to stop me? You are a funny old priest. What makes you think you can stop the most powerful force in the universe? Tell me old man; I would really like to know."

The beast loosened its grip on his throat and dropped him to the floor. The flow of fresh air into his starving lungs caused Thomas to bend over to hack and cough. He stood up and with a hoarse voice, looked the beast in its demonic eyes and said: "I will stop you with a force far greater than you, the power of the Lord my God. He will crush you under His great shoe like a gnat."

The roar of laughter from the beast sounded like a pack of wolves fighting over one piece of meat. "Stupid priest, your life will end with the knowledge that your God does not exist and, as my prisoner, you will be mocked for all eternity for your pathetic misbeliefs."

He knew the beast would finish him at any second and all he could think about was how he had failed Chloë. The sadness of that reality overwhelmed him and then he heard the beast roar again: "Your death is near, priest, but not tonight. I'm not finished with you yet." Thomas looked up at the beast, confused by what he had just heard, because he was certain that death had swung open its doors for him. The beast stared back at him, its eyes still burning with incendiary hatred, and spoke once more, but this time in a human voice, "Enjoy the performance, Father."

****

Ann stared at the empty chair beside her and wondered what had happened to Father O'Sullivan. The show's producer, Adam O'Reilly, had informed her earlier that he and Chloë had arrived. Where was he? The duet performance was about to begin. She watched as the conductor finished up a piece, then turned and walked to the podium and announced: "Ladies and gentlemen, the RFE has a very special treat for you tonight. As advertised, we have a special performance from fifteen year old Michael Lockwood, the singing sensation from London. What you do not know is that he will be joined by our very own singing phenomenon, fifteen year old Chloë McClosky. Please give a warm welcome to Michael and Chloë as they perform a trio of songs handpicked by the RFE, starting with the beautiful duet, 'The Prayer', as performed by Celine Dion and Andrea Boccelli."

As the crowd showed their appreciation at the surprise inclusion of Chloë McClosky, Ann was relieved to see Father O'Sullivan as he made his way to the seat beside her. As he approached her, she was shocked to see that his face was badly bruised and swollen. He walked awkwardly and seemed to be holding his ribs. He had been beaten. No one paid much attention to him as he struggled to sit down beside her; they were too busy cheering for Chloë and Michael.

"Father O'Sullivan, I am Ann Lockwood. What happened to you? You look like you were hit head on by a dump truck. You need to get to a hospital."

The symphony started playing, followed a few seconds later by Michael, beginning the duet, when Father O'Sullivan leaned in closer to Ann and spoke: "I'll be okay, Ann. You must leave here at once with Michael. You are in grave danger."

"What happened to you, Father? Who attacked you? We are safe here. We are surrounded by hundreds of people."

Looking in her eyes, Father O'Sullivan clutched her forearm as he spoke with a very deliberate and clear voice, although it was hushed to avoid attracting attention and disrupting the performance: "The beast is here. He almost killed me just a few minutes ago. He is planning a major attack on mankind, Ann, and somehow, Michael and Chloë are part of it."

"I know that, Father. I have known that about Michael for a very long time and most recently I have put together the connection to Chloë, which is why I arranged to meet you here tonight."

"The fact that you and I are still alive is by design, Ann. He could have killed me tonight, but he let me live. He is using us in his master plan, just like the kids. We must find a way to stop him." Father O'Sullivan explained urgently.

Ann sucked in her breath with a thought that rocked her in her seat. She gazed at Father O'Sullivan, a look of horror stretched across her face, as she whispered: "Father, what if there are other kids, just like Michael and Chloë that are also part of the demon's master plan?"

Chapter 8

Father David Beckstead, leader of SOSL, and family priest to the Oakley family, tried in vain to reach Father O'Sullivan in Dublin. The murder of Peter Highfield, the personal assistant to Ann Lockwood, in his office at the Lockwood home the previous night was one of the most brutal murders seen in London in many years. The last vicious killing in London, of that extreme nature, was the one that also happened in the same home more than fifteen years ago. That was during the rape and attack on Ann, which also resulted in the slaughter of Dalton Lockwood. Several months later, the Lockwood estate was the site of the beheading of Ann's mother, Emily.. It certainly appeared as if the family was cursed and the tabloids would have a field day with the latest murder. It further cemented the growing legend of the Lockwood estate as a haunted home, which could never be sold if it ever went on the market..

Early that morning, Scotland Yard detectives had notified him of the murder and asked if he could come to the Lockwood home to console Ann and Michael. They informed David that Ann and Michael were in Dublin earlier in the evening attending a concert with the RFE National Symphony Orchestra, where Michael had performed with special guest, Chloë McClosky. David had hoped to get input from Thomas before meeting with the Lockwoods.

To complicate things even further, Sherman Oakley, the

estranged father of Ann and one of the wealthiest men in Europe, was wasting no time instructing his lawyers to begin legal proceedings against his daughter to gain custody of Michael, based upon unfit and dangerous living conditions for his grandson. David had been the family priest to the Oakley's since he entered the priesthood and began his work at St James Roman Catholic Church in London more than thirty two years ago. Sherman had proven over the years to be a tough person in business and even tougher toward Ann, when he cut off all ties with his daughter after Michael was born. He had tried to counsel Sherman over the years to be more accepting of his daughter's plight, but the old man would hear nothing of it. The Oakley's financial contributions to the church were enormous and the church elders insisted that David stay out of the conflict between father and daughter, because they did not want to risk losing such large donations.

David's PhDs in both economics and political science would have afforded him a successful career in business, but his unwavering desire to help his fellow man through the word of God brought him to the priesthood. The majestic and historic St James was his platform to exact change in mankind, not the podiums of politics. He chose simplicity over conflict, passion for the spiritual word of God over the shallow words of political leaders. He knew the world was quickly heading towards a Judgement, a reckoning of sorts with God, a day when man would account for his history and David believed the time was near. Not only was he the Roman Catholic Church's foremost expert on the biblical beliefs about the end of times as foretold in The Book of Revelations, he was also the head of the Vatican's secret committee called SOSL. The acronym stood for the Special Office for Spiritual Longevity and its mandate was to study, track and report world events that led to the theory that Judgement Day was imminent. David had been chosen by Rome to be a member of SOSL soon after he had taken his vows of priesthood. He led SOSL in its early days, before handing the leadership over to a young priest from America, Father Kevin Zorn, who eventually rose to the level of Cardinal, before his tragic death in Ireland three years previously. David was tasked, once again, to take over the leadership of SOSL after the Cardinal's death. During the past three years, David and Father O'Sullivan had become quite close through their interaction with SOSL and Thomas's firm belief that Satan was actively at work on earth, plotting a diabolical plan to destroy mankind. The McClosky girl, Thomas believed, was somehow a part of that plan.

David could not deny that the emergence of Michael Lockwood and his incredible talents both as a musician and singer at such a young age and his meteoric rise in the music world were eerily similar to the history of the McClosky girl. David was anxious to vet this theory of similarity with Thomas. The surprise concert last night in Dublin with both Michael and Chloë was a smashing success and the music world was abuzz about those two. "What is going on here?", thought David.

Although David was still unable to reach Thomas in Dublin, he arrived at the Lockwood estate, a sprawling and private property in the heart of downtown London. Police cars filled the driveway and uniformed officers monitored the entryway to keep the press at bay. David was met at the door by investigators and quickly ushered into the study, where Ann was waiting. Sitting in an arm chair next to hers, he took her hand and said: "I'm very sorry to hear about Peter. He was a fine man. How are you holding up, Ann?"

She looked at him with eyes that reflected little sleep, but they also showed a determination. He was surprised at her directness when she spoke: "Let me be frank, Father. It is not even noon of the day after the grisly murder of my trusted assistant in my home when I am served by my father's lawyers, seeking custody of my son. What is the meaning of this? You are the Oakley family priest and spiritual advisor. You have been a part of this family for as long as I can remember. Have you spoken with my father and can you explain what he is trying to do?"

Looking at her sitting there, all alone in this big house with her son, having lived through so much tragedy, David's heart went out to her when he replied: "Ann, I am so sorry. I knew your father was planning something drastic, but I never thought he would take it this far and the timing is appalling. Sherman is a very determined man, Ann, and I must warn you, he will not stop until Michael is safely in his permanent care."

She was furious when she replied: "The nerve of that son-of-a-bitch, excuse me, Father. He had nothing to do with the raising of Michael, ever. He has invited Michael to Oakley family gatherings over the years, but they are few and far between. Michael barely knows him!"

David shifted in his chair, so he could look at Ann directly, when he replied: "Ann, you are right in what you say, it's outrageous. Your father is a very powerful man with deep connections right up to the Royal Family. He will stop at nothing and the power of his money and influence will know no boundaries, Ann."

She looked at him with a look that David could not avoid, a look of disgust directed at him. "Father, you are his priest. Talk to him for Christ's sakes and tell him Michael belongs with his mother. He is almost sixteen years old, his musical career is exploding and he needs me now more than ever. It's just been him, and I, all these years since he was born. We are survivors Father, and be damned if I will let my power hungry, ruthless and heartless father ruin Michael's life. I won't. That is exactly what he will do if he gets his hands on Michael. He will force him into giving up his music to come and work for Oakley Steel."

Cringing at Ann's choice of words in using the Lord's name in vain, he suppressed it because she was right. Sherman, would do exactly what she said by making Michael work in the family business rather than allowing him to continue to pursue what he was born to be, a musician. "Ann, the Church will not allow me to get involved in this matter; my hands are tied, and I am sorry."

"Your Church? You mean to tell me the Church elders are more concerned with the precious donations from Sherman Oakley than the welfare of a child? That is abhorrent, Father, and disgusting. Excuse my directness Father, but I would like you to leave my home now and when you see the leadership of your Church next, please pass on a message to them from me. Tell them the generous support of the Lockwood Foundation to the St James, though not as large as Sherman Oakley's contributions, is finished. Goodbye Father."

He left the Lockwood estate feeling about as low as he had ever felt in his entire career and life as a priest. He came to console Ann, for her loss of Peter Highfield, and instead their meeting had quickly disintegrated into a heated discussion regarding the pending legal action by Sherman Oakley. The situation forced him to look weak and foolish in front of Ann. He decided right there and then that he would do everything he could to stop Sherman Oakley in his bid to use his power and money to interfere in the life of Michael Lockwood. He also had influence with certain politicians that attended his

Church and he would not hesitate to use it. As one of the most respected clergy in all of England, he would also use that in a family court to testify on Ann's behalf. It was the least he could do for that woman. He knew he would feel the wrath of the Church elders for his defiance "but to hell with them", he thought to himself, as he continued to fume.

He arrived back at the St. James and stopped by the administration office for any messages and to let Helen, the office administrator, know to contact Sherman Oakley to schedule a meeting. "Let him know, Helen, that I would like to meet as quickly as possible and his office is fine. I am feeling a little off, and I am going to lay down for a bit, so give me an hour before you disturb me. Thank you."

For some reason, he felt uneasy all of a sudden. He needed to take a Gravol to settle his stomach and then lie down. The sensation that something terrible was about to happen was growing inside of him. As he made his way out the side exit of the rear of the Church and down the twenty foot walk to the Rectory, it felt like a mile. He was starting to sweat profusely and struggled to open the door. "Is this it for me? Am I having a heart attack?" he worried. Finally, he was able to get his shaking hand to navigate the key to open the door. When he entered his quarters, he wished he had never gone to the Rectory. In fact, he wished he was as far away from there as he possibly could be.

A young boy, twelve years old at the most, one of the newest choirboys, was naked and hog tied on the middle of his bed. Standing over him was a creature that could only have come from Hell. It was huge, it's body almost filling the entire room. The oily, greyish skin covered disproportionate muscles stacked onto an almost eight foot frame, making it terrifyingly hideous. The head was almost as wide as its massive shoulders.

Its ears were large, grey and slimy. Folds of skin gathered at the protruding forehead above the eyes, almost shielding the sinister red eyes that glowed from within. At the end of its massive arms were claw-like talons that the creature manoeuvred like fingers.

The boy was struggling against the rope tied around his neck, then down to his feet and then to his hands behind his back. Any second, he would lose his ability to keep his neck arched before the rope would then tighten and strangle him. David struggled against the severe pain resonating through his chest and arms. Looking at the beast, he cried, "Leave him alone! You are here for me! Let him go in the name of God!" With one hand, he held himself up against the wall as he tried to move his feet forward, but they were stuck like they were encased in cement. He couldn't move.

The beast screamed at David, "You think you can help Ann Lockwood by testifying against Sherman Oakley? Michael belongs with his grandfather and away from that stinking whore. You are a weak and pathetic priest that has the courage of a mouse. If only O'Sullivan was weak like you. Your God laughs at your weakness, like I do."

David fell to his knees and prayed for the life of the boy, "God have mercy on this boy and release him from the clutches of your enemy. Sacrifice my soul for his, dear God. I pray this in…"

The beast boomed, "Silence, you fool. He's not listening and there is nothing He can do to stop me if He was. Do you feel your heart being squeezed Father? That's right, you do feel it. Before your heart stops beating, watch this helpless boy die, Father, and take with you when you see me in Hell, the knowledge that your legacy is that of a sick pedophile. You had a heart attack Father, while molesting this child." The beast's hoarse laughter shook the windows of the tiny Rectory.

David fell to the ground onto his side, gasping for air as his heart no longer fed oxygen-rich blood to his lungs. He died with the image of the boy's shaking arms no longer able to withstand the tension of the rope around his neck, as they went weak, and the rope tightened around his throat with ferocious force. They were both dead in seconds.

The beast now transformed himself into a naked man. He walked to the priest's closet, took a set of his clergy clothing and proceeded to get dressed. Once he was satisfied that the black shirt and black pants were suitable, he surveyed the room and was quite impressed with how he had set this little ruse into play. The famous Father Beckstead, leader of the Vatican's SOSL, and respected priest, would now shame the Church like so many before him with the scandal of being a pedophile priest, but with a twist. This well-respected priest would be exposed, not only as a pedophile, but also as a child murderer. He could see what the headlines in the tabloids would read, 'High ranking Catholic priest dies of a heart attack after molesting and killing a twelve year old boy. Laughing so loud that he thought he would burst a vein in his temple, Robert Best, dressed to look like a normal priest, took an extra minute before he exited the Rectory, to position Father Beckstead's now naked body, on the bed beside the bulging, wide-eyed and very dead boy.

****

Father Thomas O'Sullivan, rested comfortably on his trusty armchair, and sipped a cup of his favorite Irish tea, blended Assam and Ceylon from Sri Lanka laced with more than a dash of whole milk. He opened the New Testament to Matthew 7:24-27 and began reading and preparing for his upcoming sermon on 'Obedience to God'.

"Therefore, whoever hears these sayings of Mine, and does them, I will liken him to a wise man, who built his house on the rock." "And the rain descended, the floods came, and the winds blew and beat on that house; and it did not fall, for it was founded on the rock". "But everyone who hears these sayings of Mine, and does not do them, will be like a foolish man who built his house on the sand." "... and the rain descended, the floods came, and the winds blew and beat on that house; and it fell. And great was its fall."

Thomas went on to include further passages from the Books of Matthew, Luke and John in his sermon. "How man has become so disobedient", thought Thomas. God was ushering in his fury onto this world because of it, Thomas knew. Man has fallen a long way in his obedience to God and Thomas took some responsibility for that. It was his job and that of the thousands of other Christian clergy around the world to bring back obedience to our Maker. They were failing miserably. The Anti-Christ was marching on this earth and he was winning the war. Soon God would cleanse this earth of its sin and when He did, Satan would be there to collect the lost souls of men like fish in a giant net. Thomas would strive with his last breath to stand before him and defy him what he coveted the most. Closing his Bible, and setting it on his lap, he reflected on the events of the last fifteen years and his many confrontations with the beast. Thomas has tasted death on many occasions, staring directly into the eyes of Satan himself, but he had survived. God was using him in this fight; otherwise he would have been dead many times over. What He had in store for him, Thomas didn't care; he just knew that when He needed him, he would be ready.

The cordless phone rung and pulled Thomas out of his thoughts. "It is getting late, so who could be calling me now?"

he wondered. He hated cordless phones, because he could never remember where he had left them the last time he used them. He could see the handset of the phone turning bright orange with each ring, underneath the tea towel on the counter. Finding it, he looked at the caller I.D., and saw it was a call from Rome. Answering it on probably the tenth ring, as he had no voicemail to interrupt the rings, he said, "Father O'Sullivan."

The voice on the other end was high pitched and sounded panicked. It was Italian. He did not recognize the voice, "Father O'Sullivan, I am Father Acconci, the Vatican public spokesman. I apologize for calling so late in the day in Ireland. I am sorry, but I have terrible news to share with you. It involves Father David Beckstead. I am afraid that he is dead." Father Acconci went on about a story of severe scandal brewing in London regarding the torture and sexual molestation of a twelve year old boy in Father Beckstead's rectory. Both were discovered dead, lying naked beside each other, the young boy tied and strangled with rope. The newspapers and tabloids were going crazy. The Vatican wanted Thomas to leave for Rome at once to discuss the Church's response to this terrible crime and the whiplash of scandal to the Church as a whole.

He hung up with Father Acconci and collapsed into his arm chair. He was shaking and thought he might be sick. "Father Beckstead a pedophile? A murderer? Impossible!", thought Thomas. Then the phone rang again and this time the caller I.D. said 'private'. His mind was still reeling from the news of Father Beckstead, as he answered, "Hello."

"O'Sullivan, what did you think of the news of your buddy Beckstead? Pretty sick motherfucker, isn't he Father? Too bad he's dead and couldn't see the scandal it'll bring to your beloved, but broken church, Father."

The beast.

His shaking hands stopped, replaced by a swelling anger, he screamed at the demon on the other end of the line, "You're a coward demon! Just like the word of God teaches. You're a liar and a coward. You killed a child! I will kill you with my own hands when I get the chance!"

The laughter coming through the phone turned his blood to ice. He gripped the phone even harder. Then the beast bellowed with a voice so demonic it sounded like it was coming from a burning inferno of hatred, "Your old and withered hands couldn't crush a grape, Father. Who do you think you are? You think you are surrounded by the protection of God? Do you think Father Beckstead thought that too, O'Sullivan?"

Before Thomas could respond the demonic voice continued, "I'm coming for you, Father. Be ready and then we'll see who the coward is. Shredding you like cheese will be the highlight of my day." The following laughter was deafening.

The phone line went dead.

Angrier than he had been for a very long time, Thomas hurled the handset into the kitchen, and watched it smash to pieces against the kitchen wall.

He gave his anger a minute to subside, then he prayed.

Chapter 9

Marie Jimenez sat on her back porch in the same house in Maracaibo, Venezuela just as she and her late husband, Rafael, had done almost every night of their married life. They would spend hours at a time just sitting and holding each other after he had stuffed himself with the arepas which she cooked and he loved so much. They would sit and dream about starting a family. Now, after an unbelievable fifteen years, she still missed him terribly and could feel his presence around her when she was alone and feeling sad. Their son, Juan, now fifteen years old, was away on a concert tour in Florida. He would be performing for the thousands of South America fans in Miami, Orlando, Tampa Bay and Jacksonville in concert venues seating five thousand people. The concerts would sell out within hours of the tickets going on sale. Soon, he would be performing in front of crowds of twenty thousand or more as his popularity grew. Unfortunately, the demands of Marie's work as executive assistant to Antonio Jose Escalona, VP of Exploration for Heavy Oil at Petroleosde Venezuela S.A., Venezuela's state-owned oil conglomerate, kept her from attending most of Juan's performances. Since he had turned South America upside down with his performances when he won the 'Cuanto Vale El Show', Venezuela's version of 'America's Got Talent', he had skyrocketed in popularity. His American manager and producer, Robert Best, had Juan working around the clock, practicing and preparing, not only his singing abilities, but his choreographed dance moves as well. His concert shows included up to a dozen dancers and the precision execution of their dance moves was extraordinary. Juan was a heart throb that sent the pubescent girls into frenzy when he danced. His voice was silky smooth and had such a beautiful tone to it that, when he would sing a ballad, the girls would try to rush the stage to get a piece of him. Most of Juan's music was original, supplied from the growing collection of songs written by Patrick Benning. He sang all of the songs in English, with the exception of the few Latin American songs he included in his concerts.

Marie was worried that Juan was working too hard and that being away from home for so long at a time couldn't be good for him. She often thought that perhaps she should slow him down by informing Mr. Best that she wanted to give her son more time to develop his musical career. What was the rush? He was only fifteen years old. He was still so young to be faced with the pressures he had. She was feeling guilty about all of that and she decided to have a discussion with Mr. Best once Juan was back from the Florida tour. Her sister, Sophia, was adamant that Juan needed to slow down and she was constantly nagging her to tell Juan's manager so.

Sophia was picking her up in a few hours, as they were having a girl's night. There would be some shopping, then dinner and if they still had the energy, maybe a movie. Marie loved her big sister and her husband and children. They had been there for her and she knew she never would have made it through the tragic death of Rafael without them. The success of Juan's career allowed for the two of them to help Sophia and her family out financially, by getting them out of a cramped apartment and into a home of their own not far from where she and Juan lived. The money Juan was making had not made him rich yet, but he was getting very close. He pleaded with his mother to leave her job at the oil company and be part of his management team, along with Mr. Best, but she refused. She loved her job and she also felt that it was important that Juan make his mark in this world without his mother's direct influence. Besides, Mr. Best was one of the best in the business and she knew that Juan was well looked after, even if he was working too hard.

Marie made her way from the peaceful tranquility of her back porch and into the house to get ready before Sophia arrived and became cranky when she was not ready. Her spirits lifted as she thought about spending time with her sister; it would be a fun night, which was something she needed.

Two hours later, the two of them clinked their wine glasses together after they had settled in at their favorite restaurant, the Katamaran, a popular local eatery that specialized in seafood and Columbian cuisine. Sophia looked radiant in her yellow and white sundress with white high heels. Marie chose to wear a tighter fitting white mini skirt with a navy blouse with sparkly sequins. The two of them had drawn the stares of the men in the restaurant, as they had walked to their table earlier.

After toasting to a great evening, Sophia said, "Marie, you look so damn good, why don't you date? You have been alone for so many years. The time is long overdue for you to meet someone and start a relationship."

"Sophia, can we please just have a fun night without talking about men or dating or any of that stuff? I have my hands too full with work and Juan's career to even think about going out on a date."

"That is a load of crap and you know it, sister. We have been having this conversation for years and you keep saying the exact same thing. Oh sister, I have to work and Juan is singing this weekend and blah, blah, blah. Come on, Marie, you are not getting any younger, you're beautiful as hell and you are alone half the time because Juan is always singing somewhere with that creepy manager. Juan is getting older, Marie, and it won't be long until he will be a man and making his own decisions or at least the ones that Best guy will let him make."

"That's not fair, Sophia. Mr. Best is strict because he has to be in this business and look at Juan's career; it's taking off in leaps and bounds."

"I never said he wasn't a good manager or producer or whatever he is, but there is something about that guy that creeps me out. Just be careful with him okay, Marie? Just some friendly advice from your big sister, is all."

"Just to put your mind at ease, I have been thinking about Juan and his music career a lot lately and I think he is moving too fast. I am going to speak with Mr. Best about slowing down some and giving Juan a break to let him be a teenager for awhile."

"That is the best thing I have heard you say in a while. If you need some help putting Best in his place, let me know and I would be glad to help you with that."

Laughing, Marie replied, "Oh, I am sure you could put him in his place. Juan will not be happy with me as I have tried talking with him about slowing things down before and he just shrugged me off. You know how teenagers are. However, he will thank me in five years, when he still has his sanity."

****

After shopping and dinner and too many glasses of wine, Sophia and Marie decided to call it a night. Sophia drove her little sister home, watched till she was safely inside and got the usual wave from Marie through the window that everything was okay, then drove off for home. Driving the short distance, Sophia reflected on Marie's incredible journey over the years. Her story could be made into a movie, it was so unbelievable. Fairytale wedding to a man who should have been a major league baseball star, then savagely beaten while watching her husband being murdered. Her husband's unborn child grew up to be a major singing star. What a ride it had been.

A block from home, Sophia was about to make the turn onto her street when she was startled to suddenly see police lights flash behind her. "Shit", she thought to herself, "I'm being pulled over a block from my house?" She quickly calculated the amount of wine she drank tonight, but she was confident that the glasses were well spaced, so she should be okay. Why was she being pulled over? The cop better have a good explanation. The cop came to the window, asked the usual bullshit line for license and registration, then returned to his car without so much as a response when Sophia asked why she was being pulled over. The prick was probably letting her stew for a while, figuring that the more scared she got, the more of a bribe she would be willing to pay. She knew she would paying some sort of pay-off to the cops tonight, that's how it worked, but what this asshole didn't know was who he was dealing with. He'd end paying her money just so she would leave him alone. "Bring it buddy", she uttered under her breath.

At least another ten minutes had passed before Sophia finally saw the cop step out of his cruiser. She was steamed and she took a few deep breaths to calm down. She had no patience for scumbag crooked cops. They were all on the take and it made her sick. The cop had the classic look she hated; big belly, unkempt and very likely, untrained and on the take.

Acting like he thought was competent, he appeared at her window and commanded, "Ma'am, please step out of your car and keep your hands in the air as you do, so I can see them."

Then she lost it. This son-of-a-bitch was going to have her lean over the hood of her car so he could have a free grope session. Not with her he wasn't. "You can kiss my ass, officer. You are making an illegal stop, as I have done nothing wrong. What is it you want? You want to feel my tits up before you rob me of my money? Not going to happen. You either step aside and let me be on my way, or I will speed dial my lawyer right now." Sophia demanded.

Before she even had a chance to speak her next sentence, the cop had his handgun out of his holster and pointed straight at her head, only inches away, "Get the fuck out of the car now, bitch, before I blow your brains out all over the dashboard. Now move it."

Now she was scared. This cop was a psycho. He would likely take her to a secluded place and rape her first before he robbed her. Right now, with a gun about to go off at the side of her face, she decided to play it cool until she had an opportunity to either run for it or disable this cocksucker with a powerful kick to the nuts. "Alright, alright, I'm getting out. Take it easy, Mr. Policeman."

Once she was out of the car the cop did what all cops in this city do - take advantage of innocent people. He handcuffed her hands behind her back with a force that wrenched her arms awkwardly, shooting pain up and down them and then he snapped the handcuffs so tightly that she could feel her wrists go numb instantly from a lack of blood supply. Then he shoved his groin into her ass and groped her breasts through her dress. Not a single car in this neighborhood was in sight. Then he barked, "You like this, don't you? You probably make it a habit to break the law so you'll be pulled over in the hope that some poor cop will feel sorry for you and give you some attention."

Her blood boiled, thinking of what a loser with a badge could do, "Fuck you, asshole. I'll have your badge and your dick on my fireplace mantel as a trophy, once my lawyer is done with you and your corrupt police department."

The officer sneered, "Good luck with that, okay. Keep it up and your lawyer will be determining if you ever made a will."

The cop grabbed her by the arm and walked her to his cruiser, where he threw her into the backseat. Then, he got in the front seat, turned off his roof lights, pulled onto the road and sped away.

Sophia knew she would be badly beaten and raped tonight and would be lucky to survive. If she did, she wouldn't stand a chance if she tried to press charges. Nobody in the police department would believe her. Every one of them was crooked and they all backed each other up and supported each other as they ran roughshod over this city. He pulled the cruiser into the deserted parking lot of an abandoned school yard. This was where it was going to happen. Sophia surveyed the school grounds and could see that any residential homes were at least three blocks away. It would be a long run to find safety in those homes, if they would even let her in and help her before the cop threatened them with the same fate. The cop got out of the car, opened the back door and, rather than drag her out, he climbed in beside her. He would beat the shit out of her right here in the backseat of his cruiser. This was the first time she was able to get a good look at the cop's face and he did not even appear to be Venezuelan. He was likely not even South American. In fact, he looked American. Sophia thought he looked familiar, then when he spoke, she knew and the terror filled her veins like ice water.

"You know, you and your sister should stop worrying so much about Juan. He's in very capable hands."

Sophia hissed, "Where is Juan? What have you done with him? I swear to God, you will not leave here tonight alive if you so much as laid a finger on him."

Robert Best laughed hysterically at her before responding, "Your hands are handcuffed behind your back. What are you going to do? Drive one of the heels of your pretty shoes through my skull?" Best continued to laugh when Sophia made her move. She catapulted herself, shoulder first, into Best, making contact with his jaw. She could hear it snap. Using the car door she kicked off her heels and braced her feet into the door and aimed another shoulder at his head. This time, she connected flush in the middle of his face, breaking his nose. She drove hard again a third time slamming her shoulder with all the power she could muster into Best's face. He slumped over and Sophia wiggled her armless body over top of him and out the open door. Kicking herself free from Best, she fell onto the gravel of the school parking lot, bruised and bleeding from the struggle. As she was trying to right herself so that she could stand up and make a run for it, she heard a loud roar come from the car. Lying on her side, she looked up at the police cruiser and wished she hadn't. It was no longer the American, Robert Best, masquerading as a Maracaibo cop, but a monster. The cop's uniform was shredded and hanging off of the huge upper torso of a demonic beast. Its head was massive and grotesque with eyes that glowed a bright red. She was about to be ripped to pieces by this thing, whatever it was. She began to pray out loud. She prayed, not for herself, but the life of her husband and children and the life of her sister and Juan.

The beast screamed in a voice so hoarse and demonic that Sophia could barely discern what it was saying: "Don't waste your breath, bitch. He can't hear you, never has and He never will. Your husband didn't put up nearly as much of a fight as you have. Too busy trying to protect those youngsters, I guess."

When Sophia heard that he had killed her husband and kids, she rolled face first into the gravel and sobbed. Pieces of gravel made their way into her mouth, yet she continued to sob uncontrollably as she struggled with the realization that her family had been destroyed. Suddenly, a huge and powerful claw wrapped itself around her throat and lifted her off the ground. As she was forced to look into the glowing red eyes of what surely had to be Satan himself, Sophia sealed her fate by spitting into his face. She yelled, "Go ahead and kill me, you evil fuck. I will seek revenge for my family, through God, in my next life."

The look of utter hatred in the beast's eyes deepened with the mention of God's name and the claw around her neck tightened and squeezed all the air out of her lungs. Sophia realized that her life was quickly ebbing away but her thoughts of her life and her loved ones were interrupted by the demon's final words to her: Die knowing that Juan is my son. It is I who fathered him and not the pathetic Rafael like your sister wanted you to believe."

****

At the exact same time that Robert Best had crushed the neck of Sophia Mendoza, he also waited off stage with a cold bottle of water and a towel for Juan as he finished his second encore performance at The Mahaffey concert hall in St. Petersburg, FL. Best's glowing red eyes were not seen by anyone amongst the lights reflecting everywhere from the light show sweeping the stage. The frenzied, sold out crowd of just over three thousand, mostly of South American descent, would leave the concert tonight and continue to spread the word of how fantastic Juan Jimenez was in concert. His plan was right on target and, other than a few hiccups along the way with the murders of Jonathon Green, Peter Highfield and the Mendoza's, his musical prodigies were becoming more popular every day. Soon, he would have all seven of them performing individually to sold out crowds around the world.

Soon after, the world would be his.

Chapter 10

The performance by Chloë and Michael Lockwood last week was a smashing success. The chemistry the two shared on-stage was obvious, instant and amazingly rare, considering the two had never met each other, never mind sang together. When Ann Lockwood arranged the surprise duet for Chloë and Michael on the concert stage in Dublin, she knew it was a risk. She had no doubt that they would perform brilliantly together, but she worried about the consequences of their meeting. She was not the only one. What is he up to?" worried Thomas, who assumed that the demon was, as usual, behind it all. Thomas rose from his bed to begin his day. His seventy-three year-old body still had some youthfulness attached to it. The years of paying attention to what he ate and keeping up a modest workout regimen was paying dividends today. He knew that he would need every ounce of strength and energy he could muster in the coming months. His body was still sore from his encounter with the beast last week at the concert hall. He stood and stretched his creaky body, then dropped to the floor to begin his daily stretching, pushups and sit-ups routine. Thomas always slept in his boxers, not liking the restrictiveness of pajamas. When he went through his brisk twenty minute workout on the floor in his boxers, he would be a sight to see if anyone charged into his rectory. Once he was finished, he stood and stretched some more, reaching for the ceiling. Straightening himself out, he walked over to his kitchen window to glimpse the construction workers arriving to begin their day on the renovation and expansion of the Church.

Thomas finished his shower and dressed for the day. During the week, Thomas chose to wear his usual clerical clothing consisting of a black long sleeved shirt, black pants and his black nylon bomber jacket, if the air was cool. He always wore his white roman collar, the trademark signature of a priest. He knew of others who flaunted the strict rule of the Church about priests wearing clerical clothing at all times. Their casual and cavalier attitude towards their responsibility angered Thomas, because it showed a lack of respect for the profession and the Church.

He always rose at 7:00 a.m. and almost always left the rectory and walked over to the Church at 8:00 a.m. It was a routine he had followed for decades. The other routine was prayer. Thomas prayed every morning when he rose and before he started his exercises. It was like he was letting God know that He was his priority before everything else. Plus, he wanted God's blessings, wisdom and guidance spelled out before he started his day. Thomas prayed all day long and all night. Sometimes his prayers were specific in nature or for a particular person. Often they were long but, at other times, they were short little bursts of conversation with his maker. The Lord, omniscient, knew of the circumstances surrounding Chloë and Michael, and he prayed to Him daily for his guidance. Thomas knew without a shred of doubt that the Lord Almighty was also planning the destruction of this demon. He would stay strong and on guard and wait for God's word to guide him. He would seek the guidance from the SOSL group next month, when they were scheduled to convene in Rome.

The final routine of the morning was breakfast. He loved

fixing himself eggs and bacon or sausages plus two slices of rye toast. Like prayer, starting his day with a full stomach was mandatory. Once he was ready for the day, he made his way to his office in the church. He took a minute to speak with Mrs. Beckeridge, the Church Administrator, to see if she had any pressing matters that required his attention. He got his usual morning scolding from her as he liked to call it when she brought him up to speed on the church affairs for the day. Giving her a series of head nods after each item that drove her crazy, he would send her off with a wink that would cause her to roll her eyes in frustration. The routine complete, Thomas made his way to his desk to settle in for the day. He had a meeting at 10:00 a.m. with the contractor for an update on the progress of the renovation. He also had a luncheon with the Deacons' wives to discuss the church's plans for the upcoming Christmas season. "Oh joy", he thought to himself, "a luncheon with the Deacons' wives." Oh, how he disliked those luncheon meetings. Thank goodness he had another meeting at 1:30 p.m. that would pull him away from the cat fighting that was sure to take place amongst these women.

He was interrupted from his thoughts when Mrs. Beckeridge entered his office, "Excuse me, Father O'Sullivan. Sister Agnew from St. Patrick's Academy is on the phone for you. Would you like me to take a message?"

His first thought was that something was wrong with Chloë. Fear instantly began to build in his stomach. He replied a little too quickly, "No I will take it. Thank you."

"Yes, Father," answered Mrs. Beckeridge as she turned to return to her desk, she too sensing his heightened anxiety.

Picking up the phone, Thomas yelled into the phone, "Sister Agnew, is there anything wrong? Has anything happened to Chloë?"

The pleasant voice of Sister Agnew replied, "Good morning to you to, Father. There is nothing the matter with Chloë, but I am calling about her."

Thomas instantly calmed down, "I'm sorry, Sister, just a little antsy when it comes to Chloë. What is happening with her?"

Her voice had a ring of excitement as she continued, "Her incredible journey in life has taken another exciting turn, Father. I have received a request from a Mr. Dylan O'Hara, the manager of the Irish quartet, Celtic Woman, to have Chloë join them on their North American tour. One of the ladies in the foursome has fallen ill and the tour begins next week, too late to cancel, so they want Chloë to fill in for the tour."

Thomas should be thrilled for Chloë, this was certainly incredibly good news and a fantastic opportunity for her, but he was not thrilled. An unimaginable danger stalked her every move and Thomas would not have her out of the sight of Sister McGarrigle for one second. "Sister, you must tell this Mr. O'Hara that we are very grateful for the opportunity for Chloë, but unfortunately, at this time, it is not in her best interests."

Disappointed, Sister Agnew replied, "Father, are you sure? We are talking about the beloved Celtic Woman? This is such an honor for Chloë. To deny her this opportunity would be very unfortunate."

She was right. To withhold Chloë this chance would be downright shameful. He could not hold back the rising talent that Chloë McClosky possessed, regardless of the circumstances of her birth. He thought of something.

"Sister Agnew, I know what you are saying and you are right. Chloë deserves this opportunity. I will agree to the tour as long as Sister McGarrigle accompanies her and never leaves

Chloë's sight."

"Excellent news, Father O'Sullivan, and a wise decision. Chloë will be so thrilled.   I can't wait to tell her. Of course Sister McGarrigle will also be thrilled and she is like a protective mother to Chloë, so I am sure they will be fine, Father.

****

Chloë left for Dublin the next day in order to join the other three members of Celtic Woman to cram in rehearsal sessions in advance of the tour. They had less than a week to prepare, but the women gelled like they had been performing together for years. Chloë knew most of the songs anyway and in her solo performances, she truly excelled. Her incredible beauty and angelic voice made her an instant star with the older and more experienced ladies. They loved her already and gave O'Hara the thumbs up that they were ready after only a few days of rehearsals. The tour was slated for six months, starting in New York and making their way across the Midwest at a torrid pace of a show every second night and sometimes every night. The illness that came over the performer who Chloe replaced was mysterious. Doctors were mystified as to its cause and could not accurately diagnose the illness. Rebecca Murphy was healthy and singing beautifully one day, and the next she couldn't get out of bed. Choosing Chloë as her replacement was natural as she was not only the best singer available, she was clearly a star in the making, and her popularity in Ireland was skyrocketing. The Irish people were thrilled when the news broke that Chloë had joined the famous Celtic Woman group. Ticket holders in the United States were less than thrilled as Rebecca was one of their favorites and they had never heard of Chloë McClosky. O'Hara promised the concert promoters that they would be thrilled when they heard how good this young girl was.

Thomas was able to attend a few of the rehearsals at the group's studio in Dublin and he was simply amazed by how quickly Chloë had adapted and fit right in. She had been able to learn the choreography for all of the songs so quickly that she now moved with the other girls as if they had been performing together for years. He was so proud of Chloë that, when it came time for them to leave for the United States, Thomas embraced Chloë and was surprised that he found himself fighting back tears. He looked her in the eyes and spoke: "Chloë, I am so very proud of you. You are an amazing young woman and you have accomplished so much. You have earned this opportunity, young lady, with your hard work and dedication. I wish you all the success on the tour. Finally, the world will get to hear how incredibly talented you are."

With tears quickly forming and sliding down her cheeks, Chloë hugged Thomas, not wanting to let him go. Looking up at him, she said: "Thank you, Father, for everything you have done for me all these years. You and Sister Agnew and Sister McGarrigle have given me such a wonderful life and I will work very hard on the tour. I promise and I give thanks to Him for his blessings in giving me this talent. I love to sing, Father, it's what I was born to do."

He could see how happy she was and it warmed him so. He watched as Sister McGarrigle joined Chloë and the rest of the entourage as they said their final goodbyes before climbing in the van taking them all to the airport.

Little did Father O'Sullivan know, the next time he would see Chloë, it would be under considerably different circumstances.

****

Chloë was like a giddy little school girl on the long flight to New York City. The other three women were enthralled with Chloë, taken in by her boundless energy and excitement. Though she was only fifteen years old, she looked no younger than the three older women in the group. Strikingly beautiful, her long blond hair that reached the small of her back, high cheek bones and full lips made her the star attraction for the boys whenever she ventured outside of the Academy. However, she was never too far away from the watchful eye of Sister McGarrigle. She carried herself with such dignity and class that you had to pinch yourself to recall that she was only fifteen years old. The group had become somewhat stale over the past few years as they ground out the tours. Chloë was a breath of fresh air, energizing the three of them as well as the musicians and dancers. When the flight's captain announced over the P.A. that the Celtic Woman were on board, they were bombarded by other passengers with requests that they sing for them. If it wasn't for Chloë, the other Celtic Woman members would have been fast asleep during the seven hour flight over the Atlantic, but suddenly, they were harmonizing songs together, their beautiful voices rising above the drone of the jet's engines, bringing cheers and hollers from the passengers for more. The women urged Chloë to sing a solo, but winked when they said to sing it loudly in order to reach to the back of the plane. Without hesitation, Chloë broke into song, singing the beautiful 'Over the Rainbow'. She sang as if she was the only person on the plane. She closed her eyes as she let her voice soar to the ceiling then travel down to every nook and cranny in the plane. Flight Attendants stopped what they were doing, enraptured by her voice. You could have heard a pin drop. Even the steady hum of the jet's engines seemed to evaporate.

Chloë stood in the aisle, lifted her arms in the air and let her voice touch the heart of everyone on the plane. It was an incredible moment for everyone. The other Celtic Woman members were entranced, their eyes hung on every note coming from Chloë's mouth. People felt like they were in the presence of an angel singing to them; it was that beautiful and, combined with the clouds whipping by all of the windows, and the bouncing of the plane, they could have been in heaven for all they knew. They were all so caught up in that perfect, memorable moment.

When Chloë finished and her arms dropped to her sides, she opened her eyes and smiled. The passengers took a few seconds to register and get their bearings before they all exploded in applause and cheers. The ladies of Celtic Woman were stunned and dabbed their eyes with tissue before their mascara wreaked havoc. Juliana, the incredibly talented fiddle player, spoke up and said to the rest of the girls: "I felt witness to a star being born. I know she is good, I have heard all the stories and heard her last week in rehearsals, but that went way beyond anything I have ever heard. This young girl will be a major, major star and this tour is her coming out party for the world to see and hear. I couldn't stop the chills running up and down my spine."

All the other girls agreed and when Chloë sat back down with them, they felt an instant draw to be close to her, to protect her, the innocence emanated from her like a warm and welcoming blanket.

****

The passenger sitting in the window seat next to Sister McGarrigle was the only unmoved passenger on the plane. It was because Robert Best, music producer and manager, expected that reaction from the passengers before Chloë even began to sing. It was still a treat to see it happen though; the beautiful Chloë McClosky had them mesmerized.

Sister McGarrigle was beaming like a mother seeing her little girl sing solo at the kindergarten Christmas concert. She could easily pass for her mother; she was about the right age and her attractive looks gave credence to the impression that Chloë could be her daughter. She was not wearing her usual habit; instead, Sister Agnew thought it best that she wore civilian clothes, and she helped her shop for some outfits before she left.

"Wasn't that an incredible performance, Sister?"

Beatrice McGarrigle was startled to hear the passenger sitting next to her had addressed her as Sister. Was it that obvious? "Yes, it was incredible. How did you know that I was a nun?"

Best looked into her eyes, burrowing into them until he saw the recognition click in. "Don't you know, Sister, that all nuns have an aura that surrounds them. Only true believers of Christ can see it."

"Do I know you? You look very familiar to me. Have we met somewhere before?"

Best's eyes not only delved into her, but they now glowed a bright, crimson red, cutting into her mind until the connection clicked. He had possessed her body many times in the past and will again when the time was necessary. The fear that projected from her eyes with recognition was intensely beautiful. "Yes, you do know me Beatrice. You have known me for centuries."

****

The tour began with great reviews and full houses. Americans loved everything about the Irish, especially in New York City, and these four beautiful women could put on a concert. The music reviews in the local papers of the cities in

118

which they performed were raving about the newcomer, fifteen-year old Chloë McClosky. Not only stunningly beautiful in her long gowns and with her long blond hair flowing freely as she moved around the stage, her voice could out sing an angel, they would say. In a concert in Rochester, NY, Dylan O'Hara, the group's manager and producer, decided to let Chloë sing instead of Lisa Doyle, when it came time to perform the hauntingly beautiful ballad, 'May It Be' from the soundtrack of the Gladiator movie. Chloë's amazing talent shone through and it was this night that the audience got to catch a glimpse of her incredible talent. She breathed incredible depth into the song, allowing it to swirl around the souls of the audience, making them sigh as she took them on a rollercoaster of emotions. Upon the completion of her solo, the group were several verses into the next song before the audience caught up and realized the group was singing a different song. They were that stunned by her solo performance.

After the Rochester concert, the tour would take a few days off before their next show in Syracuse. When Chloë finished changing into a comfortable pair of blue jeans and top in her dressing room, she and Sister McGarrigle left for the hotel and hopefully, somewhere good to eat. Asking the doorman at the VIP entrance of the concert hall to call for a taxi, they were interrupted by a well dressed man approaching them from the other side of the lobby.

"Excuse me, you must be Chloë McClosky. You look so much younger dressed in casual clothes than you do on stage. You are a beautiful young lady, I must say. Let me introduce myself, Ms. McClosky. My name is Robert Best and I am a music producer and manager. My record label is Blackstar Studios." Looking at Sister McGarrigle, he continued: "And you being so lovely yourself, I'd assume you must be Chloë's mother. Very nice to meet you Mrs. McClosky."

"Thank you for the compliment Mr. Best, but I am Chloë's caregiver, Sister McGarrigle." The recent encounter on the plane was completely gone from her mind.

"Oh okay, well, very nice to meet you." Looking at Chloë, he said: "You were amazing tonight Chloë. You made me want to rush out after the concert to look for a video store to purchase the Gladiator movie."

Chloë looked at Best in utter amazement and found herself fumbling for words when she replied, "I am honored to meet you, Mr. Best. I can't believe you are here in Rochester and took the time to see us perform. You are, like, the biggest name in music," she gushed.

"I came to see you specifically, Chloë. It is you I am interested in. Have you ever considered singing pop music? Your voice has so many layers to it, you would be a natural. With your age, beauty and your incredible voice I could make you a star. I understand you are filling in for the sick Rebecca Murphy for a little longer yet, but when she returns to the tour, I would like you to spend some time in my studio working with a few more of my young stars like Connor Asker and Juan Jimenez. How does that sound?"

She looked at Sister McGarrigle before answering: "Oh my gosh, Mr. Best I can't believe I would be working with Connor Asker. I can't believe this, I am so excited. I would love to, it would be a dream come true, but of course I would need Sister McGarrigle and Father O'Sullivan's approval first."

Sister McGarrigle looked at Chloë, her face masking the terror she felt and said, "I think it would be an opportunity of a lifetime for you my dear. Don't worry about, Father O'Sullivan, I'm sure he will feel the same way, I promise you."

Chapter 11

Marie could not even remember the police being in her home. Yet they had just left, she could still hear the sound of the front door latching as they closed it behind them. In fact, they were climbing into their cruiser out in front of the house. "It sure seems that way", she thought. They came to tell her that Sophia had been brutally murdered last night. Now that was really strange because she could still hear her sister laughing as they clinked wine glasses just a few minutes ago or maybe it was a few hours ago. She was having a hard time focusing. The living room she was standing in seemed distant. All of a sudden, she felt like a visitor standing in her own house. It felt unwelcoming. "Very weird", she thought to herself. "Sophia was dead? Impossible." The police said she had been attacked by a gang of thugs in a violent robbery attack. They said she was torn to pieces. "Impossible!"

She turned to look out the front window to see if the police were still in her driveway because she needed to check their story again. They had the wrong person. It wasn't Sophia. Suddenly, she realized she wasn't standing at the window anymore, but instead was standing in the middle of her kitchen. "What the hell was going on? This had to be a nightmare she was caught in. That's right, this couldn't be real." A knock at her door broke the confused silence. She knew instantly that it was Sophia and she would wake from this bad dream when her tough older sister would knock her across the side of the head. She started to step towards the front door from the kitchen and then she was suddenly standing in front of the door. "Whoa things were getting weird." She opened the door and two uniformed police officers were standing on her step. They looked just like the two who were just here, telling her the bizarre, but obviously false story about Sophia being torn to pieces after she dropped her off last night. They were the same cops. Back to tell her she could come to the station and pick up the box of pieces of Sophia's body.

Opening the door to greet them she said, "You're back? Did one of you forget your radio?"

"Excuse me? Why would you ask that? Forget it. My name is Officer Hector Vesta and this is…"

She finished the introduction for him, "Yeah, I know, Officer Penelope Olozabal. You were just here. What can I do for you officers?"

"Ma'am I don't mean to be rude but we were not just here. We have never been here. We have some terrible news for you I'm afraid. May we come inside?"

"Come inside to tell me what? You can't find one of my sister's arms? The attacker threw it so far away you lazy bastards missed it?"

"How did you know that? Who told you that? Mam, her limb was discovered in a patch of tall grass beside the parking lot of the school. My sincere apologies for having to confirm such terrible news, but I am shocked that you would have known this. We came here to tell you that your sister had been brutally murdered last night. I was not aware you had already been told by other officers before us."

Marie closed her eyes for a split second to control the rage building up inside of her at the ineptitude of her country's police department, but more so for the shock of hearing the officers confirm her statement of finding Sophia's arm in the grass. This was insane. She opened her eyes, only to find herself in her bed. She bolted upright, the fear pulsating through her veins. She had been having a terrible nightmare. The relief at the discovery of her being locked in a horrific nightmare and not reality was palpable and it washed over her like a tidal wave as she slumped back into her bed. "What the hell was happening to her?", she worried, as her misgivings took shape. Maybe she was missing Juan so much and the worry of not knowing if he was okay or not was affecting her mind. She needed to speak with him more often, daily in fact. She would no longer tolerate his excuses that he was busy rehearsing or getting ready to perform.

Her head was beginning to pound and she needed to close her eyes for just a little while before she got up, showered and then tried to reach Juan. "What time is it?" she wondered? She was pretty sure it was early in the morning. It felt like it. Her eyes finally closed and she was instantly bombarded with images straight from a horror movie. She could see a cop in the distance, getting out of his squad car and opening the back door. She was standing on the far side of a school parking lot, watching the cop open the door of his car. She watched as he climbed into the backseat and closed the door behind him. She watched from far away as he began assaulting the woman. The rear window of the cruiser was misty and not clear, but it looked like she was kicking the cop. Good for her! The woman looked familiar but she was so far away she wasn't sure. Then the cop began to run his hand up and down her body, groping the woman's breasts. Marie felt herself beginning to yell out. She had to stop this. Then the car door was kicked open and the woman fell out and onto her back. Her hands were handcuffed behind her. She was struggling to get away. The woman's hair and her clothes looked so familiar to her. She knew this woman, but who was she? Then the lady began to scream. The recognition jolted Marie. It was Sophia! At the same time, she could see the creature crawling out of the backseat of the police car and onto the parking lot. "Oh God, it was the beast! The creature was the monster that had raped her all those years ago and killed her husband!" Suddenly she heard a pounding, like someone was pounding on her door. It was getting louder. She awoke to the sound of the front door knocking again. Her body was soaked in sweat. What a horrible dream.

Climbing out of bed, she searched for her housecoat while the person at the door continued to bang away. "Alright, enough already," she yelled out in the direction of her front door. After she retrieved her housecoat from off of the back of the bathroom door, she made her way to the front door. Then she vaguely remembered being visited by two police officers. They were telling her about…wait yes to tell her about Sophia! "Sophia! She was dead!" The cops had been here to tell her Sophia was murdered. "Oh my God." Her body began to tremble with fear as she struggled with the images flashing through her head. The door was banged again, startling her, it was so loud. She checked through the peephole and expected to see the police again, but it was a man. A well dressed man and very handsome. She cracked open the door enough to look out and ask, "Yes, how may I help you?"

"Excuse me for disturbing you Ma'am, but I am hoping I could speak with you. May I come inside?"

"Who are you and why would I let you in my house You can ask me what you need to ask right there."

"My name is Robert Best and I am here to talk with you about your son, Juan."

She could feel the panic rise within her as she asked, "What is the matter with Juan? Has something happened to him?"

The man walked up towards the door, his face apologetic and reassuring, as he replied: "I am sorry if I have alarmed you Ms. Jimenez. There is nothing wrong with Juan. I am from the United States. I represent your son in the music industry. I am his producer and manager."

The name and face looked very familiar to her, but she could not pin it down. What was he talking about him being Juan's music producer and manager? This is crazy. Maybe she was still dreaming? "I'm sorry sir, you have the wrong house. My son is only fifteen and he will be home from school soon. I have to go now. I'm sorry." She closed the door and leaned against it, trying to make sense of the images pouring through her head again. She could see Juan singing on stage and thousands of people cheering and screaming. "I need some sleep", she thought. "This is insane."

There was another loud knock on the door again suddenly, causing her head to snap back. "Jesus, what the hell is the matter with this nutcase?" She opened the door and was about to shout an obscenity, but she could see there was no one standing there. He had disappeared. He had just banged on her door a second ago. Then the images in her head came back again. This time, they were of the creature crushing Rafael's throat and his head falling to the floor. "What is going on?" She slammed the door closed, leaned against it and closed her eyes tightly, trying to force the terrible memories to leave her mind. It wasn't working. Then she heard the man's voice again, "I let myself in. I hope you don't mind."

Opening her eyes, she was horrified to discover that the man who called himself Best was standing in front of her.

"How did you get in here? Did you come in the back? Get out of my house right now before I call the police."

"I told you I wanted to speak with you about Juan."

The fear in her was rising and she was finding it harder to breathe. This man was so familiar now. Who was he? "How do you know my son? I have never met you before. Now I will ask you one more time to leave my house before I call the police."

The next four words spoken by the stranger brought her to her knees in gripping terror.

"I am his father."

Then she heard a voice that wasn't coming from inside her head. It was a sound she had not heard in a very long time. Sixteen years to be exact. The beast had returned. She opened her eyes and the monster was ten feet away from her. The fear shuddered through her body like an electric current. The tears streamed down her cheeks and the memories of Rafael were as vivid in her mind as if it had just happened. Then a greater fear gripped her. "Juan!"

"Where is my son? What have you done with him?"

The beast took a step towards her, its eyes burning bright, "He is not your son and he never was. Your body was used to give him life but you're not his mother."

Marie knew she was about to die. She had given birth to the Devil's child, and now she was no longer needed in whatever plan he had for Juan. She had to protect Juan. She defiantly shouted back at the approaching monster, "You even touch him and I swear to you, the God I love, the Creator of all life will show you no mercy."

The demonic laughter that erupted from the beast shook the walls of her tiny house. She braced herself for his attack. She prayed. Opening her eyes, she was suddenly standing in her kitchen. The room was completely white, including the cupboards, walls, countertops and windows. All bright white. What was going on? "Am I in Heaven?" she wondered.

Then she heard the demonic voice again. She glanced quickly around the white washed room but she did not see the beast. Only a voice calling out to her in her head. She couldn't take much more of this. She needed to get to her son. She yelled out to the voice, "What do you want from me? Leave me alone! Leave my son alone!"

"It's too late for that now, isn't it?"

She whirled around and the ghastly site of the deformed creature, standing just a few feet away, in the brightness of the white room made the sight of it even more frightening. Then a barrage of images came flooding into her mind again as if the creature had stepped inside of it and began playing its own picture show. "Wait what was that?" She saw herself standing in the parking lot of the school again, watching the cop climb out of the backseat of the police car. Her sister, her hands handcuffed behind her back, began to whimper and backpedal on the pavement, away from the car. The beast had stepped out of the car now, its enormity and rage coming after her helpless sister. Marie cried out, "Sophia, run! Get up Sophia! Please dear God, don't let her die!" Sobbing uncontrollably, she was helpless to stop the images in her mind showing the brutal slaying of her sister by the beast.

"You fucking bastard, I'm going to kill you!" She rushed the beast in a rage she had never experienced before. Before she reached it, the beast snapped out one its massive claws, catching her violently around the throat. It lifted her high in the air and screamed, "You're already dead!"

She gasped for air as she tried to pry apart the vise-like grip the claw had on her throat when suddenly, she dropped to the floor. She was alone again. The beast was gone. She cried as she wrapped her arms around herself and curled up into a ball on the floor. She couldn't stop the images of her sister dying, of Rafael's decapitation and her son Juan all alone somewhere. Then through her tears, she saw the blood. It was all over her hands. Sitting up on her knees, she was horrified to see blood all around her on the floor. The contrast of the scarlet blood on the whiteness of the room made it even more frightening. Looking down at her hands, she screamed. She had a large butcher knife in her hand and it was covered in blood. She was now no longer kneeling in her kitchen, but lying in her empty bathtub. She shook in fear as she looked down at her other hand and began to gag and wretch when she saw her left wrist had been slit wide open. "What is happening to me?"

The beast appeared at the end of the bathtub its sight no longer frightening, in fact she felt a sort of comfort from its presence. Then it spoke to her in a human voice, "Do you remember now?"

She looked at him and the terror returned. "Oh my God, what have I done? No, no, it's not possible! I couldn't have. Please God, save me from this madness!"

"He can't help you now. His love and protection disappeared the second you plunged that knife into your wrist. God does not love those who do not love themselves."

She looked down at her mangled wrist again and now saw the full memory of her suicide play out in her mind. The despair at the death of her sister had sent her over the edge. "Oh God, please save me! I didn't know what I was doing! I must find Juan. He needs me."

The human voice of the beast was gone and replaced, once again, by the hoarse and guttural shouts of pure evil. The laughter also returned, "Don't waste your time praying anymore because He can't hear you. The angels of heaven will no longer play their trumpets in anticipation of your arrival. You are mine now."

The despair was crushing into her chest like a heavy weight, when she spoke, "Am I in Hell?"

"Yes."

She cried again when she asked him, "What will it be like?"

The beast moved its grotesque head within inches of her face and then it replied: "Look around you. This is your home now. For all eternity, you will be forever locked in this room. You will live everyday like you lived the previous day in complete and utter despair and misery. You will look down at your wrist every minute of every day for all of eternity and ask the same question over and over, 'Why did I kill myself?'"

"What will happen with Juan?"

"My son will help me destroy mankind very soon and then forever live by my side in triumph over the defeated and destroyed body of Jesus Christ the Saviour."

Marie closed her eyes in complete shock and when she opened them, the white light of her bathroom was replaced by blackness, despair and death.

****

Juan bolted upwards off of his bed. His mother. Something had happened to her. Something terrible. He needed to get home to her. He climbed out of his bed and quickly dressed. He didn't want to wake Connor or Mr. Best. He had an overpowering sense that he needed to return to Venezuela immediately. He would take a taxi to the airport and wait for the next flight available to Caracas. He would call Mr. Best from the airport. He would understand. He would miss Connor's performance tonight , but that was no big deal. Opening his bedroom door in the large hotel suite, he looked over across the hall to Connor's door and then to Mr. Best's. Both of them were dark and quiet. "Sound asleep", he thought. He stepped out into the hallway, closed his door silently behind him and turned towards the door leading out to the elevators, when he heard a voice behind him.

"Juan."

He turned at the sound and discovered both Mr. Best and Connor, fully dressed, standing in the hallway in front of their bedroom doors.

"Mr. Best, something has happened to my mother. I need to get home as soon as possible. I will return in a few days when I know she is okay."

In the shadows of the massive room, the only light was from the moonlight splintered through the blinds covering the glass windows that surrounded the suite. Mr. Best spoke again, "Sit down Juan, there are some things I need to tell you."

Juan felt drawn to Mr. Best as if he was a metal filing and Best was a powerful magnet. The pull was very strong. It was much different than he had ever felt before. It was kind of weird. He sat down and he felt like he was in the presence of someone or something that was supremely powerful. He knew, right at that second that his mother was no longer of any importance to him. Mr. Best was some sort of God and he wanted to be with him forever. He did not know why he felt this, but he did and it felt great. He listened intently as Mr. Best spoke.

"Juan, your destiny was revealed to me over sixteen hundred years ago…."

Juan could see both Mr. Best's and Connor's eyes shine a bright crimson red as he listened to the incredible story of his new life. What a beautiful color their eyes were. He wondered if his eyes were also shining as bright a red as theirs were.

Chapter 12

There was something special happening in Las Vegas when Guy Laliberte, the CEO of Cirque du Soleil, and Celine Dion announced a press conference at the brand spanking new Meritzia Sky Resort. Members of the local and national press were all over the story, anticipating a major new Cirque du Soleil production starring Celine Dion. The city was desperate for good news, having suffered more than any other American city during the recession. The whole country would be encouraged by the announcement as a further sign that the economy was recovering.

Everyone assumed that the press conference had been called because Guy Laliberte wanted to announce a brand new, state of the art, eye popping production with Celine's seductive voice as the centerpiece. Unlike Celine's previous show in Las Vegas, *A New Day*, this show promised to be more Cirque du Soleil than Celine Dion. The announcement had been kept top secret and, as hard as the press worked their contacts looking for a leak in order to be the first to write the story of the show that 'would save Las Vegas', the news did not leak, so the excitement filling the new state-of-the-art theatre hall in Meritzia Sky, was palpable. The Mayor of Las Vegas was as giddy as a school boy on the first day of school. The Governor of Nevada was even in attendance at the press conference, hoping the announcement would revitalize the cornerstone of his state.

The press conference finally began in the un-named theatre. It was widely suspected that the name of the hall would reflect the mega production about to call it home. The V.P. of entertainment for Meritzia Sky opened the press conference with introductions that included Celine Dion, Guy Laliberte and a beautiful young girl nobody in the room seemed to recognize. It was left for Guy Laliberte to introduce the young girl.

He took the stage, thanking the resort executive as he did so and looked out at the impressive audience and said, "I would like to thank Meritzia Sky for the opportunity to bring this incredible new creation to Las Vegas. This show is a culmination of many of my dreams, both as a child and as the creative force behind Cirque du Soleil. The video presentation you are about to see represents the most ambitious and expensive show ever seen in Las Vegas or anywhere else in the world. It is truly spectacular, as you will see in a minute. Before we show the video, I would like to bring up Celine Dion to introduce our special guest. Celine, if you may."

The beautiful Celine Dion took the podium and her signature French accent shone through as she spoke, "I would also like to thank the executives from Meritzia Sky for their commitment to this show and the commitment they have shown me for so many years. They are the true innovators of Las Vegas and I applaud them for leading the charge to restore Las Vegas as the top tourist destination in the world. Before I introduce the young lady to my right, let me begin by telling all of you what a pleasure it has been seeing her grow from a extremely talented little twelve year old girl to the beautiful fifteen year old young lady you see here today. She is the most talented singer and musician I have ever seen at such a young age. Her future is so bright, it is difficult to imagine where she will be three years from today. In the meantime, the world will be blessed to see her raw talent blossom in this spectacular show Guy has built around her. Without further delay, it is my pleasure to introduce to you today, the star of the new Cirque du Soleil production, 'Panterra', from Montreal, Quebec, Canada, Elizabeth Leroux!"

Standing and then embracing Celine, Elizabeth made her way to the podium. Wearing white slacks with a light pink, sleeveless, satin blouse, decorated with a necklace of pink and pearl beads around her neck, she looked stunning. Her hair was a shimmering auburn color with long, sweeping, wavy curls that accentuated her high cheek bones and full lips. She looked like a much younger version of Angelina Jolie. She was not nervous in the least, only excited. Her beauty and confidence instantly had an impact on everyone in the room. Her smile was so infectious that people felt drawn towards her, waiting for her to speak. When she spoke, her English carried only a slight tinge of French, "Thank you Celine, for those wonderful words. I had the pleasure and the honor of singing in front of Celine Dion and her entire family three years ago and it was something I will remember for the rest of my life. She is truly a hero and an inspiration in my life. When Mr. Laliberte approached me several months ago about Panterra, I was truly blown away that he would bestow such an honor on me, a virtually unknown performer. He showed great confidence in me right from the beginning and now, after all these months of hard work in rehearsals, I believe I am ready to give you a great performance every night. Thank you."

Guy Laliberte returned to the podium, "Panterra was kept purposefully under wraps right up to this announcement. The fact that we were able to successfully keep it a secret all this time, even during the construction of the stage in the new theatre, plus at our top secret rehearsal facility in Montreal, is a testament to the commitment of everyone involved in this production. Panterra is signed to perform five nights a week at Meritzia Sky for the next three years. The show will open in two weeks and tickets will go on sale beginning tomorrow morning. Panterra is the best show I have ever made. I will run the video trailer for the production and return to the podium to answer any questions. Thank you."

A giant screen behind the head table rose towards the ceiling and stopped when the full twenty feet of its height was in place above the heads of everyone at the table. The lights dimmed and the video began. The narrator described a beautiful world, untouched by the spoils of society, tucked away in a secret place on earth. Its inhabitants were perfect in every way, both physically and intelligently. They had existed for centuries. They kept their world hidden from society by using a series of gigantic mirrors, thousands of them that surrounded their massive compound that was the size of a small country, by automatically shifting and turning to reflect a vast forest of wasteland to anyone or anything that encroached either by land or air. The hundreds of thousands of mirrors, camouflaged to reflect the surroundings, were controlled automatically by a central computer system. The mirror system was created by advanced technology in the last century, as society threatened their discovery.

Alexis, the central character played by Elizabeth, longed to explore the world outside of the mirrors. No one from her world had ever been outside of the mirrors, so it was only the stories of legends told through the ages that filled their dreams of what it would be like. Alexis possessed the voice of an angel and was soon enslaved by the King and Queen of the Royal Palace, forced to sing to them to soothe their troubled souls every day for the rest of her life. Finally managing to escape the castle with the help of a brave and handsome soldier, exiled from the royal family, she found a way to escape her world through the mirrors. Facing a modern day world, she was not prepared for the danger and chaos. She longed to return to the safety of her world but she could not find her way back. Her world was obliterated by the giant mirrors she could not see.

The incredible video ended, leaving the audience spellbound. They erupted in huge applause and cheers, the room buzzing with the excitement of the incredible new show and its star, Elizabeth Leroux. Guy Laliberte returned to the podium and opened things up to questions. The reporters began shouting trying to get their questions heard, hoping to get a direct quote for their publication or news channel. Steve Ross from the Las Vegas Journal, always having written about Cirque du Soleil in a positive light, was rewarded for that by being given the honor of the first question.

"Guy, I have heard that Panterra is the most expensive show ever produced in Las Vegas and the world, for that matter. With that much on the line, why was the decision made to cast an unknown as the lead character?"

"That is a great question Steve and thank you for asking it. First of all, for the lead character of Alexis, it needed to be someone young and beautiful, smart and very, very talented. I was introduced to Elizabeth through Celine and the first audition was the last. There was no need to audition anyone else. We knew we had someone very special, a major star in the making, when we discovered Elizabeth. She is an experienced and well known musician and singer in her native Canada. Panterra will allow the rest of the world to enjoy this incredibly gifted young lady."

Questions came fast and furious and Guy handled them with patience, taking his time to answer as many as he possibly could.

"What is Celine Dion's role in Panterra?"

"She is the technical advisor to the show and to Elizabeth personally."

"If Panterra fails to gain an audience, will this be the end of big productions in Las Vegas?"

"Panterra will not fail, in fact, we are predicting it will be the most successful show ever in Las Vegas. There will always be big productions in Las Vegas; it is why people come here. To be entertained like nothing they have ever or will ever experience anywhere else. That is the magic of Las Vegas."

The press conference ended over an hour later with Guy and Celine heading off for individual interviews with some of the bigger media outlets. Elizabeth joined her father back in her suite at Caesars. Exhausted from the long day, all she wanted to do was get some rest. On her way up to the suite, her dad informed her that he had a very special surprise for her. A very special person wanted to meet her. Though very tired, Elizabeth was excited to know who would be waiting for her.

She entered the suite and was shocked to see Connor Asker and an unknown gentleman getting up out of their chairs to greet her. Smiling from ear to ear, her father introduced them, "Elizabeth, may I introduce you to Connor Asker and his manager, Robert Best. They are here to support you on your big day and to help you celebrate!"

Connor extended his hand to her and said, "I am very pleased to meet you Elizabeth. Congratulations on Panterra. You must be so excited."

She was very nervous even shaking his hand. Connor Asker was in her hotel room congratulating her! This was unbelievable! Finding her voice, she replied, "Thank you Connor. I am such a huge fan of yours, ever since 'America's Got Talent' three years ago to your new album. "Follow Me Follow You" is so incredibly good, I listen to it all the time on my iPod."

She extended her hand to Best and said, "So nice to meet you Mr. Best. I can't believe I get to shake your hand. Wow, what a day, I must say."

Robert Best took her hand and replied, "The pleasure is all mine Elizabeth. I watched you perform three years ago in front of the Montreal Symphony Orchestra and I knew right then and there that you were a very special talent and, after today, I know that I wasn't mistaken."

"You were at that concert three years ago in Montreal? That is incredibly humbling. So tell me Mr. Best, why didn't you sign me back then?" giggled Elizabeth.

Elizabeth's father spoke up and said, "Honey, that is why Mr. Best is here right now. He wants to talk to you about your career."

Sitting down in one of the large suite's many couches and chairs, Best began, "Elizabeth, you have a very special voice, a gift that is very rare. Have you ever considered singing pop music?"

She looked first at her dad, then at Mr. Best and said, "That has been a dream of mine for as long as I can remember. I grew up listening to Beyonce, Brittany Spears and Rhianna. I have only been performing classical music and opera, so I don't know how I would do in pop music. It never presented itself, so I never pursued it or let it go beyond my dreams."

"What I have been discussing with your father, Elizabeth, is having you take some time over the next several months to work with Connor on some collaborations and see how you like it and how you do. I think you might be very surprised at how well you can sing pop music."

Again she looked at her father before answering, "What about the show? I cannot take any time away from Panterra."

"Certainly not Elizabeth. You have a one year contract with the Panterra show that you will fulfill with an option for another two years. What we have been discussing is for you to take a shot at dabbling in pop music when the show takes its breaks. Connor and I will rent some studio time here in Las Vegas so you don't have to travel and we can have some fun. What do you think?"

"As long as it's okay with my dad, I would be honored and thrilled to sing with Connor."

****

Halfway across the world from Las Vegas, Nevada, as the press conference ended, forty foot tsunami waves were rushing towards the shores of the Philippines as a result of a devastating 9.0 earthquake seventy five miles out in the South China Sea. The shock waves generated sent a wall of water hurtling towards the densely populated Manila. By the time weather experts picked up on it from reports coming in from fishing vessels caught in its path, it was too late to give any meaningful warning time to the people living in Manila and the surrounding towns and villages in the path of the tsunami.

When the waves made it to shore, the ensuing devastation was beyond belief. The water made it almost ten miles inland, wiping out buildings and structures like they were match sticks as it swept along. The overwhelming destruction was far worse than a nuclear bomb. There were hundreds of thousands of casualties in Manila alone, in addition to the mounting death tolls all along the Philippine coastline. The northern tip of Malaysia also received heavy damage and deaths in the thousands.

The reaction from around the world was swift and generous. China itself, the brunt of so many natural disasters this past century, sent supply ships packed with aid immediately. Australia, India and Japan sent in ground troops to begin the search for survivors. Russia, The United States, Britain, and Canada sent aid ships, troops and cash. All the countries around the globe helped in some way, either through direct aid, monetary donations or offering refuge to the hundreds of thousands of survivors left homeless from the devastation.

With so many expatriate Philippino's spread around the world, the outpouring of grief for their homeland was overwhelming. The Pope, grieving for a country with over 80% of its population Roman Catholic, spoke out for the industrialized nations of the world to do more in their relief efforts to help the millions still stranded in the flood waters.

Religious zealots around the world took to the streets in demonstrations announcing that the end of the world was near. God's patience with man was wearing thin and the recent tsunami's in Japan and now this one in the Philippines were the first of many more the world would endure in the coming years.

A dark force on earth, a wicked evilness, rejoiced in the devastation of his adversary's wrath, knowing that the time was near for this world and mankind. The deadly storms, earthquakes, tornadoes, tsunamis and hurricanes would increase in the years ahead. It was soon to be God's time to make the necessary corrections in the timeline of mankind. He allowed them to take what He was the most proud of, their intelligence and compassion, and use it to seal their own destruction. Man was flawed from the very beginning, when Eve bit into the forbidden fruit and soon the timeline would come full circle, when God made His ultimate correction by destroying mankind and starting anew.

Father Andre Picard-Belisle, head priest of the Notre Dame de Paris in Paris, prayed for the families of the people killed and the survivors still being pulled from the wreckage of the tsunami wreaking havoc and mayhem in the Philippines. He agreed to lead the secret office, SOSL (Special Office of Spiritual Longevity), at the Vatican, with the death of Father Beckstead and that took him to Rome for special meetings every quarter. His heart felt heavy, not only for the carnage in the Philippines, but because of the signs that continued to mount, pointing towards the final judgment of God's fury. He knew it was foretold in the Bible, but the realization that it was coming to pass was another matter. He never in his wildest dreams felt that Judgment Day would happen in his lifetime, but now he was sure of it. The time was near. The members of SOSL would soon need to prepare the Christian faith around the world for this reality. The wickedness and evilness plaguing mankind would be cleansed in one fell swoop, with Armageddon destroying the human race, leaving behind only the true believers to start a new world with Jesus Christ as their King. His strong belief in this reality, combined with his educational background, were the reasons he was chosen to lead SOSL.

He thought about his friend and fellow SOSL member, Father Thomas O'Sullivan. He knew he was in a spiritual battle with Satan ever since the birth of the child Chloë McClosky. He prayed for Thomas and his fight with his beloved God's enemy.

Chapter 13

Detective Samuel Showenstein of the LAPD Homicide Division entered the apartment of Bentley Paxton to deliver the terrible news of the death of her boss, Jonathon Green of *Music Talks* magazine. The shock hit her hard and Sam suggested they take a seat in the living room, as she looked like she might faint.

"I was just speaking with him on the phone earlier. Oh my God, this is so terrible. Who would have done such a thing?"

Sam took a seat on the living room chair facing Bentley, while his rookie Detective partner, Daniel Ryerson, stood nearby. As he flipped his notebook open, Sam asked: "Bentley, tell me about the phone conversation please."

Bentley shifted nervously in the loveseat as she remembered the phone conversation with Jonathon: "Jonathon flew into Los Angeles this morning from New York. I picked him up at the airport as he wanted to make a proposal to me over lunch. I had no idea what that was, but during lunch he revealed that the board of directors of *Music Talks* wanted me as the new V.P. of Business Development and Licensing for the magazine. It was a huge offer but it meant that I would have to relocate to New York. That is just something I was not prepared to agree to over lunch. I needed some time. Jonathon stated that he expected that, so he would spend the night in L.A. and come by in the morning to get my signature on the contract before he flew home. Jonathon can be very persistent when he wants to be."

Sam studied Bentley as she spoke and could see the pain in her face at the loss of her boss. She was an incredibly lovely woman, smart and well educated. No wonder the head office earmarked her for a V.P. position. Sam asked her another question, "Besides yourself, who else would have known he had decided to stay overnight in L.A.?"

"I would think the office in New York would have known."

Sam looked back at Detective Ryerson and instructed, "Dan, call the head office of *Music Talks* and find out exactly who knew that Green was planning on staying the night."

Bentley looked up at Detective Ryerson and stated, "Here is my card Detective, the number to the head office is on it. It will be a lot quicker for you if you ask for Diana Williams. She is Jonathon's personal assistant. If you don't, then the switchboard operator will send you through a maze of departments just because she can and she will make you sweat. Oh and mention your name, Detective Ryerson. That should work."

Ryerson gave Bentley a smile and disappeared into the hallway to make the call. Sam knew he was as smitten as a twelve year old getting his first kiss. Once they were back in the car, Ryerson would go on and on about how much Ms. Paxton was into him.

Sam turned his attention back to Bentley and the line of questioning, "What did Jonathon say to you when he called you on his cell?"

"He called me when he had checked into his hotel room. He was frightened about something or something had frightened him. Then he said that he thought Nathan's killer was after him as well."

"Who is Nathan?"

"Nathan Steck, he was the nationally syndicated afternoon DJ on KJAY 960 in New York."

Now Sam remembered the grisly slaughter of seven people working at the radio station. Steck was one of the seven victims. "Why would Green think the killer would be after him?"

"Jonathon was friends with Nathan and they often

socialized together with their families. Jonathon felt the killer was some sort of psychopath religious freak blaming people like Nathan and himself for spreading evil to the masses through music."

"That seems to be a bit of a stretch, but I will pass this onto the investigators in New York. They may want to speak with you. What else did Green say on the phone?"

"He began telling me about a photograph sent to his email inbox. When he opened the attachment, it was a photo of Nathan Steck murdered in his office. It had to have come from the killer, right?"

Sam thought about this connection and how it tied the two murder scenes together. Green was torn to pieces in his hotel room in L.A. similar to the murder scene in New York. Sensing what he was thinking Bentley continued, "He was about to hang up when I heard him shout like he was yelling at someone who had just entered his room. All I heard was 'What the fuck are you' and the sentence was cut off and the phone went dead. Then I called 911 right after that."

"I have seen the photo on Green's phone. Underneath the picture of the Steck murder scene a caption said, 'See you soon' like whoever had sent it knew where Green would be staying and that he would be meeting him there. Are you sure, Bentley, there was no one else besides you that he was scheduled to see?"

"No, no one that I am aware of."

Sam then looked at Bentley and asked, "Do you know a Robert Best?"

She looked at him, startled. The name registered. "Yes I do, he is very well known, one of the top music producers in the country. Why do you ask?"

"Green had received an email from Best requesting a meeting before he returned to New York just before he received the photo of Steck."

"I am not sure how Best would have known Green was in L.A. but the request for a meeting would not be unusual. *Music Talks* is the top mag in the business and the movers and shakers in this industry are always trying to be heard."

Just then, Detective Ryerson returned to the living room and announced, "I spoke with Diana Williams. She stated that Jonathon had called this afternoon questioning if a Robert Best had made inquiries as to his whereabouts or if he happened to be in L.A. He seemed upset and impatient. She said she hadn't but Jonathon had insisted she check with the switchboard operator. Diana checked with switchboard and discovered that she had indeed taken a call from someone asking for you and she let slip that you were away in L.A. on business."

Sam could see that Bentley was visibly upset about this latest development and asked, "Ms. Paxton you seem quite upset. Can you share anything more with me ?"

Bentley's hands were shaking when she said, "Best is a dangerous person. Don't ask me how I know that because I don't know. It's just a feeling I have whenever I happen to run into him. He gives me the creeps. I think you know what you need to do from here Detective."

"Would you happen to know where I could find Best?"

"I do and the only reason I know that is because in this business whether you like a person or not, it doesn't matter when the magazine needs an interview or a quote. You have to be connected enough to be able to pick up the phone and call that person direct and not through agents, managers, lawyers or spouses."

"Let me guess. You're connected."

"I am connected Detective. Best owns Blackstar Studios with offices here in Los Angeles as well as in New York. Give me a minute and I will get you the contact info for both offices." Bentley took a piece of paper and wrote down the info from her Blackberry contacts for Best and Blackstar Studio's.

Sam took the piece of paper from her and thanked her for her cooperation and her time. He told her that she should expect a call from the NYPD in the near future regarding their ongoing investigation. Ryerson took an uncomfortable extra minute to linger with Bentley and thank her all over again.

"What a putz!", Sam thought.

Back in the car, Sam instructed Ryerson to drive. As he pulled out into traffic, Ryerson looked at him and with a grin like the cat that caught the mouse said: "Did you see the way she was staring at me? She's got the hots for the badge, I can tell. Whoee. I can tell."

Sam glared at the rookie homicide detective with a look of disgust and said, "You ever try to schmooze a potential witness in front of me again, and I will personally kick your ass and have you transferred out of this department and back on the street writing parking violations. You got me Ryerson? I have sixteen years in Homicide, which means you were still in grade school when I investigated my first murder. You are a rookie grade level one detective and I am a veteran grade three detective, which means you fucking behave when you work with me. Act like a God damned professional" The look he gave Ryerson backed up the words.

"Jesus, Sam, take it easy. I was just a little caught up in those movie star good looks, you know. I never meant any harm."

"Okay, got it but don't let it happen again. Let's get back to headquarters and start tracking down Best."

Ryerson looked over at him with a great big cocky smile, "You got it boss."

Sam tried to contain himself but couldn't hold it back any longer and broke into laughter when he said, "Wipe that grin off your face rookie. Yes, I will give that to you, she was one beautiful looking lady. Zowee!" The two of them drove on to HQ, laughing some more at Ryerson's awkwardness around Bentley.

The mood may have gotten lighter in the car on the way back to HQ, but Sam knew they had a very good lead on a fresh murder and he could feel the noose tighten around Best's neck.

****

Back at headquarters, Sam went to work trying to track down Best. He had Ryerson begin the paperwork by opening the files necessary to start the 'murder book' or investigators' case file. Everything related to this investigation would go into the murder book. Detective's notes, photocopies of everything including warrants, lab results etc. Absolutely everything goes into that book. His boss could stick his nose into the book at anytime and feel reasonably comfortable he was up to date on the investigation. If detectives were lax in their paperwork and got behind in keeping the murder book up to the minute, they would feel the wrath of Homicide Captain Rodney Bitters, a cantankerous veteran homicide detective whose personality closely matched his name, bitter. By-passed over the years for promotion, Bitters was stuck in homicide. Caught-up in a messy divorce five years ago that drained him financially, he was forced to stay on the job well past his retirement eligibility because he simply couldn't afford to retire, which made him even more pissed off at the world. He has been Sam's boss for the last fifteen years. There would be a very good chance Sam would retire before Bitters. Not interested in sitting behind a desk pushing paper, Sam fought hard over the years to resist the Department's desire to move him behind one. Sam was well educated and an excellent detective and the Department wanted him upstairs. However, he loved the streets, loved the thrill of opening a murder investigation and then closing it with the perpetrator securely behind bars.

There was one murder investigation that never got closed. The investigation of his ex-partner, Steven Benning murder, fifteen years ago. It was a strange and bizarre case that haunted Sam to this very day. Lots of blood and DNA were collected at the scene, but were never able to be typed or identified by the lab. The lab couldn't even determine if the DNA, other than Steven's and his wife Chelsea's, was human. The case was quickly closed by the Department and Sam was forced to drop it and move on. Although he was officially unable to investigate the murder of his partner, Sam never stopped investigating on his own. He never was able to put together who killed Steven, but he swore that someday he would find out who slaughtered his partner and make them pay for what they did.

Sam started looking for Best by calling Blackstar Studios in Los Angeles. A pleasant sounding receptionist answered, "Blackstar Studios, good afternoon. How may I direct your call?"

"May I speak with Robert Best please?"

"I'm sorry but Mr. Best is not here at the moment. Would you like to speak with anyone else or if you could tell me what you are calling about I could direct your call to someone who could help you."

"I really do need to speak with Mr. Best. How may I reach him?"

"May I ask who is calling please?"

"I prefer not to leave my name, I only wish to speak with Mr. Best."

"Mr. Best travels frequently between our New York office and Los Angeles so I never for certain know where he might be. I can certainly take your information and forward a message to him. I am sure that, within a few days, you will hear back from Mr. Best or his personal assistant."

Sam was getting frustrated. He should have showed up in person at Blackstar and used his badge to get past this gatekeeper. "Can you please transfer me to your New York office?"

"I'm sorry sir, our New York office is closed for the day. It is after 5:00 p.m. in New York."

He hung up the phone as he was getting nowhere. He was naïve thinking he could just call Blackstar, speak with Best, then meet him to interview him. Grabbing his suit jacket, he barked at Ryerson to join him for the drive over to the offices of Blackstar Studio's to rattle some chains. As they made the thirty minute drive over to West Hollywood to Blackstar, Sam filled Ryerson in about the run-around he got over the phone from the receptionist. "I bet the prick is sitting in his office when we walk in."

They arrived at Blackstar and Sam noticed an expensive looking Mercedes parked in the stall reserved for Robert Best.

Looking at Ryerson he said, "That could be his car. We might get lucky."

Sam and Ryerson walked into Blackstar, where they were greeted by a ridiculously beautiful receptionist, whose cleavage spilled all over her keyboard when she looked up to greet them. "Welcome to Blackstar Studios. How can I help you gentlemen?"

"Robert Best please."

The blonde bimbo, the same one who Sam had talked to earlier on the phone, stood up behind her desk, revealing a body dripping in surgery, and with a phony voice asked, "Who may I say is here?"

"LAPD Homicide Detectives Showenstein and Ryerson."

"Excuse me for one minute please." Sam watched as the receptionist wiggled her body that seemed to be trapped in a straight jacket of a dress, out of sight around the corner.

Returning a few minutes later and with a look of triumph on her face, she announced, "I am sorry, but Mr. Best is not here at the moment. Is there someone else here that can help you?"

Sam had enough and, looking at his partner, he motioned him to follow, "Well, maybe you can show me his office so I can see for myself that he isn't here."

The bimbo started to protest, but Sam and Ryerson had already brushed past the dress- restrained woman instead of hearing her protests as they made their way to Best's office. Taking the corner from where the receptionist returned, he was surprised to see only two offices in the back and another door with a sign that read, 'Studio in Session'. Well, it wouldn't take long to determine which office was Best's.

The first office, when they approached, seemed much larger than the other one. Sam entered and a well dressed man in an expensive suit and tie was sitting behind it talking on the phone. It was then that Sam noticed the impressive looking brass sign on the door that he never noticed when he approached, as the door was open. The name on the door read 'Robert Best, President'. The man motioned them to come in and take a seat. He observed Best talking on the phone and noticed he was definitely a ladies' man. Sam knew he was not the best looking guy on the block, with his stereotypical big Jewish nose, balding curly dark hair mixed with grey and a frame that reached 6'5' but was basketball skinny. Sam could eat anything he wanted and as much as he wanted and never gain an ounce, the curse or gift of his family genes. All of his brothers and his father were tall and skinny. Best was very handsome and looked to be in great physical shape. His short-cropped, black hair was tinged with a little grey, so he figured Best to be in his mid to late forties. His eyes were incredibly dark, the darkest eyes he had ever seen. Spooky dark, but he was sure the women fell hard for them. His eyes looked like they had seen a lot of terrible things over the years. They reflected anger. He suspected Best could be very intimidating if he wanted to be. "Why aren't my eyes as black as coal with all the shit I've seen over the years?", thought Sam.

After he finished up his call, Best looked at the detectives and stated: "Detectives Showenstein and Ryerson I presume."

The blonde finally made it to the doorway and shouted, "Mr. Best, I am so sorry, I tried to stop them!"

Robert Best quickly dismissed her, "It's alright Gina, I'll take it from here. Thank you."

He turned his attention back to the detectives, held his hands in the air and stated, "Gentlemen, what brings two determined policeman into my office so late in the day?"

Instantly disliking the smug Best, Sam replied, "We are investigating the murder of *Music Talks* executive Jonathon Green." He paused to study Best's reaction.

Best appeared truly shocked and replied, "My God, Detective, that is horrible. How did it happen?"

"He was ripped to pieces in his hotel room early this afternoon."

Best's eyes seemed to grow in size in horror at the news. "Jesus Christ, detective. Who would have done something like that and why?"

"We're hoping you could shed some light on that for us

Mr. Best."

"How could I possibly shed any light on the murder of Jonathon Green?"

"For starters, you can tell us your whereabouts today, starting at around noon."

Best looked at Sam with a look of disgust on his face, "That is easy; I was in the air flying from New York to Los Angeles. I landed at LAX approx two hours ago. I was picked up by the Blackstar limo and brought straight here. I hope that eliminates me as your number one suspect."

Sam knew he was telling the truth but he'd grind him some more anyway, "I'll need to see your boarding pass or a confirmation number that I can verify."

"Certainly detective. I believe my boarding pass is still in my suit jacket pocket." Best stood up and made his way around his desk to his suit jacket, hanging on a hook on his office door. He reached into his jacket and pulled out his boarding pass and handed it to Sam.

Satisfied that Best did indeed have a solid alibi, he folded the boarding pass and stuffed it into his shirt pocket and replied, "I'll hang onto this for verification if you don't mind. Do you mind if I call you Robert? Thank you. Tell me Robert. What was your relationship with Jonathon Green?"

"Jonathon was not a friend, only an acquaintance and a colleague in this crazy business. From time to time, I would receive a call from Jonathon requesting an interview with one of my clients to be conducted by one of his journalists out in the field."

"Who would those clients be?"

"*Music Talks* has featured Watermark, Devon Devine and Connor Asker."

Now Sam delivered the punch line, "Was there a particular reason you would be sending Green an email requesting a meeting just minutes before he was murdered?"

"Yes, there was Detective. I was trying to meet with him tonight regarding getting two of my most recent clients an interview with the magazine. I sent Jonathon an email from my iPhone while I was boarding my flight in New York at approximately 1:00pm eastern time. Would you like to see my outgoing email box on my iPhone?"

"How did you know Green was in L.A.? Why wouldn't you have just met with him in New York? You have an office there, and you are there frequently."

"To be perfectly honest detective, I was hoping to meet with him tonight over a drink and convince him in person, here in L.A., to do the interview the next day with their journalist, Bentley Paxton."

"Any particular reason you would want Bentley Paxton to write the interview?"

"Detective Showenstein, Bentley Paxton is one of the most renowned and respected journalists in the business. I like to make sure my clients are afforded every advantage. An interview by *Music Talks* magazine conducted by Bentley Paxton is great publicity for my clients, I can assure you."

"I'm sure it is Mr. Best. We will leave you alone for now. Thank you for your time. Here is my card. Call me if you hear anything regarding this case."

****

Best watched the two detectives exit his office and, as Showenstein turned the corner, he called out, "Detective Showenstein."

A second later the detective stood in his office doorway with a look of 'What the fuck do you want' all over his face. "I just wanted to say give my best to Bethany and Sebastian."

The look that crossed the detective's face went from surprise at the mention of his wife and child to deep anger, "You motherfucker, how the hell did you know the names of my wife and son?" The detective looked like he might pull his sidearm and use it, he was so pissed as he crossed the room towards Best's desk.

Chapter 14

Chelsea Benning was a happy woman and she could finally say that. It had been so long since she truly felt happy. It was over fifteen years ago that it happened. Namely, the brutal attack and rape by a monster that also took the life of her husband Steven. It was still a memory that would never go away and something that she thought about every single day. She focused her energies on raising her son Patrick and she was very grateful to have been blessed with such an amazing child. She knew that God had not abandoned her and Patrick. Despite her son's demonic creation, he was a miracle from God. She knew He had blessed her child.

Her good friend Sam Showenstein, a LAPD Homicide Detective and former partner of her deceased husband, urged her to begin opening her heart to a relationship. She slowly but surely did just that. She had gone out on a bunch of different dates for the first two years and, though nothing serious materialized, she really got to know herself once again. She would find herself comparing her dates to Steven, but then she quickly put a stop to that. It wasn't until almost three years after opening herself up to a new relationship that she felt that she had met Mr. Right. For the past three months, she had been seeing a man who wasn't a cop, a fireman, or a lawyer, any of the jobs where guys tend to bring the job home. Her new guy was a dream. He was a successful accountant who didn't work nights or weekends and who hated to talk about his job. Now safely in her forties, Chelsea was still considered a beautiful woman according to everyone in her office. She always took care of herself, and successfully avoided the mid-life weight gain. Her blond hair needed touch ups now and then to keep the grey at bay, but overall, she was happy with the way she looked. Her boyfriend Clint seemed to be satisfied so that was a good thing, she laughed to herself. Thinking of him always made her smile. Always. They took it slow for the first month, but both of them realized they were crazy about each other and couldn't stand to be apart. Sleepovers were a common occurrence. It was awkward at first for Patrick when she introduced Clint to him because, other than Sam, he had never had a male figure in his life. Her son soon warmed to Clint and they became fast friends. She was nervous about introducing him to Sam and Bethany, but they loved him. Now they often got together on the weekends, either at her house, Clint's or Sam's.

They had just spent a wonderful evening together. The two of them attended a benefit concert by the eighties rock band Journey for the Philippines Relief Fund. The band's lead singer, a mega-talented Filipino, was personally affected by the tragedy of the tsunami that killed hundreds of thousands and the band was doing benefit concerts nonstop all over the world to help raise funds for the victims. Clint was just so easy going and fun to be around that Chelsea found it more and more difficult to say goodbye at the end of the evening during the week. She wanted to make sure she was always there in the mornings to see Patrick off to school, though he hardly needed her to do that.

Clint dropped her off at her house after the concert, the two of them still humming the song "Don't Stop Believing" as they pulled up. They exchanged hugs and kisses with promises to get together on the weekend. Waving goodbye to Clint as he waited to ensure she was in her house, Chelsea entered her home and noticed that all of the lights were out and it was eerily quiet. Where was Patrick? He would likely be in his bedroom, listening to music or watching TV, but he always left some lights on for her if she was out. She put her purse down on the living room couch and headed up the stairs to check on her son.

She turned on the lights as she made her way to Patrick's

room. It was dark as a cave in her house. She didn't remember the last time she walked through her house with all of the lights completely off at night. It was barely 10:30 p.m.at night.

She made her way to Patrick's room and knocked on the door. Hearing no response, she rapped on the door again. She leaned her ear against the door, but heard nothing. Even if he had his earphones on, she would still be able to hear him as he always sang out loud to the songs or beat his drum sticks against his pillow or the bed frame. He was so cute when he was into his music. Many times, she had watched him in amazement as he beat his sticks against the dash of the car to the beat of the song coming over the radio or when he was wearing his ear buds, listening to his iPod. Patrick's drumming abilities were way beyond that of a kid fascinated with the drums. He was as good, if not better, than a professional. He was hired on many occasions to do studio work for local musicians recording an album. They chose Patrick, not only for his talent, but because he came cheap. He was better than the session players and their outrageous union rates, so to save some money they would hire Patrick. Word had spread throughout the music scene in Los Angeles of the boy wonder who could play percussion better than anyone.

Once musicians found out that Patrick was just as proficient on the base guitar as the drums, it lead to all kinds of opportunities for him. He was in demand all over the music scene. Local bands playing the nightclubs often brought in Patrick as a fill in for someone that was sick or unable to do the gig. No one questioned whether or not he was of age, as he easily passed for someone in his twenties. She and Clint would often sit in the crowd at the clubs to watch Patrick perform. Clint loved watching him play and was amazed at how talented he was.

She was getting no response from inside the room. He was not home. Where would he be? She never allowed him to perform at a club on a weekday during the school year and never without her consent. She was worried. Chelsea ran back downstairs and grabbed her cell phone out of her purse and quickly dialed Patrick's cell. It went straight to voicemail. She left him a message and then texted him, asking him to call her immediately. Occasionally, she allowed him to play with a band if they had a Thursday to Sunday gig at a club and they were really stuck and Patrick had no exams at school. His marks were at the top of his class so he got a lot of leeway from his teachers. The rule was that she would drop him off at the club after she met the manager and she would pick him up. She allowed no exceptions to that sensible rule.

Patrick always kept his room locked. Chelsea did not have a key, but she allowed Patrick this privacy as long as he never did anything to break that trust. If he ever did, she told herself, then the lock would come off. His reasoning was that he hated to be disturbed when he was deep in thought, playing music, writing or listening to music. She would make random inspections of his room to make sure it wasn't a pig pen and nothing hanky-panky was going on. He never stopped her from coming in and the room was always immaculate so she trusted him. He kept his key in the bathroom as he always entered the bathroom before he opened his bedroom door. It was a routine she had heard from her bedroom for years. She checked the bathroom for the key, but she could not find it after looking in all the obvious places. It would have to be somewhere easy to get to because he was only in the bathroom for a second before opening his bedroom door. With her hands on her hips, she scanned the interior of the bathroom looking for potential hiding spots for a key. She opened the medicine cabinet and lifted up all the vitamin and pill bottles in a search that proved to be futile. She checked underneath the soap dish and toothbrush holder. No key. Stepping back, she looked at the mirror. The mirror was oval with a wooden frame and it was attached to the wall with a hook behind the mirror. The outer rim of the frame was recessed towards the wall. With one knee on the countertop, she hoisted herself up onto the counter so she could look down on the top of the mirror. The key was nestled on the recessed part of the frame that you could not see from looking at the mirror straight on.

The key rested against the wall. It was the perfect spot to hide something. Kids are imaginative when they want to keep something a secret. She grabbed the key, got down off the countertop and turned towards Patrick's bedroom. She suddenly felt guilty that she was invading her son's space. He would be furious. Her fear of not knowing where he was overcame her sense of guilt.

Chelsea opened the door to Patrick's room and entered, calling out his name as she did so in case he was just sleeping on the chair on the other side of his room, "Patrick, are you here baby? Just wondering where you are as you didn't answer when I knocked on your door."

She was about to turn and leave when she noticed something on the far side of his bedroom on the wall. Curious, she walked over and was mortified to see dozens of black pencil sketches of mutilated bodies, grotesque images of limbs torn off bodies with blood spilling and splattered everywhere. She was completely taken aback: "Did Patrick draw these? He must have, but why?" These drawings were so dark and evil looking that it scared her to her soul that Patrick was capable of drawing something so horrible. There was a theme to every drawing. They all had an evil looking face with a pair of bright red eyes depicted on them. "What did that mean?"

Then it hit Chelsea like a tidal wave. It was the eyes. The beast. "Oh my God", she thought. Dropping to her knees, she buried her head between her legs and sobbed. The nightmare of the attacks fifteen years ago had returned. Her biggest fear was that Patrick would somehow know his origins. Now it was a reality. He knew. "He was drawing the red burning eyes because he knew!" She thought she would be sick so she stood up and bolted out of the bedroom into the bathroom where she emptied her stomach. She finally got a hold of herself and stood up and looked at herself in the mirror, thinking she would see the beast standing behind her, ready to thrust a claw through the back of her skull. She splashed cold water on her face, washed her hands and returned to Patrick's bedroom. She sat on the corner of his bed gripping the bed post fearing her shaking would plop her off the bed and onto the floor. The drawings were so demonic looking and evil. "What was going through his head when he was drawing those images? How much does he know about himself? Has the beast visited him and shared his evil beginnings?" Too many questions floated through her head in quick succession. Then she saw it and the sight of it sent her falling to the floor, fainting from the reality of what her son was.

She awoke a few minutes after dropping to the floor. She took a few seconds to focus her eyes on where she was and what she was doing. Then the reality of the situation became clear and the fear returned. As she lifted herself up off the floor, she almost fell down again with the headache from hitting the floor pounding in her skull. She looked back at the drawings and she began to cry again. This time she really cried. Her sobs resonated through the house. Her son was a killer. One of the drawings depicted the mutilated bodies of Bill and Evelyn Crittenden, her former neighbors who were brutally murdered three years ago. Stapled to the bottom of the drawing were three graphic and developed iPhone pictures of the slaughtered corpses of the Crittendens. Below the graphic image was the message that read: 'Killed by Patrick Benning'. In fact, most of the drawings were depicting either animals or humans being mutilated, usually with a man standing with a severed head or limb in his hand. Below each image, in the corner of the drawing, were always the words 'Killed by Patrick Benning. Often there were additional details such as First Human Kill and the date. They were horrible images. The Crittendens' drawing was the only one with real pictures attached to it. One of the pictures was a disgusting image of Patrick laying on the floor beside the corpse of Bill Crittenden with his face caved in, Patrick's arm around his neck and shoulders, smiling like a hunter with his trophy deer proudly displayed. The picture was taken by Patrick holding up his phone like kids do taking pictures for Facebook.

The killers of the Crittenden's were never caught. It was because her son had killed them. No one would ever have suspected Patrick. Chelsea knew without a doubt her son, the spawn of Satan, was a cold-blooded killer. She shook like a leaf as she made her way out of the bedroom and down the hall. She had to think of what to do. Patrick would walk through the door any minute and she didn't know how she would react when she saw him. She would call Sam. If she did, then Sam would have no choice but to arrest Patrick for the murders of Crittendens. This wasn't Patrick's fault. He couldn't stop himself because of who he was. He needed her help. She would call Sam. She trusted him not to arrest her son until they thought this through. She picked up her phone and dialed his number.

After several rings he finally picked up, his voice groggy; she had awakened him from a deep sleep he had likely just started. With a sleepy voice he said, "Chelsea its 11:00 p.m. Why are you calling me so late?"

Between sobs, she managed to get out, "Sam, I need you to come to the house right now. Please hurry. Please."

Sensing the fear in her voice, he was instantly awake and clear when he replied, "Chelsea what the hell is the matter? What is going on?"

"It's Patrick. I need your help Sam, please hurry!"

"Is he okay? Do you need an ambulance Chelsea? I can call one on my way over!"

"No, he's not here right now. Just get here now please."

"I'm on my way Chelsea, I'll be fifteen minutes."

She dropped her phone on the floor and fell back against the cushions of her living room couch, burying her face in her hands, the sobs wracking her body once more. Her life was over as she knew it. Patrick would be arrested, thrown in jail for the rest of his life. Clint would leave her, never wanting to be associated with the mother of a serial killer. Maybe she should go upstairs and get one of Steven's old pistols, still kept in a locked gun case in her closet. Then, when Patrick walked through the front door, she would blow him away and then take the gun to herself and end this madness once and for all. Her thoughts were wrenched away by the sound of the front door bell. Sam was here.

She didn't know how she was going to do this other than just bring him upstairs and let him see for himself what she saw. Let the chips fall where they lay. Getting up off of the couch, she walked towards the front door but it seemed like it was miles away. She felt as if she was walking for hours to cross the few feet from the couch to the door. Taking a deep breath, she reached down to the knob and turned it, opening the door slowly, and her strength seemingly draining by the second. When the door was swung completely open, she just wanted to fall into Sam's arms, wake up and know that this was all just a bad dream. What she saw made her freeze in fear; the blood quickly drained from her face as the fear of who was standing on her doorstep materialized in her brain.

The beast had returned.

****

Sam got dressed quickly while explaining to his sleepy wife, Beth, that Chelsea was in trouble and wanted him to come to the house immediately. She was scared out of her mind about something. He strapped his pistol to his waist, grabbed his coat off of the hook on the back of the closet door, reached down and gave Beth a kiss and told her he would call her as soon as he got to Chelsea's. Sam climbed into his unmarked, grey Ford Crown Vic, threw on his police lights in the front grill, back window and sped off for the ten minute drive to the Benning's home.

All the way over to Chelsea's, he tried calling her phone but she didn't pick up and it just went to voicemail. Then he tried her cell phone. It also just rang and rang till it finally went to voicemail. "What has her so spooked?" he worried. She was hysterical and crying, going on and on about Patrick, and urging that Sam needed to hurry over. His stomach had taken on the familiar feeling of dread, as if preparing him for something very bad that was about to happen. When he pulled onto Chelsea's street, he gunned it to her home and came screeching to a stop in the driveway. He jumped out of the car and bolted up the driveway to the front door. He rang the doorbell and pounded on the door. Hearing nothing, he checked the door and it was locked. Something was very bad; he could feel it in his bones. Panicking, he shouted her name into the door and continued to pound. No response. He took off of the step and raced around the side of the house to the back door. It was locked. Sam thought to himself: "son of a bitch, what the hell is going on?"

He pounded on the back door, shouting her name and Patrick's. It was dead quiet inside. He pulled his 9mm from its holster and used it to smash the window of the back door. He reached in, unlocked the door and ran inside. Clicking off the gun's safety, he held his gun shoulder high as he walked through the back of the house and into the kitchen. He continued to shout Chelsea's and Patrick's name. Then he heard what sounded like crying or more like wails coming from Patrick in the living room. Steven bolted into the living room and straight into the pit of hell.

Patrick, covered in blood, sat on the living room floor, cradling what was left of Chelsea. The look on Patrick's face was something that would forever be etched into his memory. Patrick was rocking back and forth holding what appeared to be the partial shoulder, head and other shoulder of Chelsea, the rest of her body was torn to pieces all over the living room. Sam thought he would pass out; the scene was right out of a horror movie. He instinctively whipped out his cell phone, called into dispatch a 187, requesting ambulance and paramedics. He asked Patrick if there was anyone still in the house, not expecting to hear anything back, the boy was lost, holding his shredded mother. Sam quickly checked the rest of the house to see if the perpetrators were still in the house and, after not finding anyone, returned to the living room. He then knelt down beside Patrick, the look of a boy completely destroyed etched right through him. Sam put his arm around his shoulders and whispered to him.

"Patrick, I am so sorry. I am so very sorry. Please let her go. The ambulances will be here any minute. Come outside with me on the front step and we will wait for them together."

Patrick looked up at Sam with a look on his face that made his heart ache and said, "What the fuck is an ambulance going to do for my mom huh Sam? Put her back together again like Humpty Dumpty? Leave me alone Sam, I'm not leaving my mom."

"Come on Patrick, let her go please. This is horrific for you, come on let's get out of here."

Patrick began rambling like he didn't hear what Sam just said, "Who could have done this to my mom, Sam? What did she ever do to deserve this? She's torn to fucking pieces." Patrick dropped his chin into his chest and sobbed, his body heaving with the sobs.

Sam reached over and gently took Patrick's hands off of the severed head and shoulders of Chelsea and placed the remains on the floor. He stood up and bent down and gently took Patrick by the arm and lifted him up off of the floor. The sirens of the police cruisers and ambulances could now be heard. Patrick didn't appear to be hurt, so Sam just eased him slowly out the front door, down the steps and into the front seat of his police car.

Sam let Patrick know that he would be right back, that he was going to have a talk with the police and then he would take him home to his place where Bethany and Seb would be waiting with some food and then a warm bed.

Talking with the uniformed policemen, explaining the scene and what they needed to do, Sam noticed the arrival of his partner, Daniel Ryerson. Sam instructed Ryerson to take charge of the crime scene; that he was taking Patrick home to his place so Beth could comfort and take care of him and then he would return.

As he climbed back into the driver's seat of his car, Sam buckled up and looked over at Patrick, who was staring blankly out the window towards the front of his house, quiet, likely in shock. He would take care of Patrick from this day forward, he knew. He would keep him safe. Whoever or whatever brutally killed his father and now his mother, Sam swore that he would protect Patrick to his death.

Chapter 15

Sam helped Patrick out of the car and into the house. Sam had taken a minute to call Beth and give her the horrible news before he got back in the car with Patrick to take him to his house. Beth and Seb were waiting on the front step for them when they arrived. Beth, crying, hugged Patrick for what seemed an eternity. Wiping his face with his sleeve, Patrick turned and gave Seb a hug. Not many words were exchanged between everyone, just lots of hugs. Beth and Seb led Patrick into the kitchen where she had just pulled one of her famous homemade pizzas out of the oven. It was almost 1:00 a.m. so everyone was tired. Patrick was the only one that had an appetite and almost ate the entire pizza by himself. When he was finished, he looked up at everyone and said that he was tired and would like to get some sleep.

Beth took Patrick upstairs to the spare room, made sure he was comfortable and then returned to the kitchen to cleanup. She was stunned by the tragic and brutal killing of her friend Chelsea Benning. That family seemed to be cursed. First the murder of her husband and Sam's partner and the rape and violent beating Chelsea suffered. Now she was dead. What was going on in this city? Who would want to do this to her? Poor Patrick would spend the rest of his life without both his parents now. How tragic.

Beth was able to catch Sam as he was walking out the door, "How bad was it for Patrick, Sam? I feel so awful for him, I can't imagine what he must be feeling."

Sam looked at his wife and with a look of sorrow written all over his face replied, "It was the worst crime scene I have ever seen Beth. She was literally torn to pieces like a wild animal had had its way with her. I found Patrick holding onto a piece of his mother. Comfort him Beth, as best as you possibly can. We're all he has now. I have to go back there so get some sleep okay? I love you." Sam swung his big arm around his wife, giving her a hug and a kiss as he backed down the stairs and into his car.

Beth watched her husband pull out of the driveway, and wave to her as he sped off down the street. "These are dark times", she thought as she turned to walk back into the house. She silently prayed for her husband, like she always did when he left for work. This time was different. Something evil was out there; she could sense it. She didn't know how she could feel it but she did and it scared the hell out of her.

****

Sam arrived back at the Benning house and this time the place was surrounded with blue and whites, their lights flashing. The whole block was cordoned off. Emergency vehicles were parked on standby at the end of the block. An ambulance was parked on the front lawn of the house, its emergency lights turned off. There was nothing left of Chelsea to save; it was just a matter of scraping up her pieces.

He walked into a house that was full of uniforms and detectives. Captain Bitters saw him walk in and made a move towards him, "Sam, Jesus Christ, I'm so sorry. What a fucking mess in there. Ryerson is on it, he is coordinating things until your return. Are you sure you're good on this one Sam? I can totally appreciate you taking a pass on this. You don't have to take it. I'll put Booker and Russell on it, outside of you, they're the best."

"I'm good Cap. I need to do this, okay? I failed Steven, I'm not going to fail Chelsea."

"Good, I was hoping you would stay on this. How's the kid?"

"In shock and will be for a few days. Beth has taken the rest of the week off and will be there for him through this. I found him holding the head and shoulders of his mother for God's sakes. The kid has been through hell."

"Fucking awful. Whoever did this is a fucking maniac. You and Ryerson have the full resources of the LAPD at your disposal. You will be given top priority on everything. You need extra bodies, you got 'em. Overtime, no problem. Lab work and autopsy will be given top priority. Get the motherfuckers who did this to Chelsea, Sam. You hear me?"

"I hear you boss. Thanks Cap and don't worry. When I catch the cocksuckers who did this they're going to wish they were never born because when I'm done with them, even hell won't want them."

"Go easy Sam. Be careful, by the book remember. Keep me updated."

Sam quickly located Ryerson and was brought up to speed, "CSI will be here any minute to try and make sense of this. There is a lot of blood Sam, as you could well imagine. Hopefully, some of it is from the killer. I have uniforms canvassing the neighborhood to see if any of them saw anything or anyone near the Benning home that looked suspicious. We had a look around the house, but saw no footprints or anything out of the ordinary. There is no forced entry other than the broken back door from you. Robbery was not a motive. Nothing appears to be stolen and there are no signs that the killers tried to rob the place. Everything is intact."

Sam was deep in thought before he replied, "Good work Dan. I bet Chelsea knew the killer. The front door was locked. She must have known who it was, let them in the house, then whoever killed her locked the door on his way out."

"If that's true Sam, then wouldn't the killer be tipping his hat by letting investigators know he was known by the victim? Why wouldn't they have trashed the place as if they were robbing it to throw us off?"

"The killer doesn't care what we think. He believes he won't be caught. The murder scene is very similar to the Jonathon Green murder don't you think? This is a madman savagely killing innocent victims but they are connected somehow. Come on, let's finish up and head back to the office. Murders with no motive, no robbery, no rape, just a brutal attack and over kill. That's what this is Dan. Whoever did this is a raging, out of control psychopath. Whoever did this will not stop. There are going to be more victims and I bet if we start checking, we'll find previous victims besides Chelsea and Green."

Forty-five minutes later, Sam and Ryerson left the Benning house and called it a night with a plan to get started first thing in the morning. It was 1:30 a.m. and both of them were exhausted. They needed sleep because they both knew they were not going to get much for awhile.

****

Sam arrived home by 2:00 a.m., exhausted and hungry. He debated whether to just head to bed and worry about food in the morning, but his growling stomach convinced him to make a pit stop at the kitchen first. Digging around the fridge, he was hoping to either find some left over spaghetti from a few nights ago or even some of the cupcakes Beth brought home from the store. He didn't care, he was starving and the sooner he satisfied that craving the quicker he could get to bed and get some sleep. He settled on making a ham sandwich with mayo and cheese, so he carried everything over to the table to begin building a mountain sized sandwich.

He damn near dropped everything on the floor when he noticed Patrick sitting at one of the chairs at the table, silhouetted from the little bit of moonlight slicing through the partially opened blind on the kitchen window. "Jesus, Patrick, you scared me. Is everything okay? You having a tough time sleeping?"

"I want to go back to my house, Sam. I want to be close to my mom`s spirit. I can`t sleep here knowing her soul is lingering back at the house worried and wondering about me."

"Here we go", Sam thought. He knew he would be having a conversation soon with Patrick about the loss of his mother but he didn't figure so soon. "Patrick, I know you are hurting and you miss your mom, but she is gone. She is truly gone to a better place. She will not be lingering at home for you Patrick; she is here with you right now. She will forever be right there with you. I believe that Patrick. Your mom will always watch over you, from heaven."

"You can stop with the heaven bullshit Sam, you don't believe that and neither do I. My mother`s body may have been shredded but her soul is intact and it`s in hell Sam. Life on earth may be under God`s watchful eye, but once your body dies, your soul becomes the property of the dark power. My mom is with the dark power now Sam and she needs me, but I can't hear or see her unless I return to my house. She is waiting for me there."

This poor kid was so traumatized and tired he was delusional. Sam knew he needed to get Patrick to bed so he could get some rest. "Patrick I understand, I do. This is a conversation that we need to have tomorrow. You and I are so damn tired we cannot even think straight. Will you do me a favor? Will you go to bed and promise me you will sleep so tomorrow you and I and Beth can talk more about how you are feeling?"

Sam watched as Patrick seemed to withdraw from their conversation like he was fading into the shadows of the moonlight coming through the windows, his long wavy hair catching pieces of the moon's light. Then in a voice so quiet it was barely a whisper that made the hair on the back of Sam's neck stand-up, he spoke: "Sam. He's coming for you."

"Who is coming for me Patrick? What are you talking about? Okay, enough for tonight okay Patrick. You have had a very rough day and its time you got some sleep. So let's go before I wake up Beth and then you know you'll be in big trouble. You don't want to piss off Bethany Showenstein at 2:30 a.m. in the morning. Trust me. It can be brutal. What do you say; will you do us both a favor and get to bed?"

He seemed to snap out of the little mini trance he was in and rose from his chair and looked down at Sam and just stared for a minute before he said, "No one can stop him Sam, no one. Not even your God can stop him now." With that he turned and headed up the stairs to the bedroom Beth had prepared for him. "Who is coming and not even God can stop him? That was weird", he thought while watching Patrick disappear into the shadows as he climbed the stairs.

****

The next morning Sam awoke, his eyes opening suddenly, afraid instantly that he had slept in. Looking over at the clock, he was relieved to see it was only 7:00 a.m. Beth was already up, likely preparing a special breakfast for Patrick and Seb. He needed to be at the office soon, Ryerson would be there bright and early, ready to go. As he made his way into the shower and let the hot needles of the water wake up all of his senses, he began to recall the details of last night's horrific murder scene at Chelsea's. Whoever butchered Chelsea also killed Jonathon Green, Sam could feel it. The savagery and brutality of the murders were very similar and they needed to start connecting the dots as quickly as possible before the next victim turned up.

Sam made his way into the kitchen to hear Patrick pleading with Beth to let him go to school. She would not hear any of it. Child and Family Services were likely to be at the house today to talk with Patrick. Knowing he could not win against Beth, Patrick resigned himself that he would be staying in the house today. He was acting like nothing happened last night and not like he had just lost his mother in a vicious murder. Maybe school was a way for him to be around his friends and his peers in order to take his mind off of the loss of his mom. He glanced at Beth and got her attention by nodding his head towards the living room. The two of them met in the living room and he asked her, "Maybe we should let him go to school. Being around his friends might be his way of coping with all of this. What do you think?"

His wife is one of the smartest people he knew and Sam was always amazed by how she broke things down so that they made perfect sense and this was no exception: "Honey what you need to understand about Patrick is he deals with his problems by internalizing them. He has not mentioned her nor has he acted like anything is the matter. He is putting up this front that he is okay, that he can handle this. He can't Sam. He loved his mother more than anything in this world. They were so close, as close as a mother and son could possibly be. Less than twelve hours ago he was holding the head of his murdered mother in his hands. How could he possibly be okay? Child and Family Services need to assess him, get him to the right doctors who can help him deal with this. They will want to see him as quickly as possible, likely today. He is not going to school until he has had some counselling."

"You're right. I feel like an idiot. How could I possibly think he would be okay going to school so soon? I love you Dr. Showenstein."

"I love you too and besides, I took the week off to make sure Patrick gets the help and support he will need. What do you say we let Child and Family Services know that we would like temporary custody of him? At least for the time being."

"How about we let them know right from the start that we would like to adopt Patrick permanently? Where else can he go? We are like his aunt and uncle anyway. He knows us and he trusts us. Plus he and Seb are like brothers. I believe it's our duty to Steven and Chelsea that we make Patrick ours to ensure he is loved and wanted. What do you say sweetheart?"

She wrapped her arms around his neck and replied, "I say that is the best thing you could have said. That would make me very happy and I'm sure Seb would be completely thrilled."

He gave his wife a big kiss and hug then looked in her eyes and said, "I love you so much. You are the best and I am so lucky to have you as my wife. Listen, I will drive Seb to school and talk to him about all of this, okay? I know it's a long way from reality but we should let Seb know what we are thinking, as he will be affected by all of this too, don't you think?"

"Of course it is. Driving him to school and having a talk with him is a great idea. You had better get going."

****

Sam glanced over at Sebastian as he pulled out of the

driveway to take him to school and asked, "It's been a crazy time hasn't it son? Terrible times for Patrick but he is lucky to have a good friend like you to lean on."

His son, fifteen years old, tall and lanky like himself, but athletic where he wasn't and likely headed to college on a basketball scholarship, replied: "I know Dad, don't worry I'll be there for him."

Sensing something was wrong with his son he asked, "Is everything okay Seb? You seem off about something. Would you like to share it with me?"

His son looked over at him, not saying anything, just staring for what seemed like an eternity, when he finally replied: "Dad, is he going to be living with us forever now?"

"Your mom and I have talked about that and we both agree that would be best for Patrick. There is a long road ahead before that will happen but I know that is what Chelsea would have wanted. Don't you agree son?"

He stared out the window, quiet, watching the houses and parked cars fly by before looking back at him and replying, "I guess that would be okay Dad. Patrick needs this family."

"You don't sound so thrilled son. Are you sure about this? Your mother and I will not pursue this unless you are 100% on board. Being best friends one day with Patrick and step brothers the next might be too much for you. Your mom and I will understand."

Sam pulled up into the parking lot of Seb's school and put the car in park. Looking at Seb, he continued, "You don't have to tell us right now whether or not you are okay with this. Take your time. Let it sink in for awhile before making a decision. Okay?"

"Dad, he scares me."

Sam wasn't sure he heard Seb correctly, "What did you say son? You are scared of Patrick?"

"No I'm not scared of him, I'm terrified of him dad."

"Jesus, Seb where did that come from? What do you mean you're terrified of him? You guys have been best friends since you were born. I don't understand."

"Did you know that when he sleeps over he never falls asleep? Not ever."

What the hell was his son talking about? He never sleeps, what was that all about? "Seb, I know Patrick can be a little high strung at times but he does sleep, he has to. Everyone needs sleep."

"You think I don't know that dad? I'm telling you, ever since I have known Patrick, my whole life, he has never slept. I wake up during the night and he's always sitting on his bed either slapping imaginary drum sticks in the air or is furiously writing stuff down on a pad of paper. He has even told me he never sleeps. He hasn't slept in years."

The words Patrick spoke last night at the kitchen table before he went to bed came back to Sam now: "He's coming for you. No one can stop him Sam, no one. Not even your God can stop him now."

All of a sudden, those words, dismissed last night by Sam as coming from a traumatized boy, took on a whole different meaning.

Chapter 16

Alive Records was exactly that today, *Alive*! Jenn Steinart, the beautiful office manager for Alive Records, or as Avery would tell her, the backbone of the company, was run off of her feet. There was so much going on she was setting new personal levels on multitasking. She wasn't complaining, in fact, she revelled in the haywire atmosphere taking hold. Alive Records was spearheading a benefit concert at the Staples Center this weekend in support of the tsunami relief efforts taking place all over the globe. All of the Alive clients were participating, in addition to the stars volunteering for the event. There were so many artists wanting to get involved, Avery was forced to close the registration because he couldn't fit anymore in. Natural disasters like the tsunami brought the musicians out in droves because they knew they could make a difference. It was great to see.

Jenn wrapped on Avery's door before entering. That was her routine; give him a split second warning that she was coming in. She saw that Avery was buried in paperwork and not about to look up and acknowledge her. This meant that he wanted her to be brief and then leave him be. Interrupting his concentration, she said, "Avery, I have the final schedule for the concert completed. I will need you to go over it and give it final approval so we can send out the press kits by courier this afternoon. When will you give me the time?"

He looked up at her, took off his reading glasses and replied, "How about right now? Can you grab me a Coke first, I'm dry as hell, and then we can grind this thing out okay?"

"Sounds good. I'll be right back with your bottle of water."

****

Avery chuckled to himself when Jenn left to go get him a bottle of water. Months ago, she made it her mission to wean him off of his addiction to Coke and to get him to start drinking water. He hated water; it was tasteless and did nothing for him. He liked his two cups of coffee first thing in the morning when he arrived at the office, but the rest of the day he would devour three to four Cokes and even more if they were recording into the evening. Today would be a long day and his craving for a Coke would pick up steam later in the day. Jenn knew this and would watch him like a hawk from about 2:00 p.m. onward. This whole water thing with Jenn really took hold almost like an intervention when he was railroaded over drinks after work with Jenn and later by Bentley. Jenn would nag him all the time that he should stop drinking Coke and start drinking more water. When Bentley got involved in the debate, the two of them joined forces and now Avery couldn't even enjoy a Coke over lunch or dinner when he and Bentley were out together. Bentley was as bad as Jenn. He enjoyed rousting the two of them about it just to get a reaction because he knew they were so serious about it. When Jenn returned to his office, a bottle of water each for the two of them, he protested, "Wait a minute Jenn, I need a Coke. This is a stressful day and I need to calm my frayed nerves so I need a damn Coke."

With a curt smile and a wink she replied, "Nice try Johnson. I'm the one with the frayed nerves and all the stress okay. Enjoy the water. Now let's get busy."

"You like seeing me suffer, don't you Jenn? You get some sick and perverse satisfaction from it I bet."

"Hey, listen to me Mr. Healthy. You expect to someday marry the beautiful Ms. Paxton? Then you better start adopting a healthier lifestyle."

Laughing Avery said, "Okay, okay, you win. Don't tell Bentley I asked for a Coke okay? What do you have to show me for the schedule?"

Jenn laid out the itinerary for the mega concert that would

begin Saturday at noon and end around midnight, twelve hours of nonstop music by some of the top acts in the world.

"I like it that you have scheduled the Asker kid to kick things off. That will get the crowd there early and that little dynamo will get them worked up."

"Good. I am also doing it again after the break from 6:00 p.m. to 7:00 p.m. with Juan Jimenez, the fifteen year old heartthrob from Venezuela. He'll get everyone cranked up for the heavy weights to follow."

"I know who the fifteen year old heartthrob from Venezuela is Jenn. You're trying to distract me from the fact you snuck in another one of Robert Best child prodigy clients. I hate that prick but those kids are damn good and will sell tickets. Okay, again good move Jenn."

"The big stars all want to perform in the evening. They think the place will empty out with of all the kids and be replaced with their moms and dads for the rest of the evening. There's a problem because I don't have room for them and I need to fill the rest of the slots during the day. I have everyone performing a minimum of six songs and some acts upwards of ten"

"Okay, then let's decide first who will close the show. Then we will slot them in as best we can and to hell with what they think. This is a benefit concert for Christ's sakes, not Woodstock. They don't like it, tell their managers to go to hell. They're not getting paid but I can guarantee you that they want the exposure this concert will generate. They will grumble like spoiled school children but they'll be there."

"I'm thinking we should let Aerosmith close it up. If there's any dollars to donate left in the fans' wallets, Steve will get it out them."

"I agree and let's get Arnel Pineda from Journey back on to join Aerosmith in their encore. He can give a little thank you speech to the fans and to the other bands for their time and talent to the cause for the people and victims of the tsunami."

"Okay, Avery, if you're okay with the rest of the lineup then we're done.

"Is the curtain backdrop with the Alive Records logo and the tsunami relief fund logo for the stage complete and installed at Staples Center?"

"Yes it is. I saw a proof and it looks awesome. Did you want me to email you a copy?"

"No, it's okay, I'm just messing with you. I was down at the Staples Center last night when the crews began assembling the stage and I got a glimpse of it as they rolled it out on the arena floor to attach the cables. It looks incredible Jenn, it really does. This concert is a real coup for Alive Records and I owe it all to you. Thank you."

He watched as her skin turned just a tinge of red. He liked that look and needed to compliment her more often. If this compliment caused her to blush, then wait until she walked into the parking lot and was what was waiting for her there. "Her face will bleed red", laughed Avery laughed to himself.

"Will Bentley be joining you backstage? Will she need VIP backstage credentials?"

"No, she is working the event for *Music Talks*. She has all the credentials she will need. Will you do me a favor and make sure the limo that will be picking her up has flowers and a mushy card from me? You know what I mean."

"I know what you mean. How is she doing Avery? With her boss Jonathon's awful murder, I mean?"

"It's been a tough week for her, without a doubt, but she's a trooper and I think she's looking forward to working again, so this concert will be good for her."

"I think what's really been good for her is being able to curl up to you every night. You guys make a great couple and she's crazy in love with you, Avery."

"Oh come on Jenn, don't be starting rumors. It's too early for that."

"You think so? I say bullshit. I know when a woman's in love and I'm telling you that girl is swooning. You know what else?"

"What, she got an 'I love Avery Johnson' tattoo?"

"Don't flatter yourself Avery. I think you're as much in

love with her as she is with you."

She just knew how to cut to the chase. He looked at her with a smile on his face and said, "Alright, enough already, get out of here and get some work done for once."

Returning Avery's smile, she grabbed her notebook and paperwork and got up to leave. Before exiting his office he called out to her, "Oh by the way Jenn, would you mind going out to my car and grabbing the bottle of champagne? I forgot to bring it in for our little celebration."

"Celebration, Avery? Now you have me running out to your car for errands? The things I put up with in this place," joked Jenn as she closed the door to his office.

He waited about thirty seconds and then hustled out of his office and down the hallway to the exit door leading into the employee parking lot in the back. He got there just in time to see Jenn's stunned reaction when she saw what was waiting for her. It was Jenn's 35th birthday and he had had a brand new, candy apple red Maserati GranCabrio Sport convertible wrapped in red and white ribbons and balloons delivered for her.

She looked back at Avery and broke out in tears. "Oh my God, Avery this is incredible! What a beautiful surprise. You bought me a car, my favorite car, a Maserati for my birthday. Thank you." With that she ran towards him and jumped the final few feet into his arms, bear hugging him and squealed like a little kid. "This is the most incredible thing that has ever happened to me. Wow, I'm in shock."

"Jenn you haven't even gone over there and looked at it yet. Yes, it's a little crazy buying my assistant a Maserati, but you so deserve this. *Alive Records* is what it is because of you and I mean that. This is a small token of my appreciation, okay a large token of my appreciation. Happy Birthday Jenn, now get over there, rip those damn ribbons and balloons off of that beautiful car, listen to the patient salesman who delivered it on how everything works and go have some fun. I'll see you in the morning."

"Okay I will. Thank you so much Avery. Unbelievable.

Oh shoot, I almost forgot to tell you who called. He has been calling all day requesting a meeting with you. I kept putting him off, knowing you wouldn't want to be disturbed."

"Who was it?"

"Robert Best from Blackstar Studios."

"Jesus, Jenn, why did you have to ruin the moment, huh?"

"Sorry Avery, but he is very insistent that he meet with you. His number is on my desk. Grab it and call him okay? He has cleared the schedules of both Asker and Jimenez to have them there for the benefit so he deserves at least a meeting."

"Alright, I'll call him. Get going and wait till you leave the parking lot before you start laying down some rubber on the pavement okay?"

****

Avery wrapped up things at the office and rushed out to the parking lot to his BMW. Now that Jenn had the nicest car in the parking lot he might have to consider getting some new wheels one day soon. He was running late to meet Best over drinks after promising Jenn he would call him and agree to meet. Best suggested they meet at the Whale and Ale in central San Pedro for some fish and chips and a pint of British ale. He said he was bringing a client and no, not to worry, it wasn't Devon Devine. "Best actually sounded human", thought Avery, who also informed Best that he was bringing a friend along as well.

While guiding his SUV into late commuter traffic, Avery dialed up Bentley's number, feeling the butterflies dancing around in his stomach like a kid asking out a girl to the dance. She answered on the second ring, "Hi Avery! My busy day of work has drained my energy but talking to you lifts my spirits. I miss you sweetheart, what's up?"

"You must be having a positive influence in my life. I have agreed to have drinks with Robert Best from Blackstar Studios."

"Holy cow, that is a 360 degree turn. What prompted that change in attitude?"

"Not sure, maybe professional courtesy, the new me

because of you, Jenn asked me to or just why the hell not? I would like it if you joined me though. He's introducing me to a client and I would like some company so I don't have to be alone. I might lose it and with no backup I could get hurt."

Her laugh warmed him inside when she spoke, "I doubt that very much Avery. It would be great to join you. Where are you meeting?"

"At a British pub in San Pedro, I'll be driving right past you so if it's okay with you, I'll pick you up. Be there in fifteen minutes. Does that work?"

"Perfect. I'll be ready. Bye, see you soon."

Fifteen minutes later, Avery pulled up in front of her apartment. She was waiting on the sidewalk in front and walked up and got in the car. She was incredibly beautiful and when she climbed in his car, he took a second to admire her beauty. Dressed in dark navy pants, high heels and a meshed light blue shawl over top of a white blouse, she had different colors of blue beads cascading down the front of her top. He leaned over and gave her a kiss. "Great to see you beautiful."

Avery wore black dress pants, a white dress shirt with an open collar and no tie, with a black suit jacket. Jenn would tease him when he wore this because it reminded her of an Amish man. He would shoot right back by telling her he doubted if an Amish man wore a stainless steel Breitling watch. He wore his custom leather black slip on dress shoes, his favorite. He owned several pairs of the exact same style. The drive to San Pedro went way too quickly with Avery enjoying every second as Bentley reached over and cradled his hand in hers as she told him all about her day. Then she finally said, "I must admit to being a little uncomfortable meeting with Best. It was just a few days ago that I attended Jonathon's funeral service and one of the first suspects the police questioned was Best."

"I completely understand Bentley. If this makes you to uncomfortable then let me know and I can take you home. Just try to remember that he was questioned by detectives then quickly dismissed as a suspect due to the fact he was on the other side of the country when the murder occurred. "

"I know that, it just adds to the creepiness that I've always felt about him. I'll be fine as long as you are. I think I'll just keep an eye on you to make sure you don't lose it," laughed Bentley.

"I'm going to go into this with an open mind but the second he gets weird, we're out of there before I do lose it!"

They arrived at the Whale and Ale only fifteen minutes late and were promptly escorted to a rear table by the hostess, who was expecting them. As they approached the table, Robert Best stood up out of his chair to greet and shake hands with Avery. "Thank you for taking the time to meet with me Avery." Looking at Bentley with a broad smile, he continued, "What a pleasant surprise to see you again Ms. Paxton. I am so glad you're here. Please, both of you, I want you to meet Juan Jimenez from Maracaibo, Venezuela."

So this was the rising young South American heartthrob making his way onto the American music charts. He reached out his hand, followed by Bentley's hand, "Nice to meet you Juan. Congratulations on your success and thank you for taking the time for the benefit concert."

The young man was around the same age as Connor Asker but looked much older and more mature than his age. This kid would have no problems getting into nightclubs, no one would think twice checking his I.D. He looked at him and Bentley and replied, "Nice to meet you Mr. Johnson and Ms. Paxton. Mr. Johnson, I am honored to meet you. In the music industry in South America, you are a legendary producer. Ms. Paxton I am a huge fan of your magazine and I look forward to the day when maybe you can interview me."

Bentley glanced over at Avery before she replied, he could tell she was impressed with the kid, "The way things are going for you in South America, *Music Talks* might have to stand in line to get that interview!"

The kid was a charmer, an important character trait to have in this business. Drinks were ordered with Avery choosing one of the micro breweries' house blends and Bentley choosing a glass of house red wine. Avery turned his attention to Best: "Tell me Robert, what brings us together today? It has been awhile since our last business conversation many years ago and if memory serves me correctly, that didn't go so well."

Best was an impeccably well-dressed man, his dark navy suit looked professional and reeked of expensive tastes. The lighter blue dress shirt and tie matched so well he had to have had a tailor choose his ensemble for him. His face was unmarked, the skin perfect, his looks couldn't have been sculpted any better by a skilled plastic surgeon. He was a very good looking guy and for the first time, Avery felt a little uncomfortable sitting across from him with Bentley beside him. He was not jealous in any way because he knew Bentley loathed him, it was his personality. He projected immense power and stature. He was an intimidating man both in his looks and his confident personality. Best could control a boardroom full of executives with ease, Avery was sure of it. Women that were not as rock strong as Bentley would easily fall prey to his charm.

Breaking out into a smile, exposing too perfect and straight white teeth, he replied, "Thank you for the reminder Avery. That was a very long time ago indeed. Let's just say I have come a long way in this industry, both in the quality of my clients and myself as a person and a producer and manager. Let me get right to the point on why I wanted to meet with you. My company, Blackstar Studios, is working on a mega project that I will share with you in the near future because I believe you will want to participate in the opportunity. In the meantime I have the careers of young major talent coming on board and plain and simple, I need help. I want you Avery and your studio Alive Records, to take over the career of Juan Jimenez. He is on the verge of superstardom, not only in South America but in the United States and around the world as well. I would like for you to produce his debut CD and manage his career. What do you think?"

This caught Avery by surprise; he was not expecting Best to offer up a potential Latin American superstar like Juan

Jimenez. These types of clients don't fall out of trees every day. There would be a catch, Avery knew, and what price would it be? "That is a very generous offer Robert but I have to respectfully decline. Alive Records is currently not accepting new clients, our stable is full to the point it's getting unmanageable. I'm sorry Juan."

"I beg you to reconsider Avery. I know you're busy because I know who your clients are. Most of your clients, however, are established veteran stars who require little babysitting or managing, including in the studio. Most of these vets show up at your studio with a team of producers and you end up being a minor collaborator, am I wrong? Taking on someone like Juan offers you an opportunity to start at the ground floor with a mega-talented but green kid like Juan and launch his career. He'll be putty in your hands. You can shape him anyway you like."

He was impressed. Best was right about his veteran clients. That was the natural progression in the industry. A lot of the stars that had been around awhile had so much money that, once their contract expired with their record companies, they would start their own labels, build their own state of the art studios in their mansions and keep all the margins. That is why the studios were always looking for the next big stars, trying to be there to launch their careers. Avery didn't have songwriters and lyricists on staff, but he had a stable of them to contract out that would write music to fit the personality of a potential new star. "What does Juan have for original music?"

"We have twelve English singing songs ready to go. Pop songs with hip hop flair. Guarantee three of them will be mega hits both in South America and around the world."

Avery rubbed the stubble on his chin while he was thinking. He stole another glance at Bentley, whose eyes were projecting 'Yes, Yes' and he replied to Best, "It sounds interesting enough Robert. But why me? With our unsavory history, why did you come to me? There are other good producers out there. What's the catch here that I'm missing?"

"Quite simply, Avery, I know you're busy and I know you

don't like me so if I can sell you on Juan and his potential, you will look past all the other stuff and do it. You're the best, Avery, I'm not going to lie. There isn't anyone any better in the industry and Juan needs the best. His career is going to be that big. That's the catch. So come on what do you say? Can we be partners?"

"I want full creative control Best."

"You got it Avery. All I'm asking for is the final say on the production cuts and for Blackstar to be listed as a contributing producer."

"No, I won't agree to that. No one gets the final say on the final cuts but me. I want full creative control and that includes from A – Z. I will decide when the album will be released, when and where he tours, merchandise control, everything Robert or you can find someone else."

Best clenched his teeth, relaying to Avery that he was pissed. Then he looked at him for a few seconds without saying a word, then broke into a smile and reached his hand over the table to shake his and said, "You got a deal Mr. Johnson. You ask a lot but I expect a lot in return so let's make this happen, shall we? I will have my lawyers draft up the contract within forty- eight hours and it will be couriered to your office for your signature. You will find the financial numbers very generous Avery. I am not interested in doing this necessarily for the money so that will not hold up the deal, I promise you."

After a few feeble attempts to engage in conversation on topics other than the career of Juan, Avery and Bentley rose to leave. Avery knew this would be a straight business relationship. The way he felt about Best and the way Best felt about him would not change. And that was good enough for him.

Chapter 17

He may have had the full resources of the LAPD at his disposal for now, but Sam knew he would not have that luxury for long. Soon the department would start scaling back the overtime, reassigning detectives to other cases, and returning detectives on loan from other departments, all in response to the lack of progress on the investigation of the Chelsea Benning murder. When it slowed down, then resources were taken away. That was the nature of the beast in police work. The rule of thumb in homicide investigations was the forty-eight hour rule. Most murder cases were solved within the first forty-eight hours. Beyond that, the percentages of solving the case went down dramatically. Witnesses changed their minds because they were scared and stepped back into the shadows of their unanimity, forensic evidence deteriorated, suspects slipped through the initial dragnet of momentum when the investigators were first assigned to the case. The 'rush' of the first forty-eight hours was critical on many fronts. Investigators assigned to the case were super focused and their instincts were razor sharp because they knew how important the first few days were in the case. Like the evidence, they had a tendency to slow down as the case dragged on. Lack of interest and the excitement to catch the next 'rush' wreaked havoc. A good homicide department captain anticipated this ebb and flow and kept his team focused and motivated. Captain Bitters was the best of the best in leading a group of skilled investigators for the LAPD Homicide and Robbery Section. Turning down opportunities for promotion in other sections to stay in Homicide, Bitters became the quintessential leader of the most highly paid group of cops in the force. He chose to accept it and his attitude had improved dramatically ever since. Sam learned to respect his boss immensely and the feeling was mutual and as a result, Sam saw himself turn into a career investigator in Homicide.

Sam caught the rush just like everyone else but, unlike the other detectives, he understood and accepted the fact that some cases, especially the psychopathic killings where the murderer killed in a precise and deliberate way, could take months and sometimes years to solve. Bitters steered these cases to Sam and his new partner Ryerson because he knew that Sam had the patience that resulted in the thorough and quality investigation required in long term cases.

It was Tuesday morning and Bitters wanted an up-to-date report on the Benning investigation on his desk by 10:00 a.m. Sam had been at his desk since 6:30 a.m. and he was joined by Ryerson an hour later in an effort to lay a quality and detailed report on Bitters' desk, knowing it would be going up the chain of command. Decisions on whether or not to begin the scaling back the process would be made based on this report.

The truth of the matter was that Sam had nothing. The investigation into Chelsea Benning had turned up no witnesses, no useable DNA, no murder weapon and certainly no motive, just theories. It had been six days since the slaughter of Chelsea and, right from the beginning, he knew this would be a very difficult case. He was convinced that there was a serial killer on the loose. So far as he knew, Jonathon Green and Chelsea Benning were the first, random vicims of the sick mind of a crazed killer. There would be more and he needed to start piecing things together soon before the department resources dried up. He needed every bit of help he could get to stand a chance to catch the killer. Someone this sick would make a mistake at some point and they would catch him. It was just a matter of time, but how many innocent people had to die in the meantime? The theory that he and Ryerson were spinning into their report for Bitters was the connection between Green and Chelsea. The savagery of the murders was almost identical. The bodies of Green and Chelsea were ripped to pieces like they could have been attacked by a pack of wolves. Their body parts were spread out all over their rooms. Whoever or whatever killed them was extremely angry and violent with no fear or remorse. By connecting the two murders, they could show a crazed and violently sick serial killer was on the loose in L.A. in the hope that the department resources would continue to flow until they could jar loose fresh and useable leads that would solve this case.

The search of the Benning home was difficult for Sam, especially when they made it to the garage, where Chelsea had stored many of Steven's belongings. Sam let Ryerson sift through the eight or more Rubbermaid containers full of his life-long things and memories.   Sam worked on searching Patrick's room and was puzzled at the lack of 'stuff' in his room. His dresser drawers were empty outside of a few pairs of socks and boxers, the closet had only a few shirts hanging. The laundry room was void of any clothing. There were no pictures, books, games, Xbox, or anything in Patrick's room. It was like a hotel room. Like Patrick had been living from a suitcase. The house was still in lockdown until the crime scene was completely scoured by investigators. Yellow LAPD tape, crisscrossing over the width of the door frame kept anyone, except Sam and Ryerson, away.

Crime Scene Investigators, veteran officers of the LAPD, all highly skilled and trained, were completely baffled at the lack of forensic evidence. They couldn't believe that the killers had used such brutal violence and yet had left not a shred of DNA behind. The eerie similarities to Steven Benning's murder scene in this very same house almost sixteen years ago were disturbing, to say the least. Sam pondered these similarities as he tried to come to grips with another murder of someone close to him that left more questions than answers. He could not let this investigation get away from him; he needed to find the killer or killers soon.   Otherwise, he knew he would turn his badge and gun over to Bitters and walk away from a career with the knowledge that he had failed.

He pulled out the crime scene photos from the Jonathon Green murder and laid them in a row on the top of his desk and below, he placed the photos from Chelsea's murder scene. Then he had a thought. Although he was not sure why, he wanted to lay out the photos from Steven Benning's murder scene as well. He left the photos on his desk, while he went down to the basement to Records to retrieve the files from Steven's investigation.

He greeted Records Room Supervisor, Tony Kirsch, with the usual banter about requesting the Benning file once again. He found it weird that he replied with, "Which one Sam? You know there are two Benning record boxes now. Bitch of a thing to say, isn't it? I know that Chelsea was close to you and Beth. Give my best to your wife for me, will you Sam?"

"Thanks Tony. Get me Steven's; I have everything I need in the files upstairs on Chelsea." The file box for Chelsea would be almost empty, as most of the items gathered and tagged at the scene would still be at the labs for DNA testing.

A few minutes later Tony came back with the box containing the evidence remaining from Steven's murder. He box included the murder book, blood, hair and fibre samples with the lab results attached and, of course, the photos. Sam took the photos signed for them, gave the rest back to Tony and returned to his desk. He proceeded to spread out the photos underneath Chelsea's. His desk was covered in gruesome crime scene close up photos of the bodies of Green, Chelsea and Steven. The murder weapon had not even been determined yet in the Green and Chelsea murders. CSI were calling it a possible sword with very sharp and large serrated teeth along the blade. CSI suspected that the strength required to strike the blows, even with a devastating weapon like the sword, would need to be enormous. Though not chopped to little pieces like Chelsea and Green, the ability to twist Steven's neck completely around would require similar strength. The chills that were causing Sam to suddenly shudder were not from a cold draft but from the realization that the person or persons who killed Steven almost sixteen years ago could very well have come back and killed his widow. Why? Who would be hunting Steven and then decide to come back after all these years and murder his widow? The three murders could easily be classified as coming from the same killer, if there was more evidence besides the photos and gut feeling.

He stood in front of his desk transfixed by the photos, trying to see if he could find a connection or maybe see something that was missed. "What am I missing?", thought Sam. He pulled his mind away from the photos for a second and thought about other similarities that could connect the crimes. There was no sign of forced entry in any of the crime scenes. That meant that Chelsea and Green might have known their assailant and willingly let him in. "Wait a minute", he thought. "There was no forced entry when Steven was killed. It's because he arrived after the killer was already in the home and assaulting Chelsea. She might have known the assailant sixteen years ago and again last week." He then thought again about the claims by Chelsea in the beginning of the investigation that they had been attacked by a demonic monster, a non-human creature that had spoken to her in Latin. He had tried unsuccessfully to convince Chelsea to agree to hypnosis by a LAPD-trained professional in order to recollect the events of the attack and, hopefully, the Latin spoken by her attacker. She reluctantly agreed and only did so because Sam had pleaded with her that it was critical to his investigation. It turned out to be of little use as Chelsea, once under the spell of the hypnosis became hysterical, screaming uncontrollably, shouting unrecognizable references to what seemed like the name 'Babken' and reliving the attack in her deep slumber. Sam finally couldn't take it anymore and instructed the therapist to shut it down. He asked Chelsea a few weeks later if she would agree to go under hypnosis one more time in the hope that she would reveal something that could be used, but she would have nothing to do with it. When she changed her story later, she stated that she was mistaken about being attacked by a demonic monster and she was really attacked by a gang of thugs. At that point, the case really hit a dead end and became cold. He needed the hypnosis to explore the Latin words spoken by the killer, not to prove it was a monster as earlier claimed by Chelsea, but in the hope that the words would shed some light onto the identity of the killer. It was like she had decided that it was a crazy story that no one believed, she had a son to raise and it was in their best interests to put it behind her and move on. Sam did give his rabbi brother Jacob a copy of the interview between the therapist and Chelsea in the hope he could make any conclusions. He was reaching for anything at that point, but in the end Jacob, not only found nothing of use from the tape, he also found nothing on the name 'Babken'. Jacob felt he needed to scold his little brother for unnecessarily traumatizing Chelsea in his bid to soothe his soul about the death of his partner.

He knew with every fibre in his body that whoever killed Steven sixteen years ago had also killed Chelsea and quite likely Jonathon Green. He knew that if he could solve Chelsea's murder he would also be solving the murder of her husband and his former partner so long ago.

His thoughts were suddenly interrupted when his Blackberry vibrated on his hip. Pulling out his phone, he saw from his caller I.D. that it was Beth, so he answered the call: "Hi honey, let me guess. You're taking time away from your day off to take me out for lunch. How sweet!"

He could hear her chuckle before she replied, "Not far off buster. I am on my way down to see you though. You don't remember do you?"

He quickly searched his mental to-do list and was drawing blanks, "Sorry Beth I am drawing a total blank. What am I forgetting?"

"Well, considering I am coming up the elevator to your office right now it's too late to turn around and go home, so whatever other plans you made, you'll have to change them. You told me to drop off the boys for a few hours while I did some errands and you would show Patrick around, spend some time with him and Seb."

He forgot about that, but it was just a suggestion. Beth obviously took the suggestion to heart. "Okay, that is fine sweetheart. Where are you? You're not in the elevator because you wouldn't have cell service."

"Look to your right."

He looked to his right and the three of them were standing in the doorway to Homicide, all of them with great big grins on their faces. Beth gave him a hug and a kiss, careful not to embarrass him, not that he cared. She had been up here many times over the years and was well liked by the other detectives. "Okay honey, I'm going to let you be for a few hours while I do some personal maintenance down at the salon. I'll pick them up when I'm done in a few hours okay?"

After Beth had left, Sam turned to the boys and said: "How about some lunch? Are you guys hungry? Detective Ryerson has offered to buy, so I think we should do the right thing and oblige. What do you guys say?"

Ryerson looked at him before rolling his eyes about being suckered into paying and said, "You know Seb, your dad owes me a week of lunches. He thinks his rank allows him to mooch free food off of me on a daily basis. Now do you think that's fair? Can you talk to your old man about that sometime for me? Okay, let's go get some chili and fries around the corner."

An hour later, after some incredibly spicy chili loaded on a few fries, they made their way back to the office. Daniel was amazed at how much Patrick could eat. In addition to the meal- sized chili fries, he packed away two jumbo hot dogs. Joking with Patrick, he quipped, "You'll have gas tonight Patrick. I think, Seb, you better take cover in a bunker somewhere safe tonight otherwise the mortar fire could get ugly", he laughed.

Once back in Homicide, Captain Bitters caught them coming in and motioned to Sam for him and Ryerson come in and see him. Sam instructed the boys to sit tight for two minutes. They entered his office and closed the door so they were out of earshot from the boys. Sitting down in front of Bitters' desk, Sam asked: "How did it go this morning regarding the briefing upstairs?"

He leaned back in his chair and crossed his arms before he replied, "That's why I called you guys in here. You're still on it full bore, but you need to start turning over some leads sooner rather than later. They want to see some real progress on the murders. Your report tying Green and Chelsea's murder together worked for now. I want you guys to start busting some street heads. Get the guys in Narcotics and Gangs to start hitting the streets to kick some ass and look for someone who might have heard or seen something about the lunatics that are carving up victims. Check with your contacts with the Feds and discreetly find out if there are similar victims in other cities that we can cross reference. We've got to give the brass what they want and if we can't give them an arrest then let's give them information that we are making progress."

The knock on the door interrupted Bitters, causing all three to look in the direction of the door. Seb stood in the doorway with a strange look on his face as he spoke: "Dad, its Patrick, you better come out here."

Sam jumped out of his chair, quickly followed by Ryerson and Bitters. He looked at his son as he walked out into the hallway asked: "What is the matter Seb? Where's Patrick?"

"He is sitting at your desk staring at the pictures Dad. I took one look at them and turned away, they are horrible, but Patrick sat down in your chair and…and studied them. He has a look on his face like he is enjoying looking at those pictures of his mom. Dad I want to go home."

"Ah Jesus, I forgot about those photos. Stay here Seb. Let me go talk to him."

Sam walked over to his desk and saw Patrick sitting in his chair and holding up a photo of Jonathon Green's severed head. He seemed to be transfixed by the photo, turning it in his hand, studying it, not even noticing Sam standing right behind him.

"Patrick, you shouldn't be looking at these pictures. These are crime scene photos of active murder investigations. Come on, let's go, I am driving you and Seb home now okay?"

Patrick didn't turn his head to speak to Sam. He just kept studying the photo, then placed it on the desk and picked up another one: "These are really great pics Sam! Did you take them? They're fucking morbid as hell."

Sam glanced back at Ryerson and held up his hand to stay back with Seb. He then watched Bitters walk back into his office shaking his head.

He reached over Patrick's shoulder and took the picture from his hand and said, "Come on, enough show and tell for this day Patrick. Let's go before Beth kicks my ass for not getting you guys home."

"I thought she was picking us up here Sam? We just got here. I want to look at more of these pictures, they're fucking cool."

Sam looked at Patrick, stunned at what he was hearing. The kid was still suffering from discovering his mother chopped to pieces. Bringing him here was a big mistake, leaving the photos on his desk, unattended, with him and Seb nearby was incomprehensible. Beth would have a nuclear meltdown if she found out about this. He needed professional help. How could he be so stupid? "Listen Patrick, stop fucking around. Enough already. That's your God damned mother for shit sakes. Now let's go and I mean now."

His eyes burrowed into Sam's as he replied, "Okay, okay, already. I didn't root through your desk and find these pictures. Next time, put the fucking pictures of my dead mother's severed body away so that her son can't see them!"

Sam watched as Patrick walked out of Homicide, towards the elevators down the hall, followed closely by Seb.

Sam thought to himself: "What the fuck was I thinking?"

Watching Patrick and Seb walk away, he had a burn that began to churn inside his gut and it wasn't heartburn. It was fear. He wasn't afraid for himself, he was afraid for Seb. Something was not right about Patrick and the burn smoldering in the pit of his stomach was telling him he was dangerous. Seb was scared of him and now he understood why.

"Patrick was dangerous!"

Chapter 18

The past year went by in a flash for Avery and his studio, Alive Records, with the explosion of Juan Jimenez's career after the release of his first album, *Standing In Line.* When Avery and his team were mixing the tracks laid down by Juan, everyone knew it would be a tremendous success. The kid could sing and the new Latin heartthrob was taking the U.S. and the rest of the world by storm. The first single, "A New World", sky rocketed to the top of the charts and stayed there for seven straight weeks until the follow-up to "A New World", "Join Me" took over the top spot on the Billboard Top 100. Sales of the album were through the roof, setting records, including the record for most downloads of a single song in iTunes history, set earlier in the year by none other than Connor Asker and his huge hit "Follow You Follow Me".

Around the world, the music scene seemed to be taken over by the kids with huge followings, resulting in sold out concerts and massive album sales. The success of the phenomenally popular Cirque de Soleil musical, *Panterra* ,led by the incredibly talented voice of Canadian sixteen year old gifted Elizabeth Leroux, was setting attendance records at the Meritzia Sky in Las Vegas. During a break from Juan's tour dates, Avery and Bentley, were able to catch a concert by the popular Irish quartet, Celtic Woman, led by sixteen year old Chloë McClosky. Her voice brought tears to Bentley's eyes as she was truly moved by the power and beauty of her voice. Brittany Campbell's success a year ago on 'X Factor' had pushed her into a spotlight that wouldn't go away, as her fans eagerly anticipated the release of her first album. Michael Lockwood, the sixteen year old British hunk whose stunning tenor voice was filling concert halls all across Europe, including a private concert for the Royal family, was beginning to build a following on this side of the Atlantic. It was insane, what was happening with these kids, there had never been anything like it in the history of music.

It amazed Avery and Bentley that they all were discovered by Robert Best. It appeared as if Best was a genius with the innate ability to recognize raw talent at a young age and nurture it along to produce a major star, over and over again. He used the perfect mix of marketing and timing to showcase each star's unique gifts. His success with these strategies was, quite simply, incredible. These kids were blessed with looks that made the youth around the world scream in delight while their parents worried that their kids would never take their iPod ear plugs out of their ears. The war chest of written music from which these young stars chose their next songs to record was filled with melodies and lyrics perfectly suited to them and to what popular music buyers wanted. Best pushed all the right buttons and he had turned out to be a pleasure to work with. This was a surprise that left them shaking their heads as to the about face in Best's attitude. He went from being a mega control freak and an arrogant asshole to an agreeable contributor and a professional partner.

"You know what Bentley, I have to hand it to this guy. He comes out of nowhere sixteen years ago with a couple of one trick pony acts in Watermark and Devon Devine to this. It blows my mind."

Bentley looked at him, not saying anything, lost in thought. He asked: "What are you thinking about sweetheart? It looks like I lost you somewhere in this conversation."

She tapped her chin slowly with the side of her hand, as she replied: "I'm sorry honey, it's just when you mentioned Watermark, that brought back all those old, creepy feelings that I used to have about Best. Do you remember what happened to those guys from Watermark? They all died sad deaths Avery. Alone and abandoned by the man who controlled every aspect of their lives, Robert Best. Don't forget that Avery."

"We don't know for sure what really happened to the members from Watermark. It could very well be that he tried to help them after their careers petered out, but maybe the drugs are what took them down."

"I don't think so Avery. He walked away and couldn't care less about what happened to them. What will happen to these kids when they lose their youthful charm, the music runs out and the fans move on? Will he abandon them too?"

"I understand your concerns and your lack of trust for Best. I'm not completely on the Best bandwagon just yet either. I still am dragging one foot on the pavement, but it's been a very long time since Watermark and he has worked incredibly hard for these kids. I think we should cut him some slack but still watch over our shoulder to see what might be coming up behind us. You know what I'm saying?"

She looked up at him with those beautiful and dreamy eyes of hers and said, "I know what you're saying baby. You know the interview with him for *Music Talks* is coming out next week and then the music world will know that he is the brainchild behind all these kids. He is giving one hundred percent of the credit for the success of Juan Jimenez to you and Alive Records. He is not afraid to spread his success around. I'll give him that."

"Let's be serious. A high school kid with an iPhone could have recorded Juan's album, the music Best provided for the record was that good."

"Give yourself more credit than that, Avery Johnson. Remember, you are still the best and most respected music producer in the country. You're certainly the best looking," she smiled.

Their conversation was interrupted by the sound of Avery's iPhone ringing. He reached into his pocket, checked the caller I.D. and declared: "Well, I'll be damned. Speak of the devil, its Best calling."

Bentley looked at him, just sitting there with the phone in his hand and said: "Why won't you answer the phone? Maybe he's going to send another child prodigy your way."

He wasn't amused as he let the call go to voicemail. Bentley knew she had pushed a button she shouldn't have and back pedaled. "Listen honey, I'm sorry. I shouldn't be making comments on your business, that's not fair. Won't happen again, I promise."

"Don't apologize. It's just that I'm not quite there yet with the relationship, even though he has been purely business. I'll get there."

He checked the voicemail message from Best that said: "Avery, its Robert. I was hoping to chat with you about the major project I have been working on. It's just about ready so we need to talk. Give me a call when you have a minute. Take care."

He repeated the voicemail to Bentley before asking her: "What the hell kind of major project could he be working on that he'd want my input? I guess I better call him back."

Avery called Best back and the call was picked up on the first ring: "Avery, thanks for calling me right back. I bet you must have been with Bentley so I won't keep you long. Listen, when we first met at the Whale and Ale, I mentioned to you I was working on a major project. Well that project is almost ready to launch and I want you to be a big part of it. I need your help and expertise to make this work."

He looked at Bentley while he listened to Best talk, raising his eyebrows as he listened and making faces to convey shock. It was driving Bentley crazy with curiosity. He replied to Best, "You definitely have me curious about what you're working on Robert. I can't make any promises about whether I'll get involved, but I'll certainly hear what you've got to say."

"That's great Avery. I am in New York at the moment but I will get a flight out of here first thing in the morning. Let's plan to meet at Blackstar Studios tomorrow afternoon. You'll be happy with what you're going to hear Avery. It will change your life."

He made a face crunching grimace, sending Bentley falling back in her chair with silent laughter, as he replied: "I don't know about the life changing stuff Robert, but I'm looking forward to tomorrow. I will see you then."

He hung up the phone and Bentley almost shouted: "What the hell is going on Avery? He is going to change your life? Sounds kind of creepy doesn't it?"

"He wants to share his mega project he has been working on, stating that I would play a major role in it and that he needed my help to make it all come together. Come to think of it, that does sound kind of creepy."

****

Robert Best was satisfied that his plan to bring together the musical child prodigies he had fathered was nearing completion. The final phase of his plan to destroy mankind would then take shape. He relaxed in his New York office before he prepared to leave for L.A. and his meeting with Avery Johnson. The success of Brittany Campbell, Connor Asker, Elizabeth Leroux, Chloë McClosky, Michael Lockwood, Patrick Benning and Juan Jimenez was phenomenal, to say the least, and way beyond what he had expected or needed. It would make the final phase easier and smoother. Now that he was about to succeed in having the industry's top producer and manager take them over the top, it was just too much good news for him to take. He needed to get out tonight and have some fun, celebrate, before leaving for the west coast in the morning. He would kill tonight, maybe several souls. Not just anyone either, someone powerful. Take out a politician and his entire family. Make it look like a terrorist act maybe. Shake things up a bit. Get the country scared and paranoid before unveiling his plan that would make them all feel good again.

He thought about the few wrinkles he needed to smooth out in his plan. Ann Lockwood needed to go but it had become very difficult, if not impossible, to get to her. His adversary was protecting her and he was baffled as to why He had chosen her in His desperate bid to stop him. It was all pathetic and sad and there was nothing He could do to stop him, but it still pissed him off. He needed to get Michael on board with the rest of the kids, and soon. It was okay, he had a plan to circumvent the bitch and still bring Michael in, but he'd find a way to kill her regardless. If nothing else, just to darken the light that surrounds Him.

The other wrinkle was Patrick Benning and his wild antics. The crazy little bastard was out of control and threatening his plan. He slaughtered his mother in the hope that it would settle him down and it did for a while, but he was at it again. He was on another killing spree in L.A. and, now that he was living with the Jew cop, he couldn't take any chances. He was on a short leash, but he needed him more than any of the other kids. His talent for writing music was a complete surprise, but one that solved so many problems for him. He didn't have to go elsewhere to find the music and the lyrics he needed. Plus, he would need his killing prowess, if only he could control it better. Benning was a growing problem but one he could handle.

The crusty old priest from Ireland should have died from old age already but he also had the cloak of protection that he couldn't penetrate. However, his presence was minimal. The priest could not stop Chloë from achieving her destiny. Father O'Sullivan could sense his darkness and he would have to be careful. He was entering the most important phase of his plan and he must control even the most insignificant details to ensure complete success.

****

The world awoke to the headline news of the brutal killing of the Governor of New York and his entire family. Governor Sexton, his wife and two teenage daughters were found in their bedrooms, stabbed to death over one hundred times each by Islamist extremists. Their own blood was used to smear anti-American messages all over the bedroom walls announcing "death to Americans" and "this was just the beginning." An anonymous caller phoned into CNN New York with the ominous message of death to all who call Jesus their Saviour. All the major networks picked up the story from there and were running it full-time. News agencies from around the world began to converge on New York to cover the exploding fireball of ethnic backlash already brewing on the streets of America. Within forty-eight hours, riots had broken out on the streets of New York as well as in other major cities across America. Muslims across America stepped back into the shadows to avoid the anger swirling all around them. The level of paranoia toward Muslims by Americans was palpable. Most people made an instant association between all Muslims and the Islamist extremists whom they assumed were the perpetrators of the killings of the Governor and his family. They never even considered that it could easily have been radical, underground, atheist, American militia who killed the Governor.

When the morning the news broke about the murder of the Governor, Best was comfortably relaxing in executive class of the American Airlines flight to LAX. "What a shit storm I have created with this one", thought Best. Most of the passengers were just hearing of the killings on the small screens in the seats in front of them and the looks and gasps reverberated throughout the plane.

No one even noticed the handsome, well-dressed businessman, with his eyes closed and earphones covering his ears, laughing hysterically to himself.

Bentley and Avery, in what was becoming commonplace, spent the night together in Avery's spacious condo, awakening to the reports dominating the morning news on the slaughter of the Governor's family from New York. Avery fixed them each a strong coffee as they snuggled together on the bed, watching the news, Bentley wrapped in Avery's housecoat.

"My God Avery, when is it ever going to stop? Terrorists are having a field day in this country it seems. Killing the Governor and his family? That's horrible."

He had become numb to the news of a new terrorist attack happening somewhere around the world, it happened so often now, but this was different and much closer to home. When they killed a top politician and his young family, it was scary. After a few more minutes of watching the news unfold with constant updates and the breakouts of rioting happening already, it was enough for him. He reached for the remote and turned the TV off. "I know what you're saying, it seems endless. I can't stand to watch it anymore."

She snuggled in closer to him. "I agree. I'd rather watch you step into the shower. There is so much more to see." Bentley purred and she emphasized the word 'more'. The two of them quickly found themselves under the covers once again, naked, heated with passion, embracing one another with a lust that went way beyond the physical. They were falling in love with each other and they both knew it, but had yet to verbalize it. They kissed each other slowly at first, then picked up speed as the heat between them rose. His hand caressed her back before reaching down to her perfectly shaped buttocks, reveling in how perfectly her body was sculpted. Her moans drove him further down until he was between her legs, feeling the warmth combined with her wetness. She opened herself up to him and he rolled her onto her back and climbed on top with ease, as though they were one. Smothering her neck and then her breasts in wet kisses, he moved as her body moved, slowly at first but then she began arching her back towards him, physically begging him to enter her. Within seconds of entering her, she stiffened, her soft screams of climax stifled as she bit into his shoulder. The pleasure combination of her orgasms and his own building climax touched off more spasms coming from her that led to a jolting orgasm that took the strength from him, dropping him flat against her for a brief second before he got his elbows to work again and he lifted himself up.

He looked down into her beautiful eyes, rimmed with sweat, and reached down, kissing her deeply, using his index finger to lightly wipe the sweat away from her eyes. Looking at her once again, both of them not saying a word, just staring into each other's eyes, he interrupted the star gazing with a gentle whisper, "I am the happiest I have been in my entire life Bentley. It's because of you that I am. I have fallen in love with you. I wished I hadn't waited so long to be with you like this. I love you Bentley Paxton."

The sweat that was just seconds ago rimming her eyes was

now replaced by tears that came spilling out and ran down her cheeks, causing her to sniffle before she replied: "Avery, I have loved you from the moment I met you all those years ago. There is a reason our paths have crossed once again. I believe that. We were meant to be with each other. Oh jeepers, listen to me, babbling like an idiot. I'm sorry Avery for being a cry baby, but you're not the only one who's happy. "

He reached for her again and drew her close, holding her, enjoying the feeling passing between the two of them. Soon the two of them were fast asleep, the comfort of each other relaxing them both to where they quickly dozed off. Thirty minutes later, the vibration of his iPhone on the dresser awoke him from his slumber. Careful not to wake up Bentley, he reached for the phone as he stretched across her to check the caller I.D. It was Jenn and checking the time he saw that it was already 9:30 a.m. Shit, he'd better answer it, knowing it would wake up Bentley. He needn't have worried, as she stirred beside him, "You better answer that baby, or Jenn will start blaming me for your tardiness."

He pressed the answer button on his phone as he smiled down at her, and then lifted the phone to his ear, "Good morning Ms. Steinart. Calling to tell me Juan Jimenez has gone multi-platinum I bet?"

"Hmm, Ms. Steinart, huh? You must be with Bentley. No I'm not calling about Juan and by the way he went multi-platinum months ago if you were paying attention to your clients, but I am calling about him in an indirect way. Blackstar Studios called and they want you over there for a 2:00 p.m. meeting."

"Did you have a bad date last night? Pretty crusty to your boss, just to let you know, who just happens to be the best boss in America."

"Buying me a Maserati does qualify you as the best boss in America, I'll give you that. I'm not crusty, Avery, just busy, and that's your fault. You get to sleep in and have incredible sex, while I'm here photocopying and preparing reports since 7:00 a.m. this morning".

"Okay, you win, but being busy is a good thing. I'm sorry if I came across like I don't respect what you do. I do appreciate you keeping the office running smoothly. Thanks for the heads up on Blackstar. I won't be in before the meeting unless you need me for something."

"No I'm fine, good luck in your meeting Avery. Say hello to Bentley for me."

****

Avery held the door to his BMW open for Bentley as they left the bistro around the corner from his condo. They had grabbed a quick lunch before the meeting at Blackstar, their morning of lovemaking still fresh in their minds as they held hands all through lunch like two school kids. Once they were in the car, Bentley reached over and took Avery's hand in hers, with the fingers of her right hand lightly running up and down his arm. That morning, they had told each other that they loved each other and now, back in the car with Bentley holding his hand, he felt something new, unlike anything he had ever felt before. She made him feel special and her words and her touch drew him closer every minute they were together. She drew his hand to her lips and kissed him gently as she spoke: "I hope that you and I can take off together for a few weeks, a week, or even just a few days before everything gets crazy. I don't want this feeling between us to end. I'm so crazy about you Avery Johnson, I'm afraid your career and mine will keep us apart more than we will be together and all I want right now is to be with you."

"Nothing will keep us apart, I promise you Bentley. I'm not sure the direction I'm going in with Best and Blackstar Studios, but I will never let business compromise what I have now with someone who has become the most important thing in my life."

Chapter 19

Sam decided to keep Patrick's behavior at his office to himself and not share it with Beth, at least not now. It would only frighten her and he needed to figure things out with Patrick before he shared this aggressive behavior with his wife. Patrick's bizarre attraction to the crime scene death photos of his mother Chelsea and those of his unknown father Steven, plus the pictures of the grisly hotel room depicting the shredded body of Jonathon Green was disturbing. Originally, he just wrote it off to the traumatized mind of a teenage boy dealing with the murder of his mother, but now he wasn't so sure. Something just wasn't right with Patrick. His actions did not reflect those of a grieving boy who had lost his mother in a terrible fashion. Instead, he was behaving like a thug. To top it off, his son Sebastian was so frightened of him, he stayed in his bedroom, rarely venturing out except for dinner. He had convinced his mother he was busy with school work to justify why he was always in his room, but Sam knew better.

On the way up to his bedroom after calling it a night, he stopped in front of Patrick's room and contemplated knocking on his door to talk with him. He felt he was losing him and the fear of Patrick never recovering from the trauma he had experienced at such a vulnerable age scared Sam. He decided that he would seek professional help for him, whether Patrick voluntarily agreed to it or not. Sam would drag him by the arm if he had to. Deciding it was too late and Patrick was likely asleep anyways, he turned to head to his bedroom, when he almost bumped into Seb standing in the hallway.

"Jesus, Seb, you scared the hell out of me. Why aren't you in bed? It's pretty late son."

"I haven't been able to sleep much lately and I heard you coming up the stairs so I thought I would talk to you about something."

Seeing the concern on his son's face, Sam answered: "Sure we can do that. Let's go in your bedroom to talk so we don't wake up Patrick and worry your mother by whispering in the hallway."

Sam followed his son into his bedroom, closed the door behind him, leaned against the door frame and waited for his son to talk. He watched as Seb, dressed in sweats and his Clippers basketball shirt, his black curly hair impossible to mess up at the length he always kept it, looked up at him and said: "Dad, I don't think you need to worry about Patrick waking up."

Sounding a little confused, he replied: "Why's that son? Of course I would worry about waking Patrick up just like I would be careful not to wake you up if I knew you might be asleep."

"What I meant Dad is that I don't think Patrick ever sleeps. Remember when you dropped me off at school and I tried to tell you? He never slept in all the years growing up when we would have sleep overs as kids at each other's houses. Now that we're older and don't do the sleep over thing anymore, I have been listening to see if he falls asleep since he's been staying with us and he doesn't Dad."

"How could you possibly know if he never sleeps son? I'm sure he has trouble falling asleep like a lot of people and especially now, with the death of his mother, he might find it hard to nod off, but he has to sleep at some point Seb. Otherwise, he couldn't function and you know as well as I do that it's impossible for the body not to fall asleep."

"I get that Dad, but trust me on this okay? Since we were kids, he has always told me he never, ever sleeps and never has. That is why I was always so exhausted as a kid when we would do the sleepover thing, because he would keep me up all night with him. Since he has lived with us, I hear him all night, either singing or beating his drum sticks on the bed frame, dresser, closet door or whatever else he finds in the room that will make a sound."

"Are you sure Son? I mean, I've never heard him. Making that kind of racket at night, your mother or I would hear that. He's just down the hall."

"No, he waits until you are asleep. I don't know how he knows you are asleep because he doesn't leave his room to check on you, but he knows because he has never woken you or Mom has he?"

"I guess not, but why doesn't he wait till you are asleep?"

"He doesn't care if I hear him. I think he wants me to hear him."

Sam could feel his blood pressure jump. Patrick was starting to piss him off. He was getting out of line. "Well, that is going to stop as of right now. I will go into his bedroom and talk with him Seb and put an end to this bullshit. You need to get your sleep, for God's sakes."

Seb's voice suddenly took on an air of urgency when he responded to his Dad going into Patrick's bedroom. "Wait. That's not all that he does Dad. During the night, when he believes that even I am asleep, he sneaks out of the house and disappears. Sometimes for hours and sometimes he barely makes it home before you or Mom wake up. One time recently, he snuck back into his room when Mom had already gone downstairs to start the coffee and you were in the shower. I think he goes out every night."

An unmistakeable burning began to form in the pit of Sam's stomach as he listened to his son describe Patrick's strange behavior. He wished he was in his police car so he could reach under his seat for the bottle of Tums that was standard issue for most homicide cops. His thoughts were interrupted as his son continued: "One more thing Dad. I know this sounds crazy, but I think Patrick is killing small animals in our neighborhood and his old neighborhood."

"What the hell are you talking about? You think he's killing small animals? What do you mean?"

Seb walked around from the foot of his bed where he had

been leaning on the footboard and sat down on the bed, pausing for a few seconds before he replied. "One night, a few years ago, when Patrick was over for a sleep over, I followed him out of the house when he left in the middle of the night. I had to keep a distance from him in order not to be discovered, but I wanted to know where the hell he always went during the night. I followed him for about five blocks, even thinking of just turning around at one point as he didn't appear to be going anywhere in particular and I didn't want to get caught. All of a sudden, he darted behind this house. I carefully made my way around the side of the house to see where he had gone and what he was doing. I thought he might be breaking into the house. Then I heard a large dog growl in the backyard of that house. I darted over to a tree that would cover me and give me a view of the backyard. The back of the house was so dark, I couldn't see anything, only hear. I was terrified that Patrick would hear me and discover that I had been following him."

Sam was stunned at what his son was telling him. The burning in the pit of his stomach was threatening to turn into a full blown heartburn. He interrupted Seb when he asked: "Why didn't you come to me or your mother about this Son? We would have spoken with his mother about it so she could put a stop to it."

"Dad let me finish. I didn't get a good view of what Patrick was doing because of the darkness, but the dog's growling woke up the next door neighbor. The neighbor turned on his back porch light, which partially lit up the backyard we were in. Dad, I watched Patrick grab this big dog, a lab I think, and swing it by its tail like it was a small cat and slam its head into the tree, killing it instantly. It was horrible. It made me sick to my stomach.

Sam was horrified and sat down beside his son, and put his arm around him and said: "My God, Seb that is terrible. What did you do after seeing that Son?"

"I bolted from behind the tree and ran. I was so scared to be discovered, not only by Patrick, but also by the neighbor. I ran the fastest I have ever run in my life."

""What did Patrick do? Did he see you?"

"I don't think so. I was always a lot faster than him anyway and I was so scared, he never would have caught me. I ran home and got into my bedroom and jumped into bed, terrified that he would come home and slam me headfirst into the wall like he did to that poor dog."

Sam remembered the story a few years ago of this dog being brutally killed. It was in all the papers. It wasn't the only time that something like this had happened in the neighborhood either. There were other incidents, now that he thought of it. "Unbelievable Seb. What happened after that?"

"A little while later, he came home and knocked on my door, waited for a second, then just opened it and came in and sat down in the chair. He didn't say anything for a while, like he was waiting for me to say something first. When I didn't, he finally leaned forward in his chair towards me and said that he killed the dog because it was threatening to attack him. He did it to defend himself. I didn't know what to say back, so I never said a word and so then he just got up from the chair and left my room. He never mentioned that night to me again and I never asked him about it. I think he's forgotten about it, like it never happened, but I never forgot. Now do you understand why I'm scared of him Dad?"

"I do Son and I'm so sorry that I never knew this was happening in our house and you had to deal with Patrick on your own. Your mother and I will move him to a place where he can get some help for his problems, I promise. This is so hard to believe Seb. I am shocked and your mother will be too, but she needs to know immediately. In fact, she might know a good therapist that is able to help Patrick through her contacts at work."

"Thanks Dad, for helping Patrick. I know he's been through a lot and needs help. That will be the best thing for him right now."

Rising off of the bed, Sam looked down at his son and replied: "I agree. Just remember Seb that Chelsea meant everything to your Mom and I and we will do whatever we can to make sure that Patrick is taken care of okay? So don't worry. I'll get out of your room now so you can get some sleep. Hopefully you can, Son. I'll talk to your Mom about him tomorrow when she gets home from work and we'll decide the best path to take for him."

Peeling off his bright yellow jersey, Seb fell back into his bed and looked up at him as he opened the door to his bedroom and said: "Thanks Dad. Goodnight."

Sam stepped out into the hallway outside of his son's bedroom and closed the door. He walked silently over to Patrick's bedroom door and listened. Dead silent. He was most likely waiting for him to return to his bedroom and fall asleep, so he could once again step out into the night to stalk innocent animals. He thought about knocking on the door, but decided to wait. He needed to let his mind absorb all of this before he spoke to Beth about it. She would be horrified.

****

Rabbi Jacob Showenstein could not sleep. His tossing and turning would soon wake up his wife and he didn't want that. Josephina was not a happy person when she was awakened in the middle of the night by her restless husband. Jacob leaned over to his side of the bed to look at the time. It was 4:30 in the morning and he knew it would be a long day. Made even longer by the lack of sleep. He had received a call late last night from Sam to discuss Chelsea's hypnosis once again and, in particular, the name that she had constantly shouted out during the hypnosis, 'Babken'. His brother, the cop, would not let this go and he had to admit he would do the same if he was in his shoes. Sam was the lead investigator on the murder of his partner, then years later, his dead partner's widow's brutal slaying. It was a lot for anyone to handle. He promised Sam he would look into it further in the morning.

The name 'Babken' sounded like a biblical name, but it had no biblical reference that he could find when he looked into the name originally. However, the only check he had made was a Christian bible database check that had turned up nothing. He never pursued it any further because he thought the name was insignificant at the time, but he knew now that was a mistake.

He carefully climbed out of bed and dressed quickly and quietly, so as not to wake up Josephina. He would drive over to his office at the synagogue to do some more research. He had a few ideas he wanted to check out on the computer, but he chose to go to his office in case he needed to get access to some Hebrew books. He also didn't want his wife discovering him on the family computer downstairs doing Google searches in the middle of the night. He slipped out into the garage, climbed into the family SUV and risked the electric garage door giving him away. He turned off his cell phone to avoid the phone call that was sure to come, had he awakened his wife. He left the garage door up, so as to minimize the risk.

He entered his office through the back door of the synagogue, turned on his desk light and got to work. Bringing up the computer search engine, he typed in the name 'Babken'. He was surprised to see multiple hits on the name come up. Reading down the list of links, they all referred to the name of a thoroughbred horse that had success in the 1960's, racing for the Triple Crown, but broke a leg after winning the Preakness and had to be put down before he had a chance to win the Kentucky Derby. Then he saw it. It was about five links down the list of the Google search results. The one line sentence of the link referred to a great warrior, son of King Tiridates of Armenia. Jacob opened the link, bringing him to the Wikipedia website, where it described in length the legend of the seven sons of King Tiridates, one of which was named 'Babken'. It was believed that in 400 A.D., the country of Armenia had come under attack from the Prince of Darkness, Satan, because of their fierce loyalty to God and their embracing of Christianity as the state religion. Babken and his brothers, along with the King and his armies, fought back the invading armies of neighboring countries, empowered by the Devil, and his unholy war to stop them. The King and his sons successfully defeated the Satan's army's attempts to wipe

Armenia off the face of the earth.

"What did this have to do with the name that Chelsea had shouted over and over?" he wondered. Jacob then remembered Sam telling him after the murder of Steven Benning that Chelsea had insisted that it was a demonic monster that had murdered her husband. Then, a few years later, she changed her story completely and refused to talk about it any further. "What had happened to her back then that caused her to change her story after sticking to the demonic attack of events so staunchly for so long?" He could feel the hair on the back of his neck begin to rise. He hit the back button to return to the search page. He scanned the list of links again, but nothing more referenced this story. He then typed in King Tiridates and hit enter. A long list of links also came up, with the first one being the Wikipedia link again. He opened the link, but it just talked about the rule of King Tiridates in Armenia and nothing else. He hit the back button once again to click on a new link, when he heard a loud bang from somewhere out in the worship area that nearly made him fall out of his chair. He decided to investigate the sound, gathered himself, and walked out of his office towards the main doors leading into the Hekhal, the synagogue's main sanctuary. He stopped to turn on the hallway lights, when there was a second bang was so loud and unexpected that he felt someone had discharged a firearm in his ear. The shock of the loud bang caused him to fall back against the wall. He could see through the windows of the Hekhal from where he was leaning against the wall and it was pitch black. Or was it?

He thought for a second he seen two balls of red light suspended high up in the ceiling. It had to have been just a reflection on the window from the red exit sign that glowed further down the hallway. He felt like a child, scared of the dark. He reminded himself to get a grip and he opened the doors to the worship area and entered the pitch black room and fumbled to find the light switches in the dark. Finally, his hand hit the area of the wall that housed the bank of switches and dimmer knobs. He flipped the first two to give him some light in the back of the auditorium where he stood. There was nothing. He flicked the switches on and off, but no lights came on. "What's the matter with the lights now?" he thought to himself. He reached over to flick on the other lights, but none of them came on either. He pushed in the knobs of the dimmers and none of them came on. "Did the breaker shut off for this room?" he wondered. "What happened to the light of the Ner Tamid?" Then he heard it before he saw it.

A voice so evil and hideous, it only could have come from hell, called out from behind two glowing red orbs in the blackness that surrounded him: "Working late I see, Rabbi?" Then a laugh boomed through the worship room before it continued: "Doing a little investigative work are we? I thought your brother was the detective, Rabbi?"

Frozen and unable to move with a fear he never knew existed, Jacob called out to the glow of the red demonic eyes that shone through the darkness. They eyes could have been right in front of him or at the back of the room. They seemed to have no discernible depth to them: "Who are you that you think you can come into the house of God with such evilness?"

The Hekhal suddenly began to shake violently, the whole room thundering. Jacob lost his footing in the shaking and fell to the floor. The lights flicked on for a split second, but not long enough for Jacob to see what was behind those menacing red eyes. He tried to crawl back to the door leading out to the hallway, when the violent shaking ended and the thundering roar stopped. It was eerily quiet. He felt he was falling into an endless abyss as his body adjusted to the black stillness that enveloped him. What happened next went beyond reason. Growing up in the faith of Judaism, trained as an orthodox rabbi in the teachings of the Hebrew bible, he did not believe in a physical demon, only that his God was the Creator of both good and evil and it was up to mankind to choose which path they would follow. Staring at the entity before him, Jacob knew without a shadow of a doubt that he was in the presence of Satan the beast.

The darkness was pierced by a white light that surrounded the serpent, whose size was ten feet off the ground. Jacob tried to stand but an unknown force held him steadily on the ground. The entrance doors into the Hekhal from the hallway opened and slammed shut repeatedly with tremendous force. Priceless works of art were peeled off the walls like postage stamps and flung across the room, smashed to pieces. The holy Torah ark floated in the air before being thrown upside down on the floor. It was madness and the roar of sound was deafening. He began to pray a blessing, "Barukh atah Adonai Eloheinu melekh ha'olam, ha'gomeyl lahayavim tovot, sheg'malani kol tov."("Blessed are You, LORD, our God, King of the Universe, Who bestows good things on the unworthy, and has bestowed on me every goodness.") He continued, "Odeh Adonai be'khol layvov b'sood yishorim v'aydah."(I shall give thanks to the LORD wholeheartedly in the assembly of the upright and the congregation).

The beast roared, its massive bulk bearing down on Jacob, ready to shred him to pieces with its claws. Jacob was stunned at the sheer rage emanating from this being. Its red eyes glowered like beacons, a long and bleeding tongue danced in and out of its mouth filled with fangs, when it spoke in a voice guttural and hoarse: "Silence, you fool! Your God will not save you now!"

Jacob continued to pray blessings, "Ho'ayl shegmolokh kol tov..." (God who has bestowed on you every goodness ...). Suddenly, fire erupted all around him, making any attempt at escape impossible. The flames spread reached the upholstered chairs in front of him and they were immediately engulfed in flames. The beast had moved to within a few feet of him, standing like a huge dinosaur, the flames all around him when it screamed: "Die rabbi, in the knowledge that I killed your brother's partner and raped his wife. Know that the Benning son, Patrick, is my child who will join me in the destruction of all of mankind."

Still held frozen in place by unseen forces, Jacob watched as the huge structure of the synagogue was completely on fire.

The smoke that was filling his lungs made it impossible for him to breathe. Then he could hear the faint sound of approaching sirens. He knew his bones and the wood beams of the surrounding structure would be reduced to charred ash in seconds. He looked up to see that a large cross wood beam had become dislodged high above him and teetered for a second, before falling downward towards him. Before the wood beam would crush him, he thought of his brother. Sam didn't even know the son of Satan was living in his house and was best friends with his own son. He thought of Josephina and how much he would miss her. He looked up through the smoke and flames towards heaven and whispered to himself that he was coming home.

The wood beam entered his chest like a giant spear, killing him instantly, just as the flames had found their way onto his body.

Chapter 20

As he sat back in his spacious office, right on Independence Avenue in Washington, across the hall from the Secretary, Deputy Secretary Robert J. Ramirez of the U.S. Department of Health and Human Services had seen it all over his twenty-four years of public service. Or at least he thought he had; until now. He read the memo on his desk. He read twice just to make sure he wasn't reading it wrong. He buzzed his secretary: "Nancy, can you arrange to have the Commissioner of ACYF attend a meeting in my office by the end of the day please."

"Certainly Mr. Ramirez, any time in particular? Your calendar is clear as of now."

"Check with the Commissioner on his schedule, but make it sooner rather than later. Push for 1:00pm. Thanks."

A few minutes had passed when his phone rang. He picked it up and asked his secretary: "Does 1:00PM work for him?"

"Sorry to disappoint you Bob, but its Bruce Petersen over at ACYF. Got a call from your secretary a few minutes ago looking for a one o'clock over at your office? Listen, if it's all the same to you, would you mind meeting over here? I have a video presentation to show you. We have it all setup in the boardroom. We would be ready to go at 1:00PM. Will that work for you?"

Commissioner Petersen of the Administration on Children, Youth and Family was one of the hardest working public servants he had ever known. He would be a shoe-in for his job when he retired next year. Not only was he a smart, hard-working department head, he was a great guy, which was why this memo was so strange, coming from him. Regardless, he needed to deal with it. "Bruce, tell me why we're meeting about a bunch of kids creating a frenzy at some live concert venues? Talk to me about the spiraling out of control teenage pregnancy issue, not a couple thousand kids who think jumping into a mosh pit is their idea of a good time."

"You must have thought I'd lost it when you got that memo Bob and I understand what you're thinking, but the trend developing here with these kids is serious. I need you to see what we've got, then you can tell me if it's just a group of kids suffering from concussions after a night in the mosh pit."

"Okay Bruce, you've got me intrigued. I'll see you in a few hours."

****

Ramirez decided to take advantage of the mild weather and walk the one mile from his office to those of the ACYF at 14th and Madison. He would grab some lunch along the way from a street vendor and take the chance to get away from the constant hustle and bustle in his office. Still relatively healthy after thirty seven years in public service, he loved to get out of the office and walk, taking in the sights and smells of one of the most fascinating cities in the world. Out here on the sidewalks, no one knew who he was. Inside the office, everyone knew he was retiring soon and they acted like he was a dead man walking. The importance that came with the position as Deputy Secretary diminished to that of figurehead the minute he announced his retirement plans. Could he care less anyway? He would soon be another portrait on the hallway walls depicting past Deputy Secretaries. No one would remember him and he wouldn't remember them. That's how it was in government work.

He found the food cart he was hoping for a couple blocks down Madison. It offered Mexican enchiladas, tacos, burritos and the best Mexican fries in D.C. He was famished for some reason and he didn't hold back, ordering a half pound burrito with sour cream and a large order of fries. He then smothered all of it with hot sauce, making an already hot lunch, inferno hot. One of his favorite past times was to people watch and it didn't get any better than Madison Avenue. A curious combination of the multitude of government office workers, tourists and beggars that combined with the aromas of the food carts lined up along the sidewalks; it was a people watchers delight. Finding an open spot on the stone ledge of a retaining wall that held an assortment of shrubs and flowers, he dove into the spicy hot cuisine.

Soon his thoughts drifted to what he was being dragged into by Petersen. He remembered reading newspaper articles on the phenomena of these young kids turning the youth of the country upside down with their music and caught some television highlights of young girls going berserk at a concert, but so what? It had been happening ever since the Beatles and Elvis Presley ruled the day. The fact that they were so young was kind of cool. The only reason he even agreed to hear Petersen out was to find out why he was wasting department resources even looking at this. The Secretary, his boss, would have a shit fit if he found out the ACYF was studying or focusing on the popularity of these kids. "Should be interesting" he thought, as he rose to throw his trash into the nearby garbage bin and make his way the rest of the walk up Madison.

As he entered the office, he was greeted by the receptionist, who was waiting for his arrival and promptly led him down the hall and into the boardroom where he was greeted warmly by Commissioner Petersen, who had been slumped over his laptop queuing up what looked like a Power Point presentation.

"Thanks Bob, for coming over. I hope it's not too much of an inconvenience to come here instead of meeting back at your office."

"I guess we'll see, won't we Bruce?" he replied with just a tinge of sarcasm that wasn't lost on Petersen.

"I know it sounds kind of silly Bob, but after my presentation you might think differently. So why don't you have a seat and I'll get this started."

Though the next thirty minutes, he was bombarded with slide after slide of an increasing wave of youth hysteria sweeping the country that was clearly getting out of control. Concerts and appearances by the singers in public had caused rioting and mayhem to an alarming degree. Album release dates and the rush to purchase the CD's were scenes of all out fighting and mob- type rioting in the stores and malls, as rumours of an appearance by one of the singers spread like wildfire. The slideshow progressed to serious injuries occurring during these events. Recently, two teenagers were beaten to death in the parking lot when they refused to give up the hoodies they had purchased at the show.

As the presentation ended, he was in disbelief at the level of hysteria surrounding the popularity of these kids. He looked at Bob for a brief second before asking, "Jesus Bob, these kids are out of control. Where the hell are the parents in all of this?"

As he found a piece of paper in the pile stacked on the table, Petersen replied: "Our office received this letter from a newly formed organization of concerned parents called 'PAMC' or Parents Against Music Coercion. They claim these young superstars are brainwashing their children with severely negative lyrics, combined with heavy doses of over the top sexual exploitation. They want us to stop it or introduce legislation to have it dramatically toned down. They are saying its Justin Bieber and Brittany Spears times ten. Instead of the young fans screaming and fainting like they used to for Brittany and Justin, now they are killing each other."

"I agree, it's out of control Bruce, but I think it's safe to say, that it's just a passing fad among the youth of our country that will be forgotten in a few months. Don't you agree?"

He watched as Bruce took off his glasses, reclined back in his chair, then replied, "No, I don't Bob. If it was limited to just one superstar that was tearing up the musical landscape, then I would agree. The fact that it is three of them in the United States alone, all sixteen years of age, incredibly good looking, talented and with what seems an endless supply of hit songs, I believe it's only going to get worse. There is also a kid in London that is creating a furor, also sixteen, plus a sixteen year old from Canada who headlines the mega popular musical Cirque de Soleil production in Las Vegas that is creating its own case of hysteria. On a smaller scale, there is a young Irish girl who critics say has the voice of an angel, who is touring the United States with the ladies from Celtic Woman, who are also now attracting all kinds of attention. Do you want to guess how old she is?"

"Don't tell me, she is sixteen years old as well?"

"Yup, you win the prize."

The coincidence of all of these young talents springing up out of nowhere around the world, all sixteen years of age, was eerily bizarre. Bob looked at Bruce, shaking his head before replying, "This is crazy Bruce, but you have to admit, it's a pretty darn good story. I can't believe the TV networks or the internet haven't been all over this."

****

In Swords County, Ireland, Father Thomas O'Sullivan was alone in his parish rectory at St. Colmcille's, his weathered, leather bound King James Bible opened to 1 Peter, where he read 5:8 again and again: "Be sober, be vigilant; because your adversary the devil walks about like a roaring lion, seeking whom he may devour."

Thomas knew he was being drawn into the snare of the demon, his soul was warning him through revelations placed there by God. His body was feeling the strain of his seventy-four years, but his mind was sharp and focused. He was still alive, he knew, for one reason and that was to be a soldier of God and fight His battle here on earth against His biggest adversary.

The horrible deaths of his close friends and colleagues Cardinals Kevin Zorn and David Beckstead were sobering reminders of this battle. He would not survive this, of that he had no doubt, but he would live long enough to rip the soul of this demon from its earthly body for all eternity.

Thomas thought again of his beloved Chloë, touring with

the Celtic Woman in concert performances all over the world. Her rising star was making her the most popular of the troupe and the hope of having her return to the Academy anytime soon was fading. He needn't worry, he knew, she was under the watchful eye of Sister McGarrigle, who updated him regularly by email regarding their well-being. Chloë's talent was immense and way beyond her years. He was very proud of her, like a real father would be. Her real parents, Katherine and Grew McClosky, would have been very proud of their daughter. That thought lasted only for a brief second as the haunting memory of Chloë's real birth snapped back into his mind. The poor girl had so much to look forward to in her singing career, but she also faced a dark future of horror and fear that was surely to come her way. He would be ready for that uncertainty, even if it killed him.

****

Robert Best, with Connor Asker and Juan Jiménez sitting on either side of him in the sold out Civic center Music Hall in Oklahoma City, watched as Chloë McClosky sang to the audience in her beautifully manicured voice. The audience members felt as if Chloë was alone with them in their own living rooms singing; it felt that personal. The concert goers appreciated the talent of the other women in Celtic Woman, but they were clearly here to listen to the phenomena sweeping the nation, Chloë McClosky and her hauntingly beautiful voice. The media covering the Celtic Woman had been limited to the local press wherever they were performing. Not any longer. National news channels, entertainment networks and even *Music Talks* magazine were running stories on the amazingly talented Chloë McClosky. The media were finally starting to pick up on the storyline of the hottest talent in the music industry today. It was finally noticed that they were all kids and they were all just sixteen years old. It was no surprise that Bentley Paxton of *Music Talks*, was the first to print a feature article showcasing the amazing talents of Connor Asker, Juan Jiménez, Brittany Campbell, Elizabeth Leroux and now Chloë McClosky. The article was well written, capturing the fact that they were all exactly sixteen years of age. It further fueled the flames of the frenzied fan base growing dramatically every single day.

Best looked over at young Connor, sporting his new, short-cropped hair style, his long blond locks that made him look vulnerable and soft were gone. That look was now replaced with a more aggressive look, still very alluring, but definitely a more mature look. Connor sat transfixed, listening to the voice of Chloë, when he asked him: "Do you think your pop voice could sing alongside Chloë?"

Connor looked back at him with a sparkle of excitement in his eyes when he replied: "Are you kidding me? Her voice would bury mine, it is so beautiful."

"I'm not so sure of that Connor. I think you would be great together. Both you and Juan would sound great with her. How about all three of us go backstage after the encore and meet with her. What do you guys think?"

Juan had also gone through a personal makeover at the insistence of Best. His long dark hair was now styled with subtle blond streaks to break up the black and gel pulled his hair in a sweeping direction down the side of his face. Juan had been listening to them talk through the sound of Chloë's soaring vocals. He leaned in close and asked him: "Mr. Best, could you really arrange for us to sing together? The three of us would sound amazing together."

He looked at Juan with a smile and said, "I know you would Juan. Both you and Connor would sound great with Chloë. Come on, let's get out of here and go meet her."

In an audience full of concert goers not familiar with the two young pop stars that were making their way down the aisle with the distinguished gentleman, the three of them slipped backstage unnoticed.

****

The final encore performance finished and the twenty-five hundred people, leapt from their seats and gave the women a thundering applause as each of them walked across the stage and bowed before gathering as a group in the center of the stage, their arms interlocked, and bowed once more to the audience as a group. The fans went crazy, reminding Best of a reception reserved for a rock concert and not a concert of Irish ballads and Celtic dance favorites. He waited off to the side of the stage alongside Sister McGarrigle who, much to his bemusement was looking less and less like a nun every time he saw her. Tonight she was dressed in dress slacks, a blouse and a fashionable sweater. Her hair was styled simply, but pleasantly. She even wore a little makeup with a hint of lipstick. He chuckled as he wondered what O'Sullivan would think if he saw McGarrigle now. The two of them stayed out of view of the audience as they seemed to be in no hurry to leave the hall, still thinking the Celtic Woman would come out for a third encore. They watched as the women dispersed to their dressing rooms while Chloë made her way towards them. Connor and Juan waited further backstage, amusing themselves with the pretty stagehands that had recognized the young stars.

When she approached them, her smile widened with delight as she recognized who was with Sister McGarrigle. Giggling like a little girl, she reached out to shake his hand before saying, "What a surprise to see you here! I didn't know you were watching, but I'm glad I didn't know because I would have been so nervous!"

"I doubt that very much Chloë. You are a true professional. You were amazing tonight. The audience loved you. Congratulations."

He watched as she blushed slightly before she replied, "Thank you Mr. Best. Coming from you, that means a lot."

"Chloë if you have a minute there are a few people that I would like to introduce you to."

"Certainly Mr. Best, I would be happy to."

"Okay great, they are big fans of yours and are just backstage." Robert led her backstage, where he found Connor and Juan helping a cute stagehand load a large sound board into a travel case.

"Guys, I would like you to meet Chloë McClosky."

His words were drowned by the squeal coming from

Chloë when she recognized Connor and Juan, "Oh my God! I can't believe you guys were here in the audience! This is just the coolest!"

After a few minutes of letting the three of them get to know each other a little bit more, Best stepped in and said: "Chloë, have you ever given any thought to singing pop music? I think with that voice and your look you could be a major star. What do you think?"

"Me a pop star? Oh I don't think so Mr. Best. These two guys are pop stars. I'm just an unknown Irish singer toiling away in music halls across the country." In an embarrassing tone she continued, "So no, Mr. Best, I don't see myself singing pop songs."

"Well these two pop singers think you could be a star and would love the opportunity to record with you. Isn't that right guys?" Best looked at the two of them, the shock registering across their faces that quickly turned to a look of excitement before they turned and faced Chloë, "Yes, that would be so amazing! We would be honored to sing with you Chloë. Please say yes!"

Best looked at the three of them and said, "Chloë, I am working on a major project right now that will turn the music world upside down. In two weeks, when your tour concludes, I would like to invite you and Sister McGarrigle to my Los Angeles studio for a meeting where I will propose an opportunity to you of such magnitude that it will change your life. Sound alright to you?"

She looked at Sister McGarrigle for reassurance and, after receiving it, turned towards him and the boys and once again squealed, "I would be honoured to meet with you. I can't imagine what it would be you're proposing, but if it involves singing with Connor and Juan, then count me in!"

Chapter 21

The European economy was taking a pounding on the markets, driving the economies of the most powerful industrialized countries in the world to scary levels. Smaller, weaker countries were brought to their knees from the worsening economic crisis. Governments were left to make backroom deals with companies to keep them from moving their operations and the jobs that came with them to other parts of the world. It was quickly becoming chaos and people were beginning to panic, they were certainly losing faith in their governments to pull them out of this mess.

One man was not panicking through all of this, and that was Sherman Oakley of the Oakley Steel Empire. The British economy was a disaster, but exports of steel were at an all-time high. The Chinese government couldn't buy enough of it, because their economy was one of the few in the world that was growing while the worldwide recession gripped everyone else. He also used the opportunity to squeeze even more tax breaks from the British government, with a threat of massive layoffs if he didn't get them. The Conservative government was barely keeping its head above water with the upcoming election, so the magnitude of the layoffs Sherman was threatening was political suicide.

Ann Lockwood loathed her father in every sense of the word. She hated him for his greed and his cruelty to her mother while she was growing up. He was a terrible man; you either hated him or feared him. Most people feared him and allowed him to trample all over them just to maintain the appearance of a relationship. He was that powerful, not only in Britain, but all over the world. Countries everywhere needed steel and Oakley Steel controlled more than 40% of the world's steel market. His voracious acquisitions of steel foundries across Europe during economic downturns over the past thirty years had given him too much power. Power was not a good thing for someone like Sherman Oakley. If Sherman Oakley wanted something, he got it. However, there was one thing he has been unable to obtain: his grandson Michael. He went to court after the death of Ann's husband, Dalton, to obtain custody of Michael when he was born, using Ann's outlandish stories of being attacked by a monster as the means to have the courts declare Ann as incompetent and incapable of raising a child. The courts kicked his money, power and political influence to the curb. The infuriated Sherman cut off all ties to his daughter after that and never gave up the fight to gain custody of Michael. Ann had money as well, lots of it and she used it to keep her father away from her grandson, at least in the courts, through the years. She felt, however, that she should allow Michael to get to know his grandfather, aunts, uncles and cousins in carefully arranged get-togethers at Christmas and on other special occasions. She was confident that Michael would see his grandfather for what he was, a ruthless and cutthroat man bent on power without any influence on Ann and he would reject his grandfather. For the most part, Michael did not have much of a relationship with him, other than attending the two or three special occasions over the course of a year.

Sherman hated his daughter as much as she hated him. She poisoned him to his grandson and he never had any chance to have a relationship with him. He would make her pay for her selfishness one day, he promised himself. So, when his assistant approached him about American record producer Robert Best's request to meet with him regarding the musical career of his grandson, he agreed to it. He knew his grandson was a talented musician, he had attended many of his performances over the past few years, but to attract the attention of one of the world's most prominent record executives was impressive.

Sherman assumed that Mr. Best figured he would not get to first base in signing the boy if he couldn't get the approval of his powerful grandfather. He would like to think that was true, but in reality, he had no say in any decisions regarding Michael. His daughter made those, all of them much to his angst. There was a knock on his door, pulling him from his thoughts. His assistant stepped in to announce that Robert Best had arrived. Sherman instructed: "See him in, please."

A tall, handsome, well-dressed man, who looked to be in his mid-forties, stepped into his office, his assistant, left the room after him, closing the door as he left. The man stepped confidently towards him, his hand extended, "Mr. Oakley, pleased to meet you, Robert Best."

"Nice to meet you as well, please sit down," Sherman gestured Best to the leather couches situated in front of large windows offering a spectacular view of the 'Square Mile', the London downtown business and banking district. Oakley Steel's head offices were downtown, while his flagship steel foundry factory was located over in Silvertown on the north bank of the Thames in Greater London.

Sherman, pushing sixty-eight years old, looked much younger. He kept himself in impeccable shape, did not drink alcohol, nor had he ever smoked. His thick, silver hair was smartly styled with a touch of gel, giving him a very distinctive and powerful look. Most men who had the opportunity to be in his presence found him intimidating. His steely blue eyes could be as cold as ice. Sizing up the American businessman, Sherman sensed that this man was very powerful as well and carried himself with extreme authority and confidence.

"Mr. Best, or if I may, Robert, can I offer you something to drink? Coffee or tea? It's early but I can get you something a little stronger to kick-start the day."

"Robert is just fine, if you will allow me to call you Sherman. Tea would be great. Just black, thank you."

Sherman stepped back to his desk, punched a button and barked out to his secretary to fetch tea and biscuits. Returning to his seat opposite Best he asked, "So what brings you all the way to London, Robert, and in particular, to my grandson, Michael?"

"As I'm sure you are aware, your grandson is an incredibly talented musician and singer. I want to make him a major star, not only in England and America, but all over the world."

"I am aware of your background, Robert, and the list of stars that are clients of yours. Most impressive, and I'm honored that you feel so strongly about Michael's abilities. But you have not done your homework regarding me and my relationship with my grandson. It is cordial at best and his mother, much to my dismay, has full parental decision-making control in Michael's life and his music career."

"I am aware of that. I have a proposal for you that will get you into a position of having a say in his career. Would you be interested in hearing about my project?"

Sherman studied Best for a moment before answering. Being a part of Michael's career would be fantastic, but he knew Ann would never allow it. "I'm afraid that is impossible Robert. My daughter would never allow me to have any say in Michael's career."

Leaning back in the supple leather of his chair, Best continued, "Have you ever heard of Connor Asker?"

"Of course I have, who hasn't? Incredible young man."

"Connor is my client. Have you heard of Elizabeth Leroux?"

"I believe so. Is she not the young lady starring in the Vegas production, Panterra? I caught that show last time I was in the U.S. Fantastically talented young lady."

"How about Juan Jimenez?"

"The young Latin heartthrob who is turning all of the young women in the world inside out? He just performed in London recently, I believe. I presume these young stars are also clients of yours?"

"Correct. What about the young lady who won 'X Factor' in the United States, Brittany Campbell?"

"No, I haven't. Let me guess, another client? What is your

point Robert? I don't need a rundown of your client list. Let's get back to Michael and your proposal, shall we?"

"Certainly, my apologies Sherman. Based upon what you know and what you have heard, would you agree that these young stars are at or near the top of the music industry?"

"I know fans here in London went crazy trying to buy tickets to Asker's concert. A fan that had been waiting in line for two days went berserk when he made it to the front of the line, only to be told that the concert was sold out. He stabbed the clerk behind the ticket counter to death and almost killed one of the security staff who tried to subdue him. I don't like that kind of music myself, I'm a little old for that stuff, but I am certainly not oblivious to the impact these young stars are having on our youth."

"What if I was able to bring all of them together into one rock group? A superstar band, which brings together the top young music stars in a generation into one explosive band that will set the world on fire with their music. I have the hit songs already written and the commitment from all five of them. I am missing two young stars before the band can be complete. Your grandson Michael, and the Irish girl, Chloë McClosky. Chloë will be part of the fold soon, but your grandson and his mother are another matter. I need your help and this is what I am proposing to you. This group will need a year or two to come together, to practice and rehearse and release a steady stream of hits before they go on the road and tour. I need a corporate giant to finance this. A corporation like 'Oakley Steel'. I am talking about purchasing a state of the art studio for them to rehearse in and record in away from the public eye. A secluded mansion for them to live in. A massive stage production, never seen in the history of live shows, will need to be built and prepared. Tour buses, dozens of trucks to haul everything from city to city. Private aircraft to shuttle the kids from concert to concert and carefully selected public appearances. What I am talking about here, Sherman, is a carefully constructed superstar band the likes of which has never seen before. It will dwarf the Beatles in comparison.

Social media will fuel the frenzy like nothing ever witnessed. These kids, all on their own, could create social chaos, but together, it will be mayhem amongst the youth of the world. Imagine Justin Bieber times ten.

Sherman sank back in his chair, his mind swimming with possibilities.

Best continued, "Now, you could imagine the exposure for Oakley Steel that this would create? Not that you need it, but what I'm talking about is an opportunity that rarely, if ever comes around. I need your money and connections, but most importantly, I need Michael. What do you think?"

"I think you could get any corporation in the world to finance this, the potential is huge, but Michael is someone that I cannot buy. When Ann finds out it's Oakley Steel financing the group, she will pull Michael immediately. You may not get him. You might if I wasn't involved."

"I thought of that, but let me explain what I was thinking. Once Ann knows that your involvement is strictly financial and you are not involved in Michael's musical decisions or any of the kids for that matter, then I think she might relax somewhat. You could make a case that this project involves an incredible amount of funding and what better company to do that but that of Michael's grandfather. Leave it to me, Sherman. My team and I will convince your daughter to let Michael go. At the end of the day it will be Michael's decision. If he wants to come on board, do you really think his mother can stop him?"

His hands steepled to his chin and deep in thought he replied: "I just don't know. The hysteria and the hype of the band could spook Ann and convince her that's it too much pressure for Michael at such a young age."

"The kids will have the very best tutors your money can buy teaching them. Their privacy will be a top priority and they will be protected from the media and the outside world. Security will also be the very best. This is an opportunity of a lifetime for Michael, and his mother is not stupid. It may take some convincing, but she will let him go, trust me. So tell me

Sherman, is Oakley Steel in or out?"

"You convince my daughter to let Michael join and Oakley Steel is in. I will give you a blank check to put this together, how is that?"

Best rose from his chair, took Sherman's hand and shook it as he replied: "Consider it done. All I ask is that you keep this conversation strictly confidential between you and me. A leak at this juncture could jeopardize everything. I will get back to you shortly on the next step."

"Answer one last question for me before you leave."

"What question is that Mr. Oakley?"

"I'm curious. What will you call this super group?"

"Vasallus."

"Vasallus? That is odd, I must say. What does it mean?"

"Vasallus is Latin for 'servants', Mr. Oakley."

He watched as Best left his office and was thinking of the name, Vasallus. Latin for servants. Interesting. He liked it.

Best left his meeting with Oakley, successfully securing the funding he needed to fund the band and the tour. He didn't need his money, he could get the money a number of different ways. What he needed was a clean and legitimate source. Just another small piece. Oh, and Oakley Steel's name would never be associated with Vasallus. The old bastard would be furious when he discovered he'd been duped. That is, if he lived long enough.

****

Jenn knocked on Avery's office door, and then stepped in to declare: "Robert Best is in the board room waiting for you. Would you like me to have anything brought in?"

"Okay, thanks Jenn. Let's just start with tea and coffee for now. We'll see how long the meeting lasts, then we can think about bringing in something to eat. I am meeting Bentley for dinner so I can't let this last all afternoon. Let Best know I'll be right there."

Avery gathered his files and made his way into the board room of Alive Records. His record company was now in control of the careers of Connor Asker, Juan Jimenez and

Brittany Campbell. All of them had been transferred over from Best's Blackstar Studios. Their careers were in full swing and it blew Avery away how talented these young kids were. He was running out of superlatives when he met with Best.

He walked in and immediately Best left his seat to shake his hand and flash a warm smile: "Good afternoon Avery. Thanks for taking the time to meet with me this afternoon." The turnaround in Best's personality was still sort of new to Avery and still an adjustment from the prick he was so good at before.

"No problem Robert, I'm sure a meeting was due with these kids' careers skyrocketing like they are. There is lots to talk about, so I'm glad we're getting together."

"Yes, there is a lot to talk about Avery. Why don't you go first?"

"Okay, let me start with Connor. It's time we took him off tour and put him back in the studio. He needs to release a new CD. His music is now showing signs of wear. I have got some ideas on song selection for the new CD. My writers have been putting some stuff together."

"Let me interrupt you Avery, if you don't mind. I know you have some great ideas for Connor's new album. It's why you're the best in the industry, but song selection will come from my song writing team. That was my only stipulation when your studio took over their careers. Has that changed?"

He could feel his anger rising when he replied, "Managing their new material is the heart of managing their careers, Robert. Wouldn't you agree? Not allowing me a say in what they are going to record, you might as well record their albums yourself over at Blackstar. You don't need me."

"Not true, their careers would not be where they're at without you and Alive Records. Song selection is an important piece of the puzzle, but it's just a piece. Tour dates and city selections, press conferences and chart positioning are all just as critical, Avery. Why am I telling you this? You already know that. I feel the like the student lecturing the teacher. Besides, the songs have done very well, have they not?"

He was right. The songs were perfect for their vocals and they were churning out hit after hit like a vending machine dispenses candy. Why mess with a good thing, right? Who was writing these songs? It didn't matter anyway; the songs coming into Alive Records for these kids were incredible.

"I am not here to discuss the song selection, Avery. I have something else I need to talk to you about. Remember when I asked you to take over the careers of Connor and Juan because I was working on a major project that needed my time?"

"Yes I do. Do I get to hear what it is now? Do I need to?"

Best shifted forward in his chair, his arms extended over the table as he began to speak, "I have been very fortunate, as have you, to be involved with some of the best young talent to come into the music world in decades. Would you agree with that statement?"

Avery nodded in agreement, so Best continued: "I have recently signed on Elizabeth Leroux, the Canadian girl starring in Panterra in Las Vegas."

Avery was stunned. How was he doing this? "Jesus, Best, how the hell are you getting these kids? Why you? Why are they not signing on with other record companies? You're not the only successful producer in L.A."

"That is true, Avery. What I offer is a track record and history of success with rising young talent. We both do. The agents and the kids' parents know we are partnered and that we know how to make these kids stars so they want to sign with us. It's that simple."

"Okay, I get that, but how are you finding these kids? Leroux and Asker were already known, but you had Campbell before anyone even knew her name until 'X Factor'. The same with Juan, and he was just some kid from Venezuela."

"Like a successful baseball organization, Avery, I have a vast network of scouts everywhere. There is talent out there, you just have to be prepared to turn over the amount of stones required to find them. It's just hard work. I could say the same thing with the talent you have discovered."

"Mine were not all at the same time and all the same age. Kind of bizarre, don't you think? The fact they are all just sixteen years old?"

"Kind of, but not really. Think of the NFL draft. How is it that some years produce the biggest crop of star quarterbacks? In 2004, the draft produced Manning, Roethlisberger and Rivers. The 1984 draft produced Elway, Kelly and Marino. Our kids came from one hell of a good draft class, don't you think?"

Not quite the analogy he would have used, but it worked. "Quite astonishing, to be honest. The world is barely recovering from Bieber fever when *wham* here come four more and all at once and far more popular. It's crazy."

"Let me get back to what I came for here today. What would you think if we put all of them into one group? A sort of super group. What do you think of that idea?"

"Holy shit, Best. Are you even serious? The fucking world would split wide open at the seams. Fans would tear apart stadiums just to get a chance to get close to them or, God forbid, touch them. You can't be serious?"

Smiling now from ear to ear, Best replied: "As serious as a heart attack, Avery."

"Jesus Christ, this is nuts. How can we make this work? Leroux for one is still contracted to Panterra, plus how can this many stars share the stage?"

"It's all just semantics, Avery. Nothing we can't work out. Leroux's contract is ending with Meritzia Sky soon, plus we will need a year or maybe more to get them together, figure out who sings what, then rehearse and practice them to the bone. We need the time for song selection, marketing, promotion, and legalities. Once again, it's just semantics."

"Okay, I'm with you. I like it Robert, no, I love it. This will be the best thing since the Beatles. They will make the Backstreet Boys look like a garage band. Holy shit!"

"In order for it to work, we must get two members for the group that we are missing. That's where I need you and your world class charm to convince some stubborn people that this is a good idea."

Now Avery stood up in the board room and began pacing, then stopped and looked at Best before speaking: "Wait a minute. Do you have any idea how much it is going to cost to get this off the ground? This is a massive undertaking that requires major sponsorship."

"Let me interrupt you right there. It's taken care of. I have secured corporate funding that is going to finance the whole package, including putting together the biggest stage show the world has ever seen, a mansion to house the kids, the best school tutors, tour buses, transport truck and trailers to haul all this around. Marketing and promotion campaigns. Everything. We have a blank check, Avery."

"Who have you brought in this quickly?"

"Sherman Oakley from Oakley Steel out of London, England. He will finance everything. I have yet to work out the legal terms of the agreement or the payment schedule from record royalties, tours, and merchandise, but it won' be outrageous, I assure you."

"And why is that?"

"This is where your charm and powers of influence come into play, Avery."

"I thought you already had Oakley Steel in play?"

"I told you the super group needs two more members, well actually three, but for the two, I need your help."

"Okay, and who is that?"

"Michael Lockwood, the grandson of Sherman Oakley and Chloë McClosky, the Irish girl touring with the Celtic Woman. I need you to talk with Michael's mother in London and the Irish girl's caregiver, Father Thomas O'Sullivan."

"You're kidding me, right? I know both of them and their talent is out of this world. Bentley and I saw the McClosky girl at a concert and she has a voice like nothing I have ever heard. If I wasn't so busy, she would be a rising star that Alive Records would pursue. Lockwood is insanely talented. Adding these two would add a European flavor that would give the band tremendous versatility and a broader appeal. They are both incredibly good looking kids, to boot. All of them are good looking. A marketing bonanza. How old are these two?"

"Would you believe sixteen?"

"Fuck off, enough already. That's impossible."

"Sorry to disappoint you, but they are exactly sixteen."

"Unbelievable. The next thing you're going to tell me is they all share the same birthday too."

Looking over at Avery Johnson, he struggled from breaking out into laughter. "If you only knew Johnson, if you only knew" he laughed to himself.

Chapter 22

For his dinner with Bentley, Avery chose a booth in a quiet corner of the restaurant. They had lots to talk about as Avery could barely contain himself when he had called her in the late afternoon for dinner arrangements. He had said something about one of the most exciting things he had had a chance to be involved with in all the years he had been in the music industry. He wouldn't disclose anything over the phone, choosing to tell her over dinner and a glass of wine. The reservation was for 6 p.m. and he asked her to take a taxi to meet him at the Tavern in Brentwood as he was coming from the opposite direction. It must be something big, Bentley thought to herself, because she had never heard him so excited about anything. Well maybe he gets this excited when he thinks of me, she chuckled to herself.

As she made her way to the upscale Tavern in the backseat of the taxi, she reflected on her relationship with Avery. It was going so well she couldn't be happier. It was heading in a direction that could turn permanent someday. She felt it in her heart and she knew he did too. Then why was she fighting a feeling gnawing anxiety, deep inside of her? Was it the relationship that was causing it? Was she somehow missing the signs that he no longer felt the same for her as she did for him? That wasn't it, unless she was a complete idiot, and being fooled was something she had never let happen to her. Not ever. Then, what was eating away inside of her? Hopefully, his news at dinner would alleviate the doom that was crawling around inside of her stomach.

She arrived at the Tavern right at 6 p.m., paid the driver and made her way inside. Avery had taken her to the Tavern before and it was one of the best Mediterranean restaurants in the city, if not the best. As the hostess showed her to their table, she recognized a well-known Hollywood executive schmoozing a beautiful, young woman that was definitely not his wife. It used to be that celebrities would be a little more discreet in their extra-marital affairs, but not anymore. They were all players and taking a vow of marriage was no different to them than signing mortgage papers. It could be sold today and they could buy something new tomorrow. She hated that side of the entertainment business; it was why she had never married. Her parents had been married for almost fifty years and they were still madly in love. Making her way to the table, she could see Avery standing and holding out a chair for her. He was so damn handsome, that she melted every time she saw him. Wrapping her arms around him, she hugged him maybe a little tighter and a little longer than she normally would. *Bentley wondered what was wrong with her tonight.*

Avery must have sensed something, because he looked her in the eye for a moment before he spoke, "What's the matter, sweetheart? There's something bothering you. You have tears in your eyes. Come on and sit down. I have our favorite merlot on its way over to the table."

There was a padded bench on one side of the table and two chairs on the other. Avery directed her towards the bench and then slid in beside her. He wrapped his big arm around her shoulders, pulled her close, and then whispered to her, "Hey baby, what has you so upset? I have some great news to share, but maybe that should wait till later. How about we just start with you telling me how your day was?"

For some reason, the tears just spilled out uncontrollably. She buried her face into his chest and bawled like a baby for a good minute. Every time she thought that she could stop and lift her head, the tears came again. Finally, the crying stopped and she looked up to where Avery had a cloth napkin waiting for her. She wiped her eyes, knowing full well that her mascara was all over the place. She looked down at Avery's chest and was horrified to see that, not only was there a big wet spot, but it was black with mascara. "Oh my God Avery, look at your shirt! I'm so sorry. I can't believe what a cry baby I am today. This has never happened before. I am so embarrassed."

He reached out and stroked her hair to the side before he spoke in a reassuring voice, "Don't worry about the shirt honey, it can be dry-cleaned. Why don't you take a minute to go to the ladies room and freshen up? I'll fill your glass while you're doing that."

She stared at herself at the mirror, thinking what a nutcase he must think she was. She carefully re-applied her makeup, including her lipstick, took a deep breath and made her way back to the table. Avery was on his phone and, when he saw her coming, he quickly ended the call, stood and took her by each arm and asked if everything was okay.

"I don't know what came over me, Avery. On the way over here in the taxi, I was thinking about the good news you wanted to share with me when I was suddenly overwhelmed with this sense of dread. Like something bad was about to happen, you know? It was really strange and very powerful. Next thing I know, the taxi pulls up I walk in and just lose it. I am so sorry. I must have made quite a scene."

"You never made a scene honey, I promise. In this place, you could scream 'bomb' and nobody would even notice, they're all too into themselves. Tell me about this feeling of dread. What do you think it was about?"

"Doesn't matter, Avery, now let's forget about me and instead talk about the good news you were so excited to tell me about before I ruined it."

Lifting her chin up so their eyes met, he whispered, "I love you, Bentley, I want to make sure you're okay though. You scared me, baby."

She sat up tall on the bench and reached over to cradle his hand before replying, "I'm okay honey honest. Tell me before I go crazy with curiosity already."

"Okay then, but first let's fill our glasses, or should I say my glass. You haven't even touched yours yet," laughed Avery, as he reached for his glass of wine and held it up to Bentley's, where they clinked glasses. He continued, "Here's to one of the most historic nights in music history!"

She reached over and gave him a playful punch on the arm, then almost shouted, "Enough already, Avery. Tell me, for heaven sakes!"

He shifted in his seat so he was facing her directly and then continued, "How would you rate the success of the young stars that we are managing now, Connor, Juan and Brittany? How do you think their careers are going?"

She gave him a playful smile, and then replied, "I would say their careers are skyrocketing. I would also say they are the most successful, most popular artists in the music business today. Their songs are at the top of the charts, their concerts are sold out and their fans can't buy enough merchandise. I think they're doing pretty well."

Avery continued, "Now in a different vein of music, what do you think of the careers of Elizabeth Leroux, Chloë McClosky and Michael Lockwood? Not in comparison to where their careers are at with the other three but more about talent and potential?"

She couldn't stop her eyes from widening in amazement, "Don't tell me you have signed those three? No way Avery, are you kidding me?"

"Best signed Leroux and is close to signing the other two. He needs my help with the Irish girl, McClosky."

"I thought Leroux was locked in with the Panterra show at the Meritzia? They would never let her go from her contract. She is the heart and soul of that show; without her it sinks."

"I agree, but the show's producers only signed her to a one year contract, not knowing exactly how she would do in the lead role at such a young age. They had every intention of signing her long term, but were blindsided when she informed them she was leaving the show after the year is up next month."

"I don't understand. Why would she even think of leaving Panterra? She could perform that role for another three years minimum and make a small fortune before she ages out, but instead, she's opting out now after the world is just waking up to her? She could fall flat on her face on her own."

"She's not leaving the show to be on her own."

"What the hell do you mean she's not leaving the show to be on her own?"

She watched Avery as he pulled closer to her, glanced around him as if to check if anyone was listening through the racket of the restaurant's busy dinner crowd and continued, "Do you remember the night we met Best at the Whale and Ale when he asked me to produce and manage the career of Juan Jimenez?"

"Yes, of course, so what does that have to do with Leroux not going out on her own?"

"Well, when I asked him why he would give up Juan's career and turn it over to me, of all people, he replied that he was working on a major project that needed his full attention and that he would need me on it as well.."

She looked at him intensely, waiting for him to go on, "Yeah, okay, continue."

"That project is now ready to launch, and he shared it with me this afternoon and you're not going to believe it."

She damn near pulled her fist back to cold cock him before he finished, "Robert Best has signed all these superstar kids, these child music prodigies to bring them all together in one explosive rock band!"

She thought she would fall to the floor. She was stunned, almost speechless, then she replied, "Oh my God, you're not kidding are you? All these kids, together, in one band? This is going to be epic Avery, on a scale never seen before."

Now he was smiling from ear to ear and his eyes sparkled when he replied, "Bigger than the Beatles, Bentley. The impact on the youth of this world will be like a giant tsunami, a tidal wave of fever never seen before. It's crazy, and guess who Best wants to produce and manage this new super group?"

"The only music producer who could pull it off and I'll give Best credit for seeing that right up front. You'll do a marvelous job, honey! I'm so excited for you!"

"Thanks. This could be the greatest thing in the music industry ever, or it could be a total disaster. These kids are still fairly young and naïve, but as they get older, it will get more and more difficult to manage their egos."

"Tell me how the McClosky girl and the British kid, Lockwood, fit in this band. They are both classical singers in every sense. The same as Leroux. How will that work?"

"Best is a genius and he proved it when he insisted they

all have to be in the group or there will be no group. He knew this would only work if he had them all. Their voices give a layer to the sound that will differentiate them even more. Plus, they are seriously good looking, athletic and very mature and committed to the group. It will be out of this world when they hit the stage."

"I agree. I am super excited as a fan, but to write about this for *Music Talks* will be mind blowing."

"Glad you brought that up. We have to keep this under wraps for some time. A long time actually. Best wants them to go into the studio to gel as a group, become friends and as close as possible, before the pressure and spotlight hit them. He wants them practicing and rehearsing nonstop for at least a year, maybe longer. It will give us enough time to set in place the hype that will create a feeding frenzy unparalleled in this industry. The kids will continue building their individual careers, that's part of the hype, but on a much more controlled and limited schedule. Best has it all figured out. He has put an awful lot of thought into this, Bentley. It's an incredible and ambitious project, but I think it can work. You, however, will get first dibs on the story when it's announced. I didn't even have to ask him for that and he volunteered it."

She sank back on the bench and exhaled, "Wow Avery, this is indeed a good news story. Pour me another glass, will you?"

****

At LAX Avery and Bentley boarded the Delta Airlines flight to Dublin with a stopover at JFK in New York. Bentley informed her new boss, Jeremy Jyles, or as he preferred to be called, 'JJ', that she was taking a few days off to spend some time in Europe with a friend. She didn't know if it was just men in general, but JJ had the same instincts that Jonathon used to have. They both could read right through her, especially when it came to her relationships. He told her, "No problem Bentley, take as much time with him as possible. Maybe you'll come home with a ring on your finger, what do you think?"

"I think that you think too much, JJ. Why is it that men think they have women figured out all the time? I don't get it. Do I question you on your quest to find someone who would even consider wanting to be with you? No, I don't, because it's none of my business. To answer your probing and nosy question, yes, Avery and I are off to Dublin to relax in the warmth of the Irish. No ring exchanges, I'm afraid. Avery has some business over there, so I get to tag along. You jealous?"

"Jealous because it's Ireland, or jealous that you're going with the most eligible bachelor in L.A.? I'm not gay, Bentley, if that's what you're insinuating."

"Sure, okay, we'll leave that for another day. I'll touch base with you when I'm back."

Five hours later they landed at JFK and decided just to stay in their seats rather than deplane for a break, like most of the other passengers. They only had a half hour and they both were content to hold hands and talk about their visit to Father O'Sullivan.

She shifted sideways in her seat, so that she faced Avery when she asked, "So what do you know about Father O'Sullivan anyway? You told me he was the caregiver for Chloë, but what else do you know about him?"

Avery had removed the cuff links from his expensive dress shirt with the monogrammed *Alive Records* logo on the cuffs so he could roll up his sleeves. The tie had come off before they sat down in their seats back in L.A., so he was getting comfortable for the long six and a half hour flight across the Atlantic. Looking at her for a second, letting his eyes linger, he replied, "God, you are so beautiful Bentley. I love you so much. Have I told you that yet today? How much I love you?"

Giggling, she reached down and locked her fingers into his before replying, "Hey, I asked you a question, so don't be dodging your journalist girlfriend. It's my job to ask questions, but since you said you loved me, I'll cut you some slack. And no, it's the first time you told me that today. I'm keeping score you know. I love you Avery Johnson. Very much. Now that makes me ahead by one, because, if you recall, I believe I told you that before you stepped into the shower this morning!"

Pulling her hand towards him, he kissed it then looked up at her and said, "No that makes it tied, because you couldn't hear my reply from the sound of the water in the shower when I told you I loved you back."

"Okay, we're even. Now tell me about O'Sullivan. What are you expecting he'll do? You need his consent because Chloë is a minor. Do you expect any problems?"

"Best said that he was an old, crusty priest, stubborn as a mule, but a very wise and fair man. At the end of the day, he loves Chloë very much and her happiness is everything. He'll give his consent."

"Is that why you brought me along? To show him that she'll be taken care of?"

"I have to admit, it will help, but no, that's not why you're here and you know it. We'll meet with O'Sullivan and then you and I will spend the weekend sightseeing. I'm looking forward to making those horny Irish men jealous of the beautiful American woman on my arm."

"What if I'd rather just spend the weekend in bed with you?" she asked.

She looked in his eyes as he leaned in close to her, kissed her passionately, and then replied, "Sounds good to me!"

****

They arrived in front of St. Colmcille's Parish Church in Swords County, Ireland, with a few minutes to spare for their 11:00 AM meeting with Father O'Sullivan. Even with GPS and a map, it was difficult navigating the Irish countryside, but the scenery during the drive was stunning and well worth any aggravation caused by the lack of directions. Climbing out of their rented BMW sedan, Avery commented to Bentley, "This church must be a hundred years old."

They made their way up the walkway to the entrance to the parish as Bentley replied, "Looks like they have added an addition to it recently. Kind of spoils the historical aspect to it, doesn't it?"

"It does. They don't tear down institutions very easily here. They'd prefer to renovate or add on."

Before they opened the door to walk in, he commented, "Never in my wildest dreams did I ever think I would be travelling to a small village in Ireland to ask permission from a Catholic priest to sign a fifteen year old Irish sensation to a pop singing contract."

They walked into the church lobby and looked around, wondering where the offices might be, when they heard a pleasant, Irish-voiced lady coming down the hallway towards them, "Good morning, I'm coming." A few seconds later a tiny, older woman with a shock of white hair that looked like she had her finger stuck in an electric socket too long, came around the corner. Her complexion was rosy and she had a pair of reading glasses hanging by a string from around her neck. The glasses were resting on a rather large, matronly bosom. She broke out in a wide smile and with her thick Irish accent, called out, "You must be the music people from America! Welcome to St. Colmcille's. I'm Mrs. Beckeridge, the parish administrator. Father O'Sullivan is waiting for you down the hall in his office. Please follow me."

Avery looked over at Bentley and gave her a playful wink as they turned to follow Mrs. Beckeridge down the hall. Avery looked at the walls along the hall and took in the framed photos of previous parish priests who had served this church in the tiny hamlet in Ireland's green pastures. They continued to follow her down the hallway, smiling at each other as they listened to her hum an Irish song. They stopped in front of an office as Mrs. Beckeridge knocked on the open door, announcing the guests from America. She showed them in and they were greeted by a tall, athletic, and white-haired priest dressed in traditional black, his white collar giving him an air of authority. He extended his hand to them both with a firm handshake and a smile that instantly warmed the room. Any feelings of anxiety were quickly melted away by this man whose presence seemed to exude goodness. His thick Irish brogue added to his warm personality.

"Welcome to my humble parish, Mr. Johnson and Ms. Paxton. How was your flight to Dublin? I see you found Balbriggan with no problem. Please sit, we have lots to discuss. Mrs. Beckeridge will bring us tea and biscuits shortly."

They turned to catch a glimpse of Mrs. Beckeridge flash a look to Father O'Sullivan that exuded, "Oh I will, will I?"

Avery smiled as he replied, "Thank you Father O'Sullivan. You have a wonderful church here. The countryside was breathtaking as we made our way to Balbriggan."

Avery was drawn to Father O'Sullivan's eyes as he spoke; they projected confidence and compassion. His congregation must love him, he mused. Father O'Sullivan looked at Bentley this time when he said, "Have you both been to Ireland before?"

Bentley, with her intoxicating beauty filling the room, was clearly charmed by the priest and replied, "This is the first time for both of us, Father, and we're looking forward to seeing more of it."

Father O'Sullivan looked at them both for a brief second. He seemed to be putting together the fact that they were not a married couple, but a couple. He replied, "Good to hear. I hope you enjoy your stay. There is an old saying in Ireland, Ms. Paxton, "May you have the hindsight to know where you've been, the foresight to know where you're going and the insight to know when you're going too far."

Father O'Sullivan continued, "Enough ramblings of an old man, I must say. When we spoke on the phone Mr. Johnson, you talked about Chloë's music career and the plans your company has for her. Why don't we start there? Sister McGarrigle and Chloë will be arriving shortly from the Academy, so getting a good background from you before they arrive would be helpful. You can imagine how excited an impressionable, young fifteen year old girl could be at the prospect of fame and the bright lights of America."

"Certainly Father, and please no formalities. Avery and Bentley are fine. Let me start by saying that Chloë is a very special young girl. She is not only an extremely talented singer and musician, but very mature and focused for such a young age. It is obvious that she has been raised by people who love her very much and who have given her the confidence and maturity to pursue her dreams. We are putting together a group of young people from different parts of the world, all similar in age, to form a pop band that will generate instant excitement and success for all of them. It will give Chloë a stage to showcase her beautiful voice to a worldwide audience. The kids will spend the next year to two years practicing together, rehearsing and recording before they go out as a group. They will continue to build their individual careers during this time, however, at a much slower and more controlled pace. Only when we feel that they are ready, will we proceed with a potential concert tour, promotional appearances and so forth. In the time they will be together, practicing and rehearsing, they will also grow as a group. Friendships will be formed, and trust will be built amongst them. At such a young age right now, all of them could go out on stage and sing their hearts out and the world would love them. They already do, but we feel that it is critical to their long term success as musicians, that they learn to appreciate all of the aspects of a professional career before they embark on this together as a group. We project that this group, Father, will be mega successful. Make no mistake, there will pressure heaped upon them, but they will be carefully protected from outside pressures, like the demands from the media, so that they can keep their identities intact and still be kids."

Father O'Sullivan stepped in and said, "Sorry for interrupting Avery, but you keep referring to 'we'. I am assuming that you mean you and Bentley, or is there someone else involved? I am fully aware of your career and success as a music producer and manager of talent, Avery. You have a very strong and respected reputation in the industry, which is why I am even considering this proposal for Chloë. You never mentioned anyone else."

"My partner in this is Robert Best from Blackstar Studios, one of the biggest names in the industry, Father. Between the two of us, we have nine Grammy Awards as producers and collaborators and over thirty Grammys won by our clients."

Bentley looked over at him before looking back at Father O'Sullivan when she stated, "Sorry for the interruption sweetheart, but bragging about your achievements is not something you're comfortable with, so let me do it for you. Father, I am a journalist for the music industry's largest print and online magazine, *Music Talks*. Our publications have covered both Avery and Mr. Best's careers over the years and they truly are the best in the world at what they do. Chloë will be in very good hands with them. They will nurture her into a superstar in due time, when she and the others are ready."

"Thank you Bentley, for that. I also know about your success and your career. Very impressive to say the least. I also know about Robert Best and his success. You're probably wondering how an old priest in the middle of nowhere can be so current on the music scene in America. Well, if it wasn't for Chloë and Sister McGarrigle I wouldn't be, I can assure you. Ever since their return from the tour with the Celtic Woman in America, Sister McGarrigle has become this passionate fan of American pop music. She is like a mother to Chloë and loves her very much. She is also someone deeply rooted in faith and her love for Christ is unmatched. She is fully in favor of Chloë taking this next step in her musical career and it is for that reason that I am agreeing to allow Chloë to go to America to pursue her dreams. It is also why I insisted that you come here to Ireland to meet with me. I wanted to look in your eyes, Avery, and see the man behind the reputation. You're a good man and not the money-mongering, shallow person that is typical of the entertainment industry."

Avery was truly moved by his words. He could feel the strength and compassion of God running through this man, "Thank you, Father. I assure you, Chloë will be taken care of and only her best interests will be the priority. All of them will be treated and managed with great care. She will stay in California in a secluded home with the rest of the group, where they will be able to focus on their music and schooling. They will have the very best of tutors and a full-time, highly qualified teacher living in the home to work with them. You will be kept abreast at all times of Chloë's development and her career. It is a tremendous opportunity for her Father, and I am glad that you agree."

"I have one condition before I agree to let Chloë go."

"What is that Father?"

"Sister McGarrigle must accompany Chloë to America and be with her at all times. She will be my eyes and ears, Avery. Keep in mind that Chloe is still a child and her care is my responsibility, as the representative of this church. Do you understand?"

"I understand Father, you have my word. Please feel free to contact me at any time regarding Chloë," Avery replied, handing Father O'Sullivan his business card.

Suddenly there was a commotion outside in the hallway and they could hear Mrs. Beckeridge squeal in delight. Avery looked at Father O'Sullivan, who replied, "Chloë is here, as you can tell. Mrs. Beckeridge will miss her dearly when she leaves."

Sister McGarrigle, dressed plainly in her habit, walked into the office first, followed closely by Chloë. Avery and Bentley rose from their chairs to greet them. Avery was stunned by Chloë's beauty and presence, as he gave her a hug. Her smile filled the small office and radiated warmth as if the sun had somehow been placed in the room. Her long, blond hair fell onto her shoulders and down the back of a wool knit sweater that had colors of green woven in amongst the dominant grey. She wore brown corduroy pants tucked into tall, brown, leather boots. Her natural colouring captured her beauty elegantly. He and Bentley stole a glance, and he could tell she was also overwhelmed by Chloë's presence. Everyone sat down and Father O'Sullivan spoke first.

"Chloë, I have been discussing your future with Avery and the lovely Bentley Paxton, and we all agree that sending you to America is in your best interests. How would you like Sister McGarrigle and you to travel to Los Angeles to begin work on an ambitious new project?"

Everyone watched as Chloë leapt from her chair, giggled with delight and turned and gave Sister McGarrigle a big hug before replying, "Father, are you serious? Thank you so much! This is a dream come true!"

Father O'Sullivan replied, "I'll let Avery and Bentley explain what they have told me, and unless you change your mind, I would suggest that you begin to prepare yourself. I have a sneaking suspicion that your life will never be the same. Let's just hope and pray it's for the best my dear."

A couple of hours passed as Chloe listened to Avery while he outlined the plans for the super group and Bentley added her reassurances. Her joy and delight were interspersed with feelings of adventure and pure excitement. She fired questions at him in rapid succession at times and had to be cooled down by Sister McGarrigle. Her excitement was palpable, and who could blame her? He was outlining the opportunity and adventure of a lifetime. It was one that included fame and fortune. It was a surreal experience and as they wrapped things up and said their goodbyes both he and Bentley felt like they were witnessing something historical.

****

When everyone had long gone and Thomas sat alone on the recliner in his rectory, he reflected on the significance of the day. If only Avery and Bentley knew that Chloe truly was the child of Satan. As he prayed to God for His guidance, he asked Him in prayer to take Chloë under His wing. She was His now, and there was nothing more that he could do for her.

Thomas was certain that God had a plan for Chloë and that her birth was significant in His plans for mankind. He prayed one final time for her protection and safety, and for the hand of God to cleanse her blood of the demon's that flowed through her.

Chapter 23

Sam rolled towards Bethany, hoping he had at least another hour of sleep. He needed it. His restless night was punctuated with images of Patrick, with one dream that yanked him awake and temporarily left him disoriented because it was so real and frightening. He dreamt that Patrick was swinging Bethany by her ankles, crashing her head into the side of the dresser. This was crazy, and he knew he had to do something. He rolled back onto his back trying to reclaim the night, as Bethany slept soundlessly beside him. Suddenly, his cell phone came to life, vibrating insistently on the nightstand. He snatched it up and walked into the bathroom while he checked the caller I.D. He did not recognize the number. He thought about hitting the end button, but his cop instincts answered it.

"Detective Showenstein."

It was Jacob's wife, Josephina, and she was out of her mind: "Sam! Sam! I can't find Jacob! I don't know where he is, Sam! The synagogue is on fire and Jacob is not home! Sam! The police are here! Do you know where he is? Oh my God, Sam!"

Sam snapped to attention, instantly fully awake: "Josephina, calm down, I can barely understand you. What are you talking about a fire? Where is Jacob?"

Suddenly there was a bunch of commotion and loud scratching sound on the phone as if Josephina had dropped the phone. Then a man's voice was on the phone: "Is this Sam Showenstein?"

"Detective Showenstein, LAPD Homicide. Who is this, and what the hell is going on?"

Bethany appeared in the doorway of the bathroom, a

serious look of concern etched on her face. Sam held his hand up to her, indicating a plea to give him a second, while the man's voice on the other end of the phone continued: "This is Officer Jensen, North Hollywood Station. I think you need to get over here to your brother's house, Detective. The Temple Ivy Ann is currently engulfed in flames and your brother, Rabbi Jacob Showenstein, is missing."

Sam dropped the phone to his side, looked at his wife and said: "Get dressed Beth, and fast. The synagogue is on fire and Jacob is nowhere to be found."

****

Twenty minutes later Sam and Bethany came to a screeching halt in front of Jacob's house. There was just the one patrol car in the driveway. They made their way up the walk quickly and they were met in the driveway by an officer who introduced himself as Officer Jensen: "Detective, thank you for coming over so fast. Mrs. Showenstein is in hysterics."

"This is my wife, Bethany. Honey, why don't you go inside and comfort Josephina while I talk with Officer Jensen?" He waited until Beth made it into the house, then looked at Jensen: "When did the fire start?"

"It's been at least an hour. There's not much left of it, I'm afraid." Jensen hesitated before he continued: "There's a body, Detective. The talk on the radio is pretty gruesome."

Sam turned and ran into the house and found Bethany comforting Josephina in the living room. A female police officer was sitting on the edge of the recliner across from them. Sam walked up and knelt in front of Josephina; he tried to comfort her fears: "Listen Josephina, I know it looks bad. I'm going to go over to Temple Ivy now and see what I can find out. Hang in there my dear, it'll be okay. Bethany will be right here."

Her face was stained with streaks of tears and as the minutes clicked by with no word from Jacob, she seemed to slip further into an abyss. She nodded at him, indicating she'd be alright. She leaned into Bethany, staring down into the carpet. Sam stood up and squeezed Josephina's arm, gave Beth a reassuring look, and left the house.

Temple Ivy Ann was only twenty minutes away and Sam made it in thirteen with his emergency lights flashing all the way. The blaze was controlled by multiple fire trucks pummeling the fire with water from all directions. Sam headed towards the fireman with the white helmet amongst the sea of yellow-helmeted firemen.

"Chief, Detective Sam Showenstein. My brother, Rabbi Jacob Showenstein is missing. Is there anything you can tell me?"

"Detective, I heard you were on your way. I'm sorry about your brother, we're doing everything we can. We do have a body, I'm afraid. Impossible to identify at this point, as you could imagine. The body has been removed to the morgue. It could take days for identification, but it's quite possible it is your brother."

He knew it was Jacob all along. If it wasn't, he would certainly have contacted Josephina long ago to reassure her that he was okay. "Any conclusions at this point as to the cause of the fire?"

"Too early to tell, Detective. My men have the fire under control and should have it completely out within minutes. Then we can begin the process of investigating how this all started."

Sam continued, "Have any of the other Ivy staff been contacted and accounted for Chief?"

"Executive Director Wanda Levi is here now on site and has been able to reach the entire staff of Ivy. Everyone, that is, except your brother, Sam. I'm really sorry, but there is something else you need to know."

He looked into the Chief's eyes and he could see that this wasn't going to be good. He braced himself when he replied: "What?"

"As soon as we were able to get a section of the building's flames out, we entered the area and discovered the body. There was half of a burned support pillar impaled in the chest of the victim. A large pillar, Detective, must have been a foot in diameter. It was clean through the chest and out the other side."

"Okay, but you're talking about a beam that fell from the ceiling. That can happen?"

Now the Chief began to shift from one booted foot to the other before replying: "Oh shit, Detective, there's no other way to really say this other than just tell it to you straight."

"God dammit Chief, what is it?"

"Each of his eyes was replaced with a cut out in the shape of The Star of David."

****

For the rest of the morning, Sam stayed at Jacob's helping Bethany care for Josephina. Bethany tried to make some food, but no one was in the mood to eat. Sam's cell phone rang a few minutes before noon. It was the coroner's office. Thankfully, it wasn't the Chief Medical Examiner, Eunice Epp. He wasn't in the mood for her sarcastic attitude. Even though it was his brother who was the likely burn victim found in the synagogue, she would get a dig in. The Assistant Medical Examiner, Victor Robertson, was on the line.

"Sam, I'm sorry to have to be the one to make this call. We found a piece of jewelry burned into the right wrist. The body was cinder, Sam, and the bracelet was buried in the charred remains and what was left of it literally fell onto the autopsy table. Did your brother wear a gold bracelet?"

Sam found it hard to swallow and then even harder to speak: "Yes, he wore a gold chain bracelet with the chai symbol charm."

There was a brief pause on the other line before Sam heard Robertson reply: "I'm sorry Sam, it's Jacob."

He exhaled loudly before he replied: "Thanks Victor, for calling me personally. I'll be down before the end of the day to officially identify him and sign the paperwork. I don't want Josephina to see that."

"No problem Sam, we'll see you soon."

He was about to say goodbye, but asked Robertson: "Victor, do you know what the chai symbol stands for?"

"No I can't say that I do, Sam."

"It's Hebrew for 'living'. Kind of ironic, don't you think?"

****

A few days had passed since the fire and, though his life would be forever altered with the death of his brother, Sam never told Bethany about the Magen Davids embedded in Jacob's eyes or that the case was being investigated as a murder. Nor had he shared with her the discussion he had with their son regarding Patrick. He lay under the covers, deep in thought, as he waited for her to come to bed. The weight of what he carried in his conscience was getting too heavy to bear and he knew he would have to talk with her sooner, rather than later, about Patrick. His mind suddenly drifted to an image of Patrick driving the stars into the eyes of Jacob, his own eyes ablaze in flames as he pounded the metal blades into Jacob's skull. The macabre images disappeared when he heard his wife open the door to the bathroom and make her way to bed.

She crawled in beside him,snuggled close, and said: "You looked as though you were sleeping. I was hoping that was sleep. You could sure use it, Sam."

"Patrick has to be moved, Beth."

"Patrick? What are you talking about? What's he done in all of this chaos that would make you say something like that?"

"There's something not right with him. He has our son terrified to even go to sleep at night."

He watched as Beth leaned up on her side, resting on her elbow so she could look down into his eyes when she spoke: "Patrick has our son terrified. My God, Sam, what's going on?"

"He's a killer. Of animals, Beth. He leaves this house every single night and goes out into the neighborhood looking for animals to kill."

Now she was sitting straight up in the bed, clearly upset: "You're not making any sense? Do you know how crazy that sounds, Sam?"

"He's been doing it for years. For as long as Seb can remember. One night, years ago when Patrick was over on a sleep over, Seb followed him for several blocks till he entered the backyard of a house as if he knew what was in the backyard waiting for him. Seb snuck around in time to watch Patrick swing a large dog by its tail like a sack of hammers, over his head, and then slam the dog's head against a tree. Seb was scared out of his mind and raced all the way home."

"Sam, this is horrible, just horrible. For Seb to see that is just awful. I can't believe this." She fought back the tears, trying to maintain composure. Then the anger took over. Her eyes narrowed. "How dare him, Sam. To expose our son to that. I'm going to get his ass in this bedroom right now. We'll get him to explain himself."

"Hang on Beth, just calm down. We have to think this through more thoroughly. We can't just barge into his room and start accusing him of these things. He needs help Bethany. He's sick."

"You damn right he's sick. I'm sorry Sam, he's going to hear from me. Right now!"

He reached out and grabbed her arm before she had completely swung out of bed, "No, honey, wait. There's more. I think it's worse than that. Much worse."

"Worse, Sam? My God, what can be worse than that?" Then she realized at that second what he was referring to and it caused her to buckle over in the bed, clutch her stomach and sob. He could only watch as she sobbed into the pillow. He stroked her hair until, after a couple minutes of crying, she regained her composure and asked him: "Do you really think he's capable of murder, Sam?"

Sam knew it was going to upset her, but he had been thinking this over and over for the last few nights and replied: "I have no proof he is killing people, Beth, but my instincts are telling me he has and is."

She just stared at him, unable to speak, stunned at what he had just said. He continued: "Do you remember the night Chelsea was murdered? Okay well, I discovered him in the house Beth, cradling Chelsea's head and shoulders in his arms. He was covered in blood and the look in his eyes was of pure death. At the time, I just took it as strange behavior by a kid faced with the slaughter of his mother. Now I'm not so sure."

Beth continued to search his eyes for some sort of explanation, so he continued: "Three years ago, the murder of the Crittenden couple right behind Chelsea's house was just as brutal. There were no clues, no DNA, no suspects and no witnesses. Just days after Chelsea's murder, the day I had Patrick and Seb with me in the office. Do you remember that day?"

"Yes, I brought them to your office while I ran some errands. What happened in your office?"

Now he paused, looking down at the bed before looking his wife in the eye: "I fucked up that day, really fucked up. When you and the boys showed up unexpectedly, I was engrossed in crime scene photos on my desk. I never..."

"Oh Sam, for the love of David, you never what?" She demanded.

"I got called into a meeting with Bitters and left the boys alone in the office. Seb interrupted my meeting to tell me that Patrick was sitting at my desk staring at the pictures of his murdered mother's ripped body. I ran out, only to discover that Patrick wasn't just staring at the pictures, he was studying them, enjoying them like an adolescent boy would enjoy looking at porn. It was sick. Real sick, Beth."

"Oh my God, honey. What the hell are we going to do?"

"I know what we're not going to do, and that is we are not going to breathe a word of this to Patrick. The police or anyone else either. I have no proof, just a gut instinct, but it all makes sense in a sick way." Bethany was a well-known and successful plastic surgeon and she would know how to get the right help for Patrick. "He needs professional help Beth, by a doctor that can help him sort out the demons in his mind. Do you know of anyone? Until we can figure this out, I'd like to keep this between just you and me and the doctor, okay?"

"I agree Sam. He needs help whether he committed these murders or not. I'll talk to this doctor I know first thing in the morning."

Sam looked in her eyes for a brief second longer, enough to make her protest once again when he said: "There's one more thing."

"What?"

"Jacob's charred remains were pulled from the fire with a large beam piercing his chest."

"That's terrible!"

"Beth, he was also found with a Star of David impaled into each eye. He was murdered."

He heard her gasp as he continued: "When I left the Temple Ivy Ann to come back to you and Josephina, I stopped by the house to check in on the boys. Seb was sound asleep but Patrick was nowhere to be found. I picked his bedroom door, as he keeps it locked and I could smell a faint odor of smoke in the room. I checked his laundry basket and pulled a pair of blue jeans that was thrown on top and guess what?"

"They smelled of the fire?"

"Yes. Smoke. Exactly what I smelled when I was at the burning Ivy Ann. I think he had something to do with the fire and the death of Jacob. Or at the very least he was there. He was definitely there, Bethany."

He watched her shiver as if a cold breeze had crossed through the room. She lied down beside him and pulled the covers up over her shoulders and tight around her neck. She stared into the darkness of the bedroom, shivered once more and said to him: "Let's pray, Sam. Please."

****

Patrick stood in the hallway outside of Sam and Bethany's bedroom listening. He had heard every word that was said between them. They knew. They finally knew. He caught himself smiling, struggling to hold back outright laughter. Though he wasn't responsible for the death of Sam's brother Jacob, he was there! His master, the dark force that danced in his brain and controlled his destiny, manifested at the synagogue and revealed himself to that pathetic rabbi. The Jew didn't deserve the revelation. He was nowhere near worthy of that privilege. He wanted to feed him to the flames like a piece of kindling, but the master was out of his mind, bent on revealing the awesome power of the dark forces that rule this world and every other world that has ever existed. His father did allow him to inflict the coup de grace with the stars however. Now that was cool. He needed more though. Much more. His father was holding him back for some reason, and he didn't like it. No, in fact he hated it. He wanted to kill and kill and kill. His father kept repeating "In due time". "Fuck that!", he thought to himself. He was born to kill. Kill he must and he would kill. Starting right now, with the Showenstein family. Every last one of them, stinking Jew pricks. How dare that bitch Bethany think she can just pick up the phone and call one of her shrink bitch friends and say "Oh hi, Trudy. Hey I need a favor. You remember that lady friend of mine who had her head ripped from her body? Well, I'm pretty sure it was her son. Do you think you can 'fix' him? Yea! Great then. I'll bring him straight over in the morning. Thanks, Trudy. I owe you. I'll sew on some new tits for you, how's that?"

****

"Ssshh Beth for a second. Did you hear that?"

Bending her head back in the covers to look at her husband and strain to hear what he was talking about she replied: "No, I don't hear anything? What'd you hear?"

"I could have sworn I heard someone laughing outside of the bedroom door."

Sam swiveled his legs out of the bed and onto the floor. He grabbed his 9mm from its holster still resting on his nightstand and headed for the door.

He didn't even hear his wife call out: "Sam, please. Don't go out there. Sam!" He'd had enough of that bastard Patrick. The little prick was going to start talking. Especially when the inside of his mouth would taste the gun oil from the barrel of his pistol. That'll scare him into talking. The little prick is all he could think about as he reached for the bedroom door knob leading out into the hallway and Patrick's bedroom.

Then, he was brought back to his senses when his left arm was almost yanked from its socket, and his wife's seething voice seared through his brain: "Sam, no! Nooo!!!"

Chapter 24

Avery and Bentley spent a wonderful few days touring up and down Ireland, soaking in the countryside and the warm welcome they received from the local Irish townsfolk wherever they went. It was obvious to the locals that the two of them were like a couple of lovesick teenagers, and they both loved every minute of it. They were in love. The trip was exactly what they needed. They had great sightseeing during the day that ended with a glass of wine in front of a warm fireplace. Unfortunately, it was only for a few nights. They could have stayed for a month, but they had promised that they would be back. Their flight leaving Dublin for JFK was early, so they went out for dinner outside of their hotel in downtown Dublin. Rather than take a cab, they huddled together against the biting wind and walked up to the nearby O'Connell Bridge, where they took the advice of the hotel concierge and found the tiny little wine bar, D'Vine. It was a small and intimate restaurant with a great wine selection and Italian cuisine. They settled into a small table against the window facing the sidewalk where they could watch the people walking by. It was wonderful. They ordered wine and decided to share a pizza as both of them were more interested in each other rather than the food.

Avery's phone buzzed and he debated whether or not to answer it. "It's Best. Probably wanting to know if the priest changed his mind and called us back."

"Answer it honey, he's not the kind to call if it's not important."

Nodding his approval to her suggestion, he clicked on the answer button, "Avery Johnson."

"Avery, its Robert. Sorry to bother you, I'm sure you and Bentley are about to enjoy dinner, but I need a big favor from you both."

"You were bang on about us enjoying dinner. What's up Robert?"

"Would the two of you mind staying an extra day and flying to London in the morning?"

"What's going on in London?"

"The toughest test of your world famous charm awaits you in London. Are you up to the challenge?"

"You're talking about the Lockwood kid aren't you? His mother is resisting allowing Michael to come on board, is that right?"

"I'm afraid so. She is digging in her heels. She knows her old man is financing it, and she won't allow it. I need the two of you to go in there and convince her she's making a mistake."

He looked up at Bentley to get a read from her on whether she could stay an extra day and she nodded her approval, so he continued: "I guess we can give it a try. Will she know we're coming?"

"No, I felt it would be better if you just showed up unannounced. Otherwise, she would just refuse. Make it happen Avery. We're almost there."

"We'll do our best, pardon the pun."

Best laughed into the phone and replied before clicking off: "No worries, Avery. Thank you to you both. Call me when you're at the airport leaving London."

He pushed the end button on his phone and put it back in his pocket before asking: "Are you up for another sales call?"

****

The next morning, they arrived at Gatwick airport in London. They were not even given a second glance by Customs, and while they retrieved their luggage, they were met by the driver for Oakley Steel. As they were led outside of the airport to a waiting limo, a well-dressed gentleman stepped out of the back of the limo; his styled, white hair slicked back, giving him a look of extreme power. "That must be Sherman Oakley, father of Ann Lockwood" Avery thought to himself. As they approached, he extended his hand, "Avery Johnson, Sherman Oakley."

Avery took the extended hand, felt the powerful grip and replied, "Mr. Oakley it is nice to meet you. Let me introduce Bentley Paxton from *Music Talks* magazine."

He watched as Sherman turned to Bentley, took her hand in his and kissed it lightly before saying: "So nice to meet you, Ms. Paxton. Excuse me if I seem somewhat aloof, Robert Best did not adequately prepare me for how beautiful you are. Please, both of you, join me in my car as we go for lunch. I'm sure you have lots of questions before you meet my daughter and my grandson."

Avery observed how he referred to his daughter; there was a ring of annoyance in the tone of his voice. There was obviously no love lost between father and daughter. As he climbed into the back of the exquisitely adorned interior of the limo, Sherman continued: "I took the liberty of booking a reservation at the Wild Honey restaurant downtown. With traffic, we have a half hour drive. I will bore you with useless information on the city as we drive, then I will bring you up to speed on my grandson over lunch. You will need a good meal in you before you joust with my daughter. I'm just glad it's you and not me who has to convince her to let Michael leave for America."

After settling in at the Wild Honey, one of the top lunch destinations in London and surely the most expensive, Bentley ordered the Roast Pyrenean acorn-fed pork, while Avery played it a little safer with the Salad of Puntarella. Sherman surprised them both by ordering just a soda water. He chuckled slightly as he explained: "Like I said in the limo, it's you two that need your energy. Trust me. Seriously though, lunch is not something that I partake in. I have a big breakfast, then a solid workout on the weights and exercise bike before I even consider anything work related. My work day begins at 11:00 a.m. and ends at 9:00 p.m. By 6:00 p.m., I'm starving. It works for me. So let's talk about Michael, shall we?"

Avery looked at Sherman Oakley and knew that he was a very powerful man; someone who was used to getting his way and who would not accept anything less. Muscling Ann Lockwood through intimidation to convince her wouldn't work. Avery looked at Sherman: "Explain to me, if you will, the nature of your relationship with your daughter before we talk about your grandson."

"It's no secret that we are estranged. Have been for many years. She dislikes me considerably is a polite way of saying she hates my guts."

"Why is that? What happened that would cause such a divide in your relationship?"

"I'm sorry Mr. Johnson, but I don't see why discussing the issues between my daughter and I will be of any help to my grandson's musical career in Los Angeles."

"I'm afraid it is, Sherman. You're financing Vasallus. I think that has everything to do with it. In order for me to convince your daughter that Vasallus is an opportunity of a lifetime for her son, I need to be able to bridge your connection to all of this as a legitimate attempt by the grandfather to be involved, to use some of your riches to provide an opportunity for your grandson. This is what this is all about, right?"

"Of course it is. I love my grandson more than anything. Ann has never given me an opportunity to have any sort of a real relationship with Michael. Do I resent her for that? Yes, I do. That's another battle for another day between the two of us. This is about my grandson, and I want to do anything I can to help him."

Bentley, who had been quiet up to this point, stepped in: "Your daughter, Mr. Oakley, is very well off. Why doesn't she just finance Vasallus herself?"

"Please call me Sherman, Bentley. Yes, she likely has the money to finance the group, but it would take some liquidation and considerations with my trusts I have in place for Michael that I believe she would not want to enter into. That is why I think she would just stop Michael from even going to Los Angeles and push him in a completely different direction with his music career. You have to understand, both of you, the amount of money to make Vasallus work on the scale Best is talking about isn't just a few million dollars. That's pocket change, even for Ann. The mansion, cars, tutors and equipment will cost millions, make no mistake, but it's the marketing and promotional blitz packages on a worldwide scale that will cost hundreds of millions of dollars before a nickel of royalties, concert ticket and merchandise sales filter back. Robert Best does not plan to build an audience slowly and over time with Vasallus. He plans to come out of the gate with a worldwide audience already salivating at their arrival. He has the tools in place to launch the biggest marketing campaign ever seen for any event. That is why he wants the group out of the public eye for however long it takes to create the worldwide mass hysteria needed to rock the music world. Vasallus will be bigger than the Beatles, the Rolling Stones and Justin Bieber combined."

Avery was stunned. The scale of Vasallus and Best's big plans were never really revealed to him. He knew it would be big, but he had no idea it would be this big. He looked at Bentley before he spoke, and he could see a look of equal disbelief in her eyes. "Sherman, are you saying that the members of Vasallus will not perform as solo artists while they are working in the band?"

"That is correct. Best always approached this project in three parts. First, find the kids that had the kind of talent and the looks required to pull this off. Secondly, he would sequester them for a period of at least a year to come together as a group, to become closer than brothers and sisters. He did not want to risk any of them having ego or personality problems with any of the other members. They would have to be super-tight and completely comfortable with each other. During this time, music will be written for them that will harness their talent and allow them to change the face of music. They will practice and rehearse relentlessly in order to be perfect in every way when the band is launched. There will be no growing pains. They will be an incredibly well-oiled machine, ready to blow the world away with their talent."

"What is the third part?" Avery spoke what Bentley was thinking.

Sherman may have been old, but when he continued it was like he was a teenager, his excitement palpable: "A massive marketing and promotional campaign perfectly planned and executed. Television ads on all the major networks, full page advertisements in all the major newspapers around the world, billboards in every city and on every major highway, radio and much, much more. The campaign will be timed with the intent to build a controlled excitement, culminating in an epic explosion of hysteria when their songs hit the airwaves and the band takes to the stage for the first time. It will be insanity!"

"Holy shit, this is crazy. What if we can't get Michael? What if Ann does not allow him to join? Is your money contingent upon his involvement?" Avery asked.

"Not for me. The money Vasallus will generate will be staggering when it's in full swing. Best will not proceed unless he has Michael. The success of the band is critically dependent on the involvement of the seven members he has chosen. He has had this project in the works for many years, Avery. He has thought through every single scenario with meticulous attention to detail. He knows what he`s doing and what he wants, and that includes my grandson."

The hair on his neck bristled. The scale which Sherman had just described was almost spooky. He didn't know how to react to this, whether he should be excited or realistic that maybe this was just way over the top and therefore doomed to fail. He asked, "Why, Sherman? Why is Best so obsessed with creating this monstrosity of a super group?"

"That is something you'll have to ask him."

****

Avery was able to get Ann Lockwood to meet with him and Bentley after some lengthy persuasion. The woman was smart, and she would not miss out on an opportunity to sit down with one of the top music executives in the world to discuss the future of her son. Her home was only minutes from where they had had lunch with Sherman Oakley. Both of them were in awe at the size of such a place right smack in the middle of the city. It was spectacular. They were shown into a waiting area by the male servant, who took their jackets and offered them coffee or tea. They both chose red tea and sat in the expansive wing back chairs. They didn't have to wait long. A female of East Indian descent entered the room and asked them to follow her as Ms. Lockwood was ready to see them.

They were shown into a room that was large by any standards, complete with overstuffed leather chairs arranged in front of a massive fireplace with a large antique wooden table. The carved trim around the table was beautiful. On top of the table was an expensive tea set complete with three cups and saucers. They heard a voice coming from the hallway, and they turned to see Ann Lockwood walk into the room. Avery was expecting an older, plain-looking, aristocratic-looking British woman, but was surprised to see that Ann was very beautiful, not much older than he was and she had a smile that lit up the room. She surprised him again when she instantly gravitated to Bentley, giving her a hug before turning to him with her hand extended: "You must be Avery Johnson. To think my son has caught the attention of a big time American music producer is quite exciting. Please, both of you, have a seat and let's have some tea, shall we?"

Fully expecting their visit to have frost that would require finesse to be melted away before getting to the heart of the matter, it was completely the opposite. Ann Lockwood was radiant, pleasant and engaging. They both liked her instantly. He started by saying: "Thank you so much for taking the time to meet with us, Mrs. Lockwood. You have a beautiful home. We promise we won't take much of your time."

"Thank you Avery. Please, both of you, just call me Ann. I dropped the 'Mrs' years ago. Though I never remarried after the death of my husband, Dalton, I am realistic enough to know that life moves on and I have done so a long time ago.

Now, please, tell me why you are here and should I bring in Michael?"

"Not right away, if that is okay for the moment. Ann, I want to talk to you about an exceptional opportunity for your son. Hear me out, then you can ask me or Bentley questions. Is that okay?"

"Certainly, Avery, please begin."

The next thirty minutes passed with both he and Bentley explaining the ambitious new project featuring Vasallus without going overboard. He had still not quite wrapped his head around the full scope of it and there was no sense mudding the waters with Ann just yet. As he completed his presentation, he asked: "That is about it Ann. Do you have any questions?"

She seemed to sink back into the leather chair, deep in thought, before she finally replied: "Wow, this is big. Very big. Robert Best and Avery Johnson, the two biggest names in the music business, coming together to form the greatest rock band ever. Very big indeed. Do you really think I would stop my son from such an opportunity that he so richly deserves?"

"Your father, Sherman Oakley, is financing this entire venture."

"Oh Jesus Christ, Avery. That is the worst thing you could have said. I think we are just about finished here. I will have my assistant show you out. Good day." Ann rose to leave when Avery quickly replied.

"Wait, Ann, it's not what you think. Your father is strictly providing the considerable amount of capital required to make this project succeed."

"Not what I think? How could you possibly know what I think? My father is a money hungry prick who cares very little about his grandson. He sees an opportunity to make money in all of this and that is all it is to him. A business. He doesn't care about Michael. He never has. Why my father? There are plenty of billionaires in this world that would line up to fund this."

Now, Bentley stepped in, "Ann, I know what you must

think of us right now. We don't know exactly how Robert Best and your father came together in all of this, but we met with him. Just before we came here. Your father sees this as an opportunity to try and build something with Michael. A starting point. He fully accepts his failures and admitted them as much to us. He was forthright about the assessment that you would give him. He's not looking for you or Michael's redemption in all of this. He simply wants to help his grandson and he knows his money can help him. He loves Michael, always has, and he doesn't expect you to embrace or believe that. He just wants to help in any way he can."

"He can help by staying the hell out of our lives."

A voice from the other side of the room suddenly made its way into the conversation. It was Michael. "Mother, give him a chance. I believe him. I want this opportunity in America, but I also want to maybe get a chance to know my own grandfather in a meaningful way. You've protected me my whole life Mom, and I don't know why and what from, but I'm not a kid anymore."

"I'm sorry Michael, but I will not allow it. You're too young, son. You have your whole life ahead of you. There will be many more opportunities for you, I promise."

Michael was determined, "I'm going mother, and you can't stop me."

Avery felt responsible for the escalating tension between the mother and son, glanced at Bentley, then looked at Michael and said: "Michael, maybe you should listen to your mother. Maybe it's not the time."

Michael stepped closer to his mother, looking intently into her eyes before he said: "If I'm too young, then why would Father O'Sullivan allow Chloë to go to America? She messaged me on Facebook telling me of the great opportunity."

Ann looked at both him and Bentley, "Is this true? Is Chloë coming to America to join this super group?"

Nodding, he replied, "Yes, she is. Ann, it will be okay, I promise. The second you feel that Michael is in over his head, or you believe that this was a bad decision, you can take him home. You, and any of the other parents, for that matter, are welcome to visit the mansion at any time and for as long as you want. We're all in this together, Ann. In order for Michael to perform at his best, he needs to know the one person who loves him the most will support him and be there for him."

Tears began to well up in her eyes as she bowed her head to the floor, fighting the tears from brimming to the surface of her large eyes before spilling over like a large wave breaking through the levee. Sensing her mother's emotional fragility, Michael sat down beside her, wrapped his arm around her shoulders and gently said, "Mom, it's going to be okay. I love you. It's because of you that I even have this opportunity now. Your support for my music over the years has allowed me to be as good as I am and will be."

She lifted her head up and looked him in the eyes and said, "Oh sweetheart, there was nothing I ever did to make you what you are. You were born for this. This is your destiny. I love you so much son, and I will always be your biggest cheerleader and supporter. You go and join Chloë in America and make the world proud of you."

Smiling, struggling to control himself, his joy obvious, he replied, "Mom, I'd be happy if it was only you who was proud of me."

****

They stayed for a couple of hours after Avery explained how things would roll out in the next several months to Michael and Ann. The boy was highly intelligent; his questions were very mature for his young age. Eventually, he said his goodbyes to retire to his room to finish up some homework. Alone with Ann again, he touched Bentley's hand, rose from his chair and announced to Ann: "It's getting late Ann, and we must find our way to the airport. We have a flight early this evening."

"I will have my driver take you. Thank you, both. I feel much better now. You are good people, which is refreshing for your industry, apologies for the stereotyping. Promise me that you'll make sure Michael and the other kid's interests will always be the number one priority in all of this. Don't let Sherman turn this thing of beauty, this opportunity, into a business opportunity. These kids deserve better than that."

"I promise you Ann that will never happen. I'm putting my entire reputation on the line for this. I am taking this more seriously than anything I have ever done in my life."

She embraced Bentley, giving her a big hug and said: "You have a great guy my dear, but without a doubt he is a very lucky man to have such a wonderful woman like you. Look after Michael, please."

After the final goodbyes, they turned to walk out the door into the awaiting limo, when they heard Ann call out behind them: "Did you know that Sherman, just a few short months ago, began legal proceedings to gain custody of Michael? He claimed that I was unfit as a mother."

Bentley let out a gasp, "Oh my God, Ann. What happened?"

"Absolutely nothing. As quickly as he had filed the court action, he stopped the proceedings. No reasons were ever given to me or my attorney. I can't help but think that I now know why. You two have a safe flight home."

Chapter 25

Robert Best sat back in his Blackstar Studio's leather office chair and smiled. He had just received the call from Avery Johnson that Michael Lockwood would soon be on his way to Los Angeles. The final piece of his master plan, sixteen hundred years in the making, was now in place. His smile turned to laughter, causing him to stand up out of his chair for fear of falling off of it. He walked towards his office window to look down onto Clay Street in the Bunker Hill district of downtown Los Angeles. Traffic whizzed by, yet to be impeded by the ever present rush hour.

He could have gone to Dublin and London and snatched the kids from under the old priest's nose and the bitch Lockwood woman. He would have taken great pleasure in killing those two. However, there was a natural order of things that needed to be followed in his plan, even in his world. He would deal with O'Sullivan and Ann Lockwood in due time. Thinking of what he would do to them made him laugh again. These were joyous times and he needed to celebrate in the only way someone as powerful as God would celebrate. He would wreak havoc and death on mankind tonight.

He knew that natural disasters were occurring more frequently around the world as his adversary was putting in place the 'natural order' of things, towards bringing mankind to what He liked to call a 'state of correction'. If mankind only knew what was coming their way from their beloved God, they would repent and accept the Son of God as their saviour now and every single minute thereafter, exactly how it was written in their bible. Most of them would never get the chance to know Christ. They would follow him down his path instead, into eternal damnation. That reality was also written in their great book, like the option to follow Christ, but when he was done with them, following him would be their only option.

Man was born skeptical and that would be his greatest downfall. Men gathered in groups all over the world in whatever faith or belief they followed or didn't follow, and debated their fate or future from either a faith-based or scientific perspective. The complex human brain was just a mass that perpetuated confusion. He took great satisfaction in fostering that confusion, in planting seeds of doubt in everything they did in life, in encouraging them to make bad choices, bad decisions, embrace treachery and in infecting their brains with feelings of despair, sorrow, guilt and loss. It was the game he played every minute of every day with his adversary. His enemy encouraged hope, love, goodness and respect and the ability to prosper in everything they did. When God made man, He made a fatal mistake. The human soul was weak and easily influenced, making it easy prey for his evil influences. Most people couldn't sort out the confusion that reigned supreme in their brains so that they could make the choices God wanted them to make, to make-up for the one flaw He made: their souls. The brain was the key that unlocked the door to the soul. Infect and influence the brain's thoughts and voila, the soul was yours. If life was a sport, then the soul was the grand prize. It was what had fuelled the competition between him and his adversary through the ribbons of time. The fact that the end of the 'Great Game' was only just a few years away was incredible. He was very close. He not only would destroy mankind in the months ahead, but he would have their souls for all of eternity. He pressed his forehead against the glass of his window and laughed so hard that the entire office began to shake. He took a step back from the glass, feeling the power of his wickedness fulfill him, his darkness envelop him and wrap around him in a cloak of incredible power he knew he would need to release tonight in an act of total destruction and death. He also felt the presence of God around him, in fact he welcomed it, because he could also feel His fear and His sorrow for what he was about to do to His creations. Satan projected out to Him, to come along, beside him, his adversary, feel what I feel, let me feel what You feel to empower me, to strengthen me.

"Brace yourself man for I am coming", he thought with barely contained glee.

****

Terrorism was Satan's most favorite method of inflicting chaos, death and destruction. It spread fear through the confusion of the unknown. He loved it, and used terrorism all over the world. He gave this gift to the Muslim world; they embraced it like he knew they would, to combat the military might of the western civilizations.

Tonight, he would use it for his own selfish purposes. To celebrate his success, he watched and waited as six militants, strapped from head to foot in explosives, walked into six very public and populated buildings in Brisbane, Paris, Karachi, Copenhagen, Vancouver and Houston at the exactly the same time, down to the second, and detonated devastating blasts that created incredible destruction; the death toll was in the thousands. The resulting panic spread like wildfire through the civilized world, and governments scrambled their intelligence people to piece together the answers needed to satisfy the public outcry.

Terrorists groups scrambled almost as hard to distance themselves from any connection to the blasts, knowing that the military response would be crushing. Confusion reigned supreme in the days following the blasts. He soaked in the fear and panic that permeated around the world like an intoxicating drug. It gave him a high far better than any heroin addict could ever imagine or hope for. In time, the world would settle back down, their hate for the Muslim world increased, and life would continue. It always did. In the meantime, he had lots to prepare and get ready for. It was almost time for Vasallus. Very soon now.

****

To bring Patrick Benning into Vasallus was never a

problem, as the crazed little bastard had been at his side almost since his birth. However, he needed to continue his due diligence and allow the natural order of things to happen as it would, under his direction, of course. He would not need to have Avery Johnson meet with Sam and Beth Showenstein. It would be a formality anyways, and he suspected they would literally shove Patrick out the door to get rid of him. The aftermath of the bomb blasts had put the world on high alert, and in, Los Angeles, it meant a National Guard presence at all of the major buildings, airports, train stations and bus terminals. It would only last for a few more weeks before the fear would subside and normalcy would return. "This is the 'natural order' of things", he chuckled to himself.

Patrick was an extremely talented bass guitarist and drummer who would fill that role nicely with Vasallus. He was more physically developed than the other guys, and had a darker side to his personality than Juan, Connor and Michael. He would be the leader of this group. His real talent was in song writing. His abilities even surprised him, as his natural gifts continued to reveal themselves over the years. He could write the harmonies and lyrics to a hit song within a few hours. Over the last several years, he had been instructing Patrick to write songs for Vasallus that would give him a war chest of hits to keep Vasallus churning out hit after hit, week after week, month after month, year after year, though he knew he wouldn't need that long to inflict the final pieces to his plan. The lyrics were written and designed to infect the minds of the youth in a controlled and escalating fashion. Over time, the hit songs would make their way into the psyche of the adults, further imbedding the seed of his influence into society around the world in order to set the stage for the final act of his master plan. Keeping Patrick from self-destructing was a side effect that he had never planned on. He was becoming harder and harder to control. He would have to figure out a way to reign him in at some point before he threatened everything.

He decided to have Sam and Bethany, as well as Patrick, come to Blackstar Studios for their meeting. It would impress

Bethany, but he doubted anything could impress the detective. He was such a serious prick all of the time; he wondered how the plastic surgeon put up with him. Then again, he never could understand love. It was a useless feeling. The detective was still reeling from the death of his brother, so he would use that to generate sympathy with him in order to gain his trust.

He knew that word of Vasallus would soon be circulating through the social media channels. He would not be able to stop it. He didn't want to stop it, but he did want to make sure that all of the kids were securely under his physical control before the buzz really kicked in. He didn't think that the old buzzard O'Sullivan was staying up late in his parish office sending out tweets to the media, but word would get out. One mention to a family member or a friend somewhere down the line would light the match, igniting the fuse that would set off the explosion of hysteria. He was counting on it. But first thing first; the Showensteins.

****

The three of them made their way to Blackstar Studios for the 3:00 p.m. meeting as rush hour traffic was just starting to build, allowing them to make good time. They took Beth's Buick SUV and when they took her vehicle, she drove. She would not allow Sam to pull any crazy lane changing, tire squealing tactics in her vehicle. He could do that all he wanted in his police car. He was uncomfortable being a passenger in his wife's vehicle. She drove slowly, like an old woman, testing his patience like nothing else in their marriage. "Do you think you would consider using the left lane to pass this bozo? We're supposed to be there in fifteen minutes. We can't be late."

Bethany looked over at him, her face in a controlled smirk while she replied: "Patience, my dear. We have lots of time. We will be there by three o'clock, I promise."

"Not unless I hang out this window and shoot the tires out of this car in front of us. I should pull him over and write him a ticket for going slower than the posted speed limit!"

She laughed at his lack of patience and just kept driving behind the car in front of her without passing. Eventually, the driver turned off and the road ahead cleared. She continued to drive the same speed. "Honey, there is no one in front of us. What do you say; just give it just a little gas?"

Now she was getting a little annoyed, "Have you noticed that I have not hit one red light? The second I put my foot to the floor we'll lose the synchronization of the lights, and then we will be late, Mr. Big Shot Driver!"

He looked at her and couldn't contain himself any longer and burst out laughing. Patrick joined in on the laughter from the backseat, "Beth, don't listen to him, okay? You're doing great," before busting into another bout of laughter.

"Nice to see everyone is having a good laugh at my expense. I'll get the last laugh in about seven minutes."

Turning left onto Clay Street, then driving another two blocks, Sam saw the sign for Blackstar Studios on the right. He then looked at the dash clock and it showed 2:57 p.m. He snuck a look back at Patrick, who just shrugged, and over at Bethany, who was grinning like a Cheshire cat. He reminded himself to stop second guessing his wife. She was much smarter than he was.

****

They were shown into the studio boardroom by the comatose-looking receptionist that showed him and his partner into Best's office not that long ago, when they were investigating the murder of Jonathon Green. "It is a small world", he thought to himself as he took in the lush surroundings of the executive boardroom. He had no idea that Patrick's talents on the drums had attracted the attention of one of the biggest record producers in the industry. Then again, he didn't know very much about Patrick at all, it seemed. He knew he had cleansed his entire neighborhood of domestic animals. He didn't even know that until his son told him about it recently. "I wonder if Chelsea ever knew this dark side of her son?" That thought would have to be revisited another time, because he could hear Best make his way into the boardroom.

Best entered the boardroom dressed in an expensive suit, looking like a rich, successful music executive. He exuded success. "For Patrick's sake, I guess that is a good thing", Sam mused. The surprise was who followed him into the boardroom. The famous music producer, Avery Johnson, took a seat at the massive table after the introductions were completed. "Wow this is shaping up to be quite a meeting," Sam thought.

Best spoke first: "Let me start off by saying thank you Sam and Bethany, for bringing Patrick here today and meeting with Avery and I. I'm sure you have a million questions as to why we have called this meeting, but I promise you both that you'll have even more questions when we are done presenting the opportunity for Patrick here today."

Bethany spoke first and stole the words right out of Sam's mouth when she said: "Both my husband and I are quite taken aback that a major studio is interested in Patrick's drumming. No offense to Patrick, but we had no idea that he was such an accomplished percussionist. He never talks about it, nor did we even know he was playing someplace. His mother often bragged about how good he was, but we assumed it was no more than him excelling in his school band or pounding away in a garage with some friends. When Patrick told us that he knew his way around a drum kit, we didn't think much of it, until just a few days ago when you called. We are thrilled for him, but maybe we're just not sure how all this happened."

Best looked at Johnson, and smiled at Patrick before replying: "I tell you what Bethany and Sam, before we talk any further, why don't we let Patrick demonstrate to you how good he really is? Patrick, would you like to take the Showenstein's into the studio and give them a demo of your abilities?"

Patrick perked right up, "Sure, that'll be fun!

They gathered in the studio recording room, and Patrick went through a door and out into the session room, taking his place behind the massive drum set. There were guitars everywhere, dozens of them on stands along the walls. There was a beautiful, shimmering black grand piano in one corner and an electric keyboard in the other corner. Microphone stands were scattered throughout the session room. Various other instruments were neatly sitting on stands against the back wall. It was a surreal moment for Sam and Beth.

Avery spoke into a microphone on the huge mixing board full of knobs, switches and computer screens. He instructed Patrick to pick up the sticks and begin. What happened next simply defied reality, at least for Sam and Beth. Patrick picked up the sticks and began by twirling them in his fingers so fast they were a blur. He then began a drum solo like nothing Sam had ever heard, and he had been to more than his share of rock concerts over the years. He manipulated the various drums like a master, producing a sound that would cascade into the next sound and together, it was incredible to hear. Patrick was in his element, as his eyes were closed and his hands seemed to move effortlessly, magically, over the surface of the drums, the sticks moving so fast that they seemed to be invisible. He attacked the symbols in between, aggressively then subtlety, creating a lead-up to an ending that was spectacular. It was incredible; they were blown away by how talented he was. Suddenly, the deafening sound of the drums ceased and Patrick rose from the drum kit, stepped around and picked up a bass guitar. He plugged it into an unseen speaker and began to beat the daylights out of the strings with furious hand movements that created the most unique and coolest bass guitar sound. The notes were changing so fast that Sam could barely keep up with what he was hearing and what he was seeing. Patrick had world class talent, which was obvious. It bordered on musical genius; he was on par with some of the greats.

He stopped just as quickly as he ended the drum solo and moved to the grand piano. Sam could barely hear Best say: "Wait till you hear this," as he was stunned when Patrick began to manipulate the keys of the piano. It wasn't frantic like the drums or the bass guitar. He played the piano in the most passionate and heart rending way. It was beautiful, and watching him become one with the piano, Sam could feel his own heart struggle to hold back the tragic thoughts that Chelsea couldn't hear it. How wonderful it would have been to have both Chelsea and Steven Benning standing there. They would have been so proud to show off their son to their best friends for the first time. It was an intense and emotional moment for Sam.

Best brought everyone back to reality when he spoke into the mic and called out: "Okay, okay, Patrick. That's enough now. Let's get back in the boardroom, shall we?"

****

An hour and a half later, Sam and Beth, along with Patrick, walked out of Blackstar Studios stunned, in disbelief, but extremely thrilled and happy for Patrick. The plan for Vasallus laid out by Best and Johnson was incredible. They were completely blown away by what they had just seen and heard this afternoon. On the drive home, Beth could have been driving one hundred miles an hour through a red light, and Sam wouldn't have noticed nor would he have cared.

****

In the backseat, Patrick sat quietly looking out the side window, watching the fully engaged rush hour traffic inch along beside them. Beth and Sam were so excited, it was ridiculous. They were blabbing over and over like a couple of school kids. How they couldn't wait to tell Seb how great he was. Patrick didn't care one bit about any of that. Not at all.

All he cared about was later that night, sneaking out of the house, to kill. And it wouldn't be domestic animals, that was for sure.

Chapter 26

Thomas almost cancelled his trip to Rome after everything that had been happening with the recent terrorist attacks. Chloë leaving for America along with Sister McGarrigle, and the fact that he wasn't getting any younger, and the trips to Rome; it all took its toll. The subject matter was stressful and the Special Office of Spiritual Longevity or SOSL had been under attack recently. His eminence, Pope Benedict, shut down SOSL temporarily due to the scandal that broke out with Father Beckstead and the sensational murder of the young boy in his rectory.

He knew that the demon had orchestrated that whole setup with the boy, and it cost not only the tragic death of that young man, but also the death and the character of a very well respected priest. He had spent his entire life serving others, only to have his life snatched away, but also, his reputation and that of the church were taken away with the scandal. Thomas fully expected SOSL never to gather again, but in a move that surprised all of the members of SOSL, the Pope ordered the committee to continue. Thomas believed it to be a clear indication that the Vatican believed that things were not right in the world and they were not willing to concede to shutting down the secret committee of SOSL. They studied the increasing natural disasters taking place all over the world, in addition to the accelerated pace of terrorists attacks. The proliferation of unrest in the Middle East had everyone spooked, including the Vatican.

He grudgingly accepted to lead SOSL until someone else could be groomed for the position. The other members of the committee were each capable of taking over the responsibilities of the group, but that would mean a move to Rome and all of them resisted that as best they could, choosing to remain at their beloved parishes. Thomas accepted the request to lead the committee on a temporary basis, but he would not relocate to Rome, instead he would run things from his parish in Ireland. The information that came into the SOSL office from within the Catholic Church and information gleaned from outside sources was overwhelming. It was the job of the members of the committee to disseminate that information, determine what was relevant to the theory of a world ending as predicted in the Book of Revelations and report their theories to the Roman Curia. Their reports would lend a 'blue print' or working plan of action in the unlikely event that Armageddon did manifest itself into reality, and the Catholic Church could direct and inform the billions of Catholic believers around the world in a meaningful way.

The people around the world were beginning to feel the stress of the numerous terrorist attacks, global warming and natural disasters, the most recent tsunami in the Philippines and the six terrorist explosions that delivered a devastating toll on human life. There was a sense in the world that the life and the place that they lived in could no longer be taken for granted. There was an underlying feeling permeating throughout the population that there was now a real danger which threatened everyone's way of life.

Thomas arrived in Rome and made his way to the Vatican, where he would prepare for the two day SOSL conference. This conference would be different than any he had attended in the past. He would focus on the threat of the evil forces that was wreaking havoc around the world and that had nothing to do with God's fury. He had seen and been confronted by the Dark Prince, as the Bible called Satan. He had felt the demon's wickedness in his soul, but yet he survived while others around him did not. He did not understand this, he only knew that God still had a plan for him on this earth.

On day one of the meetings, Thomas would welcome the

newest member of SOSL, Father Jeremy Winters from Brooklyn, New York. Father Winters was brought in to replace Father Beckstead after his terrible death. Father Winters was a born and raised New Yorker through and through. He bled Yankee pinstripes and wore his heart and soul on his sleeve. His tireless community work during some of New York's darkest times had given him the respect of the Church hierarchy and he was dearly beloved by his parish congregation in one of the tougher neighborhoods of Flatbush. Thomas chose Winters personally for SOSL because he was as tough as nails and he could reach into the most troubled of souls, help restore their faith and turn them back into productive and contributing citizens. He had toured the United States penal system; working with some of the most notorious criminals locked away, never to see the light of day again, and had worked wonders. Not only was he changing the darkest of hearts into beacons of light, he was giving these condemned inmates, cast aside by society, an opportunity to make things right with God and the people that loved them. Words are an extremely powerful tool, and Father Winters exemplified this in every sense. He understood that the only thing that these death row inmates had left to give was their spoken word. They could choose to live out the rest of their lives in misery, trapped in the knowledge of what they had done combined with the guilt of those they had hurt, or they could choose to speak words of contrition and remorse to the victims, their families and society as a whole. He taught them not to seek forgiveness from those they had hurt, but to forgive themselves for what they had done and then reach out to those they had hurt and let their words heal the wounds embedded in the souls of their victims and their loved ones.

There was, however, another skill Father Winters was well known for within the Catholic Church. He was the most experienced priest in the Church when it came to performing exorcisms. Over the past thirty years, Father Winters had performed over five thousand exorcisms in just about every part of the world. His success had been well documented by the Vatican. His ability to connect to the demon residing in the soul of his victim was astonishing. Thomas spent a lot of time researching Father Winters' career in casting out demons on behalf of the Church. He was a fearless man and he did not hesitate in direct confrontations with the demon, instead going after the evil spirits with the same tenacity as a cornered tiger does when surrounded by tribal warriors.

Father Winters had challenged the youth of his congregation, who often talked about visiting and touring Ireland, to fundraise the $3,500 required by each of them to make the trip. He was surprised and richly rewarded when seventeen of the kids raised more than $75,000, allowing twenty-two kids in total take the trip of a lifetime. It was on this trip when Thomas arranged to have the group come and visit Dublin, with his congregation hosting them in Balbriggan. The families of his parish billeted the kids for two nights, giving them memories to last a lifetime. It was during this trip that Thomas had an opportunity to meet with Father Winters and to express his wish to have him join SOSL. Once he got past the shock and intrigue at the Vatican's keen interest in the end of times, he contacted Thomas with his enthusiastic endorsement in joining the group.

Thomas was fascinated by Father Winters' many encounters with the demon. Listening to him in the Vatican library the day before SOSL was to meet, he realized that the stories about him were true, and he was fearless.

"Father O'Sullivan, do you believe in Hell as fervently as you believe in Heaven?"

This question started an afternoon discussion that stretched into the early evening, where Father Winters explained that ninety percent of exorcisms were simply exercises in revealing the true identity of what troubled the soul of the person claiming to be possessed. They were a mixture of victims of tremendous abuse, psychologically damaged minds, nutcases or outright frauds. Then there was the ten percent, the truly possessed victims who were innocent souls, who, for whatever reason, had attracted the attention of the demon and he had come to rest in their physical bodies to take over their souls. Father Winters' success lay in his strategy of challenging the demon to reveal itself. Essentially, he would outsmart the demon into revealing itself and then Father Winters would attack it with scripture, isolating the demon from the victim and then casting it out and back to Hell from whence it came.

When Thomas revealed his encounters with the beast, it shocked Father Winters. "I have never met anyone, nor have I experienced firsthand, a direct encounter with the demon. It has always been through a victim hosting the demon. This is incredible Father O'Sullivan, please tell me more." Father Winters asked.

Thomas went on to tell Father Winters of his very first encounter with the demon almost fifty years ago, while enroute to his very first SOSL meeting after completing his training and the acceptance of his vows. The encounter at the airport in Rome caused Father Winters to gasp, then Thomas shared his second encounter in the elevator at the hospital when he was on his way to see Katherine McClosky, and then the physical confrontation in the delivery room when Chloë McClosky was born. His most recent encounters, he told Father Winters, were at the performance between Chloë and Michael Lockwood at the Academy, and the phone call he received from the demon after the slaying of Father Beckstead. Thomas explained that he believed it was the beast who murdered the young boy in Father Beckstead's rectory, as well as disguised his death as a heart attack.

Father Winters rugged, New York features seemed to soften the longer they talked. He was taken aback by these encounters: "Father O'Sullivan, that is incredible. Why do you believe all of this is happening, and to you?"

He paused for a second longer than normal, touched his fingertips in front of his face, then looked up at Father Winters and said: "I believe it's tied into SOSL and my involvement. I believe he is fearful of what this committee is doing, which lends me to believe that he is also active in the world to end the human race before God's final judgment. I believe, Father Winters, that Satan is in a race against time with his greatest enemy, our Lord Thy Saviour, to capture as many human souls for his cauldron in Hell before God wipes the slate clean with the Armageddon."

****

Back in his room, Father Winters sat down in the only chair in his tiny dorm in the Vatican and thought about all that he and Father O'Sullivan had talked about that day. It was incredible to think that the Vatican leaders not only truly believed that the end of times were near, but also that Satan was feverishly at work to end the human race before God's judgment. He always knew, not only as an ordained Catholic priest, but as a human being who read the word of God every day, that the world would end as they knew it and the Tribulation and return of Jesus Christ as King would begin. As a soldier of God and a warrior against His enemies, the thought of a direct encounter with the demon did not scare him. He had met him many times over the years, but in a much different way than Father O'Sullivan. His thoughts were suddenly interrupted by a knock at the door. "Who could that possibly be?" he thought. "Father O'Sullivan, maybe, to further discuss what we have been talking about all day? Doubt it, as he seemed very tired when we said goodnight to each other. He must be fast asleep by now." He opened his dormitory door to find a young cleric standing there: "Excuse me Father Winters, there is an urgent call for you from New York. Please follow me and I will show you where you can take the call in private."

He followed the young priest. Deep concern and worry of the unknown began to build inside him. "What had happened back home?" he wondered. A few minutes later, after taking the stairs down one floor, they walked to the end of a narrow hallway where he was shown into a small office. After he closed the door behind him, he picked up the phone: "Father Winters, how may I help you?"

A voice, dark and demonic, filling him with terror, spoke

to him: "Did you enjoy your little talk today with Father O'Sullivan?"

Father Winters regained his composure and struggled to control his swelling anger: "You enjoy this, you pathetic piece of garbage."

The roar of laughter was deafening through the earpiece of the phone, and then the gravelly demonic voice continued: "O'Sullivan is a liar trying to trick you into his little committee of fools. He thinks that meeting and talking about what God has in store for man is doing God's will. It is ludicrous. I would have thought that a priest as smart as you would not fall for this drama."

He could barely contain his hatred when he replied: "You know nothing about what God has in store for man! It is you who is the great deceiver and liar! It is your downfall and will be your demise."

Again, the roar of laughter was deafening: "I'll see you soon priest!"

Before Jeremy could reply, the phone went dead. He slammed the receiver down, his anger causing his body to shake. He gripped the edge of the desk to steady himself. What did he mean by "I'll see you soon"? He needed to speak with Father O'Sullivan about this immediately. He left the room and found the young priest who brought him sitting in a chair down the hallway. He stood and said: "Father Winters, I hope all is well. May I show you back to your room?"

He looked at the young priest suspiciously, as if he was part of this madness, but had no time to debate it so he just replied: "No, will you please take me to Father O'Sullivan's room? I need to speak with him at once."

"Certainly, you can follow me this way."

After about ten minutes of navigating several floors and hallways, they stood in front of a door and the young priest knocked on it. There was no response, so the priest called out: "Father O'Sullivan, it's Father Doucette. I am with Father Winters. He would like to have a word with you."

About thirty seconds passed when they heard a groggy

response from Father O'Sullivan, "Certainly, give me a minute to find my robe. You may go Father Doucette, and have Father Winters enter."

Father Doucette turned to Jeremy before departing and said: "When you leave, Father Winters, go to the end of that hall, down two floors and your room, of course, is A211. May I be of any additional help Father?"

"No, thank you. You have been very helpful. I will let myself in."

Jeremy watched as Father Doucette disappeared through a door at the end of the hall, and he then knocked on Father O'Sullivan's door and called out: "May I enter Father?"

"Yes, please come in."

Jeremy entered and stepped into the courtyard of Hell itself.

****

The stench in the room was unbearable. Jeremy clutched at his mouth to cover it; he could feel his reflexes wanting to wretch. The room was not a tiny dorm similar to his, but an entire floor had opened up in this room. There was no color to anything in the room, it was all black and white. Father O'Sullivan's paperwork was sitting neatly stacked on the dorm room desk. There was no sound, just a gut wrenching smell. It was the smell of death.

"Father O'Sullivan, its Father Winters, where are you?" It was eerily quiet as he made his way around one corner after another of the ever-expanding room.

Then a voice from down the hallway called out: "I'm down here Father. Please come." It was Father O'Sullivan.

Jeremy walked down the hallway towards Father O'Sullivan's voice, but the hallway kept getting longer and longer. There was no end. The faster he walked, the longer the hallway became. The loss of color in the walls and floors made him feel like he was back in a prison on the way to counsel a condemned killer, but this was no prison.

The terror he felt was replaced by a sense of fear for Father O'Sullivan. He called out once again: "Father

O'Sullivan. Father O'Sullivan!"

"I'm in here Father. Please hurry, I'm hurt."

A door at the end of the hallway suddenly opened, revealing a bright light, blinding Jeremy for a brief second, then he heard Father O'Sullivan once again: "Hurry Father!"

Jeremy ran down the hallway which once again, continued to stretch further and further away the harder he ran. He cried out in frustration: "Father, I cannot reach you." Jeremy knew he was tightly wound in a nightmare that would kill him and Father O'Sullivan if he didn't act soon. He reached down to his chest and gripped his hand around the three inch cross that hung down the front of his chest and prayed out loud: "Lord God, provider of all of our needs, hear my words. Cast out the demon that has entered your holy place. He does not belong here, Lord. Protect us, Lord, from the beast that stalks us now."

Jeremy opened his eyes and he was suddenly in a very small room unlike the never-ending room from which he had come. It was Father O'Sullivan's dorm room. He looked over and saw Father O'Sullivan lying awkwardly on his bed, unconscious with his face covered in blood. He cried out: "Father!"

"Don't worry yourself about O'Sullivan, Father. The old fool can't be saved now. Now, you, I would start worrying about."

Jeremy glanced over to the chair in the corner of the room opposite the bed where Father O'Sullivan lay and received confirmation that he was in Hell. A creature sat in the corner, nowhere close to being human, but a hideous beast whose demonic eyes burned bright red. It screamed at him: "O'Sullivan's heart just gave out; the excitement got to be too much for him. I was looking forward to tearing him to pieces, so instead I will have to settle for the rookie. You will die, Winters and I want you to bring one thing with you when you do. I want you to see something that will replay itself for an eternity in your head. Enjoy."

A sudden bolt of pain entered his head and it was so

intense, that it brought him to his knees. He slumped forward, gripping the sides of his head with his hands. The pain gripped the inside of his head like a vise as he saw an image flash across his brain to his eyes. It was his parish youth congregation. They were meeting like they always did on Wednesday nights, to play basketball behind the church before going inside for fellowship with the youth pastor. This time though, they weren't playing basketball or having fellowship. They were screaming in pain, trapped in a burning building. His beloved parish was on fire! "No! No! Please stop it. Stop this nightmare! You're a liar, beast! Your trickery will not work with me; I know you, I've met you many times. You're a coward."

He watched as the beast lifted its hulk off of the tiny chair. Its ugly grey and black skin was slimy, giving its massive muscled frame a shimmering reflection. Its arms were huge and long with claws at the end of them, and one of them was now reaching out for him. Before he could even react, he felt the incredible force of the beast wrap itself around his throat. His glowing red eyes burrowed into his as he screamed: "You're a fool, priest, a weak, pathetic fool. How can you explain my presence in the holiest place in the world? If I can appear in the Vatican and kill a priest at will, who can stop me? Do you think your experience casting out spirits in worthless souls qualifies you to have any sort of control over me? I am the truth Father. It is I who will be your master for an eternity." A demonic laugh erupted from jaws housing huge fangs, that dripped saliva all over itself like an out of control Tyrannosaurus. The cackling boomed through the room, causing the large wooden cross, attached to the wall, to drop to the floor.

Jeremy closed his eyes, knowing that his death was only seconds away, and prayed: "Heavenly Father, Your Greatness is all that matters to me, Lord. Free my soul from the grip of Your enemy and bring me to You, Lord."

The grip around his neck loosened and he fell hard onto the floor. He looked upwards and watched as the beast began to scream uncontrollably like it was dying. He watched as it flexed his entire body, wings spreading from wall to wall. Its mis-shapened head thrashed from side to side. It began to chant words in Latin. Jeremy recognized the words and knew the beast was under the control of the Lord Almighty. He had heard them before. They were random words spoken by a tortured soul. "Intereo intereo intereo intereo. EGO ago. EGO ago. EGO live. Die Intereo Die. Die intereo intereo intereo. EGO ago. EGO ago. EGO live. Die Intereo Intereo." (Die die die die. I live. I live. I live.Die Die Die.Die die die die. I live. I live. I live.Die Die Die).

Jeremy continued to pray, but this time in Latin, knowing that the beast did not like being spoken to in that language: "In nomen of Filius Jesus Sarcalogos quod Flamen , EGO to order vos dimitto procul once.The Senior to order is. Sit Righteous quod Sit Sanctus. Temerarius Suus to order Everto!" (In the name of the Son, Jesus Christ and the Holy Spirit, I command you to leave at once. The Lord commands this. He is Righteous and He is Holy. Heed His commands demon!)

The beast screamed again and again. The sound was so loud that Jeremy thought his ear drums would explode. Suddenly, the room went entirely dark except for a glow that surrounded the creature. The room filled with a bone chilling cold. "What is happening?", Jeremy wondered.

The screaming from the beast turned into a roar, and its massive wings snapped back into place with a whoosh. It was now furious, and seemed to come out of its spell and lock its fiery red eyes onto his. Its massive claw swooped down and picked him up once again by the throat, holding him to the ceiling. Jeremy's air supply was choked off and he could not breathe. He desperately tried to suck air into his lungs, to no avail. The beast burned its eyes into his soul. The images of the dying youths in his church returned. The fire that had engulfed his church and was burning the kids alive was on full display in the front of his brain, vividly captured by his eyes. He knew in his soul that it was the truth and that he had tragically lost his parish and many people had died. He now welcomed his own death. "Kill me now, demon, but know that the Lord God is coming for you. He will not stop until the earth is cleansed of your filth, treachery, and deceit."

With a movement he could not see, but only hear, the beast drove his other claw straight into his chest. He felt his lungs burst and the blood spew from his mouth. The beast roared: "See you in Hell, priest!"

Before he died, he managed to smile back at the creature and was even able to whisper the words, "I don't think so."

****

The Vatican medics desperately worked on Father O'Sullivan as they rushed him to nearby Gemelli Hospital from his dormitory room, where he was discovered badly beaten. He was alive, but barely, and any other seventy-six year old man would not likely have survived, but somehow this one had. The medics who worked on him on the way to Gemelli felt more compelled than normal to save this man. He was someone very special, they could feel it.

The destroyed body of Father Winters was removed from the Vatican quickly and quietly. Vatican leaders would keep the news of the attacks on Father Winters and Father O'Sullivan from ever reaching the public. The thought of such a vicious attack in one of the holiest places on earth, was unthinkable.

Chapter 27

The ambulance carrying Father O'Sullivan from within the Vatican to nearby Gemelli Hospital had an unknown guest that insisted on boarding the ambulance along with the medics. He introduced himself to the paramedics as Father Adalberto Gallo, and he said he would accompany the wounded Father O'Sullivan and act as the official Vatican spokesperson.

They arrived at the emergency entrance to Gemelli within minutes after leaving the Vatican and entered the hospital via an open door for ambulances. The driver entered the emergency area, barely slowing down, and came to a screeching halt that caused Father Gallo to fall forward violently. He was able to grab onto a safety handle at the last second to brace himself. He noticed the two medics did not reach out and, other than bouncing from side to side, barely moved; they seemed used to the jolt. Father O'Sullivan's gurney was strapped in securely, so he never moved. The rear doors were opened by waiting orderlies and the medics pulled Father O'Sullivan out and quickly pushed him into the hospital. Adalberto made sure he was right alongside of him all the way to the waiting doctors, mindful not to lose sight of the job at hand.

The job at hand was to ensure that the attending doctors and nurses worked quickly to save Father O'Sullivan's life, but also to ensure that no one else outside of the attending staff came into the area outside of the operating room. No information of the attack was to leave this room, and he planned to make sure that happened. No one questioned his presence. Everyone knew the Vatican was extremely private about their affairs. Many times, they had received Vatican personnel who had required emergency services and there was always an unknown priest nearby to watch over things. They were used to this and, as such, did not ask any questions when he milled about among the administrative staff outside of the surgery room where Father O'Sullivan was being worked on.

It did not take long for Adalberto to confront the first news person who came running into Emergency to inquire about the patient who was brought in from the Vatican. Among all of the tourists that were a constant outside of the Vatican, the news reporters lurked in the shadows, searching for a breaking story from the holiest place on earth. There was always some sort of newsworthy story that was made available to them on a daily basis. The age of the Pope was always a concern, and the reporters kept a close watch on his health. If his Eminence had the hiccups, it was news, and therefore, it would be made available to news agencies around the world by the reporter on the scene.

Today, an ambulance had come screaming into a private entrance in the Vatican, and left minutes later with sirens wailing. That started a firestorm of rumors of who had fallen ill inside the Vatican that needed emergency hospitalization? Did the Pope have a heart attack? Did a Cardinal pass away? The only way to find out faster, was to go directly to the hospital and determine what was going on. The reporter who came barreling into Emergency demanding answers to his inquiries was quickly referred to Adalberto, who stood nearby in anticipation of this event.

When the reporter held his recording device up to Adalberto's face, he could see that his credentials indicated he was with the BBC. It was a little unusual that a BBC correspondent was on the scene before any of the local scribes simply because they outnumbered international reporters five to one. He reminded himself that the international agencies had better and higher up sources inside the Vatican than the locals did, much to their frustration, so they usually got the scoop first. CNN and the BBC had informants in every department within the walls of the Vatican. "Tonight is no different", sighed Adalberto.

He dispatched the reporter with his usual polished spin, which satisfied the reporter temporarily. "He'll be back soon enough", he worried. Alone for a moment, he reflected on what he knew of the priest in surgery: nothing. Father Thomas O'Sullivan was a ghost in the Vatican, yet he made several trips a year to it. He had to be part of a secret committee or something kept very quiet within the Vatican. The medics acted like he was some sort of God in the ambulance. "That was kind of weird", he thought. What was he doing in the Vatican? "Well it likely won't be for much longer because the buzz around the surgery room was that he won't make it out of surgery." Adalberto was still waiting for the surgery to end and the doctor to emerge with an update so he could brief his bosses, who were eagerly awaiting his call.

Ten minutes later, a nurse emerged from the surgery room, disrobing from the surgical gown and mask as she walked towards him. She appeared badly shaken.

"Father Gallo, I am the head nurse of surgery, Agnese Moretti. Surgery is just ending and Dr. Conti will be out momentarily to brief you on the patient." She then stepped around him and continued down the hallway. Before he could even call out, she had already disappeared down the hallway. "What was that all about?" He thought, "she was acting very weird." Then he heard a voice behind him.

"Father Gallo, I presume?"

Adalberto spun around to see the surgeon standing behind him, almost bumping into him as he did so. "Dr. Conti, the nurse Moretti informed me, that you would be briefing me on Father O'Sullivan. How is he doing Doctor?"

"He is alive, Father, but I can't tell you it was because of something we did to save him. He arrived with barely a pulse from multiple blunt traumas to his upper body, including his skull. The amount of internal bleeding was very high. His heart stopped during the surgery to release the pressure on his brain. He is a seventy-six year old man, and his injuries would easily have killed someone forty years younger than him in top physical condition."

He looked at Dr. Conti with a look of shock before replying: "Dear God, will he survive?"

"The old priest has enough brain swelling to kill an ox, nine broken ribs, multiple facial fractures, a broken wrist, severe cuts and lacerations, yet he is alive. There is no explanation why he is alive, Father."

"It is a miracle Doctor. How long will he be in a coma?"

"Why don't you go in and ask him yourself? He had to be restrained from climbing off of the gurney. He demanded to see another patient by the name of Father Winters. I have been a surgeon for thirty-seven years, and I have never seen anything remotely close to what I just witnessed in that surgery room. This is beyond a miracle, Father Gallo. This is a downright intervention by God!"

****

All Chloë could think about since the day Mr. Johnson and Ms. Paxton left Dublin was going to America to be a part of the group they were forming. It was so exciting, she could hardly sleep. She would be leaving for Los Angeles within a week and she had planning to do. She had to decide what she would bring for clothes, and shoes etc: "Oh my gosh, how will I fit everything into two suitcases!" she wondered. She needed to see if she could borrow some suitcase space from Sister McGarrigle.

Chloë's best friend at the Academy, Trish Byrne, was to come by her dorm room after classes ended because they were going to take a walk into the village for some shopping. She needed to pick up some hygienic products at the drug store. Chloë loved going to the drug store, because she liked to try on some of the makeup from the samples on display. One time, she forgot to wipe it off before she got back to the Academy and, boy, did she catch it. Sister McGarrigle was the first to discover it, and then she was marched into the office of the Abbess and Sister Doyle, where a scolding took on a whole new meaning. Sister Doyle, whom had replaced Sister Agnew after her passing, was void of any compassion and administered discipline at St. Mayo Academy like it was a maximum prison. Chloë and Trish, longtime residents at the Academy, had become shrewd in the art of non-detection. They knew the Academy and its routines inside and out, so over the years they were able to make the best of difficult times. Thankfully, her singing career took her away from the Academy often, and now she would be leaving the boarding school for good and it couldn't be fast enough. She felt bad for her friend and would try to convince Sister McGarrigle to have Trish come and visit her in America.

There was a knock on the door and she could hear Trish's voice, "Chloë open the door, I have heard some very bad news!"

"What the heck is she talking about?" thought Chloë, as she swung off of her bed and opened her dorm door. Trish had a look of panic on her face. "Chloë, I have heard that something terrible has happened! I heard some nuns gathering outside of the office of the Abbess, and they were all going on about Father O'Sullivan. I think something has happened to him!"

Chloë could instantly feel her heart drop into the pit of her stomach, "Something has happened to Father O'Sullivan? That cannot be!" She pushed past Trish and out into the hallway, leaving her dorm room door wide open: "Come on, we must find out what has happened!"

Tears were welling up in her eyes as she made her way down the hallways of the Academy in search of Sister McGarrigle. Father O'Sullivan was like the father she never had. He just had to be okay; he had been there for her all of her life. He had been the biggest supporter of her music. "Please God, please take care of him and make sure he's okay", she silently prayed to herself. She turned to Trish, "We have to find Sister McGarrigle! She will know what has happened!"

Trish put her hand on her best friend's shoulder and replied: "It's okay, Chloë, we will find her. I'm sure Father O'Sullivan is just fine. Calm down a bit, okay? You're freaking out."

Chloë turned and headed off to the office of the Abbess, almost bowling over another student. Her best friend was right on her heels. They had to cross outside, through the courtyard to the administration building, where Sister Doyle's office was located. The panic in her stomach was rising as they made their way into the building and up the stairs to the office of the Abbess. You were never allowed to just barge into the office of the Abbess and Sister Doyle. You were either specially invited, or you were brought in by a Sister for disciplinary reasons. Chloë didn't care. She needed to find Sister McGarrigle. They made their way to the office of Sister Doyle, when they were stopped by an administrative nun who asked: "Children, may I ask what you are doing here? You know full well that you are not allowed up here unless you have been summoned. Now, you must leave at once."

Chloë looked defiant as she stared back at the nun and replied: "I'm not leaving until I speak with Sister McGarrigle or Sister Doyle. Now, you will tell me if either of them are here or will I look for myself!"

"That is impossible, I'm afraid, now once again, I am instructing you to leav…" the nun was cut off by a voice from Sister Doyle's doorway. It was Sister McGarrigle.

"That's okay Sister Morgan, I will talk with them. Chloë, please come in. Trish, I am afraid I will need you to return to your room. We have some personal matters to talk to Chloë about."

Chloë looked back at Trish and mouthed the words: "I'll be okay."

Chloë followed Sister McGarrigle into the office of the Abbess. Sister Doyle was sitting behind her desk. She was a very large woman and, with her habit, she seemed to fill half the room. "My, young girl, you seem to be a little bit troubled. Please, have a seat."

"Can you please tell me what the matter with Father O'Sullivan is? I have heard that something has happened."

Sister Doyle looked at Sister McGarrigle as if to indicate for her to take it from here. Sister McGarrigle gave her a look of deep concern and then said: "Chloë, Father O'Sullivan has been attacked by unknown assailants in the Vatican."

Cutting her off, Chloë blurted out: "He was attacked by intruders in the Vatican? That is impossible! Is he okay, Sister?"

"We only found out ourselves, Chloë, just minutes ago. He has been rushed to the hospital with life threatening injuries and, at this time, that is all we know. I am sorry Chloë, I know he means so much to you."

She buried her hands in her face and began to sob: "Oh please, dear God, take care of Father O'Sullivan. Don't let him die!"

Sister McGarrigle came over to her chair, knelt beside it and wrapped her arms around Chloë, comforting her. "We have all prayed for Father O'Sullivan since we heard the news, Chloë. You keep doing the same."

She lifted her face from her hands and looked up at Sister McGarrigle: "If it wasn't for Father O'Sullivan, I wouldn't be here right now. He brought me to you, Sister. I would be in some foster home somewhere, without ever having the opportunities that have been given to me in music."

"I know, my dear. Let's just pray for the best and for his recovery, so you can tell him that yourself."

"I want to go to Rome at once to see Father O'Sullivan in the hospital! I need to be there, Sister. I need to be there with him. I could never live with myself if he died and I wasn't there. Please Sister!" Chloë pleaded with Sister McGarrigle.

Sister McGarrigle looked into Chloë's eyes and replied, "Oh Chloë, I know you love him so, but you have so much to do to prepare before you leave for America. We both do. We will pray non-stop for his recovery, and the second there is a change in his condition, they will let us know. I promise."

"I am not going to America until I know that Father O'Sullivan is going to be okay and I have seen him. I cannot even think about music and America until I know in my heart that he is going to be okay."

Sister McGarrigle rose from kneeling beside Chloë and

looked over at Sister Doyle, who nodded in return. Chloë returned to burying her face in her hands and let the sobs take over, her shoulders shaking as she cried.

Sister Doyle's voice pierced through her sobs when she commanded: "Chloë, I want you to look at me."

Chloë was startled by the sinister tone of Sister Doyle's voice. She lifted her head up to address her, but when she saw what was happening in front of her, she wished that she had not done so. Sister Doyle was transforming. She had unzipped her habit and was stepping out of the flowing black robes. Her habit looked like it had been pieced together with several large curtains. Her large bulk, covered by only a slip and under briefs, stepped out from behind her desk. "What is going on?" Chloe wondered to herself.

With the head dress of her habit pulled away, a mop of grey and black hair tied together with pins was exposed. She looked garish standing in front of her, the flabbiness of her naked arms jiggling. Chloë looked over to Sister McGarrigle for an explanation as to what was happening, only to discover that she too had stepped out of her habit. "This is craziness!" Chloe thought to herself. "Sister McGarrigle, what are you doing? What is going on here?"

Sister McGarrigle had a striking figure, standing now in front of Chloë wearing just a bra and panties. She must be in some sort of nightmare. She watched as Sister McGarrigle approached Sister Doyle and they embraced each other, kissing. Sister Doyle's hands were all over Sister McGarrigle's body. She was disgusted and rose to run from the room, to run away from this nightmare and find her way to Father O'Sullivan in Rome. Then she heard another voice. A man's voice. She thought she had heard the voice before. It was the voice of Robert Best!

"Chloë, it has been awhile. Please sit down, my dear. We need to talk about your career and you're leaving for America."

"I don't know who you are or what you're doing here or what you've done to Sister McGarrigle and Sister Doyle, but I'm not going anywhere with you or anyone else to America."

She then turned to leave and run out the door. She made it to the door, but it was locked. Panicking, she yanked on the door knob, trying in vain to open the door and escape the hell she was caught up in.

Then she heard another voice call out to her from behind as her panic was turning to terror. It was Father O'Sullivan's voice. Chloë turned to look and she saw a horror show play itself out in front of her. Sister McGarrigle, with her back on the desk and Sister Doyle kissing and licking her over her bare breasts, was staring at Chloë, her eyes burning a deep crimson red and she was speaking to her, not in her voice, but that of Father O'Sullivan's: "It's going to be okay Chloë. Everything is going to be okay." Then Sister McGarrigle laughed hysterically, a demonic and awful sound. Chloë was horrified as Sister Doyle grunted like a wild beast on top of Sister McGarrigle. She needed to escape!

Then Mr. Best spoke, "Chloë, do you not know who you are? Look inside your soul, Chloë. Feel the power grow inside of you. Can you feel it?"

Suddenly she could feel herself teeter on her feet as her eyes had closed all on their own. The sensation building within her was like a hot blast furnace turning up the heat. The burning sensation inside of her caused her to collapse on the floor. But there was something else she was feeling, in addition to the intense heat: a calling. She was feeling this incredible pull towards the man who called himself Robert Best. She couldn't stop it, nor did she really want to stop it. The heat fuelling this desire was intoxicating. The calling within her was interrupted by another voice, two voices who called out her name. She opened her eyes and the room seemed to be spinning out of control. The heat of the calling from within her threatened to close her eyes again. She struggled to get back on her feet when she heard the voice again. She recognized it now. It was Connor Asker.

"Chloë, it's okay. Let the feeling inside of you embrace you. It is beautiful, Chloë, and it will be with you forever."

Now it was Juan Jimenez who spoke: "Chloë, did you

ever wonder why you had the strange birthmark on your right thigh? I have one too, Chloë, and so does Connor. We all do. We are special, Chloë, can you see and feel that now?"

She rose to her feet now, her eyes cleared and she could see Connor and Juan standing beside Mr. Best. They were all so beautiful. She wanted to be with them and never leave them. She looked around and could not see Sister McGarrigle and Sister Doyle. They were gone. Then she heard Mr. Best speak.

"They are gone, Chloë. They are all gone, including Father O'Sullivan. You're with me now. You're with Connor and Juan too. We are your family now, Chloë."

Nothing seemed to matter to Chloë anymore but the feeling she had inside, the burning, the heat and the man called Robert Best. That was all she wanted and knew it was all she would ever need again in her life. No more stifling and choking Academy. No more discipline, studying and curfews. She was free now. She had Connor and Juan and another boy who had come forward through the darkness and introduced himself as Patrick. He seemed very powerful. All of their eyes were burning a very deep, deep red. It drew her towards them like a beacon. She could feel their arms wrap around her, embracing her. She was home now.

Chapter 28

Things seemed to be getting back to normal after a whirlwind of high and low activity during the past two weeks. Sam and Bethany helped Josephina with the funeral arrangements for Jacob's body, or what was left of it. Jewish law forbids cremation, so in the case of a death that leaves the body in a decimated condition and therefore unable to be viewed, it is wrapped in cloth and placed in a closed coffin for the service, and later burial. In addition to Bethany, Josephina had many from the congregation of the synagogue there to help her with getting her affairs in order.

They also were caught up in the excitement of Patrick's incredible and surprising musical opportunity with super record producers, Avery Johnson and Robert Best. The formation of the young and talented new group they were putting together required the members to be sequestered in a mansion outside of Los Angeles. When they were told it was in Malibu, they were not prepared for what they saw when they pulled up to the beachfront mansion on the Pacific Coast Highway with Patrick. The home was a massive, opulent estate with a long, winding, private driveway that ended in front of one of the most beautiful homes they had ever seen. They were met in front by a well-dressed young man who introduced himself to Patrick and the rest of them as Michael, and offered to help Patrick with his luggage and show him around the house and to his bedroom. Sam and Bethany were just standing there alone beside their SUV, which looked ridiculously out of place amongst the richness of their surroundings. They were greeted by Robert Best, who came walking out of the front entrance, his hand extended to Sam as he approached: "Good morning Sam and Bethany. Thank you for bringing Patrick over. I see that Michael is showing him around. Please, come in for a few minutes before you head back."

Sam looked at Best and then his wife before replying: "This is where the kids will be living and practicing? Jesus Robert, someone has too much money."

He laughed at his remark, but did not reply, Sam noticed. Instead, he just commented: "It is a beautiful home that is for sure. Wait until you see the view. Come on, follow me please."

Best gave them a brief tour of the main level of the mansion, including the state of the art studio where the kids would be practicing and rehearsing. Then he led them out to the rear of the home, and he was right about the view; it was spectacular. The rear of the property went on forever it seemed, rimmed by mature trees, giving it its privacy from the surrounding estates. The view of the ocean was like nothing they could imagine. The endless view of blue water everywhere presented feelings to Sam of both solitude and excess. It just seemed surreal to him. It was happening so fast for Patrick, it was hard to wrap his head around it all. The pool that enveloped the rear of the house was beautiful and offered incredible views, no matter where you sat. In Malibu, with the limited knowledge Sam had of real estate values, this place had to be worth tens of millions. His curiosity got the better of him, so he asked: "Isn't this a little much for these kids? Why so much grandeur? Who is financing all of this?"

With an answer that didn't necessarily satisfy Sam, Best replied: "We are all very fortunate that we have someone who is very well off and believes in our vision for the band. He insists that the kids are comfortable and want for nothing so that their focus will be totally on the music."

A few minutes later, they said their goodbyes to Patrick, the young man named Michael and Best. Back in their car and leaving the estate, Beth shook her head when she said: "Even though we're less than an hour away, it seems like we are heading to the airport from here and leaving a country to head back to Los Angeles."

"I agree, I felt the same way. It just seems surreal. It's all happened far too fast. Well, at least we know he won't starve. Did you see that kitchen?"

Laughing at him, the tension that had built up for the both of them after leaving Patrick seemed to melt away with the comment: "I guess we should just focus on Patrick's happiness, as he certainly seemed to be as giddy as a ten year old let loose in a toy store when he was running around from room to room with that kid Michael. It's a heck of an opportunity for him, Sam. I'm sure everything will be just fine. If worse comes to worse, we can always just drive over and pick him up."

"Or take them by surprise and do an amphibious landing in the back entrance!"

****

Beth dropped him off at the house before she headed to her office and her job as a successful L.A. plastic surgeon. He jumped into his unmarked detective car and headed straight to work. Their son Sebastian was at school and was not interested in accompanying them to drop off Patrick. He cited that he had an important assignment to present in the morning class and couldn't duck it. He had given Patrick a cursory goodbye and the erosion of their relationship had gone full circle. Sam had admitted to being afraid of Patrick, and expressed that he was dangerous. The opportunity that seemed to come out of nowhere for Patrick and the move to the mansion was a blessing in disguise for Seb.

Sam arrived at the Robbery-Homicide Division of the LAPD on 100 West First Street just after lunch and headed up to the Homicide section located on the fourth floor. He checked in with Captain Bitters, and was given a message to contact investigators from the fire department, because they had something for him from the fire at the synagogue.

Back at his desk, Sam called the number to the fire investigations office and was directed to Officer Dirks.

"I'm sorry, it's your brother's death we're investigating,

Sam. We have a few troubling aspects of this fire that we are looking into. What we have been able to determine so far is that the church was ransacked and busted up pretty good before the fire started."

Sam gripped the phone a little harder when he heard this: "Okay. Tell me what you've got so far."

"The Torah was smashed into little pieces and was not intact when the fire destroyed it. Wall paintings and pictures were discovered on the other side of the church from where they had originally hung."

Sam thought about this and replied: "So what is the significance of that? It was a fire. Items are going to get blown around."

"There were no explosions in the synagogue, Sam. Just a ferocious fire. Besides, those expensive paintings were anchored by the frame into the concrete wall and were discovered over a hundred feet away from the wall, where they should have just melted. Very unusual."

"Okay, that is unusual. Anything else?"

There was a slight hesitation on the other end of the phone as the fire investigator seemed to struggle with his next sentence. "Sam, this is not going to be pleasant for me to explain to you, nor will it be pleasant for you to hear."

"What is it Dirks?"

"The beam that fell from the ceiling high above your brother and pierced the center of his chest. Well, we were able to examine the beam and the embers of the structure from where it came loose, Sam. I don't know any other way to tell you this, other than to just tell you straight up. The beam that broke away from the structure high above his body did not break away because of the fire, Sam. It had broken away before the flames had even reached that part of the ceiling. It was like someone, or something, had caused that specific piece of the beam to literally bust away from the support structure at precisely the area right above your brother. Also the beam, based upon its trajectory, should have landed approximately five feet to the left of his body. The chances of that beam actually falling straight down like a spear, without spinning or turning before it reached impact are even slimmer, or next to impossible."

Sam, clearly shocked, almost dropped the phone onto his desk. "There has to be some logical explanation for that beam falling the way that it fell."

"Sam, I know that it is hard for you to digest this, and especially for you to understand. We have had structural engineers go over this evidence and they have concluded, without a shred of doubt, that the beam did not fall because of the fire, but that it broke away and fell the way it did by some sort of inexplicable, deliberate action."

"Jesus Christ, Dirks. This is fucking crazy. Thanks for letting me know about this. Let me take that back. I wish you hadn't told me. This is now a murder investigation."

"I'm sorry Sam, I really am. This is terrible for you, I am sure. There is one more thing I have for you."

"Christ, what now?"

"We were able to salvage the hard drive of your brother's office computer. As soon as this turned into a murder investigation we handed all of this over to the police. I knew that Jacob was your brother so I made you a copy in addition and have sent it over to you. The contents have all been broken down into files and burned onto an external hard drive. Plug the USB into your computer and go through the files at your discretion. You should receive it by courier later this afternoon."

"Thank you Dirks."

"No problem Sam, just get the motherfucker who did this."

****

The package from Dirks arrived a few hours later, and Sam waited until everyone had gone home for the day before plugging it into his computer to begin going through the contents. He didn't want Bitters or Ryerson peering over his shoulder to see what he was doing. The night shift of detectives who would be coming in and out of the fourth floor offices would not pay Sam any attention, other than a few wise-ass jokes or comments. The sympathy comments about the death of Jacob had ended a while ago. He called Beth at her office and told her that he would be late tonight and to check on Seb when she got home, as he was a little worried about how he was doing now that Patrick had moved out. "Probably doing handstands of joy", thought Sam.

Soon, he was alone in front of his computer, opening up the external hard drive. Dirks had put all of the Microsoft Word, Excel and PowerPoint documents into separate folders. There was also a folder containing .pdf files that were all church-related documents. He focused on the Word document files first. Most of these were church-related memos, and church letters to elders regarding a wide range of church-related and administrative issues. A Rabbi was not just a preacher to the people; being the head of the synagogue was like being a CEO of a large corporation. Lots of directives and inner church administrative duties needed to be handled. Sam could tell his brother ran a very organized and efficient office as the chief administrator.

Then Sam came upon a folder marked 'Chelsea'. "Okay, what was this all about?", thought Sam, his heart beginning to pound in his chest. There was a document named 'Notes' and another named 'Reference Links'. He opened up the 'Notes' document and it was a chronological listing of Jacob's investigation into not only Chelsea's account of her attack sixteen years ago, but also of the events that had happened since then. Everything was written in order and clear, just like Jacob would do it. Sam felt that Jacob was writing this purposely in case something happened, and if anyone was to find this and read it there would be no grey areas or misinterpretation. He wanted his reports to be clear and concise. He found this to be unusual for Jacob, only in the sense that Sam felt that he was admitting that he believed Chelsea's original story.

Sam opened the report that Jacob had made on Chelsea's hypnosis session. He read over his notes and findings. He could tell that Jacob was bothered by Chelsea's repeated reference to the name 'Babken' during her hypnosis. There was a notation in the margin that read: 'see links'. He opened up the document named 'Reference Links'. He scanned down the page of website hyperlinks and found a hyperlink named 'Babken'. He clicked on the link, and it instantly took him to Wikipedia article entitled 'Babken'.

He read the Wikipedia page on Babken, and found it to be a history lesson. Babken was one of seven sons of King Tiridates, ruler of Armenia around 400 A.D. He was a fierce and brave soldier who fought many wars to maintain Armenia's independence from invading armies. Sam returned to Jacob's Notes document and continued to read. Jacob wrote about Chelsea's reference in her hypnotic state, and the fact that the beast had stated her lineage to Babken. What was the significance of Babken and her lineage? Was Chelsea some descendent of an Armenian ruler? What was the significance?

Sam continued reading Jacob's notes and theories. He switched over to the links screen and clicked on another reference entitled, 'The Great Battle'. Again, he was brought to the Wikipedia webpage where he read about the great battle fought by King Tiridates and his seven sons against the invading countries of Iberia, Albania, and Parthia. It was further down the page where Sam found it. Something in the back of his mind clicked, like a sliding mechanism falling into place in a lock. The great battle was fought because of Armenia's insistence on embracing Christianity as its state religion. IT was the first country in the world to do so and the neighboring countries had sent their armies to stop it.

Sam tried to put the pieces together that were floating around inside his brain. King Tiridates risked his country for Christianity. Chelsea claimed she was attacked by a demon, or by a beast, is what she said. The beast referred to Chelsea as a descendent of Babken. Babken was one of the seven sons of King Tiridates. The King was leading his country to adopt Christianity. "That's it!", he whispered to himself.

Chelsea believed Satan had attacked her and Steve

because she was a direct descendent of King Tiridates' son Babken. Was it about revenge? Was Satan killing off the direct descendants of the seven sons of King Tiridates to revenge the Armenia's choice of the Son of his enemy, Jesus Christ? It was crazy thinking, but Jacob obviously thought enough to write about his theories. Then came a thought which shook Sam to his very core: "Was Jacob killed by Satan because of what he had figured out and was putting together?"

Sam leaned back in his chair, deep in thought. Had Chelsea become the key to a sixteen hundred year old plot by the arch enemy of God? What plot? What was he missing? He rose from his chair to stretch. He looked at his watch, and noted that it was 9:30 p.m. He had been engrossed in the files for over four hours. He pulled his cell from his pocket and dialed Beth. She answered it, and asked if he was coming home soon. She sounded anxious to get back to watching her favorite show, 'The Bachelor'. Knowing she was distracted, he clicked off and went to the lunchroom and plugged some change into the vending machine for some coffee. As he returned to his desk, he couldn't get the theory of the revenge from the devil on the descendants of the seven sons out of his head. He went over and over it in his mind, and nothing made sense. His mind drifted back to the murder scene at Chelsea and Steven's home. There had been blood all over the walls. Steven's near decapitated head was twisted completely around. Then, there was the police lab's inability to type the blood and DNA found in copious amounts at the scene. Coroner Eunice Epp had informed him that it was DNA never seen before, not human or animal.

He thought about Chelsea's murder scene. . Her body had been torn to pieces all over the living room. Patrick had sat there, cradling her head and shoulders in his lap, because the rest of her was all over the living room. When he considered the severity of the attack, a pack of wolves was a description that came to mind. Another mechanism slipped into an unseen chamber in his subconscious. Click. He thought about Patrick, crying, cradling the macabre remains of his mother. No one else had been found at the scene. There had been no witnesses and no evidence of forced entry. Click. Investigators concluded that Chelsea must have known her attacker. Another sliding mechanism fell into its place in the lock. Patrick's infatuation with the awful and gory death photos of his mother, his father and Jonathon Green. "Wait a minute", he thought. Click! Click! The chambers were falling into place in his mind like tumbling dominos. Patrick's father was Steven. Chelsea was pregnant at the time of the attack. "Let me think about that", he persisted. His mind was crunching information, straining to bring up long buried thoughts from the past.

The doctor who delivered Chelsea's baby, Patrick. The way that he had looked at him, his eyes that flashed the deep crimson red. He investigated the doctor and he never could find any record of him other than a doctor with the same name that was deceased. The birth was not six, seven or even eight months after the attack. It was precisely nine months after the attack! Something tapped him on the side of his head. Now he knew, and his brother Jacob also knew. It was Patrick! The killer of his neighborhood's cats and dogs.

The realization of what he had just discovered resonated through his body like a highly charged electric current. The feeling in his gut was no longer a slowly building fear, it was a full blown feeling of utter terror.

"Chelsea was raped when she was attacked sixteen years ago! Could it possibly be? That means Patrick would be the son of the…!" His terror was wrenched from him when his cell phone rang, ripping through the silence of the deserted office. Catching his breath, he checked the caller i.d., but it just flashed 'Unknown'. He hesitated for a brief second before pressing the send button.

"Detective Showenstein."

The voice on the other end was a direct call from a spiritual realm that was pure evil. Chills cascaded up and down Sam's spine when he heard the demonic voice call out to him: "I'm coming for you, Detective. Be ready."

The call ended with a chorus of demonic laughter.

Chapter 29

The morning was disappearing far too fast and Nancy, checking the time on the kitchen wall clock as she passed through, almost gasped when she saw the time. They needed to get moving to the airport in the next few minutes, otherwise they would be searching for another flight. She intercepted her assistant, Leanne Renton, as she was about to climb the stairs: "Leanne, can you ask Brittany to get a move on? We're going to be late for our flights if we don't get out of here in the next ten minutes!"

"Ten minutes! I thought we had a half hour, Nancy. Okay, forget about Britt, I'd better get a move on!" Giggling, she peeled on up the stairs, yelling out to Brittany as she did.

Nancy was accompanying her daughter and her assistant to Los Angeles to see Brittany off to pursue her dreams with the super group being assembled by Robert Best and Avery Johnson, two of the biggest names in the music business. It had been quite the whirlwind year for her daughter, from winning 'X Factor', to being selected by Best for his handpicked group. The plan laid out by Best and Johnson was to house the group of kids together in a large home, equipped with a state of the art recording studio, home schooling tutors, and anything else they would need. This was to create an environment where they could focus on the material that had been written for them in order to launch a tour sometime over the next year. It was an ambitious project, and no expense was being spared for these kids. Nancy felt at ease with everything after listening to Best and Johnson. Not that Brittany would leave her much choice, but Nancy met her halfway by insisting that Leanne also accompany her and stay with her to ensure that her education requirements were being met, as well as for her overall safety and well-being.

Soon they were all in the taxi making their way to T.F. Green airport in Providence. They chatted about the long flight to L.A. and what they would do to pass the time. Leanne wanted to sleep, and Brittany wanted to be glued to the window, watching her dreams of making music bounce through the clouds like radio waves. Nancy needed to be buried in her laptop, working on some papers she needed to complete for an upcoming presentation in support of the lobbying efforts to stop a pipeline from being built over U.S. soil. Nancy never remarried since the death of her husband James, so many years ago, and work kept her busy. Her daughter's burgeoning music career was just another challenge for her to overcome, so she could be with her as often as she could.

****

Within thirty minutes of loading their luggage into the rental car at LAX, the car's GPS brought them to the house where her daughter would begin her new life. To say it was a house was a mistake. "It is a mansion in every sense of the word", Nancy thought. It was so big, so palatial, that she couldn't imagine why someone would want to build a house this monstrous and extravagant. More than anything else that had transpired since their meeting with Robert Best, the estate on Malibu Beach put things into perspective. The individuals behind this new band were serious people with serious money and the magnitude of the project was enormous. Incredibly great things would be expected of this group, that much was certain. She only hoped that her young daughter was ready for what was ahead of her.

She watched as two young men came out the front doors and approached the car. Brittany instantly began to scream: "Oh my God, it's Connor Asker! He can't be part of this?"

She watched her daughter, followed by Leanne, nervously climb out of the car and introduce herself to the boys. The guys were quite the lookers, and Brittany would be swooning.

When she was finally able to pry her eyes away from them, she turned back towards the car and noticed Nancy standing and waiting and she came running over and giggled: "Connor and Juan, this is my mother Nancy and her assistant Leanne. Mom and Leanne, this is Connor Asker and Juan Jimenez! Can you believe it?" Brittany squealed with delight.

Nancy extended her hand to them both and replied: "Nice to meet you both. My daughter is a huge fan of your music. This is quite the house fellas, do you think there might be room for us in there too?"

She had barely gotten the words out when the three of them were already ignoring her and making their way into the mansion. Leanne stood beside her, the two of them watching Brittany giggle like a little school girl as she followed the two heart throbs into the house. Leanne looked over at her and said: "Oh, come on Nancy, it's not what you think. She'll be just fine. They seem like very nice young men. Your daughter knows how to take care of herself. Remember it was you, her mother, who taught her that."

Soon after, the three of them got settled into their room, which was like an apartment within the mansion that opened up into a two bedroom spacious living area, complete with its own kitchen and living room. Leanne wasted no time claiming the couch: "The sofa is bigger than my bed, no offense Nancy, I love my room back in Providence, but this is one big-ass piece of furniture."

They all had a good laugh and then they were interrupted by a knock on the door, quickly followed by the door being opened to Connor, Juan, and a third boy they had not met. They walked in and Connor announced with a big smile: "Ladies, Mr. Best asked us to show you around the house and the studio, where we will spend almost every waking minute of our lives, does that sound alright?"

Brittany walked right up to the new guy, who had drop dead good looks and seemed older than the other two, and replied: "Sounds great! Let's go Leanne and Mom. I can't wait to see the studio."

The tour of the mansion was an eye opener in opulence and technology in a combination that left Nancy feeling a little numb. The studio, where Brittany and the others would be spending the bulk of their time was, incredible. It was recently built, so it had all of the latest state of the art equipment and innovations in sound mixing. The new boy with the long, wavy, dark hair introduced himself to Nancy, Brittany, and Leanne as Patrick, and said that he would be playing base guitar and drums. He bragged a little bit too much about being a songwriter and he said that he hoped that his music would make it into the band. There was something about this boy that struck Nancy as a little different, darker, maybe. She couldn't quite put her finger on it, but it made her cautious. She found herself paying closer attention to him than the other two boys as they made their way around the house.

When they walked out the back of the mansion and onto the rear terrace, the view of the Pacific Ocean took their breath away. It was a spectacular view, with a sandy white beach leading right up to the property and Nancy could even see what appeared to be a cruise ship far off on the horizon, just a speck in the endless sea of blue. She was now starting to understand why Best and Johnson brought them all here. They wanted to create an environment where the kids would have everything, but would be expected to work extremely hard. The luxury, views, and technology were all designed to foster that environment.

Nancy stayed one more night with the girls before she had to catch a flight to Lincoln, Nebraska for a series of meetings with state legislators. Giving Brittany a hug goodbye, she looked her in the eyes and asked: "Are you sure that this is what you want? You're still so young, you don't have to take the plunge right now. You're the best young singer on the planet, Britt, and they know that. It's why they brought you here. You are so talented sweetheart, you can do this blindfolded with a gag in your mouth."

"I know that Mom, but I want to be here. It just feels right. I was meant to be here, I can't quite explain it. I really feel that our music is going to change lives. Kinda weird, huh? Don't worry about me, Mother. Look around this place, I'll be just fine. I promise, I will keep my schoolwork up and I'm pretty sure that they will make sure I do. This is a great opportunity, Mom, that I don't think gets offered to too many sixteen year olds."

"You're right, Britt. It's scary how mature you are! I love you so much, and I am very proud of you. You are a star, Brittany, and the world had better be ready for my daughter, because here she comes!"

Nancy took a second to blow her daughter a kiss as she climbed behind the wheel of the rental car, then watched as her daughter blew her one back. She drove off and around the large circular driveway, then noticed in the corner of her eye, the dark and broody Patrick come out of the house and stand beside her daughter. There was something about that boy. Dark, for sure, but there was something else about him. He seemed a little dangerous. That was it. She hesitated as she drove down the lane, thinking about turning around and taking her daughter home. She would not come, of course, and she did not want to leave on terms where she would upset her daughter. But that boy...

****

Sam got up from his desk in Homicide, stretched, and announced to his partner Ryerson that he was calling it a day. His partner was surprised.

"You're calling it a day at 4:30 p.m.? Your day starts at 7:00 a.m., but usually doesn't begin until 5:00 p.m. I am just beginning to get used to the ungodly hours in Homicide, so please Sam, don't fuck that up."

Pointing a finger at Ryerson he said, "I'll fuck you up, alright. Tell you what Mr. Energy Bunny, why don't you go down to records and sign out the evidence boxes and murder books to the Graham Carruthers kid, Steven Benning, Chelsea Benning and Jonathon Green? I want every commonality, if there are any spelled out in point form in a report. That's what you can do."

"Oh, come on Sam. We're not going down that road again. We've been down that road so many times, if we had planted trees the first time, they would now qualify for the Rockefeller Center Christmas tree selection."

"Just fucking do it, Ryerson. There is something there we have missed, I know it. We'll go through your report in the morning." Sam grabbed his suit jacket off the hook on the side of his desk, turned and left for the elevators.

He could feel Ryerson's eyes burning into his back as he left. He knew the kid was pissed, but fuck him. He needed to get his hands dirty, and now was the time. Sam stepped into the elevator and hit P1. He was pretty sure that he parked on the first level, but he knew that he'd be searching all four floors for his car. The knowledge of what had happened to his brother, Chelsea, and Steven haunted his thoughts every waking minute of the day. He took a deep breath as the elevator doors closed in front of him. He needed sleep. That same knowledge that haunted his thoughts during the day turned his sleep into terror-filled bouts of mental torture. He was in the grips of something awful, and he couldn't shake it. He felt he wasn't pursuing a sick, cold-blooded killer, but an evilness so wicked he feared for his life.

****

Ryerson watched Sam walk out of the office and down the hallway to the elevators. There was something really bothering his partner, beyond mourning the loss of his brother. He just wasn't the same since the death of Jacob. He was on the edge, ready to explode at any minute. Ryerson had never seen him like this before. If he wanted to be home before midnight, he had better get started working on those files, he thought. The image of a cranky Sam chewing his ass out in the morning because his report was not completed was something he could do without.

A few minutes later, he made room on his cluttered desk for the boxes he had hauled up from records. He carefully placed the contents of each box into separate piles, utilizing an empty table from the other side of the office that he had dragged over. He knew that Sam had meticulously gone through these same boxes more than once, and having him do the same meant that Sam was at an impasse with these investigations. He could not move forward, because the evidence did not allow him to do so. He was searching for a clue, anything, that might have been missed, and through his desperation to find a clue, he was now asking Ryerson to give it a shot. It was tedious and boring work, but he would do his best to find something that might have been overlooked.

To read over the police reports and examine the physical evidence gathered at the crime scenes, he decided he would cross reference the evidence tag numbers to the master log sheet. He didn't quite know why he was doing it, but for some unexplained reason, it felt like the right thing to do. There were hundreds of tagged evidence items taken from each crime scene. Starting with the attack on Chelsea Benning and the murder of her husband sixteen years ago, there were dozens of random items taken in the hope of discovering useable DNA by investigators. Things like drink coasters, alarm clocks, a TV remote, paperback books, ornaments, and all kinds of stuff found in a bedroom and the ensuite bathroom. All of Chelsea's makeup and bathroom products were tagged, bagged, and included in the evidence box. Ryerson wondered why the bulk of these items were not returned to the Benning home, which would have been standard protocol after the forensic work was completed. "This is odd", he thought. Item number 157, Steven and Chelsea's bible, catalogued as being taken from the top of Chelsea's night table beside the lamp, was nowhere to be found in the evidence box. Someone did not return it into evidence. He made a note of it to ask Sam why it was not in evidence.

Another hour passed, and Daniel double-checked the evidence master log from the Jonathon Green murder scene at the hotel and almost fell out of his chair when he came to item number 157. Seeing 157 again reminded him of the log sheet from Chelsea and Steven's box. The item number 157 from the Green murder box was also a bible. Removed and then bagged, as it likely had blood spatter on it from the nightstand drawer that had been hanging open, the bible was nowhere to be found in the murder box. He felt the hairs on the back of his neck rise up. He quickly got up and went to the side table he had dragged over earlier to so that he could place the murder box regarding Chelsea Benning on it. He searched for the copy of the master evidence log sheet, found it, and using his finger, scanned down the list of numbers till his finger stopped at item number 157. It couldn't be. "This is impossible!" The coincidence of three different crime scene forensic teams bagging and tagging three different murder scenes spread out over a sixteen year time period and cataloguing a bible in each of them as item number 157 was insane. He searched through all of the evidence items in Chelsea's murder box, knowing that he would not find the bible. He did not. He walked back to his desk, slumped down in his chair and thought about picking up the phone and dialing Sam with his discovery. How could Sam have missed this? He never would have because he was the most meticulous investigator there was. The random coincidence of tagging the bible as item number 157 in all three murder scenes and the fact that now all three were removed from the boxes was spooky. He needed to call Sam now in the hope he would offer a simple explanation. Reaching for the phone, he damn near shouted out loud when it rang out just before he picked it up. Jesus, he needed to go home and get some sleep. "The timing of Sam's call is a little unnerving", he thought as he picked up the receiver, "You have no idea how you just scared the shit out of me. My hand literally reached for the phone to call you just before it rang. This is one crazy fucking night." The demonic and evil voice on the other end of the phone was not Sam.

"Looking for a little inspiration, Detective, and having a hard time finding a good book?"

****

The cell phone on Sam's night stand vibrated, slowly moving its way to the edge of the nightstand, where it threatened to plunge to the carpeted bedroom floor below. A big hand grabbed it at the last second, rescuing it from what surely would have been a rough landing.

Sam checked the clock on his nightstand before answering his phone. The bright red numbers were impossible to mistake. He groaned as he read the four followed by a zero and a five. He never bothered to check the caller I.D. as he clicked on the send button.

"This had better be good, Ryerson, or I'm going to kick your ass!"

The voice on the other end wasn't his partner, instead it was Captain Bitters. This was never good. Sam detected a sense of sadness and fatigue in his voice when he finally spoke after several seconds of delay: "Sam, its Ryerson. It's fucking awful, just fucking awful."

If he could reach through the phone and choke him right then, he would have: "What the hell are you talking about, Captain?"

"Patrol just found him fifteen minutes ago parked in front his house. Sam, he sucked on the end of his pistol. He blew his own fucking head off!"

Chapter 30

The last ten months flew by for Avery Johnson and Alive Records. His stable of stars continued to make music and tour with very little input from Avery himself. His production team did the bulk of the work in the studio, so that Avery only had to sit in in on the final sessions to give his approval on the final edits. Contract and legal work was handled by his very competent and expensive legal team, with Avery signing off on all of the contract paperwork after it had been fully prepared by the lawyers. Jenn, of course, kept everything running smoothly and did an expert job of keeping Avery abreast of everything happening within the walls of Alive Records.

She sat patiently in front of his desk while he signed a stack of paperwork. He looked up at her and said: "Don't you have something better to do than sit and watch me sign paperwork and checks? I will buzz you when I'm done, and you can come back in and take it away. Maybe I need to get rid of your assistant since you look like you have nothing to do."

He watched as she shifted in her chair in front of him. She wanted to talk about something. She did this every time she was upset with him. They would play this game of controlled silence until she broke and finally let out what it was that she wanted to say. "Why don't you just tell me what's bothering you, Jenn?"

"Thank you for the opportunity Avery, so I will. I think you're spending too much time at the mansion and with Best, and not enough time here at the studio. Your clients need to see you more than what you're giving them, Avery. Poking your head into the studio to say, 'Hey what's up' isn't cutting it, and you know it. These clients of ours pay huge fees, not only to gain access to the best studio in the world, but also for quality face time with their producer. They want to see you around here more, Avery."

"Jesus, Jenn, kind of grouchy this morning, aren't you? They will be fine. If I'm around here too much, they start complaining that they're losing creative control of their own music, and then when I'm not around they complain because I'm not around. Doesn't make any sense, Jenn."

"I'm talking about finding middle ground. Just start spending just a little more time with them when they are in town and here in the studio. That's all I'm saying. Fair enough?"

"Alright, alright already, I hear you. Keep me informed of when studio time is in session and I will be here. I might even accompany them for a few drinks in the evening away from this place to let my charm find its way into their collective souls, so they will feel soothed and wanted. How does that sound?"

"I think you sound like an idiot. Fine, I will give you lots of heads up to be here, but you better be here then."

Avery finished up the stack of paperwork and offered to carry it back out to Jenn's desk for her. She refused, of course, and reached over and took the stack from him and gave him one more little stinger: "How's everything going with Bentley?"

He gave her a look before he replied: "My relationship with Bentley is just fine. Thanks for asking just the same. Now, maybe you should get back to your desk and start processing all that paperwork you were so anxious for me to sign."

He sat back down at his desk as he watched Jenn leave his office. "Damn, she knew what buttons to push with him." Truth be told, things were cooling somewhat between him and Bentley. The demand of their careers was definitely working against them. She was constantly travelling, never for too long at a time, but enough that it seemed to be putting their relationship in stop-and-start mode all the time. They created momentum in their relationship, then it got interrupted by another interview or concert event she needed to cover for her magazine, *Music Talks*. Not to mention that there was his increasing commitment to Vasallus. He spent more time with them than any other of his clients combined. Juan Jimenez and Connor Asker were still riding the wave of their debut albums from the past year and finishing up concert dates. Elizabeth Leroux, Chloë McClosky and Brittany Campbell became fast friends, and soon were closer than sisters. Avery recognized how bright and intelligent they were as they focused on their schooling and he was amazed at their maturity and patience. They seemed to sense the bigger picture being developed around them and the band Vasallus. Michael Lockwood and Patrick Benning spent hours and hours in the studio, the two of them feeding off of each other's talents and abilities. The Benning kid was broody and a little bit unpredictable, Avery noticed, the complete opposite of Michael's calm and reassuring personality. Maybe that was why they clicked so well.

The musical talent in the mansion was undeniable, and although how they would eventually come together as one unit was still uncertain, he knew one thing for sure: the world was in store for one helluva treat. These kids were very special and it still boggled his mind how Best conceived this project in the first place, bringing all of these kids together. He was impressed, to say the least, and he couldn't wait to get them all together in the studio to begin recording.

He didn't see his pace slowing down, only increasing, as they moved closer to begin recording tracks with the kids, which meant his and Bentley's relationship would be further strained. He couldn't stand where their relationship was heading, yet he just didn't know what to do about it, short of asking her to leave the magazine and he knew he could never do that. He would have to make every minute they had together really count so that their relationship would survive. He loved her, and had never felt this way about anyone else ever in his life and he certainly did not want to lose her. He hoped she felt the same.

****

Errol Barr

The internal shuffling of responsibilities within *Music
Talks* after the tragic death of Jonathon Green and the
installation of the new Editor-in-Chief, Jeremy Jyles or JJ, put
Bentley on a plane far more often than she wanted. With her
career responsibilities, and Avery's commitment to Robert Best
and Vasallus, they hardly saw each other anymore. Neither one
of them liked it, but unless one of them walked away from
their careers, it was the way it would be. They committed to
making it work and she would do everything in her power to
make sure the relationship did not veer off the rails. He was a
great man and she loved him. The one thing they always made
sure they did, no matter where they were working, was to call
each other late at night when they both ended their days. She
noticed that lately, he was becoming less and less available to
talk late at night. The kids were getting close to heading into
the studio to begin to work on the debut album, and his time
was getting scarcer and scarcer. She made sure that she did not
put any pressure on him; there was plenty of that already, but
tried to strike a balance of giving him the space he needed and
time for each other. It wasn't easy.

****

Robert Best clipped his fingernails at his desk, a ritual he
did every day. He liked them a certain length. His nails and his
hair grew much faster than the average man. He wasn't sure
why, but it was likely because his metabolism was through the
roof. The human body he encased himself in when he was in
earthly form was barely able to keep up with the demands he
put it through. He rarely slept, or ate, like a Kentucky Derby
thoroughbred, and drank copious amounts of his favorite
beverage, Canadian whiskey. His internal furnace burned
energy like a locomotive coal-fired engine. He needed outlets
to release pent up energy, mental energy. There were times
when he would be so wound up from days of no sleep, booze
and drugs, he would burst like a time bomb and go on a killing
spree in either New York or Los Angeles. The police
departments would think there was another serial killer on the
loose, and the public would shrink further back into the

shadows, seeking safety from the danger lurking in the streets.

The time was near to announce and introduce Vasallus to the music world. He would instruct Johnson to begin rehearsals on the songs they would choose for the debut album. He would let Johnson decide on the thirteen tracks to select from the cache of songs written by Patrick. It didn't matter to him which songs were chosen, as they would all be hits and he would let Johnson's expertise decide on the exact rollout. The songs were incredible and would turn the youth inside out. He went over the hundreds of songs in the library with a fine tooth comb and tweaked the lyrics here and there. Patrick did exactly what he had been instructed to do; write songs with lyrics all pointing to one place for the listener. The words to the songs, in the beginning, would subliminally broadcast a message of obedience to Satan, then slowly progress to outright defiance of anything Christian or God-based. Kids were hard wired to their iPods today and the music they would begin listening to, day and night, all over the world, would change their very souls. Soon enough, he would have the youth of the world, and then everyone else, listening to his words and his message, culminating in their complete obedience to him.

He carefully began planting seeds with the mention of an upcoming super group being formed that would include Asker and Jimenez. In the recent concerts, they both made brief mention of something big coming together. Allusions to this on both of their Facebook fan pages also had an effect. The talk and chatter of rumours began to spread. The legions of fans for the incredibly popular Panterra production in Las Vegas were still struggling to overcome the loss of Elizabeth Leroux as the lead, and when rumours began to pop up that she might be part of some super group being formed that could also include Connor Asker and Juan Jimenez, social media began to churn the rumour mill faster than ever. Best dropped subtle hints in television and radio interviews of a possible mega announcement forthcoming. Michael Lockwood and Chloë McClosky's fans in Europe were also being tantalized with rumours of a new super group being formed by mega music moguls Robert Best and Avery Johnson. Fans around the world were beginning to hear about the rumours and the buzz began to reach a fever pitch.

****

Avery came into Alive Records early, partly to prepare for his meeting with Best in a couple of hours and partly to avoid the media that had begun to show up at his studio looking for confirmation on the rumours of an upcoming super group being formed that would include the mega popular young stars whom he managed. He chuckled to himself at Best's brilliance in the slow and subtle planting of seeds of speculation and innuendo in the media to create excitement in advance of announcing Vasallus.

Today's meeting with Best was an important one. He was about to get his first look at the music from Best's writing team.   They would go through this music and select the songs for the group's first album. The plan for Vasallus was to get them all together in the studio and introduce the songs one by one. As he did so, he would begin to get a feel about which of the kids was stronger in certain vocal ranges in order to create the harmony, or as he thought of it, 'the magic'. He knew Chloë and Brittany possessed incredible vocal ranges, and Elizabeth's unique, but very slight rasp would offer tremendous flexibility to their sound. The boys voices, led by Asker and Jimenez's powerful and beautiful vocal chops, combined with the angelic sound of the girls, added up to a dream come true for a music producer. He had waited months to get them all into the studio to begin work on the debut album, and if fans were beginning to get excited, then he was vibrating with excitement.

With a collection of the best voices that had come into the music business in years, and the incredible good looks to match the voices, it was a lethal combination if the music they chose captured their amazing talent. "We will see", he thought, as he glanced at his Breitling, noticing that Best should be here any minute. He dialed Jenn's extension and she picked up immediately: "Good morning, Avery. Did you actually get in before me this morning?"

"Been here for two hours already. Where have you been?" Avery poked.

She poked right back, "It's about time. Maybe my little pep talk with you to spend more time here worked."

"Don't flatter yourself too much, okay? Listen, Jenn, I've scheduled my morning meeting with Best here. Can you setup the boardroom for me? Coffee, tea, juice, pastries, you know, the works. We have a lot of ground to cover. We might be in there for a while."

"I never even knew you were meeting with Best today. Thanks for that. I'll get it ready but give me half an hour." The sarcasm in her voice was unmistakeable.

"Jenn, I'm sorry. Things are moving really fast. I'm trying my best to stay ahead of the storm, so be patient, okay?"

"Are you and Best ready to announce Vasallus to the world soon? The media will have the story sooner than later, and if you are planning some big surprise announcement it won't work unless you get it out there now, Avery. The switchboard is getting busier and busier with media inquiring about the rumours."

"You're right, Jenn. There were a few drinking coffee and eating donuts in the parking lot when I pulled in this morning. The announcement is coming soon. In fact, I want you to clear your schedule today and join me in the boardroom with Best today. Have Giselle look after things. We're making song selections, or at least determining the sound and look for the group today. Best has a vault full of hit songs and he wants me to make the decisions on the songs for the debut album."

"Wow, Avery, you mean to say that the music has been written for these kids and they are ready to head into the studio this quick and record?" The sound of disbelief rang through Jenn's voice as she spoke. "You don't even know what they sound like together?"

She was right, he knew, but he had spent hours listening to each one of them individually in the studio at the mansion, plus hours and hours listening to demo tapes from each of them. He listened to their demos in his car, at home, and on his i-pod just about everywhere else that didn't require his full attention. On a few occasions when they were together, Bentley had even been forced to ask him to lose the ear buds. He knew these kids' voices inside and out. He also knew that these voices, combined, would create a sound never experienced in pop music. It all rested on the music. It needed to be world class. He finished up with Jenn: "I'll see you in the boardroom. Best should be here any minute. Show him into the boardroom, then come and get me."

****

Jenn catered lunch into the boardroom, but he barely touched it. He nibbled on a sandwich and Best devoured the rest. The guy had a bottomless pit. He ate more sandwiches then Avery would eat in a week. The music compositions which Best brought into the boardroom took both Jenn and Avery by complete surprise. They certainly expected the music to be good, but the music was far more than good; it was incredibly great. He envisioned the kid's voices in the songs, as he played some of it on the grand piano out in the studio. Best took a turn on the piano to play a few of the songs, leaving him and Jenn to sit on stools looking at each other, simply stunned. Avery had Jenn bring in Amber, her assistant, who had a great voice, to lend some vocals to the piano by Best. It became clear that the music was spectacular, and once again, Avery found himself being amazed by Best. The music he had written for Vasallus was very good indeed. By midafternoon, it was apparent that they had more than enough music to go into the studio and begin recording.

He took a bottle of water being handed out by one of the girls from the office, looked at Best and said: "The music is very good, Robert. In fact, it is more than just 'very good'. Each song has hit and number one written all over it. There is enough music there for two records. It's incredible. Where did you get this stuff?"

He watched as Best took a gulp of his water, thanked the

employee as she walked out of the studio to return to the front office, and looked at both Jenn and himself before replying: "These songs are just a drop in the bucket Avery. We have enough hit music at our disposal to keep these kids at the top until they're all in adult diapers. The kid writes a hit song every time he steps in the shower, goes to bed at night, or while he eats breakfast, lunch and dinner. He is a songwriter of genius status, Avery, and you've been working with him for months."

"I have? Okay, you got me, now who might that be?"

"Patrick Benning has written hundreds, no let me correct myself, thousands, of hit songs in just about every musical genre. For the past two years, I have had Patrick write music strictly for Vasallus. He has exceeded my expectations."

An incredulous Avery looked at Best and replied: "How do you do this Robert? This kid is a modern day Beethoven, for Christ sakes. He could make a fortune in royalties writing for other artists. How did you find him? How did you find any of them?"

He thought he detected a slight color change in Best's face when he replied so strongly. It didn't turn a shade of red to indicate he was angry with him, but more of a darker shade. He seemed to adopt a more ominous look and a slightly more commanding tone in his voice when he replied: "Avery, you ask far too many questions. Decide on the thirteen songs over the next several days with the kids in the studio at the mansion. We'll make the announcement on Vasallus soon, once we nail down the first release. I want work to begin next week on the music video for the first release. You will have the very best film crew at your disposal to shoot this video. Let's meet first thing Monday morning, Avery, and decide on the theme for the video of the first song. Now I need to get out of here and let you get to work."

As Best left the studio, Avery looked at a stunned Jenn, who whispered: "I sure hope you know what you're doing. I thought Vasallus would be big. This isn't going to be big, Avery; it's going to be a God damned nuclear explosion of pandemonium."

Chapter 31

Avery rolled over in bed and kissed Bentley on her exposed shoulder. "I love this woman so much", he thought as he listened to her faint snores. They needed to find a way to make more time for each other, as the time and distance between them had become too frequent and too long. It was hard on a relationship, and he fully understood why most long distance relationships rarely survived. They both knew this, and they had committed to one another to work hard to keep the relationship strong.

He carefully crawled out of bed so that he wouldn't wake her, and made his way into the bathroom. He turned on the shower, waited until the water was hot, and climbed in. As he maneuvered the bar of soap over his body, he thought about his day and how long he had waited for this day to happen. Today, he was taking the kids of Vasallus into the studio to record their debut album, *New Beginnings*. He expected recording to last through the week and into the weekend and maybe longer, but he would need the first single completely nailed, because shooting of the music video began first thing Monday morning. He planned to be at the mansion the entire time, since they would be putting in extremely long days and he would crash in one of the many available guest rooms. He hoped that Bentley would be able to spend some time at the mansion as well. His mind started to drift back to her beautiful body, nestled naked under the covers, waiting for his return from the shower. He could feel himself begin to respond to those thoughts and he was about to turn off the water to dry off and wake up Bentley when a pair of hands slipped around his waist, exploring the front of his body.

They made love in the shower, dried themselves, then returned to the bed and made love again. Their lovemaking carried a hint of anxiety in the knowledge that the time away from each other in their relationship was catching up to them. They desperately wanted each other, both physically and emotionally, and as the two of them slumped onto the bed, he rolled on his side towards her. She did the same, snuggling in close and ran her fingers over the hairs on his chest and said: "Wow that is a great way to start the day Avery. What got into you? I'm not complaining by the way!"

He looked up at her, reached with his hand and moved a piece of her hair away from her eyes and tucked it gently behind her ear and replied: "I love you Bentley, so much, and I don't know, maybe it's just me, but we spend so much time away from each other that sometimes I think I might be losing you. Not to another man of course, but just to the time away from each other, time we cannot get back, times when you might be alone, vulnerable and I'm not around or there for you because I'm in the studio or you're travelling. I want to be there for you during those moments Bentley. Do you know where I'm coming from?"

He watched as her eyes began to fill with tears, threatening to spill over and she took his hand in hers, moved it to her lips, kissed it and moved it to her cheek before she spoke: "I love you too Avery and I too wonder what you are doing and thinking when we are apart, if you're thinking of me at all during the madness of your day, or if you miss me. We have talked about all of this before but I know it's hard for both of us. We just have to continue to promise to each other that we will be truthful to each other at all times. I don't want either of us to find out about each other's feelings in an article posted on the web or on television. Distance and time away is a bump on the road, but not a road block. Who knows what will come along in the months ahead for either of us professionally? Maybe you'll make so much money off of Vasallus that you can retire and just travel with me when I do my interviews, kind of like my personal assistant."

He pulled her close to him, gave her a deep kiss and replied: "Or maybe I can be your full time boy toy that will wait in the hotel room until you get back from your interview, give you great sex, take you out dinner, then come back to the hotel for more great sex, then do it all over again the next day."

She giggled, tilted her head back, laughed some more then let her long hair fall into his face in a teasing fashion and replied: "You are a stud baby, without a doubt, but let's face it, you're not a 'boy toy', more like a 'man toy', and 'man toys' can't keep that kind of pace, at least not for very long. I think that the personal assistant with the odd romp under the sheets is a little more realistic."

"You think so do you? Tell me something. Do you think a 'man toy' can make love three times in a row? Not a chance, so I believe I'm still firmly entrenched in the 'boy toy' category!" He then grabbed onto Bentley and spun her on her back and climbed on top of her. They made love again, their passion for each other fuelling their desire. They soon collapsed into each other, their sweat mixing, exhausted and rolled into a cradle position. Within minutes they were both fast asleep.

****

Avery awoke and instantly looked over at the clock on the night stand. It was 9:20 a.m. and both of them were late. Bentley needed to be at the airport before eleven; she was going to be pissed. He shook her awake and gingerly let her know the time. She blasted out of bed like she had been launched by rocket fuel. "Son of a bitch Avery, I can't be late for my flight, and I still have to get ready! I have twenty minutes with Madonna before she has to get ready for the opening concert of her North American tour. Dammit Avery, it's your fault! Your three times in a row is going to get me fired!"

"Listen, I tell you what Bentley. Take your time getting ready. I will have the Alive Records jet take you to Chicago. Get in the shower and I will call Jenn and make it happen."

She looked beautiful standing at the foot of the bed as she

transitioned from complete panic to relief as she said: "Are you sure Avery? That seems like too many mountains to move. It would just be easier if I got my ass moving and fixed my makeup on the flight over."

"Nonsense Bentley, I will make the arrangements. Besides, it's not every day that a man in his forties can make love three times in one morning. It's a small price to pay for those kind of bragging rights, my dear."

As Bentley made her way into the shower, Avery called Jenn and made all of the arrangements for the company jet to whisk Bentley to Chicago. She let him know that she would send over the company limo to take Bentley over to the executive jet service at LAX, where the jet was parked. With that taken care of, he jumped out of bed and quickly got dressed, packed a suitcase for the week, and made his way into the bathroom where she was already applying makeup, a towel wrapped around her body and another around her hair. He moved in close, pressing against her, kissed her neck and said: "I have to run. Call me tonight when you get a chance. I'll be at the mansion all week with the kids. It would be nice if you could come down and stay for a night."

She turned around, one hand holding her eye shadow, the other holding the eye shadow brush, and wrapped them both around his neck, stood on her tip toes and kissed him, then replied: "I would like that. I'm dying to hear them all together. I will be back in town tomorrow afternoon, then I will either come tomorrow night or the next. I will call you."

****

Avery settled into the studio at the mansion to go over the song selection for the album one more time, looking for any inspiration to change-up the rotation, but after a few minutes he had none and was ready to go. He got up out of his chair, walked out of the recording studio and down the hall to the offices where he let Amber, whom he borrowed from Jenn for the week, gather the kids and get them down to the studio. It was time.

Fifteen minutes later, all seven kids were in the studio,

sitting on any available chairs, some standing and others leaning against the wall. Avery marvelled at how incredibly good looking these kids were. They appeared to be manmade, their looks were just so perfect. Outside of maybe the Benning kid, all of them were down to earth, nice kids, not wrapped up in their individual success whatsoever, all of them eager to get started on Vasallus. They had been practicing together for weeks. Their timing was spot on and they had gelled very well together over the past several months. Now it was time to slot them into specific roles within the band.

The different cultural backgrounds from all of them added an interesting element to not only their sound, but their look and interaction with each other. Juan's strong South American accent and Chloë's Irish brogue plus Michael's contrasting clipped British cockney added to their overall flavor and identity. Elizabeth's thick Canadian French, much different than Metropolitan French, made her especially endearing when she spoke. All these accents disappeared, however, when they stepped up to a microphone.

He studied them all carefully before beginning. Chloë, with her long blond hair tied into a thick braid that rested on her shoulder, was totally casual with a pair of tiny, bright blue shorts with a tight, white t-shirt with some sort of boarding logo. Brittany and Elizabeth both wore long stretchy workout pants, Brittany boldly wore a halter top, while Elizabeth wore a plain t-shirt. Elizabeth had her dark long hair tucked behind her ears as she liked to wear floppy hats for the total hippie look. Brittany and Chloë were blond bombshells, while Elizabeth was a dark beauty, mysterious almost. All the guys wore board shorts, flip flops and sleeveless shirts which exposed their well-developed biceps. Patrick, however, wore faded blue jeans, a Jimi Hendrix t-shirt and bare feet. His beard was a few days old, giving him a scruffy look, along with his long and dark, wavy hair. Avery noticed his face looked a little puffy and he walked around with a bit of a limp. "Wonder what that was about?" he thought. The other three guys would need a microscope to find any facial hair.

Avery addressed them all together: "Do you guys think you're ready for this? Are you ready to put aside your egos, individual successes and personal interests for this band? I don't care what you have done or not done in the past, none of that matters anymore. As of this minute, we wipe the slate clean, and everyone in this room is an equal. Everything you do from this point forward is about Vasallus. Commit to the group and through that, you will have more success than any of you has ever dreamed of, I promise you."

He watched as none of them said a thing, so he continued: "The best recording and music production talent in the world are at your disposal, including myself and Mr. Best. I am your leader and the one who will walk you through the recording of your first album. Commit to me and I will commit to you. I have selected the thirteen songs that will comprise the album and I must tell you, they are very, very good songs. They will make all of you stars beyond your wildest dreams. You also need to know that it is Patrick Benning who has written these songs, including the lyrics. He is a genius in writing music, just like all of you are musical geniuses in your own right. Collectively, we are going to change the face of music forever, I really believe that. Does anyone have any questions before we get started?"

Again, none of them said a thing; they just stared back at him with wide-eyed excitement. They were like dogs on a leash that had been given the scent, and were waiting for the leash to come off so they could pursue their target. He could sense that these kids had been ready for this their whole lives and they were just waiting for Avery to say the word and they would begin making great music. He continued: "Now, since all of you are tremendous singers with beautiful voices, the challenge is to find that harmony, harness the power of your voices into one. That is what we will do today. We will work through the songs one at a time. I will change things up as we go along. What I am looking for is your strengths and weaknesses as a singing group, not as individuals. Most groups have one front person as a lead singer, but this band has seven potential lead singers and we will use that variety to our advantage. I already know you are all great singers. What I need to find out is how good you are at sharing the stage as a group, and more importantly, singing harmony. Okay? Everyone good with that?"

There was a collection of yeses and nods of heads. It seemed that, at least in the beginning, they were all on the same page. He finished up with: "This is how we are going to setup for the debut single. The song is called "Don't Hold Back", an upbeat dance number with some great harmony in the chorus. Connor will take the reins for the male lead vocals, backed by Chloë in the chorus. All of you will come in for the final chorus. Patrick, you are on drums of course, Michael on bass, Brittany on piano, Elizabeth on keyboards, and Juan on lead guitar. Again, I ask you. Are there any questions?"

And again, there were none. "This is going way too smoothly", he thought to himself. Divvying up the responsibilities for the first song, he thought there would definitely be noses out of joint, but all of them picked up their respective instruments, plugged in, got a feel for what they were doing and were ready to go within minutes. He looked down at the song sheet and went over the lyrics one last time. Connor and his smooth, engaging sound would deliver the song with purpose and then the song would almost come to a standstill while Chloë would cut in with her powerful and beautiful voice. The combination could be truly sizzling. Combined with the perfect harmony of the group, it had major hit all over it.

Don't Hold Back
Connor: You've lived your life as you've
Been told, obedient and loyal
Isn't it time you have some say
Don't forget it is your life you know
Ask for it, don't hold back

Chorus – Chloë: Don't hold back
Reach out and take a stance

Claim your life it's beautiful
Don't hold back
Be all you can be
Everyone: Don't hold back, Don't hold back

Connor: Today is a day you can take
And place a stake for your freedom
You turn around twice and your
Life will be over so stake
That claim to be free so
Don't ever hold back

Chorus – Chloë: Don't hold back
Reach out and take a stance
Claim your life it's beautiful
Don't hold back
Be all you can be
Everyone: Don't hold back, Don't hold back

Connor: Rise up and deliver to everyone
A message that you can be counted
Upon to take that stance
And be proud you did
Because it's up to you to decide
Don't ever hold back

Chorus – Chloë: Don't hold back
Reach out and take a stance
Claim your life it's beautiful
Don't hold back
Be all you can be
Everyone: Don't hold back, Don't hold back

Chorus – Everyone: Don't hold back
Reach out and take a stance
Claim your life it's beautiful
Don't hold back

Be all you can be
Don't hold back, Don't hold back

Connor: Remember to be free you
Need to be all you can be
Everyone: Reach out and take a stance
Claim your life it's beautiful
Don't hold back
Be all you can be
Don't hold back, Don't hold back

He took his position in front of the massive mixing
board, turned on the mic to speak to them behind the sound
proof glass and said: "Okay, I know all of you can read music
with ease, but you're all looking at a piece of music for the first
time except, of course, Patrick. Let's just begin with all of you
just reading the music and playing. It's going to sound like shit,
but it doesn't matter. No one is listening. By the end of the
day, however, I want this song to sound like you've been
playing it for years. Okay? Connor and Chloë, we won't need
vocals for a few takes, I'm sure, while they find their way
through. Alright on a count of three, 1…2...and 3."

What happened next defied logic. The kids broke into
song and played like they had played it hundreds of times
before. All of them were right on the beat, in tune, completely
spot on. He sat there in his chair in front of the mixing board
stunned. "This is not supposed to happen." He had worked
with some the best and most accomplished musicians in the
world, and when they were handed a brand new, never seen
before piece of music, it took them more than a few times to
get the composition down. These kids killed it the first time
they laid eyes on the music. As the song came to an end, all of
them just stood quietly waiting for Avery to say something. It
took him a minute to recover and he spoke into the
microphone and all he could think of saying was: "Okay, that
was more than incredible. Let's do it again, but this time with

vocals. Chloë and Connor, if you will, please."

They started in again, and then Connor stepped up to the microphone stand and began to sing the lyrics and it was truly a magical moment. His soaring voice took the song to a whole new level. Avery was blown away. He watched as Connor stepped back when the chorus began and watched as Chloë stepped up to her mic and began to sing. She didn't even look at her sheet, having already memorized the words. With her eyes closed, her angelic voice reached out to Avery, the sound waves piercing through the glass and into his heart, he could feel it begin to melt as she continued. Her voice was beautiful and as the chorus ended, she handed the song back to Connor who seamlessly integrated his amazing voice onto Chloë's creating a terrific one-two punch, all backed by the melody created by the rest of the kids. They played and sounded like a band that have been playing together for years. They fed off of each other like great bands do. It was a very special moment for Avery as he sat back and listened to the song wind down. It was flawless. He could have recorded that first take with no need for any further takes.

The true sense of superstardom for Vasallus hit him like a ton of bricks, and he struggled with the enormity of what was ahead for them and everyone. He knew how the music world would react to these kids, and the thought sent chills down his spine.

Chapter 32

Jake Reynolds, an aging thirty-seven year old musician, was one of hundreds, if not thousands, of struggling musicians who flocked to southern California hoping to make it big in the music scene. In L.A., musicians like Jake were just like the actors and actresses who also came to the land of milk and honey with the big dream of being discovered as the next big star. He ground out his rock-laced music in the Los Angeles bar scene for years, and once in a while, his agent got him a gig at one of the top venues in Los Angeles, including The Cave, the premier concert venue in the city. Playing at The Cave meant that you were on the verge of breaking out. The place was often frequented by record producers as a place to be seen and to check out the local music talent, looking for that undiscovered and raw talent that could push their record label over the top. If there were any producers in the audience when Jake performed there a few times, they must not have liked what they heard, because Jake never got his big break.

He had released three records, all on his independent record label, Cherish Records. That meant that his pieced together, low-budget mixing equipment was barely able to cobble together the music in a passable and useable fashion. There was a lot of great music produced in small studio apartments all over the city, in the hopes of making it big. His records sold decently well among hard core rock fans in southern California, but never found a larger audience. He needed a breakout hit, a top forty song to get him the coveted airplay on pop radio that would get him his much-deserved widespread audience.

He felt that his writing was top notch and his songs were

good. His agent told him that they were good, and to just keep writing and the inspiration for that hit song would come. His agent also urged him to form a permanent band, and change from Jake Reynolds to a group name. Rockers were not solo artists, they were in bands, but Jake resisted, instead preferring to perform solo in the studio and in clubs and to use musicians from a talent pool of struggling guitarists, drummers, keyboardists that were plentiful in Los Angeles. He wanted his music to stand alone, and he wanted full creative control over it; he did not want to be in a position of having to share that with anyone, so instead he continued to hire studio musicians and freelance available local talent to record and perform in the clubs.

A young bass player by the name of Patrick Benning, who was only fourteen-years old when he first used him in the studio, approached him several months ago with an offer to write some songs for him. The kid was an incredibly good bass player and not only had he used him in the studio, but he also got him in some clubs to perform. He looked much older than fourteen and as long as he was only used on the weekends, sneaking him into the clubs as a musician was a piece of cake. At first, Jake blew him off, but the kid was persistent and eventually he sat down one afternoon in front of his piano in his apartment and began to play some of Benning's music. The kid gave him six songs to check out and after a few hours on the piano Jake knew he had his song. Not one song, but all six were fantastic and had hit written all over them. After all the years of playing in obscurity in this business, he knew with every fiber in his body that his life was about to change.

Jake played Benning's songs on his piano at the monster popular rock club, The Brickyard, to gauge the impact of the kid's songs on a live audience. He played two of the six songs written by Benning. One was a ballad and the other was a catchy-as-hell rock song. The two songs blew the roof off the place. Jake brought the place to a standstill with the eerily beautiful ballad, 'Sometimes I Dream'. He altered some of the lyrics to better suit his style and it worked because the audience loved it. When he started up with one of his own songs to pick things back up again, the kids kind of stood around, not quite sure what they had just heard but knowing that they loved it and wanted more. The dance floor was jammed with hundreds of kids when he played the ballad but it was now empty as he played his music. He looked at the band he had put together that evening and indicated to them that they should play his other song from Benning, the guitar-driven anthem: "Meet Me in the Middle". Jake had changed the title as well as most of the lyrics, but he didn't change the arrangement. It didn't take long for the kids to return to the dance floor, jamming it full. When he finished playing it, the reaction caught Jake by surprise. The young kids, most of them in their early twenties, went crazy. They demanded that he play the song again by coming together on the dance floor and all shouting out the name of the song, and pumping their fists in the air like an army of soldiers cheering on their general. When Jake and his band broke into one of his own songs, the kids began to boo loudly. They stood their ground on the dance floor, arms and fists moving in unison and shouted their demands that the band play the song again.

The concert ended with Jake playing 'Meet Me in the Middle' three more times and the ballad, 'Sometimes I Dream' twice more. It turned out to be a surreal experience for him, but he knew he finally had his songs and he couldn't wait to get into his studio to record the album with the six songs given to him by Benning. What he would really do was use three of them and save the other three for a follow-up album. Within a few weeks after the gig at The Brickyard, he completed recording the new eleven song album that included three of Patrick Benning's compilations. He chose to take full credit for the material from Benning when he registered the songs with the Music Association of America. He did not return any of Benning's calls or text messages. "Fuck him", thought Jake. "The kid is stupid anyway and he will never know that the three reworked songs on the album were his." He had paid his dues in this industry and the kid hadn't even bought his first can of shaving cream yet. "So let him get a dose of the cruelty of this business, it might do him some good." he thought.

His agent, impressed with his new record, asked Jake where the inspiration suddenly came from: "This is a great record Jake. You should be damned proud of yourself. What the fuck have you been doing? Taking some new synthetic drug circulating around the clubs? They loosen up some of the strands of long lost creativity brother?"

He grinned at his agent, who looked like a burned out agent who finally had a client who could make some money and replied: "No drugs man, just been saving it for the right time to come out. The mind is a beautiful thing if you give it the freedom it desires. It's all about harnessing the creative energy that all of us possess man and for me, the time has come. Get ready to have some fun!"

****

It didn't take long for radio stations to catch on to the record and begin playing the first single: "Sometimes I Dream". Of course, that was after his agent sent a copy to every radio station in California and Nevada. Within a few months, he was booked to play the mega popular rock venue in Las Vegas, Hard Rock Café and he was informed by his agent that the head of Blackstar Studios, Robert Best, would be in the audience. He felt that he had finally hit the big time as his album began to garner attention in other major markets such as Chicago and New York. Lesser known record labels and producers were all trying to sign Jake to their labels as his agent spread the word that a follow-up album had already been recorded. There was only one label that Jake wanted and that was Blackstar Studios, so he waited for the gig at Hard Rock to meet Robert Best, the most influential producer in the industry, on par with the legendary Avery Johnson of Alive Records.

Jake heard a few whimpers from the Benning kid about his music, but he ignored him. The little prick wouldn't go away, he was texting him constantly and leaving him voicemails. The kid had looks to kill and talent that would someday give him his shot at the big time, but now wasn't that time, it was Jake Reynolds' time. Eventually, he paid him a visit at some swanky mansion in Malibu, and threatened that if he didn't go play in the ocean he might find himself at the bottom of it. The kid almost rolled over and peed on himself after he told him the local shark population feasted on the bodies the mafia and gangs dropped off the piers on a daily basis. The kid was scared shitless and he knew Benning would disappear for good. If he didn't, then the dumb fuck would be face first in sand, thirty feet down off of the end of the multitude of deserted piers along the Malibu Beach coastline.

The night of his performance at the Hard Rock in Vegas had arrived and so had the excitement around the music scene in Las Vegas for the new up and coming rocker, Jake Reynolds. Local radio stations were hyping the concert all week with Jake doing on air interviews with most of them. Even the giant marquee LED-lit sign of the Hard Rock pulsated with lights that changed colors every five seconds now displayed his name in big, bold letters. It was all surreal for him, but he drank it up like a fine glass of red wine. Tonight was his night and he was going to deliver the performance of his life.

****

The concert ended with the crowd going crazy and demanding an encore, stamping their feet on the floor and pounding their fists on the tables. Jake didn't know what to do; he had never performed in front of an audience that demanded an encore. His agent flew around the curtain behind the stage, almost tripping on cables taped to the floor and blurted: "Jake you've got to give them more. Listen to them, they are going crazy! Listen to me Jake, I spent the last twenty minutes sitting with Robert Best at his table and he wants you to go back out there and perform a song off of your follow-up album."

Jake gave his agent a look of confusion and replied: "How would Best know about my follow-up album? What did you tell him?"

The agent fixed him with a sheepish look that quickly hardened when he said: "Listen Jake, if you don't get your ass out there in the next ten seconds and blow Best away with that new song I heard you rehearse, you may very well be performing your next concert at a truck stop. Producers like Best, with one phone call, can put you out of the game so fast it will be like you were never in it Jake. Give him what he wants to hear and then let's bring him backstage to celebrate your future."

So he did. Jake walked back out on the stage, alone, with just his acoustic guitar and announced to the cheering crowd that he would play them a song that would be released on his next album. The stage lights dimmed except for a soft blue light that brought Jake from the darkness of the stage. The song was a heartfelt acoustic rendition of a ballad stolen from Benning. It soon had the crowd mesmerized. They swayed back and forth on the dance floor and throughout the club, their arms in the air and their eyes closed like they were listening to Steve Perry of Journey singing 'Open Arms'. When Jake finished the song, the crowd came alive and gave him a thunderous, long round of applause. It was a fantastic feeling for him as he climbed off of his stool, swung the guitar over his shoulder and exited the stage to the roar of the crowd.

Backstage, he was met by his agent who gave him a massive bear hug and screamed like a kid at Christmas. He yelled: "Get ready for the big time Jake! We have just been invited to Robert Best's suite at the Bellagio as soon as we can get over there. This is it brother! This is what you've been waiting for Jake. It's what you've worked for all of your life. It's what we've worked for! Now, say goodbye to your band, give them a hundred bucks to go buy some drinks and tell them you will see them in the morning. You fucking made it! Now, let's get going!"

He went back to their dressing room, high-fived his rented band, threw them some cash and told them all to go get drunk and he'd see them in the morning. He joined his agent in the lobby, jumped in a cab and they made their way over to the Bellagio. He knew he should be excited about getting an opportunity to meet with one of the top music executives in the industry, but there was something just not right with him. He wished he hadn't performed the new song for the encore; it was a mistake He felt guilty about playing that song. He never even gave it a second thought when he performed the Benning songs he had recorded for the first album. Playing that unrecorded new song felt weird for some reason. He had never changed the lyrics or the arrangement to it yet. It was purely a Benning song and for that, when he performed it, the realization that he was a phony hit him hard. He struggled with his emotions in the cab on the way over and could barely hear his agent as he went on and on about how big of a star he would become and how he would have to begin finding a law firm specializing in contractual work.

He even entertained the thought of coming clean with Best and telling him that the music was not his and that he had stolen it. Maybe Best would understand and say that was okay, he was meant to record that music and they would work out a way to compensate the Benning kid somehow. His agent would have a heart attack, but screw him, he needed to do this. He did not understand the overwhelming feeling to come clean, but come clean he would.

They arrived a few minutes later at the Bellagio, the limo driver dropping them off in front of the grand entrance to the resort. From there, the two of them took the elevators to the top floor as instructed and made their way to Suite 11920. After he knocked on the door, Jake turned to his agent and was about to say that he was sorry for what he was about to do, when the door of the suite opened and Jake's jaw almost dropped to the floor. It wasn't Robert Best, the famous record producer or his assistant who greeted them at the door. It was the kid. Patrick Benning. Jake struggled with the shock of the kid at the door and just stood there staring at him, searching for words, when his agent broke the silence and asked: "We are here to see Mr. Best. He has invited us up to his suite. Can you let him know that Jake Reynolds and his agent, Philip Maggert, are here to see him please?"

Benning did not acknowledge his agent or his request, nor

did he even look at him. He just stared right into Jake's eyes. A silence hung in the air while Benning continued to glare. Jake finally broke the silence between the two of them and said: "Patrick, I did not expect to see you here, but now that you are I am glad. I came up here to tell Mr. Best the truth about your music. If you will let us in, I would be happy to explain why I did what I did."

Maggert looked over at him with a dumbfounded look and said: "What the fuck are you talking about Jake? You're not making any sense. Look kid, can you just please stop staring and go notify Mr. Best that we are waiting to speak with him?"

Still not saying a word, Benning backed away from the door and motioned with his hand to come in. Jake and his agent entered the massive suite and he was about to say something to Benning when he heard the door close behind him. He turned to look behind him, but his agent had already turned around and all he could hear him say was: "Jesus, mother of Christ!"

Jake fell back against the wall, horrified at what he was seeing. One second they were knocking on a door to meet a man who would change his life forever, with an opportunity he had worked so hard for, for so many years and it had finally come together. The next minute, he had stepped into a completely different reality. Benning, unbelievably, had somehow transformed into a gigantic, monstrous beast. The mass of this thing filled the suite's hallway. Its skin was like clay, cracked, dry and broken. Its eyes were ablaze in red that reflected a horrible rage as it moved towards his agent. Maggert back pedaled into the suite, screaming, terrified as the creature raised its huge arms above its head, the claw-like talons at the end of them that were so big that they could hold a basketball as if it t was a ping pong ball. The beast swung its arm, crashing down onto his agent's shoulder, barely missed his head, and shredded his upper arm with the razor sharp talons. Blood hit the surrounding walls and furniture from the blow. Maggert cried out, and he sounded like a deer that had just been hit on the highway. Jake could only watch in horror, knowing that he would be next. The beast swung its other arm almost instantly after the first blow and raked its talons across Maggert's chest, tearing flesh and bone as it did so. Maggert was thrown over the couch by the power of the blow, and landed on the hard tile floor on the other side, his body limp. The creature flashed its crimson red eyes at Jake before he stepped over the couch and smashed its talon- tipped fist into Maggert's skull, crushing it like beer can. The sound of skull bone being smashed to bits reverberated throughout the suite.

As the beast pulled its claw out of the mangled skull of his agent, Jake began to carefully step backwards towards the door out of the suite and to the elevators to escape this nightmare. He had turned the handle and whipped the heavy door open when the beast snapped its huge head towards him, its eyes on fire. Jake made his escape to the sound of the beast breaking the coffee table as it made its way after him. He ran down the hallway to the elevator and pushed the down button. He only had a split second to spare and if the elevator did not open in that second, he was dead. He heard the miraculous *ding, ding* sound of the elevator as it arrived. After what seemed like an eternity, the elevator door began to open and yet the beast had not followed him. For a fleeting second, he felt a slight hope that he might make it off this floor and into the safety of the hotel lobby. The elevator door opened and he made his way towards it, but stopped in his tracks. The beast, all seven feet of it, came rushing towards him from within the elevator. Before he could even react, Jake felt the pierce of the talon claw burst through his chest, the pain matched only by the complete loss of air as the blow destroyed his lungs. He could feel the rush of blood erupt from his mouth.

For the last few seconds before he died, he stared into the eyes of the beast. They were a portal into hell, to where he knew he was about to journey. It was all because he stole the music from a kid. If only he knew that the kid was a demon. He'd never get the chance to know better next time. He lived another few seconds to hear the roar of laughter from the deranged face of the demon.

****

He killed the pathetic Reynolds and his agent because he was pissed off that the asshole ripped off his music. He fully intended to let him have it anyway, not because he wanted to help the loser, but just to get a kick out of seeing the success of his music through someone other than his six siblings. His master would be livid, but he didn't give a shit anymore, he just wanted to kill as many as he could tonight. The rush of death administered by his hands was too incredible to describe. He couldn't get enough of it, but he would at least try tonight.

The slaughter of Reynolds and Maggert in the Bellagio created widespread panic all down the famous boulevard. Las Vegas police closed all access onto the strip as they frantically searched for the killer or killers. Patrick decided to take his killing road show away from all of the pandemonium on the strip to a men's club a few blocks away. He walked in like he owned the place and was quickly shown a table, the beautiful and ogling hostess not even bothering to ask him for i.d. The hostess was soon replaced by a waitress, whose small breasts were ridiculously pushed together and then lifted to give the impression that she actually had breasts. She had yet to crack into the bigger money to afford the implants which all the strippers were having done these days, like newly apprenticed electricians purchasing their tool kits. He ordered their mandatory two at a time drink rule by ordering two vodka and cokes. The drinks came with the waitress sticking her shitty little boobs in his face when she placed the drinks on the table. She dragged her long hair across his face as she purred into his ear: "You want to start a tab sweetheart? Just need your credit card, honey, and then when you're ready to go, we'll charge it for your drinks and any other fun you might want to have tonight."

Patrick struggled to control his rage, but kept it in control long enough to whisper or rather shout back into her ear above the loud music: "How about you grab two of your friends, take me upstairs and we'll all pretend we're going to fuck. How does that sound sweetheart?"

Patrick could feel her tense up at his aggressive response, but she continued: "I think I can make that happen. Give me your credit card and I'll see what I can do."

He slapped a stack of cash on her tray before saying: "Will this do? My rich dad won't give me one of those things."

She looked him over for a second, trying to decide if she should just throw him out, but instead flashed a smile, winked, then disappeared behind the bar with his money and returned a few minutes later with a nervous smile: "Follow me handsome. It's time to party. Let's not keep my friends waiting, shall we?"

He followed her through the throng of horny guys all transfixed by the strip show on the small stage. The one in their section thrashed her tongue over her painted lips as he walked by her on the way to the stairway. His waitress reached behind her and took his hand in hers as she led him up the stairs. Once they were at the top, she batted her heavy, mascara-clogged eyelashes, pouted her lips and then smiled, mouthing the words "follow me" as she led him through a curtain and into a darkened room with a small mini bar and a black leather couch. She motioned for him to take a seat and went to the bar to fix him another vodka and coke. Amused, he asked: "Where are your friends? Let's get this party started, huh?"

Then he heard a voice from behind him say: "Yea asshole, let's get the party started!" He watched as two enormous, steroid-pumped muscle freaks in tight t-shirts came through a curtain from the other side of the room. The first one, with a pock-marked face, bald head, and five steel hoops in each ear charged him, shouting: "No one comes in here and acts like this place is a whorehouse. Time to feel some pain, you dumb fuck!"

Patrick slipped a pair of steel knuckles over his hand and waited until he was within arm's length of him and hammered him so hard and so fast in the middle of his face that his nose exploded in blood and broken bone like an overripe tomato. He was dead before he even hit the floor. The waitress fell back against the mini bar, screaming, and the other security guy lunged at him from behind the couch. Patrick thrust out his hand and caught the guy in the chin with his steel knuckles with a ferociousness that cracked open his skin like a split watermelon. He followed that up with a lightning fast strike with his other hand that smashed his teeth in like they were made of glass. The waitress went berserk, shouted for him to stop, jumped on his back and clawed at his face with her fake nails. He reached back and gave her a hammer strike with his elbow to her face that instantly silenced her. She fell to the floor in a heap and he followed up by driving his boot into her throat, which crushed her wind pipe and neck and made death instantaneous.

Patrick turned to the primal roar of the second steroid freak, his face covered with blood, his mouth full of black and bleeding holes, his left hand gripped an eight inch blade, ready to drive it into him. He lunged at him, but Patrick easily deflected his knife hand and, at the same time, continued the guy's forward motion by grabbing onto his other wrist and pushing him violently to the ground. The guy was flat on his stomach and braced for the death blow that was sure to come. He looked up at Patrick's blazing eyes and pleaded through his destroyed mouth: "Please, stop. I'm sorry. Just go please. I won't tell anyone what happened here!"

In a complete rage, Patrick raised his steel knuckled fist up in the air and yelled down at the condemned bouncer with a demonic roar: "I don't think so you fucking prick. See you in hell!" The force of his fist drove into the guy's face so hard that he thought his fist went right through his head and into the carpeted floor.

He stood up and let the rage fill his body. The rage was like a narcotic, hitting his nerve endings like the rush from a snort of cocaine. He ripped the curtain aside as he left the room and watched as the dancers and patrons milling about looked up at him, thinking he had just taken a bath filled with blood. The faces turned to screams of horror as people began to pour into the room behind the curtain and witness the carnage. A waitress at the top of the stairs fainted when she saw all of the blood on him and Patrick reached down, picked her up and tossed her over the rail and onto the bar tables twenty feet below. Pandemonium broke out everywhere in the bar as the patrons began to comprehend what had happened. As he made his way down the stairs, people everywhere were screaming and running towards the exits in panic.. He even could hear sirens in the distance as he walked out into the parking lot. "Too late motherfuckers", he thought, with a mixture of triumph and contempt. He thought about waiting for the cops to arrive and having some fun with them. The thought was suddenly, violently yanked from his mind and he found himself airborne, flying through the air, then landing, hard, fifty feet from where he had just stood. He landed in the front windshield of a Chevy Camaro. "What the fuck?"

The Master pounced on him on top of the Camaro. The repeated blows to Patrick's body pushed him into the front seat of the sports car. The Master was fully transformed into his true self, the Anti-Christ, and he was clearly not impressed with the carnage inside the club. He grabbed his ankles, violently pulled him through the shattered windshield and swung his entire body so hard against the hood that it was pushed right up to the front passenger headrest. The entire time, he screamed commands and orders in his native language of Latin. Although the blows did not hurt Patrick physically, the disappointment swelling inside of him with the realization that he had enraged his Master was painful. He could see that the club was completely engulfed in flames. Police cars, fire trucks and ambulances poured into the parking lot. However, the emergency personnel were so transfixed by the raging inferno, that they did not even notice the hellish spanking being administered by the most evil entity on earth to his unruly offspring.

Chapter 33

He stood to gather his carry-on bag, his weary body, once so agile and nimble, now carried the burden of a man in his mid-seventies. The physical confrontation with the demon months ago in Rome had taken its toll on his aging body, and he knew he didn't have much time left on this earth. One thing he knew for certain. He would confront the demonic beast again and he would use all the power invested in him by God himself to protect the unknowing child the beast had spawned so many years ago. He would protect Chloë until his last dying breath. Her purpose had still not been revealed by God, but he was certain that He did have a plan for her. Thomas also knew that Satan had a plan for her; he brought her into this world for a reason, and Thomas hoped that he would live long enough to see that she survived in the grace of God's mercy.

The twenty-two hour Delta Airlines' flight from Dublin to Los Angeles, with a stop in New York, was being called to board so he made his way into the line of excited, mainly Irish countrymen looking forward to a trip to America. When they saw he was a priest, he often received gestures of kindness from others, offering everything from their place in line to demands to pay for his cup of tea in the terminal. He would shrug them off, thanking them anyway, but today, when offers were made, he took them. He had a heightened feeling of anxiety about his trip to Los Angeles to see Chloë. He had not heard a word from Sister McGarrigle and only bits and pieces from Chloë. She would always have the same excuse when he was able to get a hold of her: Sister McGarrigle had just stepped out to the store, was indisposed or was running errands. Chloë seemed distant and vague. She wasn't her usual bubbly and excited self. She seemed monotone and bored. Thomas asked her if she wanted to come back to Ireland and she vehemently stated that she was here to develop her music career and would not leave. He certainly looked forward to seeing Chloë, but the familiar feeling of doom had revisited the inner walls of his stomach the second he booked the trip. He felt more like a detective conducting an investigation than an excited and proud caregiver looking forward to being part of the blossoming career of an extremely talented young lady. He would confront Sister McGarrigle regarding her carelessness in communicating with the Church. "Who knows, maybe she gave up her vows after tasting life in America? She certainly wouldn't be the first member of a religious order to succumb to the temptations of decadence." Whatever it was, Chloë wasn't talking.

His turn at the gate podium arrived and he showed the agent his passport and boarding pass and they were promptly checked, scanned and returned to him. The agent smiled as he said, "Have a pleasant and peaceful flight Father."

Thomas made his way down the gangway, adjusting the shoulder strap on his bag as he did so and then he heard a voice behind him, with an American accent: "Visiting New York Father?"

Thomas turned to acknowledge the question, but when he did, there was no one behind him, only the young couple far back at the podium gate just being handed their docs by the agent. He quickly turned back down the gangway towards the plane and there was no one there either. He was alone. "Where did that voice come from?" Too deep in thought, he must have imagined it, he surmised as he continued his way down the gangway.

The voice with the American accent spoke again, directly behind him: "What brings a tired old man of the cloth to America? A little sightseeing maybe?"

Thomas stopped dead in his tracks and whirled around, there was something eerily familiar about that voice. When he turned, there was no one, just the couple making their way towards him. He turned again to the entrance of the plane. No one. The sense of doom resonated through his stomach. He could feel the warm beads of sweat begin to break out on his forehead, causing an itchy and burning sensation. As the young couple approached, he asked: "Excuse me did you see an American man just a second ago, maybe travelling alone, in front of you?"

In a thick Irish accent, the young mane giggled and said: "No, I'm afraid not Father. Have you lost track of someone? Would you like us to go back to the gate and inquire?"

He didn't want to confuse the young couple any further, so he lifted his hand in gesture in front of him and replied: "No, that is not necessary. I'm sure he made it onto the plane in front of me. Thank you. Enjoy your flight."

As he made his way onto the plane and towards his assigned seat, he studied the faces staring back at him.. Not a one appeared to be the man who had called out to him on the gangway. "Very strange", he thought as he took his seat by the window of the large Boeing 747. Boarding took almost thirty minutes and soon they were airborne. It took less than that for a deep sleep to take him across the Atlantic.

****

Thomas awoke to a loud thud, jarring him from his deep slumber. He looked to his left to see the two passengers strapped in beside him frozen in fear, the look of terror etched across their faces like a horrible memory forever cursed in their minds. Suddenly, the plane lurched forward with such ferocity that he banged his forehead hard against the plastic screen of the small TV in the seat in front of him. Pain shot through his head like a hot knife. He brought his fingers to his head and felt the warm stickiness of blood. "What is going on?" he wondered. The plane then lost altitude, dropping thousands of feet in seconds; the rush of lost altitude flowing through his stomach forced its contents into his throat. The pilot reacted with a tremendous thrust of the plane's engines, lifting the nose of the plane up as he did so, and forcing its passengers violently backwards into their headrests. Thomas heard someone scream behind him. He looked out of his window and saw the flashes of lightning all around the plane. They were mired in a violent thunder storm. "Why didn't the pilot fly around the storm?"

Another heavy bang erupted inside of the plane as the sound of further lost altitude caused the contents of the overhead baggage compartment to lift and slam. More people screamed. The pilot came on the PA and announced heavy turbulence for the next several minutes. He cautioned everyone to remain calm and remain in their seats with their seatbelts securely fastened. Thomas leaned over to the two terrified passengers beside him and said reassuringly: "It's going to be okay. Turbulence on the Atlantic is quite common. The pilot knows what he is doing. A few more minutes and you'll feel like you're sitting in your living room, it will be so calm." The two of them looked over at him, the looks of terror on their faces not diminishing and the one sitting on the aisle replied: "You're bleeding Father. We're going to die in this plane, right now. I just hope I die on impact when we hit the ocean so that I don't have to be eaten alive by sharks."

He was going to give her a reassuring reply, when the passenger in the seat in front of him stood up and leaned over the seat and looked at Thomas with a look of desperation and screamed: "Pray for me Father. Pray for me! I don't want to die! Please Father!"

Thomas in a loud, but calm voice replied: "Sir, you need to get back in your seat and fasten your seatbelt. Everything is going to be ok…" He didn't get to finish as the plane's nose pitched downwards, shaking badly and pitching hard to the left and right as the pilot desperately tried to regain control of the plane. The passenger who asked him to pray for him was launched across the heads of the people sitting in the rows ahead of him, landing in a twisted mess against the wall of the lavatory. Passengers were either screaming, crying or praying. How did this happen? One minute he was boarding the plane and the next he was plunging into the Atlantic. He looked out the window and a sudden, bright flash of lightning illuminated the exterior of the plane. It looked like something was sitting on the tip of the wing! "That is impossible!" The flash of light was so quick that Thomas could easily have misjudged what he saw. He continued to look at the same spot, when he caught another glimpse from a second flash of lightning. This time there was no mistake. A gargoyle-like creature sat perched on the very edge of the wing. Its eyes shone bright red, blazing through the storm like beacons. They stared straight at him, not flinching or moving, locked in like radar. Another bright flash of the storm lit the sky around the creature and he could see that his death was only seconds away. The waves of the ocean surface were less than a hundred feet down, making impact inevitable and almost immediate. Thomas looked back at the creature and it was laughing hysterically. He watched as the beast spread its wings and lifted off of the plane before the plane made its deadly impact, its work completed.

Thomas made a sign of the cross on his chest and closed his eyes as impact came. Instead of the sound of horrible crushing metal and people screaming before he died, he heard a voice. It was the voice of a woman. She was saying something. He couldn't make out the words, his mind was too focused on the impact. He heard her voice again, louder, persistent. He opened his eyes towards the voice, expecting God had sent an angel to take him to Him, but instead it was the voice of an airline attendant.

"Father, wake-up. You are having a nightmare. Father. Father!"

He felt a hand squeeze his shoulder, shaking him. He opened his eyes, not to a burning carnage of torn and twisted metal and ocean water pouring through, but instead to a pleasant, smiling flight attendant looking down on him. It was just a nightmare. The relief that followed his realization was overwhelming. He immediately checked his forehead. Feeling no evidence of a gash, he slumped back into his seat, looked at the attendant and said: "I'm sorry if I caused a scene. May I ask how much longer to our arrival in New York?"

She leaned over the other two passengers and offered him

a glass of water before she replied: "The captain has begun his descent into JFK and we should be on the ground and in front of our gate within a half hour. Now, if I can get you to lift your seatback into its upright position Father, I will let you be."

****

Thomas did not even bother to leave his seat for the continuing flight to Los Angeles. He chose to remain seated, still shaken by the powerful and vivid nightmare he had experienced earlier. The two passengers sitting beside him couldn't get off the plane fast enough, looking back at him like he was a lunatic as they made their way down the aisle.. He couldn't blame them, he must have been quite the sight. Thrashing and moaning about the plane crashing. At least they would have a good story to tell their family and friends who were waiting for them in the terminal.

It wasn't long before the plane was back in the air, bound for Los Angeles. This time, Thomas was able to fall into a deep and peaceful sleep for the four and half hour flight. He was jarred awake when the plane made contact with the runway at LAX and pulled up to the gate. A sense of urgency and anxiousness came over him as he waited for the passengers in front of him to gather their carry-on luggage and make their way off the plane. He needed to know that Chloë was safe, and the faster he could get off this plane and into a taxi, the better. He struggled to maintain his patience at the incredibly slow moving passengers in front of him.

"You must be late for a sermon or an important presentation Father. You look way too impatient for a man of the cloth. Surely an event can wait for a man of God?"

It was the same voice he had heard call out to him in the gangway back in Dublin. It was the American. A chill suddenly dropped down the slope of his aging spine as he turned to the voice behind him. As he turned to face the man behind him, there was only a young woman and an elderly couple behind her. Straining to look over the couple to search for the man who spoke to him, he saw no one nor did anyone acknowledge him. He looked at a man down the aisle a ways who looked like an American, or at least like someone who might have been around the same age as the owner of the voice he heard and asked: "Excuse me sir. Did you just ask me something?"

In a thick Irish brogue the man replied: "No I didn't Father, but the aisle is open in front of you." The man gestured towards him and Thomas turned to see the plane was empty in front of him. The churning in his gut was like a meat grinder, chewing the insides of his stomach into strings of ground hamburger. He felt the presence of the demon all around him, powerful, mocking him. The lady directly behind him spoke, "Excuse me Father, but may I go around you? My family is waiting for me at the gate and I am quite anxious to see them."

Not feeling very secure on his feet, he stepped back into his row and sat down, choosing to let the plane empty, gather himself, then make his way to the baggage area. He watched each of the passengers as they made their way down the aisle carefully, looking for any clue as to the identity of the passenger who had spoken to him. Each passenger walked past his row, barely giving him a glance. Once the plane was empty, a cleaning crew came on board and got busy, not even acknowledging that a passenger was still on the plane. Thomas made his way past them, said goodbye to the attendants and the pilots as he walked off the plane and into the gangway. He was still shaky from his experience on the plane, but once he made his way into the hustle and bustle of the terminal, and saw people scurrying everywhere searching for their next gate, he began to feel a little better and decided to find a newsstand that might also sell antacids.

He made his way to his baggage carousel and discovered that the luggage was just beginning to land on the rotating and folding steel plates, working its way around to the waiting hands of eager passengers. He saw his small and plain black suitcase with a green ribbon tied on the handle (at the insistence of Mrs. Beckeridge, the parish administrator, who said if he was going to travel with the same suitcase as everyone else, then he would put up with the ribbon) fall onto the carousel. As he came around the other side to meet his bag, there was only one other person standing there. He was a well-dressed businessman, not in a big rush like everyone else on the flight to retrieve his bag, but patient to wait for it to make its way around towards him. Thomas spotted his bag with the green ribbon as it came around the corner. He stopped and waited for it. As his bag made its way past the businessman, the man suddenly bent down and scooped Thomas's bag off of the carousel and threw it on his cart with his other luggage. "What is that guy doing? Didn't he see the obvious green ribbon?" Thomas walked over to the man and said: "Excuse me sir, I believe you just picked up my bag."

The man did not acknowledge him and began to push his cart away from him, his back towards him. Thomas called out again, this time louder: "Sir, you picked up the wrong bag. Will you please stop? You have my bag!" This time the man stopped and without turning around spoke: "Don't panic O'Sullivan. You have something to hide in this bag I need to know about?" It was the voice he heard in the gangway in Dublin and again on the plane. The gale force winds began to blow through his stomach again as he struggled to keep his composure.

"Listen, I don't want any trouble young man. Can you please turn around so we can talk? It was you who spoke to me in Dublin and again on the plane. Why do you hide yourself? How do you know my name?"

The man turned around and the recognition almost brought him to his knees. The airport baggage area suddenly began to disappear all around him until it was just him and the man in front of him. Thomas blinked his eyes to make sure he wasn't experiencing another bad dream. The man was the same man who confronted him decades ago in the airport in Rome when he made his first trip to the Vatican as a newly commissioned priest summoned to the Holy City and the birth of SOSL. He looked identical, his age exactly the same. His eyes burned deep red as they bore into Thomas'. He looked at the man and said: "You! It cannot be! So many years ago!"

Suddenly, in the blink of an eye, the man was within inches of Thomas. His eyes were like burning orbs of fire. They were the unholy pits of hell. Thomas was standing in front of the beast! With shaking hands, he reached underneath his coat and clutched the cross that hung around his neck. He thrust it out from underneath the coat towards the beast followed by the prayer: "Saint Michael the Archangel, defend us in battle. Be our protection against the wickedness and snares of the devil. May God rebuke him, we humbly pray; and do Thou, O Prince of the Heavenly Host, by the Divine Power of God, cast into hell Satan and all the evil spirits who roam throughout the world seeking the ruin of souls." He had never recited the Saint Michael's prayer before, yet the words came to him as if he had been reading directly from words written on paper.

"Don't humour me, old man, with your useless words. You're only alive because I allowed it and you will die when I'm finished with you. You think you can protect Chloë, don't you? You are a foolish old man whose pathetic life is long past due. My blood flows through her, priest! That silly collar around your neck is not a shield from God to protect you from my wrath. Do you remember your friend Cardinal Zorn? Do you think it protected him?" Laughter boomed from the beast, spit flew from its mouth onto Thomas, its breath vile.

"Words of prayer from my mouth may not have an effect, but the hand of God is coming and will cut you down like the scared little sheep that you are. You're right, I may not have much time left, but I will live long enough to see you die from the mighty sword of God." Thomas steadfastly held the cross out in front of him inches from the face of the beast. He continued, "You touch one single hair of Chloë and I will cut off your head myself!"

More laughter erupted from the beast and then his fist came flying out of nowhere, striking Thomas square in the jaw. The shards of pain sliced through his brain, causing all of the blurry images surrounding the beast to turn black and he felt his legs give underneath him. He had no strength left to reach out a hand as he fell to the floor. Everything went black.

****

After what seemed like an eternity, but had only been a few minutes, Thomas awoke to a surrounding crowd bent over him, all shouting. His jaw felt like it was no longer attached to his face and his head throbbed with numbing pain. As he came to, he could see that he was lying on the terminal floor just feet from the baggage carousel. He tried to stand up but discovered his legs would not cooperate. A lady bent beside him and said: "Father, I am a nurse and I need you to remain on the floor. Medics have been summoned and will be here shortly."

Thomas looked at the concerned lady and said: "What happened? Where is my bag?"

She replied, "We all watched it happen from the other side of the carousel. A stranger picked up your bag and tried to leave until you yelled at him to stop. The man turned and belted you across the face. Can you imagine a strapping young man slugging an innocent and defenseless senior? I have never seen anything like it. He ran, dropping your bag as he did, and a few of the men you see here chased after him, but he disappeared into waiting taxi. Airport police are trying to get to the taxi before it exits the airport."

Thomas rubbed his sore jaw as medics pushed their way through the mob of concerned onlookers and replied to the lady: "No one will find him. Unless there is someone prepared to enter into hell and flush him out."

Chapter 34

After the medics checked him over in the first aid office of the LAX terminal, they recommended that Thomas get to a walk-in clinic as soon as possible to get some pain medication prescribed. His jaw was sore and his head continued to throb, but other than that he was fine. He thanked the medics and made his way to the taxi stand.

There was a line-up of about twenty other passengers waiting for taxis when he made his way out of the terminal. He took his place when the security guard who was directing the people to the taxi cabs that were pulling up approached him and said: "Father, please, if you will take the next taxi."

He looked at the young man and replied: "That is quite alright, I don't mind waiting. It shouldn't be too much longer anyway."

The security guard insisted that he take the next cab. The other people standing in line all stepped aside allowing Thomas to take the next taxi. He would never have considered taking it, but his head was pounding and he was still a little shaky on his feet so he welcomed the reprieve. Once in the cab, he gave the driver the address to the mansion in Malibu. It would be great to see Chloë again, it had been months since he saw her last. She was still considered a minor and under the care of the Church and Sister McGarrigle, but she was no child. Chloë was a young, mature woman who reminded Thomas of her mother Kathleen, determined to pursue her passions. That made it all so very strange that she and Sister McGarrigle had stopped communicating with him. When Thomas finished recovering from his injuries in Rome, he returned to Ireland, only to discover that Sister Doyle had resigned her position as the

Abbess, citing health reasons, and returned to Dublin to serve God and the Church in a different capacity. There was just too much going on and he just needed to see Chloë and ensure that she was safe, confront Sister McGarrigle and make sure they both knew that communication better improve or he would take the steps to have Chloë and Sister McGarrigle return to Ireland. It was the last thing he wanted. He strongly felt that the safest place for Chloë right now was in America and away from the danger that seemed to follow him. Music was her haven and had kept her safe, and he wouldn't change that.

He would find a way to lure the beast back into the open where it could be confronted. He had no idea how he would do this, but he would use the power of the Church and Rome to accomplish this. He would not do it anywhere near Chloë. She was innocent in all of this, and he would keep it that way.

He gathered his thoughts and tucked them away for later as the taxi rolled up to the address of the mansion where Chloë and the other kids were staying. The beautiful estate at the end of the long, private driveway was a sight to see. The home was everything Chloë had said it was, a massive property surrounded by palm trees, beautiful landscaping and the exquisite blue water of the Pacific in the background. It was gorgeous; he could see why Chloë would love it so.

As he climbed out of the taxi, paid the driver and took his plain black suitcase with the green ribbon from the backseat, he wasn't quite sure what to do next. He walked up to the front door and knocked. He was met by service maids and sent to walk around the back and surprise Chloë. He turned to the sound of an approaching car coming up the driveway. He watched as an expensive car pulled up to him, its driver's side window coming down. It was Avery Johnson.

"Father O'Sullivan, it is great to see you! Chloë told me you would be here today. Let me park the car and I'll be right back to show you inside. The kids will be in the studio rehearsing."

A few minutes later, he returned, carrying a sleek black

briefcase, dressed impeccably, like a rich business executive, with his empty hand extended: "Great to see you again Father. You must be exhausted from your trip. Please come in, and I will show you to your guest room where you can drop your suitcase and then I will take you down to the studio where you can surprise Chloë. She is going to be so excited. Let me take your suitcase Father." He never even gave him a chance to say no, which he would have. "Thank you Avery. It has been a long flight. "

As they entered the house, the size and opulence was overwhelming to him. He had never been in a home like this in his life. He followed Avery up a large and winding staircase, down a long hallway and stopped in front a room with double French doors that opened up into a bedroom that was much larger than his entire rectory back in his Church in Balbriggan. He turned to Avery before entering and said: "Wow, I must say this quite something Avery. Would it be possible if I could take a short nap before you take me to the studio? I have a terrible headache that I would like to try and let subside before I take on the noise and excitement of a rehearsal."

"Certainly Father, take your time. The kids will be in rehearsal for a few more hours. There is no rush. When you're ready."

"Give me a half hour Avery, then knock on my door."

****

Thirty minutes later there was a knock on the door, but Thomas had already risen ten minutes earlier. Feeling strangely refreshed, he opened the door and was thrilled to see Chloë standing in the hallway grinning from ear to ear, "Father O'Sullivan!" She ran into the room and embraced him, squealing with delight at his arrival: "It's so good to see you Father! I was so worried when you were hurt in Rome. I tried to see you but I was assured you were okay and they were right!"

Thomas hugged her warmly then took her by her shoulders and held her at arm's length and looked at her. She had changed so much. Her long, straight blond hair was styled into curly waves, darker highlights weaved throughout, and makeup adorned her perfect face making her look even older than her maturity already made her. She was stunningly beautiful and for a split second he thought of Katherine again and how proud she would be of her daughter at this moment. He smiled at her and said, "Please sit and tell me how everything is going."

She sat on an armchair while he sat on the opposite one separated by a small table decorated with beautiful ornaments. She giggled as she spoke: "I only have a few minutes Father, then I must return to the studio to continue rehearsal. Mr. Johnson instructed me to take you with me. You will be so amazed Father. I must admit, we are very good. We are in the process of recording the first album and we will be going on tour soon. There is a major press conference in a few days to announce the band to the world. It is so exciting!"

As she spoke, Thomas watched and listened to her. She had grown so much in the past several months it was incredible. Her small town, child-like enthusiasm had been replaced with a more serious, matter of fact tone. The band was now her life and he could see that. He was happy for her even though he and the Church would be losing her and the sweet little child who could sing like an angel. He needed to ask her about Sister McGarrigle.

"Chloë tell me, where is Sister McGarrigle? I have not heard a word from her since you left for America nor has anyone at St. Patrick's. Is she here in the mansion now? Can I see her?"

He watched as Chloë's eyes went dark, like someone had turned down a dimmer switch, the light slowly fading from them. She dropped her head slightly towards the floor and with a voice barely above a whisper said: "She left Father. She left within a few days after arriving here at the mansion."

He was stunned at the news that she had left. He shifted in his chair so he could face Chloë directly, trying to reengage her eyes but the light in them had gone out and she sat there sullenly. "Where did she go Chloë? And why? You were her responsibility?"

Without looking up at him she continued in her hushed voice: "I think that was her plan all along Father. The life of a nun, to spend her life serving God no longer attracted her. She ensured that I was safe and taken care of and then she up and vanished Father. I didn't alert you or the Church back home because I knew you would have me returned. This is where I belong Father, and it is here where I will stay."

"I see. I am just so surprised Chloë. This news is shocking to me. You understand this puts me in a difficult position my dear. Legally, you are still a minor back home and you are a ward of the Church. It is my duty, to ensure those responsibilities are met. I may very well have to take you back to Ireland. I'm sorry Chloë."

What happened next surprised him even more. Chloë leapt from her chair and stood over him, screaming: "I will not go back to Ireland, Father! I am almost seventeen years old and you or the Church cannot make me go back to that prison. That is what it is Father, a prison. Creativity and individuality is forbidden. Sister Agnew and then Sister Doyle after her, tried to control me and then stifle my love for music. They couldn't handle my going from this cute little girl who entertained the staff with my sweet little voice to a young woman who had talent and wanted to sing songs and perform in front of people outside of the Church. Touring in America with the Celtic Woman, they tried everything in their power to stop me. It wasn't until I threatened to go to you that they relented. I will not go back to Ireland Father, not ever."

The ferociousness of her rant shocked him; she was furious at him. But it was her eyes that shocked him the most. They were ablaze with a fiery crimson red. She had the eyes of the demon!

****

After Chloë stormed out of his room, Thomas sat in his chair for what seemed like hours but was only a few minutes. The horror of Chloë's rage was still fresh in his mind as he bowed his head to his chest, clutched his cross and prayed:

"Heavenly Father, Your Wisdom and Guidance is needed. I do not know what to do; I am losing Chloë like I lost her mother. The demon is inside her and will destroy her. I must do something God! I ask for your protection from the evil forces that will try to stop me. Lend me Your mighty sword for which to defeat Your enemy. I cannot do this alone."

His prayer was interrupted by a knock on the door. He looked up to see Avery standing at the doorway. "Father are you okay? What happened? I just saw Chloë down in the studio being comforted by the other kids because she was very upset."

He looked at Avery for a second before replying: "Mr. Johnson, I must go. I need to return to Ireland. There are many things I must do."

Thomas watched as Avery stepped into the room and replied: "What? You just got here Father. You haven't even seen Chloë perform. She will be so disappointed. You must stay. I insist."

Thomas had never felt as old as he felt then. If there was a mirror in front of him, he was sure it would reflect an old, withered and broken man. He raised a hand with great effort and placed it on Avery's shoulder when he replied: "Avery, Chloë is in grave danger and I must leave in order to protect her. Watch over her please, and keep her close. I will return soon, I promise."

He watched as Avery shook his head, confused, then said: "I don't understand what just happened between you and Chloë but she is in no danger Father, I can assure you. If you were to hang around here for a few days you would see that. At least stay for the press conference tomorrow."

"I'm afraid I cannot, but I promise I will look for it on the television when I return to Dublin. Be careful Avery, and have faith in God always. The bright lights of a stage or a spotlight from a camera is not the light that will keep Chloë safe. It is the light from the tip of God's sword that shines the brightest and will keep her safe. Please remember that Avery. Now take this as a gift from me." He reached behind his neck and lifted off his cross that had adorned his neck for decades, held it for a brief second, then reached out and put it into the palm of Avery's hand before continuing: "Keep this with you, Avery, whether you are a religious man or not. Keep the Lord nearby as it is He who will protect Chloë. Now I must leave for LAX. If you have a driver that could take me, that would be most kind."

****

Avery accompanied Father O'Sullivan to the waiting car and waved goodbye to the old priest as he left almost as quickly as he arrived. "That was a very strange episode", he wondered. What had triggered his sudden exodus from the mansion and his hurry to get back to Ireland after just arriving? Was it something Chloë had said to him? Maybe he had come to take her home and she refused?" Whatever it was, he would stay out of it. If Father O'Sullivan wished to ask for his help then he would oblige, but he would not bring it up any further with Chloë.

He made his way back to the studio to get the kids started on rehearsing. He felt the weight of the cross on his chest. He thought for a second, slipped it off and placed it in his pants pocket. Soon the world would discover the magic in the form of music these kids would perform on a world stage. These were the craziest of times, but he loved every minute of it.

****

The airline was able to cobble together a flight for Thomas to take him to Rome from his original flight back to Dublin tomorrow. It cost him a considerable sum, but the Vatican would pick up the difference in fees as they wanted him to come at once for a special convening of SOSL. The increased encounters with the demon and the unrest and instability in the Middle East were making the Eminence jittery and he wanted up to date information on the state of the world affairs, including the secret affairs of SOSL. The unrest in the Gaza Strip, Iran's unwillingness to stop developing nuclear weapons and Syria's refusal to stop butchering its own citizens had brought the historically troubled region back to the brink of an all-out war that would most certainly drag the U.S. and its allies right into the middle of it. Last year's terrorist bombings in the six cities around the globe still had the world at full alert. The devastating tsunami off the coast of the Philippines last year was still affecting the millions of Catholic Filipinos left homeless in that country. The Catholic people were beginning to demand that the Pope come out and denounce the tyranny in Syria, insist that the Jews and Palestinians settle their differences and plead for the United States not to declare another war.

Thomas knew in his heart that the world was fast tracking to a cataclysmic and catastrophic conclusion and it didn't even know it. Satan was making his moves in the annals of human history, bent on its final destruction and, by the look of things, he was getting closer to that event.

The outburst by Chloë was not only unexpected, but completely the opposite of her personality type. The blood of Satan had revealed itself through her for the first time. More and more, he believed that Chloë and the Lockwood boy were the keys in all of this. But in what way? The thought that these two beautiful young people were somehow tied up in the devil's final plans for the destruction of the human race was absurd, yet he couldn't shake the feeling that they were somehow connected. He was also feeling like he too was a pawn in the demon's scheme. How could he explain the fact that he was still alive after so many encounters with the beast? He was alive for a reason. There was a purpose for him and a role for him to play that had not yet been revealed. He wondered, as he settled in for the long flight to Rome, whose purpose and role would he be called upon to serve, the Lord God or Satan himself? Was he still alive because of the grace of God or because of the demon's purpose for him? He closed his eyes in prayer, asking for the Truth to be revealed to him soon so he could save the life of his beloved Chloë.

Chapter 35

The goal for the six priests of SOSL was to prepare a detailed and objective report for the Curia that would be added to a larger report being prepared for the Eminence, the Pope. Their report would include graphs highlighting the series of natural disasters that had increased in size and devastation over the last one hundred years. More importantly, conclusions and theories from the members of SOSL would be compiled into the report as one voice. As the only surviving member of SOSL from its inception, almost forty-eight years ago, Thomas had been informed by the Curia that this report would be the last as the Special Office of Spiritual Longevity would be discontinued after this final meeting.

He was surprised the committee had survived as long as it had, but the escalating wave of God's fury through storms, tsunami's, earthquakes, hurricanes and many other natural disasters over the last century kept the committee meeting three to four times a year. The Church was looking for a discernible pattern to the disasters and, combined with the violent acts of man, especially the recent thirst for terrorism by the Muslim world, to come to a useable conclusion that the Armageddon predicted in the Book of Revelations could potentially come to fruition. It was purely hypothetical analysis, but the Church as an institution demanded it, and there was a belief amongst the members of SOSL that the Pontiff secretly believed the end of times was imminent and it was his paranoia that had kept SOSL together as long as it had.

Thomas has also long believed that the end of times was near, likely in his lifetime, a belief rooted in the devil's recent activity on earth among man and his personal encounters with the demon. He planned to base the bulk of this report on the recent and frequent activity of the beast, and he also planned to include an update on the two children the beast fathered, Michael Lockwood and Chloë McClosky. There was a connection between the two, other than that they were half brother and sister and shared the exact same birthmark. The kids were conceived for the demon's purpose and Thomas believed they were born as part of the demon's plot to destroy man. Thomas knew that God would reveal his purpose to him, he believed it was the only reason he was still alive. He would never give up on Chloë's salvation and knew in his heart that his Lord had not either.

The six priests were working diligently in their assigned boardroom, keeping the administrative assistants assigned to them busy developing the spreadsheets and graphs to illustrate their findings and theories. The meeting was interrupted when an office clerk tapped on the door, entered and went directly to Thomas, and then she told him that the press conference in Los Angeles was about to start. Thomas excused himself from the rest of the committee and followed the clerk into another boardroom further down the hallway that housed a large screen television mounted on the wall. The clerk, an employee of the Vatican that was maybe in her early twenties, seemed to be as interested in the press conference as he was. The excitement of the formation of Vasallus was certainly reaching across the globe as he watched the young lady bring up the press conference on a popular Italian entertainment channel. The press conference came up and the clerk continued to stand to the side of the TV, transfixed by what was transpiring in Los Angeles. Thomas cleared his throat to get her attention and then said: "That will be all Clara, thank you."

Disappointed, the clerk left, closing the door behind her. He followed her to the door and locked it after she left, choosing to be alone and uninterrupted. He settled into a chair in front of the TV and watched as the well-dressed business man, named Robert Best, introduced Avery and the members of Vasallus, including Chloë and Michael. He wondered if Ann was watching this. Chloë looked beautiful, happy and so excited. He was so proud and happy for her, but those positive emotions were short lived because the feelings of dread and doom made their familiar appearance in the inner walls of his stomach.

The man named Best looked somewhat familiar to him, but didn't know how. He was definitely a heavy weight in the music industry on par with Avery Johnson, which was why he looked familiar, but there was something else he couldn't put his finger on. He studied the other members of Vasallus as they were introduced, none of whom he recognized or had heard of, except for Michael Lockwood. He noticed they all seemed to be around the same age. The other two girls in the band, Leroux and Campbell, were as beautiful as Chloë. Even the four guys were very good looking young men. They certainly would have an impact on the young girls of the world just because of how cute they were. The Benning kid was different though, as the camera focused on him while he was introduced. He looked older, with visible facial hair and his eyes were darker and more ominous looking. There was something somewhat sinister about this kid. He could feel it start to seep its way into his stomach. The kid reeked danger. He wasn't sure why, but Thomas had come to trust his instincts and the now familiar sense of dread.

The press conference wound down with the floor opened to the gathered reporters for questions. He smiled when he saw the first question come from Bentley. He liked and trusted her as he did Avery. He knew they would keep Chloë's best interests at heart. She asked Best where the inspiration came from to form Vasallus. He gave an answer that seemed to satisfy Bentley, who sat down after the question was answered, but it triggered something in Thomas's mind.

The interview ended shortly after and Thomas picked up

the TV remote control and searched more channels, hoping to find the press conference playing again on another channel. The channel selection inside the Vatican was limited at best and he was unable to find another channel airing the conference. What was it that was gnawing away at the inside of him about Best? He seemed too deliberate, business-like and insincere. Thomas didn't buy his sincerity about his inspiration for Vasallus. He created Vasallus for another reason. For money? For power? There was something there he could not put his finger on. What was it?

"Wait a minute", he thought. He said to himself earlier that all the kids of Vasallus looked to be of the same age, except for maybe the Benning kid. He knew Chloë and Michael were the children of the beast, yet here they were together in America with five other similarly aged kids. Thomas thought he would lose his breakfast, the bile was quickly rising into his throat. He concentrated hard to keep his stomach contents down while his mind pounded out the possibilities. "Could it be? Is it possible that the demon has fathered more children?"

The realization of who Best was hit him like a sledgehammer in the stomach. His face broke out in a cold sweat, the chills racked his body. He instinctively reached over to a bible sitting on a table underneath the TV that hung on the wall. He clutched it tightly, shaking and fighting the need to throw up. He stood up, his legs shaky and weak. He made it out into the hallway and into the nearby restroom. When he entered the washroom, he went immediately to a sink, not even noticing the other priest washing his hands in an adjacent sink. Thomas turned on the cold water tap, placed the bible on the ledge underneath the mirror and doused his face in the water. He was burning up and the water barely offered temporary relief. A voice called out behind him, mocking and demonic. "The truth is like fire licking at your soul, isn't it Father?"

Thomas wheeled around to face the voice, recognition hitting him hard: "You!"

The young priest, dressed in the traditional long black

jacket of a priest complete with the black tunic, and white collar, now transformed in front of Thomas. Large gashes opened up all over its face, its lower jaw expanding as large razor sharp teeth replaced the smaller, evenly placed human teeth. Its skin became a slimy, greyish-purple and his eyes burned a deep red. The smell of death reeked throughout the small bathroom. The temperature dropped to freezing, causing Thomas to wrap his arms around himself. He was breathing hard, the breaths exhaling in deep puffs of steam from his lungs. The beast continued to transform into a hideous creature. Its lips, stretched as the jaw extruded, split open and blood seeped out of them. It was a grotesque sight combined with the cold and the smell. Finally, Thomas gathered himself to speak: "You return to the Lord's earthly palace. You are a coward and weak. You do not scare me demon. You cannot hurt me here or anywhere. The Lord, God Almighty has cloaked my soul in his love and protection through His son Jesus Christ. I denounce you, demon, to go back to the pit you crawled from or stay and face the wrath of the Lord My God."

The room exploded as the glass from the mirrors rained down on Thomas, shards cutting into his skin. He dropped to one knee to protect himself. The booming voice of Satan filled the room: "You live old man, because it is I who chose to let you live. Your purpose to keep Chloë safe is complete and I no longer need your pathetic presence to continue in this world. You will die horribly here in the Vatican bathroom, slumped over the sink, dead from a heart attack. You will be buried and forgotten as just another useless pawn of a fictional character in the fairy tale you cherish so much, the comic book you call the Bible...."

Thomas cut in and began reciting the Lord's Prayer: "Our Father in Heaven, hallowed be thy name, your kingdom come, thy will be done on earth as it is..." He was interrupted by a tremendous shaking of the bathroom. He fell over onto his side as the room shook as if it was the epicenter of a large earthquake. He looked up at the demon. It was fully transformed, its body massive, horns protruding from its forehead like those of a ram, giant wings filled the room and it hovered above him, looking down at him, ready to crush him with its huge claws. Its burning red eyes burrowed deep into him and it screamed: "I am the true Master, priest! Your prayers are like the billions of prayers that echo around the world every minute of every day. They bounce around the atmosphere like bubbles until they burst into nothing. They are never heard, priest. There is no God; there never has been, you crazy old fool. It is time for your charade of a life to end. It's too bad you won't be around to see Chloë by my side, as the flames from my staff scorch the face of the earth to dust."

Thomas continued: "Give us this day our daily bread and forgive our debts, as we also have forgiven our debtors. And lead us not into temptation, but deliver us from evil."

The beast roared at the sound of the Lord's name, and in Latin he hissed: "Vestri lacuna planto haud dent in meus creber loricatus priest! Vicis pro man's ratio est near. Pro quoque plures centuries vir has ago per spes of eternus salus tamen nunc he mos adeo teneo suum verus fatum." (Your words make no dent in my thick armour priest! The time for man's reckoning is near. For too many centuries man has lived with the hope of eternal salvation, but soon he will come to know his true destiny.)

Replying to the beast in his tongue, Thomas spoke in Latin: "Nequitia vos have ingero in vir est haud magis. EGO to order vos in nomen of Senior Omnipotens dimitto is universitas simul. Reverto ut vestri vorago of dolor quod despero. filius of Deus Jesus Sarcalogos of Nazarus to order is! Pareo, bestia, pareo!" (The wickedness you have inflicted on man is no more. I command you in the name of the Lord Almighty to leave this world at once. Return to your pit of misery and despair. The son of God, Jesus Christ of Nazarus commands it! Obey, beast, obey!)

The room shook violently, the partitions of the bathroom stalls tore from the bolts anchoring them to the floor and flew across the room. The plumbing of the sinks broke loose, shooting water in every direction. Ceiling tiles collapsed, raining debris down onto Thomas and the surrounding floor. The entire time, the beast roared in agony. Thomas continued: "Licentia quod take obscurum of vestri dolor vobis quod permissum lux lucis of Deus fulsi perspicuus. Suus diligo quod pietas mos frendo vestri postulo ut ingero moestitia quod poena. Licentia iam scelestus unus pro telum of Senior pierces vestri scrinium quod rips vestri permaneo spiritus vobis. In nomen of Jesus Sarcalogos , filius of Deus , EGO to order vos licentia simul! (Leave and take the darkness of your misery with you and let the light of God shine brightly. His love and compassion will crush your need to inflict sorrow and pain. Leave now, wicked one, before the spear of the Lord pierces your chest and rips your last breath from you. In the name of Jesus Christ, son of God, I command you leave at once!)

The thunderous shaking in the room suddenly stopped, the beast became silent and the room was cast in darkness. Thomas was in complete darkness with the beast somewhere in front of him. He thought about making a run for it, but knew his old body would make that impossible in the darkness and the demon would lash out and cut him in half. No, if he was going to die in this bathroom then he would die glorifying the Lord in front of His enemy.

Then a strange glow appeared in the bathroom, enveloping the silent beast in enough light that Thomas could see that it was unconscious. It appeared that it was lying on its back, levitating several feet off of the floor. Its massive bulk filled the room. Then Thomas could hear a sound, a mumbling sound coming from it. He stepped towards it. He had to hear what it was saying. He approached the beast carefully and could see that it was in some sort of unconscious state, its demonic eyes were closed, and plumes of steam escaped from its nostrils as it breathed. It reminded him of the severe cold in the bathroom. He bent over, placing his ear close to the mouth of the beast to listen. It sounded similar to Latin, but Thomas did not recognize the words. He quickly thought of something and reached into his jacket breast pocket and took out his cell phone and quickly fumbled through it to open up the voice recorder. He turned on the voice recorder and placed it close to the grotesquely deformed lips of the beast and held it there. As he did so he looked over the skin of the beast and for a brief second, found himself in wonder that the most horrifying creature ever to walk this earth was lying before him. The slimy, grey and purplish skin of the beast looked thick and impenetrable. The large ram horns curved out from the top of its forehead and then back looked like decayed and cracked bone, about to be shed at any moment, falling off to be replaced by new and healthy ones that would grow in their place.

Suddenly, through the hazy glow of the bluish light, Thomas could see the light begin to glow brighter along the exposed under arm of the beast, its huge muscled bicep and forearm turned towards him. Black text began to appear along the arm, faint at first, then growing darker. It was written in Latin he recognized immediately. As the words appeared along the arm of the devil, the wonder and magnificence of the Lord revealed Himself to Thomas. The enormity of the miracle before him caused him to gasp, his hand reflexively coming to his mouth. All the years of sacrifice to Him, to the Church and to his congregation, wondering if he had made a difference in this life, all became clear to him at this moment. God was reaching out to him, the text appearing on the skin of the beast's arm were words from God. He was commanding Thomas not to give up, his work was still needed by Him. He would keep him safe; He loved him like He loved all man.

Thomas collapsed to the floor as the letters faded away. He fell to his knees below the levitated beast, clasped his hands tightly together and through his tears he prayed: "I have heard you Lord, Mighty God, Saviour of Man. I am your willing servant Lord, willing to fight evil to my last breath. Command and I will obey Lord. In the name of your Son, Jesus Christ, I pray." He sat motionless for a second, comprehending what had just taken place when he thought he heard a whisper in his head. Then he heard it again. It was unmistakeable. The voice in his head was God and He said: "Holy Water." Thomas instantly knew what he meant. He stood up, looked down at the catatonic beast and rushed to the bathroom sink. He tried all of the sinks along the wall, all of them so severely damaged they would not turn on. The last of the six sinks was still functional; he took out his blood pressure pills, emptied them into his hand and dropped them into his coat pocket. He took the empty pill bottle and filled it with tap water. He closed his eyes and prayed, needing to sanctify the water.

He turned to face the beast, still in an unconscious state, the power of the Lord rendering Satan captive. He approached the demon, held the pill bottle with the Holy Water and prayed: "God, source of irresistible might and king of an invincible realm, the ever-glorious conqueror; who restrains the force of the adversary, silencing the uproar of his rage, and valiantly subduing his wickedness; in awe and humility we beg you, Lord, to disregard this creature with your blessed Holy Water, to let the light of your sword shine upon it, and to hallow it with the dew of your Holy Water so that wherever it is sprinkled and your holy name is invoked, the assault of this unclean spirit will be baffled, and all dread of the serpents venom be cast out. May the Holy Spirit be with me Lord. In the name of Christ our Lord, I command you to banish the wicked spirit before me. Amen."

Thomas flicked the pill bottle of blessed tap water onto the beast and continued to pray the Lord's commands. The water sliced through the chest of the beast with more devastating effects than if it were a sword. The gaping wounds seemed to suck the glowing light that surrounded the beast into itself. The beast thrust open its eyes in a look that would forever be etched into Thomas's memory. The recognition, the pain and the resolution all collapsed into one lasting image. The high pitched wail sounded like the bleat of a thousand doe deer desperate to find their fawns. The beast had felt the mighty blow from the sword of God. Thomas raised the bottle again, "The Sword of the Lord Almighty is pointing in the direction of your exit, wicked one. His mighty word commands it." He dropped the bottle of holy water once again towards the beast and watched as it carved another devastating wound into the body of the creature.

Defeated, the beast recoiled away from the water in his hand, afraid of a third and final strike. Its giant wings struggled to lift its body away from Thomas. After a few seconds of desperate flapping and awkward movement it hovered high in the corner, its red eyes flickering like lanterns struggling to maintain their flame from the breeze. Thomas knew there would be no more fight from the creature tonight. He locked in a stare down with it, knowing he was staring into the eyes of Satan. The greatness and love of God coursed through his veins, he watched as the beast, in a flash, shrank in size to that of a bat, hesitated for a second and then turned and flew out the window and into the night.

****

Thomas leaned his frail body against the bathroom wall and slid to the floor. He surveyed the devastating damage in the bathroom and knew he was being called upon by God to take a final stand against His adversary, Lucifer. His encounter with God, a miracle, left him shaking as he sat amongst the broken glass and carnage of the bathroom. The Lord saved his life, gave him life to continue the battle. He prayed once again, thanking God for His mercy and reminded Him that he would be a worthy soldier ready to take his weathered old body to battle.

He heard banging on the bathroom door. It was shouts from staff and priests trying to get in. They were calling out his name. Their sounds faded as the flood of thoughts poured into his mind.

He now knew without a shred of doubt that the seven kids of Vasallus were all spawned from Satan. "That is his plan! He is using these kids as part of his plan to destroy mankind!" He needed to stop him! He must get to Avery Johnson! Robert Best, the American music producer and creator of Vasallus, is the beast, the demon, Satan. How did he not see that? He was the man almost fifty years ago that he encountered in Rome, the man in Kathleen's delivery room when Chloë was born, he was at the concert performance in Dublin of Chloë and Michael.

"I did not see it because I was blind! The Lord God has given me sight!"

Thomas rose from the floor, shards of broken glass falling from his clothes. He felt different as he stood. Much different. His body felt strong, no longer weak. He could feel the energy pour into his bloodstream. It is as if years were melting away from his body. He turned towards a portion of the glass mirror still intact on the wall. He was stunned at what reflected back at him. He saw a much younger version of himself, even though his body still looked old. His green eyes shimmered with purpose and life. The power of the Lord was in him. He felt it. He turned towards the shouts emanating from the hallway.

"Not only am I just a soldier of God, I feel like a soldier! The Lord has given me a sword and shield. I am ready!"

Chapter 36

By the end of the first day of taking the kids of Vasallus into the studio, Avery had half of the album in the bag. He was sure he could have done the entire album in one day, but he called it a day by 4:00 PM and let the kids go and relax around the pool. He did this for three reasons. Number one, they were in no hurry now that he knew they were all the equivalent of a musical savant and could easily play any music without any rehearsal or practice. Secondly, he wanted to spend the evening and listen to the recordings over and over to see if there actually was room for improvement, but he knew the answer already. The tracks were perfect. Thirdly, he wanted time to wrap his head around what he had just witnessed before they continued any further. Thankfully, Bentley was joining him tonight at the mansion and he couldn't wait to tell her how things went, but more importantly he wanted her feedback and opinion on the music, not only because she was his girlfriend and he trusted her, but also because she was one of the top music critics in the country and her opinion meant everything.

He called Best when the kids were all gone from the studio and informed him of the incredible day and how things went. If Best was surprised he never showed it, he merely accepted what Avery said without question. The momentous news that the kids had pulled off the first single on the first take was as if Best expected it. Avery asked him: "Robert, I don't think you understand what I just said to you. The sheet music to "Don't Hold Back" was placed in front of them for the first time and instead of what should have been a mish mash of a semblance of the song, they played it together like they had rehearsed it hundreds of times. In all my years of producing music, Robert, I have never seen anything like it and you act like it happens every day. What am I missing here?"

"You're not missing anything Avery. It reinforces the reason why I teamed up with you on this project in the first place. You're the best, and you obviously know how to bring the best out of a musician."

"Bullshit, Robert. I could have been a blind and deaf monkey sitting on that stool in the studio and they still would have played that song the first time. I did nothing. I never had a chance. Normally I do dozens of takes on a song with an artist working with new music, each take getting just a little better. By the end of the day, hopefully, we have a useable track or two. I could have recorded the entire album all in one day. That is unheard of with a single musician who wrote the music themselves. It is impossible with a group of young kids who have never played together to play it like they have been a group for years and have played that song hundreds of times. I'm telling you Robert, it was God damned spooky."

His voice never changed, still the same monotone, matter of fact voice when he replied: "Listen Avery, I have to run, it sounds like everything is going great and we'll be on track to begin shooting the video first thing Monday morning. The press conference for the unveiling of Vasallus to the worldwide media is next Thursday at Blackstar Studios. Film producer and director Jackson Sterling will shoot the entire video on location at the mansion. He scouted the location months ago and already has everything he wants to do in the video ready to go. Expect an army of a film crew first thing Monday. It is my expectation that the shooting of the music video will go just as well as the recording did. Any questions, Avery, you know how to get a hold of me. Bye for now." That was it. He ended the call before Avery could say another word. Things were going too well, and he knew something bad had to happen sooner or later. The law of averages always said so.

The law of averages didn't come into play on Monday when filming of the Vasallus music video for the song "Don't Hold Back" began. Lighting equipment and props were all put in place on Sunday with the crews working all day and through the night. The theme of the video was bucking authority. It would highlight all of the kids in various acts of defiance against authority figures such as parents or teachers who abused their power for their own gain. In every scene, the kids would be shown being forced to accept something they did not ask for or want. It wasn't sexual abuse or anything physical, but the theme was still somewhat disturbing and Avery, watching everything from the perimeter, did not like the direction that the video was going in. He voiced his displeasure to Best, but was told that he needed to see the final edited production before he passed judgment. The shooting of the video lasted two full days, with Sterling spending the entire evening the first night editing the day's work and when shooting wrapped, he was close to being done. He was under a deadline to have the video completely edited and finished by the end of the day Wednesday in time for the press conference Thursday. Avery did not understand the rush for the press conference, but that was Best's job. Avery's job was to produce the music and Best would promote and market the group. He had a plan and that included the press conference.

The preview of the music video was Wednesday night at Blackstar. Avery brought Bentley and Jenn with him and they joined Best in his boardroom, along with all the kids from Vasallus. The excitement going around the room was electric. Everyone was anxious to see what the rest of the world would see the next day. When the video started up on the big screen, Avery now understood why Best had spared no expense and hired one of the top directors in the film industry to shoot the video. Throughout the video, each of the kids was highlighted individually but the focus was also on the entire group together. Each band member's incredible good looks was expertly framed by the combination of costumes, lighting, hair and makeup. The video took the lyrics of the song and created a story of seven kids searching for their place in a world run by corrupt governments and authority figures. The group's defiance of the tyranny around them was a triumph for young people around the world. The music complimented the story perfectly and the kids were flawless. The video brought Avery back to the time when he first saw the video for Pink Floyd's "The Wall" and how much of an effect that song and that video had on him. This song and video would electrify the youth of the world in a similar way if not more so. The members of Vasallus were just such beautiful and believable kids, the song and video would be a massive hit. He could see that now. He looked over at Bentley and Jenn and could see in their eyes that they were blown away. It was an amazing moment for everyone in the room when the video ended. The kids were jumping up and down, crazy with excitement and high-fiving each other.

Best stood up and motioned for quiet. He looked at everyone for a second before speaking: "I hope all of you enjoyed the video. I think you will agree with me that Jackson has created the perfect video for the debut for Vasallus. It presents message of hope and courage for the youth of the world to stand up against the corruption and tyranny that lives all around them. Now, tomorrow morning at 11:00 a.m., the lobby here in the studio will be transformed for a press conference. We can expect the representatives of every news and entertainment agency of any significance to be here, led by our beautiful Bentley Paxton from *Music Talks* of course. They will all be packed into the lobby to see what you have just seen, as well as meeting each of the seven members of Vasallus. Avery will announce the upcoming tour for Vasallus which begins in one month right here at the Staples Center in Los Angeles. The tour will take Vasallus into every major city in the United States over the next three months. The group will then take a few weeks off, head back into the studio and record their second album and then begin a worldwide tour starting in London. Over the next thirty days, Avery will complete production of the rest of the album, and choreographers will work with the kids for their stage dance numbers. They will be a well-oiled machine by the time the curtains open next month at the Staples. Do any of you have any questions?"

Jenn did not hesitate and replied: "These kids are only sixteen years old, Robert. This is an incredible pace for them. What about their schooling? Their privacy? The media and fans can be ruthless and they will be pursued, prodded, poked and scrutinized like nothing they ever could have imagined. Are they ready for that?"

Avery noticed that a slight grin made its way onto Best's face when he replied: "These kids were born for this Ms. Steinart."

****

Every news and entertainment agency of any importance in the country was given a press release to break the story Wednesday night of the press conference being held in Los Angeles to announce the super group Vasallus. The press kit included the names of the members of the band, including superstars Juan Jimenez, Connor Asker and Elizabeth Leroux from Panterra fame, for a start. The press kits, which were sent to all of the online, print and TV outlet agencies, included invitations to the press conference the next morning. The released statement shot around the social media and internet like a speeding bullet. Best instructed the kids to update their Facebook fan pages, announcing the formation of Vasallus and the press conference.

The buzz circulating through the social media channels was enormous and it spread like a virus. By the time the press conference was about to begin on Thursday morning, the whole world seemed to be ready for the announcement and for more information regarding this new band, Vasallus. Best had invited all of the entertainment, music and news organizations including *MTV, Rolling Stone Magazine, Music Talks, CNN, Fox, NBC, ABC, CBS and Much Music.* He had also invited top music executives Simon Cowell, LA Reid, Clive Davis and Jimmy Lovine. The hosts from 'America's Got Talent' and 'X Factor' were also invited as part of the buzz surrounding past winners Brittany Campbell and Connor Asker. Members of the South American press, *ABN*, the official Venezuelan news agency and *El Universal,* the major English South American newspaper were in attendance. Word of the involvement of the London superstar Michael Lockwood and Irish darling Chloë McClosky brought the British and Irish press. The press conference was full of industry heavyweights and media all scrambling to make sense of the formation of the superstar band.

Avery, along with Best and the members of Vasallus, all gathered at a long table in front of a sea of cameras and journalists. The kids from Vasallus looked spectacular because Best had brought in the best hair, makeup and wardrobe teams to prepare them. Avery and Bentley marvelled at how Best was able to pull everything together so quickly and professionally. When everyone was seated and the media were ready, Best announced: "First of all, I want to thank all of you for coming to Blackstar Studios today on such short notice for this press conference and the very exciting announcement we have in store for you. I am going to start by introducing everyone at the table. I will then play the world premiere of the debut single and music video on the large screen on the wall here behind us. After the playing of the video, we will take your questions. Now without further delay, let's get started!"

An eager journalist from the London Times tried to be the first to ask a question, when he interrupted Best, but he was quickly silenced by Best: "You will have an opportunity to ask questions, as I just explained, and I assure you that your question will be the last one that I or anyone at this table will take." Everyone in the room understood what Best had meant. Anyone else who interrupted would be bumped to the back of the line to have their questions answered, no matter how big of a news agency they represented. That silenced the assembled throng in a hurry, Avery observed.

Best continued: "Let me start by saying that I approached Avery Johnson from Alive Records months ago with the idea for a project of bringing together these incredibly talented kids into one band which would impact the music world like the Beatles. We both have worked extremely hard, along with these superstars, to make this happen. We are very pleased to announce that our efforts have been realized in more ways than we ever imagined. Ladies and gentlemen, I introduce to you seven of the most amazingly talented musicians you will ever have the pleasure to meet. They have come together to form the biggest super group the world has ever seen. Please welcome *Vasallus!*"

Cameras flashed in a whir of clicks and snaps. The flashes ricocheted off of everyone like they were sitting in a violent lightning storm. The crowd buzzed, preparing to burst forth with a torrent of questions. Best silenced them all again when he continued: "All of you know and are aware of most of the members of our super group. Let me ask Avery to introduce the members of Vasallus."

He had not expected to be the one who would introduce the kids. Avery stood up, looked down the table at the kids who were all smiling, waiting for him to begin and then back at all the people assembled in the room and began: "Thank you Robert. It gives me great pleasure to introduce to all of you the most incredibly talented musicians I have ever worked with. Their talent and commitment to Vasallus is truly amazing. To my immediate left is the beautiful Chloë McClosky from Dublin, and beside her is the equally beautiful Brittany Campbell from Providence, R.I. Beside Brittany is someone who all of you know, the heartthrob we were all introduced to four years ago when he won 'America's Got Talent', Connor Asker, who has grown into an international superstar with the release of his debut album last year. Beside Connor is the Latin superstar, Juan Jimenez, the winner of the South American version of 'America's Got Talent' who, like Connor, has grown into a worldwide star. Next is someone most of you will not recognize, Patrick Benning from right here in Los Angeles. Patrick is easily the most gifted songwriter I have ever met. All of the songs on this first album were written by Patrick and when we play the first song in a minute, you will all see how talented he is. He is also a very talented musician, capable of playing any instrument, as are all the members of Vasallus. Patrick is the drummer for Vasallus. Next to Patrick is the

British heartthrob, Michael Lockwood, an extremely talented and successful classical singer and pianist from London, England. At the end of the table and the final piece to Vasallus is the hugely popular singer and performer from the hit Las Vegas musical, *Panterra,* please welcome from Montreal, Canada, Elizabeth Leroux."

Best waited for a minute while the journalists showered the table with camera flashes. He then continued: "If you could all give your cameras a rest, I will start the video of the first single "Don't Hold Back" from the debut album, *New Beginnings*. At the completion of the video, you can ask your questions. I will choose whose question will get answered. Thank you for your cooperation and enjoy the video."

An employee of Blackstar dimmed the lights and someone else started the video. The massive screen behind the table lit up with an intro to the album and the start of the music video for "Don't Hold Back". When Avery swivelled his chair to look up at the screen, everything seemed larger than life. It was a surreal moment for him. The song was incredible and sounded and looked even better the second time around. The soaring vocals of Connor and the beautiful melody by Chloë, along with the harmony of the others, captured the assembled journalists and industry executives, leaving everyone speechless for a moment when it finally ended. Avery could tell that everyone in the room believed, without a shadow of a doubt, that the song would be the biggest hit the music world had heard in years. Best then turned to them and announced: "I will take your questions now."

The room erupted into controlled chaos; everyone wanted to have their questions answered first, knowing that the world would be watching this press conference at some point. Best turned to Bentley and said: "Ms. Paxton, from *Music Talks*. Do you have a question?"

Avery was completely surprised by Best's gesture to give the first question to Bentley. Neither of them asked for it and Bentley was grateful to be the first to break the news about the group and the press conference last night. Best was full of surprises. This one was a good one. Bentley stood and asked: "Thank you. Mr. Best, what inspired you to bring these kids together? They are from all over the world, with different backgrounds in music, making it difficult to understand, but after hearing them, I understand why. What was the inspiration?"

Best, dressed in one of his impeccable looking suits, had sat back down at the table beside Avery, unclasped his hands, looked at Bentley with an approving smile and said: "That is a great question Ms. Paxton. Let me answer that by saying that I have always been a big fan of groups and classic bands like the Beatles and the Rolling Stones, and their influence on the youth during their hey days. I wanted to bring together a group of talented musicians and singers who could take well-written music to new heights and have a positive influence on the youth of the world today. I think we can agree, Ms. Paxton, that our youth could use some positive influences in their lives. By bringing together musicians from different cultural and musical backgrounds, I hoped that the diversification would create a sound different and unique and something the youth could look up too, not only to enjoy, but to learn from, to reach out and go after their dreams like these seven have. All seven members from Vasallus have worked incredibly hard on their musical careers growing up and fully deserve the opportunity ahead of them. I hope that came close to answering your question Ms. Paxton."

Bentley looked pleased and thanked Best as she sat down. Best looked at the reporter from the *London Times* whom he scolded at the beginning of the press conference and said: "I was overly hard on you, James, at the beginning of the press conference. Please ask a question."

Surprised, the journalist from the *London Times*, James Cratchert, rose from his folding chair and asked: "Mr. Best, the people of London and all of England have fallen in love with Michael Lockwood and his beautiful voice and talents in front of a piano. It will be interesting to hear how his voice and talents blend in with the others in a pop-generated music environment. My question to you, Mr. Best, is that I'm curious to know how Mrs. Lockwood ever agreed to let her son leave England for America. I noticed that she is not at the press conference today. Does that mean she disapproves of Michael being here? In fact, I don't see any of these kids' parents here at the press conference. Why is that, considering it is such a major announcement?"

An unexpected zinger that came across like a wet blanket at a pajama party, Best acknowledged the journalist for asking such an important question. His reply that each of the young members had the full support of their parents or guardians came across empty sounding and the British journalist tried to dig a little deeper, but Best cut him off and took another question from another reporter. Soon everyone never even remembered the shallow response to the London reporter's question. Avery remembered, however, and couldn't help but notice that the question hit Best hard and he struggled with that one. It got Avery thinking that he had never heard from any of the parents of these kids since they arrived at the mansion months earlier.

****

The press conference ended about an hour later with each of the members of the press conference given a press kit that included a copy of the music video for "Don't Hold Back". The excitement in the air amongst the journalists as they filed out of Blackstar was obvious. "Everything went perfectly", thought Best, "except of course that prick from the *London Times*." If he went back and started poking Ann Lockwood for an interview, it would be liking poking a hornets' nest and if it cracked open the sting from those hornets could be nasty. The last thing he needed right now was that bitch Ann Lockwood snooping around the mansion as they were about to go into rehearsals in preparation for the upcoming tour. Why were the Brits so fucking nosy all of the time anyway? The journalist wouldn't even make it to LAX. He would need to take him out. A minor inconvenience for him, and he might actually enjoy it. In fact, he would torture the fat pig.

His mood brightened considerably with that thought as he said goodbye to Avery and Bentley, the last to leave the studio.

****

Ann Lockwood caught the press conference on the television by pure chance as she was searching the TV for the weather channel. She sat on the edge of her bed, stunned; the magnitude of the band was so much more than she could have imagined. From all the excitement from the press conference and the channel airing the piece about her son, she grasped that he was certainly part of something very big. She needed to reach out to him to make sure he was okay. He was probably having so much fun with everything that was happening and the last thing he needed was for his mother to be pestering him, but there was something about the press conference that just didn't sit right with her. She needed to touch base with Michael and she would put it out of her mind. She was so proud of him and everything he had accomplished. Mr. Best, who sat beside Avery Johnson, looked so familiar to her that she felt she had met him before, but of course she had not. As she walked into her bathroom and turned on the shower, she couldn't shake the déjà vu she was feeling. Oh well. She was sure Michael would be calling her any minute, excited to know if she watched the press conference on television yet.

Chapter 37

The press conference announcing Vasallus to the world was barely twenty-four hours old when Bentley's boss, Daniel Winters, called requesting her to fly to New York immediately for a meeting. "The board of directors are freaking out after they watched the press conference and they want a strategy moving forward on how best to cover this new collaboration by Robert Best at Blackstar Studios. We need you in here ASAP Bentley."

"Alright I will leave this afternoon if I can get a flight and be in tonight. I will see you first thing in the morning Daniel."

"Sounds good, and by the way, Bentley, great job in getting *Music Talks* the first question answered at the press conference. The board is very pleased. See, if it hadn't been for me suggesting to Jonathon in getting you and Johnson together that never would have happened. Someday you can thank me. No need to now, but someday."

She giggled, listening to him go on. Daniel was a lot like her old boss, Jonathon Green, who had been brutally murdered months earlier, in that he was able to make her feel better about herself through humour. Daniel knew she was a sucker for his one liners and silly jokes, so he used them frequently. "Whatever Daniel, you give yourself far too much credit. Listen I better get off this phone and call the airline, otherwise you won't see me in the morning. I will see you when I get there tomorrow morning Daniel."

She hung up the phone and called Delta, her frequent flyer airline, and was able to get a 3:00 p.m. flight out of LAX to Newark, NJ, putting her in New York at around 10:30 p.m.. It would be midnight by the time her head would hit a pillow tonight. Before she stepped into the shower she dialed Avery, catching him on the second ring: "Good morning sweetheart, I didn't wake you did I?"

The sound of his voice instantly took away the early morning chill of her bedroom: "Nice try baby! Sleep seems to be a luxury nowadays with Vasallus keeping me busy. What's up sunshine? Are you calling to tell me how much you love and miss me?"

She pulled her exposed legs in tight to her body, pulling a blanket over them as she sat on the end of her bed: "Okay, I can go with that. I love you Avery and miss you terribly. So much so that I'm calling to tell you I'm flying out to New York this afternoon, but I'll be back tomorrow night so maybe we can get together then."

"That would be great. Bring your overnight bag to the mansion. You need to see these kids perform. They are a gift from God to a music producer. We should have *New Beginnings* completely wrapped by tomorrow night. I will give you a sneak preview when you come. What do you think?"

"I think that sounds wonderful. I'm looking forward to it. Thank you, by the way again, for getting Robert to start the press conference by turning to me for the first question. That was very nice of you Avery; my bosses at the magazine are very pleased."

There was a slight pause on the other end of the line before he replied: "Well honey, I'd love to take credit for that but that was completely Best's move. With everything going on getting the band ready for the press conference and shooting the video, I never even thought to ask him for that. Thank God he did, otherwise I would never have forgiven myself for not getting the one I love that opportunity."

"Nonsense Avery, I would never have expected that from you. Thank you for being honest about it. I am impressed that he did do that. I have really been wrong about him right from the start Avery and I apologize."

"No apologies necessary, Bentley. I felt the same way, even more so. Best was a jerk, egotistical and far too ambitious for his own good, but he has certainly surprised me with these kids. He has worked extremely hard, pushed all of the right buttons so far, has showed some compassion and professionalism through all of it and generally has been a pretty decent guy to work with. I have to give him credit as much as it pains me."

"The music world is going nuts after that press conference. The brass at *Music Talks* has called a special meeting for tomorrow morning just to discuss Vasallus. They are really having an impact right out of the gate Avery, and it's only going to get even crazier once the album is released and they start to tour."

"Wait till you hear them tomorrow and you'll get a real sense of how crazy it's going to get."

"Alright, I'm looking forward to it sweetheart. I better let you go so you can get back to work. I love you and I will see you tomorrow night."

****

Bentley tried, unsuccessfully, to catch up on some sleep on the flight to New York. Instead, she caught up on some articles for the magazine, updated her blog page and responded to dozens of tweets. Once she landed and was able to get a signal again, she would upload all of her work. By the time she caught a taxi and made her way out of Newark and into Manhattan it was midnight on the button. The magazine kept a condo on 93rd street for out of town clients visiting the city or for when she was in town. A few years ago, Jonathon had given her a budget to spruce up the condo and she used every penny of the budget and then some. The place cost the company a few million dollars to buy, simply because it was in Manhattan and not because it was a well-furnished and beautifully decorated condo. It was, however, when Bentley was finished with it, much to the angst of her former boss who almost had a heart attack when the bills started pouring in for what she had done to the place. Whenever she stayed in the condo, it made her think of Jonathon and how sad and tragic his death was. The killer or killers had never been caught.

Bentley later discovered that the lead investigator in Jonathon's death, who also interviewed her shortly after the murder, was the guardian of the drummer and songwriter for Vasallus, Patrick Benning. "We think we live in a great big world but it can get awful small in a hurry", she thought to herself as she made her way into bed.

****

The next morning, bright and early, dressed in a short black skirt with black leggings, black heels, a white blouse and her New York favorite black leather jacket, she walked down the sidewalk in front of her condo to her favorite café, picked up a sugar free latte and caught a cab into the offices of *Music Talks*, located on the thirty-second floor of the Reit Building on 33rd street, one of the priciest per square foot commercial properties in Manhattan. She was met by Daniel as she entered the office, exchanged hugs and then the wisecracks began: "You're late Paxton, and it better not be because you dragged some young stud into the condo last night, because if you jeopardize the relationship with your meal ticket Johnson it will cost you more than your job!"

Knowing there was a punch-line to follow, she played it out: "Oh yeah and what would that be?"

Taking her jacket with a smirk stretched across his face he replied: "Your love life stupid!"

A few minutes later, after she had had a minute to freshen up in the ladies room, her long dark hair taking another blast of hairspray, Bentley joined Daniel in the boardroom where the board of directors were all seated and waiting for the two of them. The chairman, William P. Beckett or Bill, was a music executive from the seventies when disco reigned supreme. He was a figurehead mostly, but still carried weight in the boardroom when things got out of control during heated debates among the directors and Daniel. Plus, Beckett was also one of largest shareholders in the company. He was one of Bentley's biggest fans and he had recommended her for a promotion before the untimely death of Jonathon. She wouldn't have taken it anyway because it involved a transfer to

New York and it would have taken her out of the field, which she was not prepared to give up yet. Beckett told her at Jonathon's funeral that he would have convinced her to come, telling her it would have been his last big hurrah before he retired at the end of the year. Bentley respected the man immensely.

Taking her seat at the large and beautifully hand crafted wood conference table, CEO Steve Knight stood and addressed the nine directors present plus an administrative assistant and Bentley. He disliked her and always did everything he could to make her look bad and today he didn't waste any time: "Thank you Bentley, for coming into New York on such short notice. As you could well imagine we were all quite taken aback by the press conference a few days ago announcing the creation of Vasallus. It was quite a shock considering, we had no idea this was coming."

She stared back at him and replied: "As it was to me as well Steve."

He held her stare and shot right back: "You meant to say Bentley, that you had no idea Vasallus was in the works before that press conference, considering your 'connections'?"

"If by 'connections' you mean my relationship with Avery, I take offense at that remark Steve. I would never take advantage of our relationship for my gain."

His attitude surprised her, it was uncalled for, even for him. A few years ago she dated him briefly, until she discovered what a true ass he really was and ended it. He never got over it and had carried a chip on his shoulder over her ever since. He continued: "It's called pillow talk Bentley. It happens all the time, it's not a crime, it just happens. The magazine would have liked to have had some prior knowledge to the formation of Vasallus. You should have informed us sooner, that's all we're saying."

Bill Beckett interjected, "No, that's what you're saying Knight. I think you should be praising Bentley for getting *Music Talks* the first question at the press conference. In my opinion, that little coup made us look pretty damned good. So if it's okay with you, I'd like for us to move on and get to the reason why we're meeting here in the first place."

Knight turned to Bentley, his mood and attitude completely changed and spoke: "Jesus, I'm an asshole. Forgive me Bentley, Bill is right. The story is just so damned big I let it cloud my judgment. It will never happen again. Getting us the first question was brilliant. Bill, I apologize."

She could feel that the apology from Knight was genuine and it surprised her, but it was the right thing for him to do. She looked at him and said: "Thank you Steve. It has been a crazy few days to say the least for all of us."

Daniel Winters then stood and called everyone's attention: "Bentley, the reason the board, as well as you and I, are meeting this morning is because that we feel we need to address the significance of the press conference regarding Vasallus and where to go from here. We have discussed some things that we want to run by you and get your feedback. Firstly, you did a great job at the press conference and your question for Best was the right question for him to be put on the spot. We also think that Best is a bloody genius for what he has done. The youth of this world are starving for this kind of music and this type of band. The timing is perfect. These kids are genuinely gifted musicians so this doesn't appear to be a one hit wonder, flash in the pan collaboration. Do you agree?"

"I completely agree Daniel. My relationship with Avery has afforded me some insight, as you can well imagine. The war chest of written music for these kids is enormous and the hits will fill albums long after all of us are long gone from this earth. The Benning kid is some sort of idiot savant or something. He has written thousands of songs, and according to Best and Avery the music is very, very good. They will be around for years if they can somehow stay together that long. I will say they have bonded extremely well at the mansion where they all live together and rehearse. Best has made all the right moves. He had them move in together into this beautiful palace where, for the past several months, they simply bonded and now they are like sisters and brothers. They are extremely mature kids, soon to be adults, and I believe they are the real deal. They are such gifted musicians, it is scary. Wait till you see them live. I saw them together in the studio performing, "Don't Hold Back" and it was an experience I will never forget."

Daniel nodded his head as she finished up and then continued: "Bentley, how would you feel about covering the group full time on behalf of the magazine?"

Bentley wasn't sure she heard Daniel correctly so she asked: "You want me to work full time covering Vasallus?"

"Exactly Bentley. Think of it for a second. The magazine asked the first question at the press conference when the band was unveiled to the world and we would be the first to commit to full time coverage. This of course would only work if you were somehow able to use your influence to get exclusive permission from Best and Avery to travel with the band wherever they go and report. I know you have told us that you will not do that, but I want you to think about it before you say no."

"Daniel, say no more. I'll do it. I think it's a great idea. Best is hungry for publicity for the band and I will supply him with all the publicity he can handle. I have already been thinking of this. The mansion is huge and might just have enough room for another full time guest."

Daniel's face lit up like the Rockefeller Christmas Tree and replied: "That is fantastic Bentley. How soon do you think you can get this setup?"

"I have a date with Avery tonight and I will run it past him. I am positive he will think it's a great idea. I am sure Best will feel the same. The top music publication in the world with a full time journalist covering the band daily will be a publicity windfall for him."

Knight piped in and said: "Maybe we can produce our own reality show starring Bentley that chronicled her life covering Vasallus. What do you think?"

Beckett quickly quashed that idea: "Don't be stupid Steve. This isn't a Saturday morning cartoon starring the Archie's.

This is history. The opportunity to be a first hand witness to music history is a phenomenal opportunity for this magazine and company. I believe Vasallus will be bigger than the Beatles and we'll be there to document every minute of it!"

****

Daniel offered to drive her to the airport after the meeting ended just before lunch. On the way over the Hudson River towards Liberty Airport, her Blackberry chimed indicating a text message. She could feel Daniel's stare as she retrieved the phone from her purse. She was hoping it was Avery and she wasn't disappointed. He is offering to pick her up at the airport. He wanted to know her flight and arrival time. She texted him back with the information and put her Blackberry back in her purse, fighting back the urge to smile, knowing it would just be a reason for Daniel to poke fun at her. It didn't matter. "Was that Avery?"

She looked over at him with a mischievous smile and said: "Maybe it was, maybe it wasn't. Or maybe it was Rihanna asking to meet for drinks to talk about her newest album."

"Fuck Rihanna, who cares about her? I know it was Johnson. The smile you are trying to suppress is not because of a text from Rihanna."

She fell back into her headrest and laughed, looked over at him and said: "Nothing gets past you Daniel. You know that, don't you?"

He laughed back at her before replying, "I know that. Let's be honest with each other Bentley, okay? You didn't fool me in that board room. The travel in this job and the separation from Avery is not helping your relationship and next to quitting the magazine, it wasn't going to get any better. Jumping all over the opportunity to cover Vasallus put you squarely into the arms of Johnson full time."

She giggled when she said: "Like I said, nothing gets past you Daniel."

"It's why I'm paid the big bucks and you're not."

****

Avery met her at the bottom of the escalator leading into

the baggage claim area at LAX, swept her off of her feet with a bear hug and a kiss, grabbed her luggage and went straight to a restaurant where they ordered food, because both of them were starving. Avery looked at her as they sipped their wine and waited for the food to arrive and said: "What's up with you? You look radiant tonight. You're glowing. Damn it Bentley, you're beautiful. I'm not sure what happened in New York, but I like it!"

She looked at him, the smile crossing her face like a school girl asked to the prom by the high school quarterback and said: "Actually I do have some good news to share, but I'm not sure how to say it without sounding artificial."

"Are you kidding me? Good news from you I want to hear. Fake or real, I don't care!" He laughed, picked up his wine glass and clicked it into hers.

"The magazine wants me to cover the kids full time. Like move into the mansion full time kind of thing!"

"You're kidding me right? Are you telling me the truth? I'm going to be pissed if this is a joke!"

"No joke sweetheart. I told them no, however. I told Daniel I would never compromise our relationship for the magazine."

Avery damn near slid off the end of the bench in their booth he became so animated: "Tell me you never said that? Get Winters on the phone right now and tell him you will accept the assignment. Do it!"

She giggled and then leaned over and gave him a big kiss. He looked at her and said: "You're bullshitting me. You did take the assignment?"

"Of course I did, are you kidding me Avery? But it all depends on you. You have to approve it, and Best I guess."

"Oh my God Bentley, this is what we have been waiting for. This will allow us to be together all the time! It's perfect! Best will have no problem with it, I assure you, and if he does then I'll quit. Simple as that!"

They finished their meal, laughed and held each other, talking about Vasallus and their plans to be together every single night.

The evening got even better when they reached the mansion and the bedroom.

Chapter 38

The reaction after the press conference, though predicted, far exceeded what Avery expected. He knew there would be excitement but he was not prepared for outright pandemonium. When tickets went on sale for the opening concert at the Staples Center, it resulted in an unparalleled rush on tickets. The rush to buy tickets online shut down the website selling the tickets, because their servers were unable to handle the volume of visitors to their site. Crowds that numbered in the thousands gathered and camped out at the Staples Center ticket window. Fighting broke out when crowds from the NBA's Lakers games passed through the tired and frustrated massive lineup of kids and adults alike looking to be the first to purchase Vasallus tickets. The media covered the riots, replayed over and over on all of the channels, further building the growing pandemonium and chaos surrounding Vasallus.

Most bands took months to prepare for a large scale tour and those were bands that had played together for long periods, but Vasallus had rehearsed for just a few short weeks. Regardless of how long they had to rehearse, they were ready. They could perform the songs from their debut album, including their first single, "Don't Hold Back", in their sleep. The choreographed dance moves the kids would perform in the moments when they were not playing instruments were perfect. The best team of choreographers in the business threw their hands up in the air after a few rehearsals and informed Avery that they were ready and he could save his money, these kids did not need choreographers. They knew what they wanted to do, what would work and the professional choreographers agreed. Everyone from Avery and Bentley to the dance choreographers, lighting and sound people were blown away at how talented these kids were. There was a sense that permeated throughout that each person involved with the band was part of music history, these kids would change the face of music for a generation and each contributor or witness felt grateful to be a part of it. That is why that, even though the choreographers had their professional egos bruised, they made no qualms about taking a backseat to the kids. Everyone jumped in with both feet, eager to be a part of it all.

The excitement of the debut concert was palpable and the media fed the frenzy, creating a buzz that attracted media outlets from countries all over the world to camp outside the Staples Center in Los Angeles on the day of the concert. Fans gathered outside holding placards highlighting their love for members of Vasallus. Signs proclaiming: "I am in love with Connor" or "Marry me Juan!" in bright colors were common. Other signs trumpeted the girls, and one sign had a picture of an angel and the slogan: "Chloë McClosky has the voice of an angel". Another read: "Vegas didn't deserve Elizabeth".

Avery and Best, along with Bentley, Jenn and an assistant from Blackstar Studios gathered in the media room of the mansion watching the news reports coming in from the Staples Center. It was overwhelming and all of them, except Best, expressed comments of wonder. Avery noticed that Best had not commented on the amount of hype before the concert so he asked: "You seem unusually quiet, Robert, as if you almost expected this kind of reaction. I knew there would be hype, but I think no one in this room expected the hype to reach this level so early."

Best picked up his drink of rum and coke with a slice of lime, took a sip then looked over at Avery, his air of confidence obvious when he replied: "You're perfectly right Avery. This is exactly the reaction I envisioned this first concert night. Prepare Avery, and all of you. This is only the beginning. Once the kids get out there and their songs begin to get more airplay on radio, it will get pretty crazy. For all of us.

A good kind of crazy, I remind you. There is going to be a lot of hard work ahead for all of us but it will also be a lot of fun. Remember this day everyone. This is a historic day in the annals of music history. Never forget where you were this day because you will be asked about it for the rest of your lives."

It was Bentley, quiet to this point, content with soaking it all in, who spoke next: "You make that sound so arrogant, Robert, if you'll excuse my directness. We all know and appreciate the potential of these kids, but you make it sound like they have already stamped their place in the Music Hall of Fame and they haven't even taken to the stage for their first concert. I think you and all of us should maybe just slow down a bit, and let the kids determine their destiny from here. You and Avery have done everything you can to get them to this point. Let them now enjoy the journey, they deserve it and remember Robert they are still kids."

Avery watched as Best absorbed what Bentley had just said to him. He bent forward towards her, adjusted his tie as he did, the gold cuffs on his shirt sleeve sparkled and then said: "Well said Bentley, I appreciate your candor but let me be clear on this. We are on the cusp of history and after tonight's concert you will have a better understanding of what I am saying."

****

It was 7:30 p.m. and the warm-up band, a local group of up and coming talent with a good following in southern California, took the stage to a vapid chorus of minimal applause and appreciation. It was clear the fans were there only to see Vasallus, but they were also excited when the warm-up band took the stage because they knew Vasallus was not far behind. The excitement in the air was electric. Bentley's exclusive access to Vasallus for *Music Talks* allowed her time with the kids pretty much whenever she wanted it. She was with them, along with Best and Avery, in the dressing room as they prepared to go on stage. Their outfits ranged from simple to the extravagant, worn by Patrick Benning. If he was going to be tucked away at the back of the stage, he wanted to ensure that the crowd would definitely notice him. His outfit consisted of bright blue sequined pants, a silver sequined dress shirt and a bright blue sequined hat. He would have made Elton John proud. The girls were beautiful in sexy but tasteful outfits. Chloë wore black leather pants, tall black leather boots with a white blouse trimmed in silver sequins telling Bentley, tongue in cheek, it was her way of showing support for Patrick. She wore her blond hair long and with makeup she easily could have passed for over twenty-one years old.

Elizabeth, a little more adventurous, chose to wear a short, tight black skirt with black high heels and a tight black top with the word Vasallus blazoned across her chest in silver sequins. She also wore her hair long. She had curled it but its length still brought it halfway down her back. Her full make-up, complete with bright red lipstick on her full lips made her sensual and sassy all at the same time. She looked fabulous.

If there was a difference between the three girls, then Brittany was probably the prettiest of the three. Her high cheek bones, full lips and huge eyes gave her a look most fashion models would die for. She was stunning. She had recently cut her hair to a medium length that was teased with hair spray, giving her a wilder look than the other two girls. Bentley looked at the three of them and marvelled at how beautiful they were. She felt like she was in the dressing room of a high fashion show and the girls were changing into their next set of clothes for another walk down the runway.

Juan and Connor screamed sex appeal. Connor preferred the Justin Bieber look of tight jeans pulled low on his waist, t-shirt and high-top running shoes. His hair was cut short with length on top that he had the stylists tease enough to give him some style. He wore at least a dozen different wrist bands on each wrist, from rope to silver chain links. His out of this world cuteness would make the girls in the front rows squeal with delight. Juan, the South American heartthrob, wore black leather pants, a white muscle shirt that exposed his tremendous physique and black boots underneath his pants. Around his neck were several gold chains that were sure to match all the sequins on everyone else for sparkle. Michael was definitely the most conservative of the bunch, choosing faded blue jeans, a white t-shirt, Nike shoes and a red hoodie of his favorite soccer team, Manchester United. He was so good looking that his plain outfit just seemed to make him even more adorable.

The warm-up band had just finished their six song set and were leaving the stage to a crowd of over 19,000 screaming fans, not realizing that it wasn't for them, but for the fact that they were finished and Vasallus would be coming next.

Bentley listened as Avery and Best stood in the middle of the room and asked for everyone's attention. Avery briefly wished all of them good luck and told them to have fun. Best looked at them all individually before speaking: "This is a great night everyone. I'm sure all of you feel the importance of tonight. This concert is the first of many that will take you around the world and back again. Make them feel what you feel. Don't let one concert goer leave this building tonight not singing the words to one of your songs tonight. Let's show Los Angeles and the world how great you kids are. Follow the song list, Patrick will lead you through them. Okay go get them."

The seven of them filed out of the dressing room high-fiving everyone in the room, including Bentley. They were all so excited to get out there. The material for her article on the first Vasallus concert was more than she could have imagined and she only hoped she could write something that would give the readers some sort of sense of what it was like to be in the room at that moment before they took the stage for the very first time. It was surreal and she would never forget it. She gave Avery a hug and found herself fighting back tears as she followed the entourage out of the dressing room and towards the stage. Security personal enveloped the kids as they made their way down the corridors of the Staples Center to the stage entrance. Stage hands, union workers, and Center employees: everyone lined the walls on both sides of the corridor, clapping and cheering the kids. As they got closer to the stage, they could all hear the deafening roar of the crowd piercing the concrete walls which separated them from the audience.. When the security guard opened the thick, steel door leading up the stairs and into the holding area to the side of the stage, the sound of the screaming crowd travelled down the stairs and out into the corridor like rolling thunder. The stage lights were suddenly dimmed, igniting the crowd into a frenzy, because they knew that the kids were about to make their entrance. Bentley and Avery stood with their arms around each other at the bottom of the stairs, the last in the line with Best and his assistant in front of them, then the kids ahead of them. They all made their way up the stairs with just faint stair lights guiding them through the darkness. When they reached the top of the stairs, security ushered her and Avery to the side of the stage, beside Best. They had a clear view of the darkened stage and other than the blinking red lights of all of the electronics and sound equipment, computers and instruments, it was pitch black. The crowd was flashing cameras in anticipation of Vasallus' entrance on stage. The place was going mad and Bentley couldn't wipe the smile off of her face. She looked up at Avery and the two of them shared a look of "Wow, can you believe this?" Then they looked over at the kids and they were like a pack of bloodhounds, straining against the leashes that held them back. Benning was jogging on the spot, his nervous energy seeking an outlet. The crowd that could see into this corner of the stage caught glimpses of the flashes of light which bounced off of Benning's sequins sending ripples of pent up excitement to cascade down from that section of the crowd. It was time. The concert producer approached the kids, gave them all wireless microphones with Connor, Juan and Chloë choosing headsets that were almost invisible, as the boom mike was skin colored and tiny. All of them wore the transmitters on their back belts, right above their tail bones. The producer indicated thirty seconds using his hands to flash the time remaining.

The kids all gathered into a circle, wrapped their arms around one another and began to bounce up and down. The producer then flashed the hand sign indicating the ten second countdown. The P.A. system in Staples boomed: "Ladies and

Gentlemen, are you ready for some music? Well then, please help me welcome to the stage the worldwide debut of Vasallus!" The kids unlocked and one by one hit the stage, led by Patrick Benning. His outfit looked like a disco ball, lights bouncing off of the sequins in every direction. The deafening roar from the crowd threatened to blow the roof off of the place. The kids all waved to the crowd as they took their positions on stage. Patrick perched himself behind the drum set, Michael sat at the gorgeous white grand piano just to the left of Patrick and the drum set. Brittany stood behind a large two tiered keyboard on the right side of the stage. Connor slung the lead guitar over his head and Juan picked up the rhythm guitar. Chloë stood beside a stand in the middle of the stage that housed several instruments including a flute, clarinet, saxophone and violin. The stage musicians at the rear left of the stage included a bass guitar player, two acoustic guitar players, as well as a man playing a large, upright bass. There were numerous other instruments propped on stands and ready for use. On the opposite side of the stage, there were four female backup singers, contracted locally in Los Angeles and brought into the mansion for rehearsals at the last possible moment.

Connor whipped the crowd into a complete furor when he called out: "Hello Los Angeles! Are you ready to hear some music? I know we're ready to give you some!" Patrick's sticks hit the drums and everyone else started in. The crowd went berserk as the band started the concert off with the extremely catchy anthem: "Out to You". Connor and Juan worked the stage like masters, switching off on the lyrics to the song while Chloë sang the chorus.

The second song featured another lead guitar driven anthem, further whipping the crowd into a fury, while, for the third song, Connor and Juan handed their guitars off to stage hands while the lights dimmed and a spotlight appeared over Chloë and the rest of the stage went dark. All of the instruments remained silent while Chloë's hauntingly beautiful voice took the band's new signature ballad: "Believe in Me" to the rooftops, stunning the 20,000 fans who had not yet heard the song. As she finished the first part, the stage lit up showing Brittany, Connor and Juan behind her to sing the upbeat chorus, their beautifully harmonized and synched voices electrifying the crowd with the sound of the new ballad. Michael remained at the piano, playing like he was dancing on the keys, having the time of his life. The song then slowed down, the stage darkened again and this time the spotlight found Chloë kneeling at the front of the stage, shaking the hands of front row fans pinned against the stage. Her voice was brilliant and there was a collective chill that ran through the crowd as they sucked in her beautiful voice and let it wrap itself around each of them. The song ended with the crowd leaping to their feet as Chloë bowed to them at the front of the stage.

Bentley and Avery had joined Best in the VIP section in front of the stage and just to the side and away from the crazed fans. The section was ringed with security, keeping fans from trying to get closer to the stage by cutting through the VIP section. Best had arranged for the parents of the kids to be sat in the section. Ann Lockwood immediately came to Bentley and gave her a big hug, her eyes glistening with tears. She hugged Avery, but never went near Best. Bentley made note of the sight, seeing for the first time that she was not the only one unsure of him. She and Avery hugged and shook hands with Elizabeth's parents, Brittany's mom, Nancy Campbell and the police detective, Sam Showenstein, along with his wife Bethany.

Soon the kids had ditched their instruments, including Patrick, and worked through a series of songs with choreographed dance moves. Each of them took turns at lead vocals that had the crowd dancing in their seats. Even the tough police detective had joined the other parents in bouncing up and down to the music and clapping to the beat. The kids worked through the songs from their debut album and played a number of the songs that would appear on their next album. The fans were getting one hell of a show, the music was incredible, and the production was first rate. They couldn't get enough of Vasallus. Towards the end of the concert, the lights on the stage darkened and the kids made their way to the holding area at the back of the stage, where Bentley joined Avery, Best and the concert producer. The crowd roared for an encore. The producer was waiting for the stage hands to put all the props in place for the backdrop to the hit debut single for Vasallus' "Don't Hold Back". Soon he indicated to the kids that everything was ready for them.

Bentley stayed with Avery at the back of the stage and watched the spectacle unfold. The kids had all changed into matching, silver-sequined costumes and when the song started, Connor stepped forward from the group to belt out the beginning of the song, the rest of them stood stoic behind him, their silver sequined hats pulled low, covering their eyes and making them look authoritarian. When Chloë stepped forward and Connor stepped back to join the others, she sang the chorus with a voice that seemed to reach the heavens, get stroked by the hands of angels, and return to earth. The kids behind her did their police state choreographed dance moves, which were simply dazzling. The crowd was going ballistic. When the song was handed back to Chloë for the second chorus, the lights on stage expanded and exposed dozens of similarly dressed extras marching in the same way as Vasallus but marching up a mock bridge that signalled freedom from authority, waiting for them on the other side.

Bentley was stunned as she took in the perfectly choreographed performance. When Connor continued, the marching silver sequined dancers were cut off on the bridge by dozens of black sequined dancers that danced up from the other side and blockaded the bridge. As the silver sequined dancers marched on the spot, unable to advance and the black sequined dancers marched on the spot, blocking passage, the song was then handed back to Chloë for the final chorus solo. The silver sequined dancers tried to advance, but the resistance from the black sequined dancers continued to halt their advance. In the fourth chorus, Chloë was joined by the rest of

Vasallus, their voices soaring in unison and then, all at once, they were lifted by invisible cables to where they were suspended high above the black sequined dancers. Carefully placed and choreographed lighting mimicked bursts of energy that appeared to cut the bridge in half with the black sequined dancers falling to the stage floor in a choreographed death fall. The music from the song continued to play as the seven members of Vasallus were lowered onto the broken half of the bridge where they all knelt in descending order and extended their arms from fingertip to fingertip underneath a cleverly placed, clear, Plexiglas bridge that was invisible to the crowd. It gave the appearance that Vasallus gave safe passage to the silver sequined dancers who marched down the bridge on the backs of the members of the band to their freedom on the other side. It was quite the spectacle and the crowd roared their approval when it was all done. The place was thundering, the roars deafening as the kids made their way off stage.

The stage went dark and the fans continued to roar, the incredible stage production for "Don't Hold Back" took everyone by surprise, including Avery and Bentley. Avery told her it wasn't even close to how it looked in rehearsal. He admitted that he had begged Best to take it out of the show, that it would look too hokey. Best would not budge and again, like every other time, his instincts were bang on.

The kids were squealing with delight, and hugging everyone and their excitement soared when their proud parents made it back stage. After about thirty minutes of everyone catching their breath, Best announced that he had reserved the entire Palm Restaurant, one of the top establishments in all of Los Angeles and just a few blocks away from the Staples Center, for a post-concert celebration. Everyone was invited, including backup performers and singers, stage hands, lighting and sound personnel, and, of course, the parents. It was an emotional moment for everyone that left both Bentley and Avery overwhelmed.

Bentley even did something that she never thought she would do. She gave Best a congratulatory hug.

Chapter 39

The reaction to the opening concert for Vasallus in their North American tour was nothing short of astonishing. Best's decision to setup a giant screen outside the Staples Center that broadcast the concert to those unable to secure tickets attracted tens of thousands of new fans. The media frenzy surrounding the concert aired interview after interview of fans watching the concert on the big screen. They were disappointed that they couldn't get tickets, but were happy they were still able to catch the historic first concert live. The media interviews of the fans pouring out of the Staples Center at the end of the concert captured people of all ages, mostly kids between the ages of twelve and twenty, accompanied by parents, and all of them were still vibrating from the excitement of the show. Their reactions were all the same, they thoroughly enjoyed the show, felt they were part of a historic event and the adults in attendance felt it was one of, if not the best, live concert they had ever attended.

The next concert in the Vasallus tour was San Francisco the following night. The kids would be on a feverish concert schedule, doing shows every other night and in some markets, two nights in a row. The tour would see them go up the west coast with stops in Sacramento, CA, Eugene, OR, Portland, OR and then ending with two back-to-back shows in Seattle. The tour then moved back south with stops in Salt Lake City, UT, Las Vegas, NV, and two back to back concerts in Phoenix, AZ. The tour would then swing back north where it would continue the pattern of south to north, north to south. The tour would see them perform in forty nine cities in one hundred and twenty days. In three months, the tour would come to an end, the kids would take a few weeks off, then head back into the studio to record and release the band's second album. The plans were still in the works to launch a worldwide tour from there.

The entourage that accompanied the kids was enormous. Ten personal assistants, who also doubled as tutors, accompanied the kids on the tour. Best handpicked these well-educated, single adults who were prepared to commit to a hellish schedule to keep the kids on top of their school work, regular doctor and dentist appointments, plus scheduling the kids' interviews with the local media in the cities where they were performing. Bentley and Avery were there every step of the way.

Best did not accompany the tour, opting to leave the management of Vasallus to Avery. He would make surprise appearances during the tour and would keep in touch with Avery for progress reports after each of the concerts. Bentley was given full access to the kids during the tour and she filed stories with *Music Talks* on a weekly basis. A film crew was also contracted by Best to follow the kids' every move. When the tour ended in three months, Bentley would be granted an exclusive interview with Best, Avery and the kids that would air on NBC Dateline as a joint project between *Music Talks* and *NBC*. Between the film crew and all of the personal assistants, concert promoters, local media interviews and Bentley, the kids were under enormous stress each and every night. Over dinner between the back to back shows in Phoenix, Bentley and Avery talked about the stress the kids were under.

"Aren't you worried about burning these kids up so early in their careers with this hectic schedule Avery?" Bentley asked.

"Of course I am Bentley, you know that, I think about their well-being all the time. It is the schedule that Best has them on and I'm just trying to keep it all together and running smoothly. I mean, they seem to be just fine, but we'll see where they are at in another few weeks when the grind really starts to hit them." Avery replied.

Bentley, radiant in her beauty as always, reached over the table and took Avery's hand in hers and said: "Listen honey, I didn't mean to imply that it is you who is pushing these kids too hard, I know that it's Best who set this crazy schedule. You are doing an amazing job at keeping these kids performing at the top of their game every single night."

He took her hand and brought it up to his lips before replying: "I know what you mean Bentley. These kids seem to have an endless supply of energy and they are ready to go every night and their excitement level never wavers. They will be just as excited to go on stage tomorrow night as they were that very first night at the Staples. They really are an amazing bunch. Benning scares me though. He has the potential to upset the egg cart, if you know what I mean."

She replied: "I know exactly what you mean. He is a ticking time bomb ready to explode. I have noticed that he has assumed the role as the leader of these kids, but I don't think it's because they respect him or want to follow his lead. I think it's more because they're afraid of him."

Avery nodded: "His song writing abilities are like nothing I have ever seen or heard of before. It's almost like he's some sort of genius that unfortunately carries emotional and mental baggage like some of the famous composers, Beethoven and Mozart. I will need to keep a close eye on him as the tour continues. The pressure could crack him, but the others seem to chug along no problem."

"Changing subjects, have you noticed the unbelievable following this band is generating that seems to be growing leaps and bounds every day? They are the talk of the country, Avery, and the youth in America have fallen in love with this band. Their popularity is through the roof. There are reports of rioting when the tickets go on sale in each of the cities. There was a shooting outside the MGM ticket office as thousands of fans were turned away from the ticket office when it was discovered that the resort only made a few hundred tickets available to the public. It's craziness Avery."

"It's spooky how much of everything Best said would

happen is indeed happening. He predicted the kids would have this kind of impact. He told us to prepare and be ready for it. We are both experienced in this industry Bentley, and I would like to think that I have seen it all, but we can both agree that we never saw this coming. Never in my wildest imagination did I expect this kind of reaction. At least not this quick. The scary thing is with the amount of great material this band has access to, there is no end in sight. It could go on for years if these kids somehow keep it together."

Bentley bit her bottom lip while she rolled something around the inside of her head before she spoke: "The songs by Benning are very good, but did you notice the lyrics all follow the same format of inviting fans and the listeners of the music to follow them in some sort of way? Even the ballads call out that Vasallus is the answer. You may want to change that up somewhat for the third album because, at some point, there is going to be a saturation factor where fans become desensitized to the music and begin to get turned off from that constant message, even if the songs are great."

Bentley watched as Avery leaned back into the leather cushion seatback of the restaurant booth and pondered what she had just said. She didn't push him, choosing to let him think about what she had just said. Finally he focused back on her and replied: "You know, you are not only a beautiful woman who I love dearly, you are clearly the smartest person I know. I had to think for a second about what you just said and I can't believe I never picked up on that myself, but you're right. It seems to be their mantra, huh?"

Bentley continued, "It's the same thing with the merchandise sales. Best is selling truckloads of merchandise at these shows and it all has the emblazoned logo 'Vasallus Nation' on everything. Excuse my language honey, but it's fucking brilliant. The kids are gobbling it up like candy."

She watched as Avery once again fell into deep thought, then refocused again and said: "Do you remember the band Watermark you covered almost seventeen years ago? The band Best managed early on in his career? You later found out that the band had broken up and all of the members had died under tragic circumstances."

"Yes, of course I remember. They were a great young, up and coming group then they just faded into the sunset, never to be heard from again. You still hear their hit song, "Balanced" on the radio from time to time. What's your point Avery?"

"My point is that Best drove that band into the ground. He squeezed every last ounce of life out of those young guys. He controlled every aspect of their lives and after they broke up, they were incapable of reinventing themselves. We have to make sure he doesn't do the same to these kids. I know he has changed over the years and he is a better guy and all but I'm worried he's pushing them too hard."

She squeezed his hand in reassurance as she spoke: "Remember, you are the band's manager and producer. If you feel they are being pushed too hard, put your foot down Avery. Best respects you and will listen to you."

"You're right and that's what I'll do. I promise."

****

The tour swung north again to Albuquerque, NM after the Phoenix concerts. The crowds surrounding 'The Pit' University Arena when the tour buses started to arrive went crazy, thinking that they would get a glimpse of the members of Vasallus, not knowing that they had flown in the night before and were comfortably resting in their hotel. Thousands of rabid fans surrounded the buses, pounding on the sides and chanting: "Don't Hold Back" over and over. The crew members refused to get off the bus for safety reasons, so the police were called in to disperse the crowds. News helicopters flew overhead capturing the out of control crowds holding the buses hostage. It was not only the opening news segment on all the local evening news channels, it also found its way onto the national news stations *CNN* and *FOX*.

Avery, busy in his hotel room working on some local issues for an upcoming concert in St. Louis, took a phone call from his office from Jenn: "Good morning Jenn. How goes the battle?"

She was in a hurry, as she blurted: "Everything is fine Avery. No worries on our end here. I am, however, sending out a UPS package of documents that I need your signatures on. It will be waiting for you tomorrow when you arrive at your hotel in Denver. Also, a Father Thomas O'Sullivan from Dublin has been trying to reach you. I told him you could be tied up in a meeting as I guess he tried calling your cell phone number. He will be in Denver tomorrow for the concert and would like to meet with you and Bentley."

He thought about that for a minute. "Father O'Sullivan will be in Denver?" Chloë was not going to be thrilled about his visit; she was very upset when the priest visited her in Los Angeles before the tour started.

Jenn broke the silence: "Hello, earth to Avery."

He pulled himself out of his thoughts and replied: "Sorry Jenn, I was just thinking. Tell him to call me tomorrow after 2:00 p.m. and we will set up a time to meet. Don't tell him what hotel the band is staying at, just get him to call me."

She sounded alarmed when she asked: "Is there a problem with Chloë?"

"Not really Jenn. The last time the priest was out he and Chloë had a disagreement and she was quite upset. I don't believe they've spoken since, so I just want to handle this a little carefully, that's all."

"Okay, you're the boss. I'll let you go and please make sure you get those documents signed and sent right back. Thank you and I'll talk to you soon."

****

The concert finished up with another perfect performance by the band. Michael Lockwood seemed to be getting more comfortable on stage, putting himself out there more, gaining confidence. The finale with the bridge was a major hit at each of the shows, so they kept using it. "It would be hard to top it", thought Avery, but they would need to change it up before they embarked on their second tour.

He suggested to Father O'Sullivan, when he called, that

they meet at a restaurant in downtown Denver where they could grab something to eat and talk. He insisted on meeting in Avery's hotel room, the nature of what he wanted to discuss demanded privacy and he did not want to meet in public. He had no idea why Father O'Sullivan was so insistent on meeting in private, but he respected Father O'Sullivan immensely and gave him his hotel room number. Avery hung up the phone, turned to Bentley and let her know how urgently Father O'Sullivan wanted to meet in private.

She sat down in a chair, freshly showered and dressed, looking stunning and replied: "It is unusual that Father O'Sullivan is more interested in meeting with us than Chloë. I wonder what it is he wants to talk about."

Avery finished, "Well I guess we'll find out shortly. He should be here any minute."

****

Thomas made his way up the elevator to Avery and Bentley's room, fully expecting to see the demon materialize. The events in the Vatican and his second encounter with the beast, and the intervention by God told him that his time was limited. Satan was making his move and the safety of the world was at stake. "God certainly does work in mysterious ways", Thomas thought, "choosing a priest from a small village in Ireland to make a stand against His arch enemy". He wasn't sure how the young couple would handle what he was about to tell them, but tell them he must. Their lives were in danger.

He knocked on the door and it was immediately opened by Bentley, who stepped into the doorway and gave him a big hug, welcoming him to Denver and then asked him inside. Avery came around the corner and shook his hand. They all sat down and then Avery asked: "You look very well, Father, I must say. Now, you have come a long ways to have a discussion. I presume you will be staying to see Chloë and Vasallus perform?"

When Thomas stepped off of the elevator on the floor to their room, he knew exactly how he was going to lay this out to them, but now he was at a loss of words. How do you tell someone they are involved with a group of kids that are the offspring of Satan and have been born as part of plot by the demon to destroy mankind? He looked at them both and started by saying: "The reason I came here to meet with you today is plain and simple: both of your lives are in grave danger. I am not here to see Vasallus nor am I here to see Chloë. As much as it pains me not to see her, I cannot and after I am done explaining, you will understand why."

He watched as the two of them literally recoiled in their chairs with Avery recovering more quickly: "What? Our lives are in danger? I'm sorry, but that is the last thing I thought you were going to say. Please Father, explain, we're all ears."

Thomas stood, struggling for the right words. He paced in front of both of them, then began: "I have been a priest since I graduated from seminary school forty-eight years ago. I came into the priesthood with a Master's Degree in Psychology because I felt if I was going to spend my life serving people and helping them get through life, I had better know how to do that on many different levels. Within a few days of completing my vows to become a priest, I was summoned to the Vatican in Rome to become part of a secret committee that was only known by a few people within the Church. That committee, after all these years, has finally been disbanded. I am the only surviving member of that committee that has been there from the very beginning."

He continued to pace the room in front of them and observed their body language for reactions to what he had revealed to them so far. He was about to continue, when Avery interrupted: "I'm sorry, Father, if I sound insensitive, but you have travelled a very long ways and I presume it wasn't to share your life story with us or to reveal the location of the Dead Sea Scrolls. What is it you are trying to tell us?"

Thomas winced at the remark, but understood the nature of Avery's comments. He got right to the point: "I was part of a committee put together by the Pope himself to study the increasing phenomena of natural disasters occurring around the world that would lead to the Church's belief that God's final fury, His Armageddon, was near. The committee was recently disbanded because the Church believes the End of Times is imminent."

He was startled when Avery leapt from his chair, stood with his arms on his hips and said: "Come on Father, please, we have a very busy afternoon to prepare for tonight's concert. If you don't mind, I would rather not engage any further in the troubles of the Catholic Church right now. Now, if you would like to see Chloë, I can have Bentley go get her."

Thomas continued: "Avery please, I understand your impatience. Let me finish, I won't be much longer I promise."

It was Bentley who spoke next: "Avery, please let him finish. You said it yourself, Father O'Sullivan has travelled a long ways to meet with us. The least we can do is hear what he has to say."

He watched as Avery, frustrated, looked at Bentley and he could see that she wanted to hear him out, so he reluctantly sat down beside her, looked up at him and said: "She's right. I'm sorry Father. Please continue."

"Thank you Avery. There is a spiritual warfare that is taking place on earth as we speak between the forces of God and Satan. Satan knows the End of Times is near, based upon what was written in the Book of Revelations. He has a plan to destroy mankind before that event…"

Avery interrupted and said: "Father, please, I feel like I'm in Sunday school."

Thomas hesitated and then looked at them both: "Satan's plan to destroy mankind hinges on the kids of Vasallus!"

Now Bentley leapt from her seat and shouted: "What did you say Father? You're saying the devil is going to destroy mankind and he is using Vasallus to do that? That's crazy Father, I'm sorry, but I think even I've heard enough."

Thomas knew his time was running out: "I met a man at the airport in Rome forty-eight years ago, when I was summoned to the Vatican. He threatened me with my life. I met the same man twenty-one years later in the delivery room when Chloë McClosky was born. I watched him as he killed

Chloë's mother in that delivery room. I encountered him again fourteen years later at a performance in Dublin featuring Chloë and Michael Lockwood. I met Michael's mother, Ann, at that performance and she warned me of this same man."

Avery walked to the hotel room door, opened it and asked him to leave. "Please, Father, I need you to leave. If you don't, I will call security."

"The man I have encountered, Avery, is the demon, the beast and he is real. This man looks identical to how he looked forty-eight years ago. This man is Robert Best!"

****

After two hours of listening to Father O'Sullivan tell the incredible story of Robert Best and the birth of Chloë and Michael, the attacks by the beast, including the most recent attack, the two of them were stuck in their seats, unable to move, horrified by what they had heard. Avery finally said: "Father you are saying that Michael and Chloë are the offspring of Satan? Do you know how hard that is to believe? Chloë is one of the most beautiful, giving young women I have ever met. Michael wouldn't hurt a fly."

"I understand that Avery. It is hard for me to understand as well, but it's the truth. I have committed my life to Chloë's salvation and I will not give up. The Lord also has a plan for her that will be revealed." Thomas said.

Avery then asked: "What about the other members of Vasallus, Father? Are they also the creation of the devil?"

"I don't have any proof that they are Avery, but it would make sense. You could know for sure if you ever got a chance." Thomas replied.

Avery continued: "How would we do that?"

Thomas cleared his throat when he said: "Chloë and Michael carry the mark of the beast."

The air left Bentley's lungs.

Avery, anguish written all over his face asked: "What do you mean?"

"They have the mark of the beast, a birth mark on their inner and upper right thigh, close to their genitals. It is three sixes that could be mistaken for three backward musical notes, but they are no musical notes, it is the mark." Thomas explained.

"How would you know that Michael carries that mark Father?" Avery asked.

"I am not one of those shamed, molesting priests, Avery, if that thought crossed your mind. I was told by his mother, Ann."

Bentley found her voice and asked: "Father, why are you telling us this? What can we possibly do to help? Best needs to be arrested and detained."

Avery looked towards Father O'Sullivan and waited for his reply: "Best is the most evil force on earth and the police will not be able to stop him Bentley. He is using these kids for a reason and I have not figured out why, but he needs to be stopped. I need the two of you to watch over them, keep them safe and observe and mentally record everything. God will reveal to me what He needs me to do in His due time. Will you answer God's call?"

She continued: "Are we in danger from Best, Father?"

Thomas answered: "No, not now. He needs the two of you to fulfill his plan, otherwise he would have killed you long ago. I'm sorry Bentley, if that sounded harsh, but it's true. I need the two of you to continue doing what you've been doing until God's plan is revealed. Be strong and be brave and know the might and clout of the Vatican and our Lord God stands beside you."

Avery and Bentley both let out a big breath, looked at each other, then back at Thomas and said: "Okay, we'll do our best Father."

Thomas looked at the two of them and said: "Thank you to you both. We are living in extraordinary times and unfortunately modern investigative techniques will not help us. The police, DNA samples, fingerprints, none of that matters here. We are at the mercy of our Lord and, for me, there is no bigger set of hands I would rather have guiding me."

The two of them sat on the couch, quiet, unable to

respond. Thomas asked: "Do the two of you believe in God? I noticed that you do not wear the cross I placed around your neck in Los Angeles, Avery."

Avery reached into his pants pocket and pulled out the chain with the ornate and beautiful cross and said: "I carry it in my pocket Father, as it is not exactly a fashion piece."

Bentley saw the cross for the first time and placed her hand over Avery's as he held the cross and looked at Thomas and said: "We believe in God, Father."

"Then there is one thing you can do and that is pray. Pray for the mercy and love of God to watch over you and Vasallus. Pray for the strength and courage you will need in the days and weeks ahead."

Chapter 40

When Father O'Sullivan abruptly left their hotel room, the two of them sat for a few moments in silence, too numb to even speak. It was Bentley who finally broke the silence: "It's such a horrible story to try and fathom Avery. But it makes sense to me. All of it does. From my first encounter with him during the Watermark interview, the change in Connor Asker from a sweet and bubbly 'aw-shucks' kind of kid, to this quiet and obedient kid the second Best took over his career. Obedience to Best. Same with Juan."

Avery jumped in: "You can say that about all of them. They all changed when Best took over their careers. Except, of course, Benning. He is evil. I have always felt that vibe from him. You know what struck me the most about Father O'Sullivan's visit?"

She looked at him like she knew what he was going to say, but he continued: "Did you notice how much younger Father O'Sullivan looked? You could see it in his face, his body stood straighter, he had more bounce in his step. He looked years younger."

She replied, "I agree. I noticed it the most in his eyes the second I opened the hotel room door. There was a change in them. Not only did he look younger and stronger but his eyes reflected something more to me. I don't know how to put this into words exactly, but they looked blessed. Almost like the spirit of God was living inside of them. I felt myself drawn to them."

"Me too and if we were to believe what he told us about his encounter recently at the Vatican with the demon, Father O'Sullivan did experience God first hand. This is a lot to take in Bentley; I just don't know what to think." Avery said.

He watched as Bentley stood, wrapping her arms around her shoulders as she walked towards the large window overlooking downtown Denver. She was quiet for a minute before she turned back towards him and spoke: "I believe him Avery. I am terrified of what's ahead, but I will do what he asks of us. Whether Chloë was spawned by the devil or not she still had a loving and caring mother who died giving birth to her, so there is as much human blood flowing through her as the demon's and I will help Father O'Sullivan to protect her and Michael."

He stood up out of his chair, approached her and wrapped his arms around her. He held her tight when he said: "I love you Bentley Paxton. We will do this together and be strong for each other. The second this becomes too much for you or too dangerous then I will not hesitate to remove you from here to a place far away from the band. Agreed?"

She lifted her head off of his chest and looked up at him, tears rimming her eyes, threatening to loosen up her mascara, she replied: "I won't leave the kids Avery. Just don't ever leave me alone with him, not for a second. I am terrified of him, but with you in the same room I can get through it. I hope Father O'Sullivan is completely wrong about all of this, but there is something in my heart that tells me he has never been so right."

"I promise Bentley, I will never leave you alone with Best, not ever. I will never let anything or anyone harm you."

"Can we do something we have never done together, or, for that matter I haven't done since I was a little girl?" She asked.

He understood what she was asking: "Would you like to pray together Bentley?"

"Yes." She said.

The two of them sat back down on the couch, he took the cross from Father O'Sullivan from his pocket and with the cross they held hands and closed their eyes. Bentley struggled for the words, but they came out beautifully, as words directly from her heart: "Dear Father, hear our prayer. Avery and I are infants in your Kingdom but we have the will of a lion. We are scared but we are ready to do battle for You. Give Avery the vision to see what is coming towards him and from behind and the wisdom to understand what that is. I pray, dear God that you watch over us, protect us, and give us the courage to do what we must do. Amen."

They reached out and held each other for a long time, when there was a sudden knock on the door, startling them both. Bentley looked at him, frightened, and Avery calmed her: "Its okay sweetheart. It's getting close to the time we need to be heading over to the Pepsi Center for the show. It's probably the road manager getting everyone moving." He went to the door to open it, thinking there could very well be a monster on the other side that would drive a spear through his chest the second he opened the door. He was relieved to see it was Elizabeth Leroux.

"Elizabeth, what's the matter? You look upset. Did you want to come inside?" Avery asked.

She never hesitated and walked into the room, towards Bentley and asked her: "Bentley, can you come to my room and talk with Chloë? She is very upset and I can't seem to calm her down. We have to leave soon for the concert and she hasn't even started getting ready."

Bentley jumped off of the couch, put her arm around Elizabeth and said: "Certainly honey, let's go over there right now. Avery, I will be back in a few minutes."

****

Bentley sat on Chloë's bed, beside her as she lay propped up against a pile of pillows. Elizabeth had disappeared into the bathroom to finish getting ready. Chloë had been crying.

"What is the matter Chloë? Will you tell me what is bothering you?" Bentley asked.

Chloë looked up at her, her eyes swollen from crying, and Bentley's heart tugged to see her so sad. She finally said: "I don't know what came over me today. I miss Father O'Sullivan. I haven't seen him since we had a bad disagreement before the press conference. I never even thought of him until today, I have been so focused on the tour. I feel terrible. He must be going crazy thinking about how I am doing."

Bentley reached over and stroked her hair away from her face and replied: "I am sure Father O'Sullivan misses you very much Chloë, but he also knows that you are very busy and this is a critical time in your music career. He is giving you the space you need right now."

Chloë shifted her body so she could look more directly at Bentley and continued: "I had an overwhelming feeling that he was here today, in the hotel and that he spoke to me. I know that sounds crazy, but it's true Bentley. It was such a strong feeling I almost left my room to search for him. He told me in my thoughts to be strong and courageous and that he loves me. He also said that God loves me very much. Pretty weird huh?"

A shiver shook through Bentley as she listened to her and replied: "Not weird at all Chloë, I think that is beautiful. You keep those thoughts close to your heart my dear."

Bentley watched as her eyes pulled away and looked off into the distance before pulling back and locked onto hers and then spoke again: "Can I show you something Bentley?"

"Of course you can Chloë. What do you want to show me?" She asked.

She watched as Chloë swung her legs out from under the covers, checked to make sure Elizabeth was still in the bathroom and then pulled down her sweatpants to her knees, exposing her bare skin except for her panties. She watched her as she spread her right leg wide and exposed her inner right thigh to her. Bentley inhaled sharply. There it was. The mark.

It could easily pass for three musical notes but just as easily could pass for the mark of the beast, three sixes, albeit backwards. It was incredible. Just like Father O'Sullivan had said. Bentley fought back the tears as she looked up into Chloë's eyes. How innocent she was, so young and how tragically born into circumstances not of her control. "That is quite the birthmark Chloë. Kind of fits doesn't it? The musical notes."

She didn't say anything just pulled up her pants, sat up on the edge of the bed and then spoke: "I think the others have the same mark."

Bentley didn't know how to respond without scaring her so she said: "How would you know that Chloë? Have you seen them?"

"No, but somehow I know. I always have. It's weird, but I feel connected in more ways than just friends to the others. I can't explain it Bentley."

"How so Chloë? Remember, you guys spend an awful lot of time together. You're together literally twenty-four hours a day. It is natural for you to feel things from the others. You guys are as close as brothers and sisters." Bentley tried to catch herself from referring to them as brothers and sisters but it just came out. Chloë surprised her with her reply.

"Maybe we are." She said.

With a smile she said, "I don't think so my dear. Listen, I can hear that Elizabeth is ready to come out of the bathroom. Do you feel strong enough now to get ready? I don't mean to rush you Chloë, but we do need to get going pretty soon."

"Can I share one more thing with you?" She asked.

"Certainly Chloë, what is it?"

"Patrick scares me Bentley. He is just so creepy and he can be really mean. All of us try and stay out of his way in fear that his temper will explode. I also think he goes out at night. All night. I hear him leave his room at night and he doesn't come back until the morning."

"That is strange, isn't it? Where do you think he goes Chloë?"

She thought for a second then just shrugged her shoulders and said: "I don't know really, he is just so different from us. It's hard to just talk to him. He keeps everything inside."

"He is a very gifted songwriter so maybe he likes to write at night and goes off to a place that inspires him. I'm not sure where sleep factors into the equation, but he is up to the task when he performs, so he must be getting some sleep, right?" Bentley jokingly replied.

"I guess so."

"Listen Chloë, don't you worry about a thing okay? I'm sure Father O'Sullivan will be back in America soon and will come and see you. As well, don't let Patrick make you scared or uncomfortable. Some kids have that brooding, isolated personality. It's not that they are bad people, but they just don't engage in social activities with others because it's not their cup of tea. Some kids are like that. I know a lot of adults are certainly like that. Does that make any sense to you?"

She nodded her head before replying, "Yea, it kind of does. Sometimes he can surprise everyone and be kind of nice. One time when we were on stage in Phoenix he came up to me after we were done and asked me if I could say hi to a couple of friends of his that were at the concert and were really big fans of mine. He said he was going out with them after the show and didn't think he would ever see them again and wanted to do something nice for them. I thought that was kind of nice, but also a little strange too."

"Strange, how so?" Bentley asked.

"Well, when I met them I made a passing remark that it would be too bad that Patrick wouldn't see them again as it must be hard not being able to see good friends and they looked at me like I was some sort of alien. I guess Patrick thought more about the friendship than they did." Chloë explained.

Bentley shuddered when she thought about the real fate of those two supposed friends. She rose from Chloë, reached over with her hand and placed it on Chloë's cheek and said: "I think it's time you start to get ready for tonight, okay sweetheart? I'll bang on the bathroom door on my way out to get Elizabeth out of there and you into it. How does that sound?"

Chloë smiled up at her and replied: "Thank you Bentley. I couldn't do this without you and Avery here you know. You guys are so wonderful, you're like our parents. It's awesome."

Bentley smiled right back and said: "I'm glad you feel that way Chloë. Both Avery and I care about you very much."

Before Bentley lifted off of the bed, Chloë reached over to give her a hug. She seemed to hang on forever, soaking in the warmth and security that came from the hug. The poor thing probably hadn't been hugged by anyone meaningful for a very long time.

Bentley left the room fighting back the tears once again.

****

Patrick opened his door slowly and quietly and looked down the hallway to where Bentley was leaving Chloë and Elizabeth's room. "What was that bitch doing in there for so long? I bet that fucking Leroux was talking smack about me. Or maybe Chloë was finking him out for something. She is a journalist writing for a magazine assigned to Vasallus. She isn't our fucking mother. Who does she think she is anyway? One thing she is, though, is a hot piece of ass and I am going to tap that one day very soon. If I can ever get her away from Johnson longer than five minutes, I will. Now that would be sweet."

It was time to pay a private visit to Leroux. He needed to teach her to keep her mouth shut.

****

The rest of the tour just seemed to get better and better at each city they played. The group only heard bits and pieces of the pandemonium that was happening in the cities when tickets went on sale. Outright rioting took place in every city. It was getting out of control, forcing police departments to take over security and costing the cities money which did not make them happy. The cities put pressure on the state and they would then put pressure on the Federal Government to help share the cost of keeping the crushing crowds under control. Scalpers, if they didn't get caught, were commanding outrageous prices in the thousands of dollars for tickets and there were more than enough people willing to pay the ridiculous prices they wanted. It was in Chicago where things got completely out of control. A scalper showed up at a lineup for tickets that came on sale the afternoon of the show. The tickets were only available at the arena box office as the facility was able to create an additional fifteen hundred seats on the floor at the last minute and made an announcement on a local radio station. The resulting crowd numbered over ten thousand, all bent on being one of the fifteen hundred. When the fifteen hundred were snapped up in short order, the thousands unable to get tickets went crazy. The not-too-bright scalper tried to capitalize on the desperation by asking five thousand dollars for one ticket. He was jumped by a mob before he even had a chance to turn and run. He not only lost his tickets to the crowd, he lost his life in the process getting stomped and punched until his brains spilled out onto the pavement.

The mob grew and attacked the fans who had bought the fifteen hundred tickets and who had lingered around to brag about their good fortune. Eleven people were literally torn apart by the attacking crowd who not only took their concert tickets, but also their jackets, sports shoes and ball caps. The mayor threatened to cancel the show, but was afraid the resulting riots would rival the Los Angeles riots of 1992. The kids took the stage that night, oblivious to the violence that had occurred just hours earlier.

As the tour wound up and down the east coast, the reviews that came out in the local papers the day after each concert carried a common theme: it was the best live show ever, topping The Beatles' and the Rolling Stones' great live performances. The kids performed like magicians every single night, and Avery ended up adding most of the songs from the band's second album into the show. That strategy created a huge demand for the second album, which would be released shortly after the tour ended. The number of requests for interviews by local and national TV stations was staggering and required careful planning. Best insisted that the kids be made available in every city, while music networks like *MTV* and *Much Music* in Canada screamed for more music videos. The video for "Don't Hold Back" was played as if it was on a continuous loop because it was so heavily requested. The following for the band was reaching cult status, young kids aged eleven to nineteen lived and breathed Vasallus and their music. When television news stations interviewed kids and parents as they left the concert, it seemed like the parents were as satisfied and excited as the kids were, sometimes even more so.

The enormity of their success and popularity and the sheer speed at which it all happened left veteran executives and musicians in the industry shaking their heads in disbelief, and scrambling so as not to be trampled by the speeding locomotive of the Vasallus Express. Avery stayed with the group on the road full-time and, if any of his other clients needed to meet with him in person, then they would have to fly to the city where Vasallus was performing. He would not leave Bentley alone with the group and she refused to leave Chloë and the rest of the kids. Jenn was freaking out, trying to keep everything together at the studio, so Avery instructed her to hire as many people as she needed to make everything run smoothly. He promoted her to Executive Vice President of Alive Records and told her to hire someone to replace her in her old position as executive assistant. He gave her full authority in everything except for contracts. He wanted to make sure it was his signature on the contract. Alive Records was Avery Johnson, and his clients expected that he was still somehow involved in the process.

****

Avery and Bentley snuggled close in bed in their Orlando, FL hotel room. The concert that night was as magical as the Disney theme parks nearby. Crowds eagerly anticipated the encore performance of "Don't Hold back". Even though it was talked about constantly in the media, it never seemed to stop thrilling the crowds.

There was one final performance for the North American tour in Miami in two days. Everyone was exhausted and looked forward to getting home. They were no longer amazed at the energy levels of the kids, as they showed no signs of fatigue and were bummed that the tour was coming to an end. Best's appearance after the concert that night was to remind them that, upon their return, they would be going right back into the studio to record the second album.

Avery held Bentley close as he said: "Did you happen to notice how differently Best seemed to act around us, especially? He was colder, more distant. His eyes were as black as black can get, don't you think? I've never noticed them like that before. Maybe it's just because whenever I see him now, I look at him from a much different angle."

Bentley adjusted her head on the pillow so she could look directly into his eyes: "What angle would that be? You're looking at him with the angle that he is the devil?"

"Yea, I guess. The kids seem to gravitate towards him though. You can tell there is a certain level of worship that exists. He treats Benning like his lap dog."

Bentley replied: "More like his pet Doberman. I'm just glad he comes around less and less. I can barely keep things together when he is around; he terrifies me to the core."

He held her a little tighter before he replied: "I'm still not convinced he is what Father O'Sullivan says he is, but he is certainly a very dangerous man. Fear permeates off of him like a body odor that can't be masked."

The two of them talked a little longer as the sound of the Orlando traffic buzzing by drifted through their opened patio doors, the two of them too sleepy to close them. Instead, they let the sounds of the night put an end to their many thoughts and allowed sleep to take them away.

Chapter 41

Sam carried the weight of the burden of his theory of who Patrick was, and what he had done, on his shoulders like a wheelbarrow full of rocks. He did not dare share any of it with anyone. Not anyone from the department and not even Beth. The death of his partner, Daniel Ryerson, went down as a cop suicide but Sam knew better. Ryerson did not die by his own hand. He was murdered by the same evil force that murdered his brother and the one that was coming after him. He was alone in this and if it was going to cost him his life, then he would not die in vain. He would find a way to expose his theory somehow. People were dying all around him and he needed to do something. Not only was his life in danger but also the lives of his wife and son.

Ryerson had discovered that three items were missing from the evidence boxes on the murders of Steven Benning, Jonathon Green and Chelsea Benning. All three murders happened over a period of sixteen years, with Steven's sixteen years ago, and Chelsea and Jonathon's more recently. Bibles were tagged as evidence at all three murders and logged in as evidence item #157 in each of the murders. The coincidence was more than impossible. The discovery got Ryerson killed, Sam was sure of it. But what did it mean?

In his home office, Sam created a master sheet that he taped on his wall. The sheet was approximately five feet square. On it, he catalogued what he had so far. Steven Benning had been murdered by the demonic beast, Satan, who then attacked and raped Chelsea. No witnesses, fingerprints or DNA. Patrick was born nine months later. Seb confided that he witnessed Patrick kill a neighbor's dog in the middle of the night. Patrick had been killing neighborhood cats and dogs regularly for years. Seb said Patrick never slept and went out every night.

He continued adding details to the master sheet by putting Chelsea's pregnancy and Patrick's birth at the top again and underneath that, he wrote: "strange doctor with red demonic eyes". He remembered those eyes so vividly from that day in the delivery room. There was no record of the doctor, but Sam discovered that he died soon after Patrick's birth. He added the strange events surrounding Patrick's birth, specifically his singing in the delivery room, instead of crying. It was the "voice of an angel", as the nurses described it, and one nurse stated that it was a miracle from God. He continued his chart with Chelsea's murder, and the details pertaining to it: Patrick was the only one at the scene, and Sam found him holding his mother's decapitated head and shoulders. Again, there were no witnesses, no DNA, and no fingerprints. Sam noted Patrick's infatuation with the crime scene photos of his mother, father and Jonathon Green. Sam also wrote down a detail about Patrick's early signs of becoming a musical genius: he recalled Chelsea's recounting of the time when he was just six years old, and he stopped to play a drum set in the mall like it was as easy as playing with Lego. The surrounding crowds were made speechless by the little kid playing the drums like a professional. Sam also charted notes about how Patrick's talent attracted the attention of music producer Robert Best and how Best wanted Patrick to join the super group now taking the world by storm, Vasallus. Sam felt the familiar sensation return when things began to become clear. A crack of understanding opened in his mind, a click of the mechanism that controlled problem solving. After a few more minutes, nothing more in his mind jogged anything else, so he continued with a different string of thought.

He went back to the top of the chart and wrote his brother Jacob's name. Underneath, he wrote of Chelsea's story of being attacked by a demonic beast, which she later recanted, and then, under hypnosis, recalled with vivid detail. The demonic attack mentioned the name Babken, over and over, and the demon's reference to Babken's lineage to Chelsea. Jacob's research of Babken took him to 400 A.D. and the country of Armenia and Babken, one of seven sons of King Tiridates. He wrote about the great battle between Tiridates' armies and the surrounding countries' invading armies, whose leaders were bent on stopping Tiridates' adoption of Christianity. He continued with the demon's revenge and the fact that Babken's lineage ended with the birth of Patrick and the death of Chelsea. In his mind he felt another click, then a sound like the roll of a coin on a wooden surface, then the sound of the coin dropping into a chamber. *Click.* He made another entry about Jacob's mysterious death in the synagogue. There was the impossible coincidence of the beam breaking off all on its own, then dropping straight down in a trajectory that would have made it land five feet away from Jacob, but it veered and landed straight as a spear into the middle of his chest. *Click and another slide and drop.* Sam, deep in thought, was suddenly wrenched away by the sound of a knock on his door. It was Beth.

"Honey, is there a need to lock the door? Please open it, I just want to make sure you're okay in there." She asked.

Sam thought for a second then called out: "Okay, Beth, give me a second." He quickly untacked his massive wall chart and carefully folded it and shoved it behind his file cabinet. He unlocked the door and invited Beth in.

"I'm sorry Beth; it's just that I'm so wrapped up in this investigation. I didn't want any sudden interruptions from Seb, or yourself opening the door, knocking me out of my train of thought." He explained.

She replied: "Isn't a knock on the door the same thing? Why are you hidden away in your home office anyway? Why aren't you just staying late at work, like you normally do?"

He put his arms around his wife, gave her a hug, then a big kiss on her cheek and looked her in the eye and said: "Listen, Beth, I know you're worried about why I'm working so much, but I am working on something important, okay? It requires an environment with no interruptions or distractions, which is why I came home. Give me another hour okay and I will come out and take a break, and maybe the three of us can go get some pizza. What do you think?"

She kissed him hard on the lips and replied: "I think that sounds like a great idea. I will let you get back to work and promise I won't interrupt you again. Love you."

A few minutes later, Sam had the wall chart back up on the wall. He pushed his chair back to the opposite wall and stared at the chart, trying to get his mind back into the train of thought he was on before the knock on the door. He found himself gravitating towards the name Vasallus. He didn't know why, but he thought about it for a while longer. A super group of incredibly talented musicians, from around the world, that were electrifying the world. In addition to all of the news reports on TV about the group, he knew how good they were, because he was at their debut concert at the Staples Center. Vasallus. Vasallus. He kept rolling that name around in his head. *Click*. He looked down the chart again at Chelsea's hypnosis. King Tiridates and his seven sons. Chelsea was an ancestor of Babken. *Click*. He looked at the name Vasallus again. He quickly stood up as a crazy thought entered his head. He wrote down the names of the seven members of Vasallus. Patrick, Connor, Michael, Chloë, Brittany, Elizabeth and Juan. Seven members of Vasallus. Seven sons of King Tiridates, he wrote on the chart, using an arrow to point toward the names of the seven members of Vasallus. The thought of the other members being ancestors to the other sons of Tiridates was absurd and he quickly dismissed it. But then he heard the familiar *click*. It made sense, at least the numbers did. He didn't know why, but there was something pushing him like a silent voice in his head to keep probing.

He moved back to his computer and entered the names of the members of Vasallus into Google, one at a time. Search results for the Lockwood kid from London showed that he was from the affluent Lockwood family, heir to the Lockwood business furniture empire. His mother, Ann Lockwood, was the daughter of billionaire Sherman Oakley, of Oakley Steel. There was no information on who Michael's father was in this link so he moved on to another and it was just more information about Michael's early childhood as a musician, and his performances with the London Symphony Orchestra as a child. The kid was brilliant. Sam did another search on Lockwood Business Furniture, London, England and came up with the company's corporate website. He navigated the site and found the company history that dated back decades, founded by Gantry Lockwood in 1951, son Cordell Lockwood took over in 1984 after the passing of Gantry. Cordell stepped aside as CEO in 1994 for health reasons. His son, Dalton, the third generation Lockwood to take the helm of the company, was CEO until his tragic death in 1996.

Sam quickly searched the death of Dalton Lockwood and came up with multiple links from news stories in the London tabloids on the vicious murder of Dalton Lockwood by a gang of thugs. There were never any arrests in the case. He looked at his watch. It was 5:30 p.m. making it 1:30 a.m. in London. He searched the web for the offices of Scotland Yard, found a phone number, picked up his home phone and dialed the overseas number. The switchboard automated system kicked in and he patiently punched in the numbers until he was transferred to Major Crimes Division. A cranky male voice picked up, and identified himself as Inspector Ingram: "How can I help you?"

He knew his chances of getting confidential police information on an old murder case over the phone were slim, but he gave it a shot: "My name is Detective Sam Showenstein, Los Angeles Police Department, Homicide and I am seeking some information on a prior murder case in London. The case is approximately sixteen years old. Can you help me?"

The Inspector sounded as if he'd been with the department for a long time. His British accent was old-sounding, and heavily slanged, as he replied: "Jesus Christ, you American cops, are such fucking cowboys. You think you can just pick up the phone, dial up the Yard and ask for investigation details on a murder. Did you ever hear of protocol? Check your department protocol for requesting the assistance of a foreign agency will you? Have a nice day cowboy." The phone went dead.

"Yeah, well, you're a pompous asshole", thought Sam as he picked up the phone to call right back, then he remembered there was a detective in Robbery who had worked a major case a few years back with Scotland Yard. He had a couple of Bobbies spend a few weeks in Los Angeles, working the case. The detective in Robbery became pretty close friends with the two guys and they stayed in touch. He could help him on short notice. Sam didn't want to use official channels for this inquiry, because he knew it would require paperwork and questions. He called Captain Bitters, and caught him at the dinner table. "Jesus Sam, its dinner, what's up?"

"Sorry Cap, but not really. I need you to do something for me right away. I'm working an angle on a case, but I need some input from Scotland Yard. I don't have the time to go through official channels, so I need the guy in Robbery who ran that case with those two London cops. They spent a few weeks over here. Can you track that down for me, boss?" Sam asked.

"When I'm done eating dinner, reading the paper and watching my DVR episode of The Simpsons, yea maybe." Bitters replied.

"Thanks Cap, just remember, if I don't hear back from you within ten minutes, I'm coming over to your place to help you finish that steak, eat your dessert, grope your wife and accidently erase the episode of the Simpsons you're so looking forward to watching." Sam chuckled.

"How about you sit at home and do nothing, but watch TV for once and maybe do a little more than grope Bethany. You work too fucking much Showenstein. Give me half an hour." Bitters replied.

Five minutes later Sam had the number to Detective Rusty Seguin or 'Penguin', as he was called in the department. He shuffled like a penguin with his feet splayed out sideways and with his name, it just fit. He saw him occasionally around the office as Robbery and Homicide shared the same floor. Penguin picked up on the second ring: "Rusty here, how can I help you?"

"Penguin, its Showenstein from Homicide. I'm sorry to bother you at the dinner hour, but I need a favor." Sam asked.

"Oh, how are you doing, Sam? It's no bother, I already ate. The wife likes to cook up homemade spaghetti on Wednesdays, you know, so I try and be here for that. I'm so full right now, I'll be on the couch for the rest of the night. What's up in Hommie, Sam?" Seguin asked.

"You remember the case you worked a few years back with those two lackeys from London? Listen, I could use some help from one of them on a case I'm working. I need a number for one of these guys, preferably one that is willing to make an inquiry or two, if you know what I mean, Rusty." Sam asked.

"Sure, no problem, Sam. Always looking to help out the guys down the hall, you know what I mean. Here, call this guy, he'll help you with anything you need. The name is Detective Matthew Kennett. Great guy and funny as hell. Tell him I say hello." Seguin added.

"Thanks Rusty. Homicide owes you one."

"You know I'll collect." Seguin replied.

Sam reached Detective Kennett, still in bed at 2:00 a.m. London time. He wasn't so funny early in the morning, Sam noticed. "Christ man, could you have waited a few more hours? What can I do for you?" He asked.

"I'm trying to track down some information on an old murder case from sixteen years ago in London. Nothing specific, just anything that was unusual about the case. You might remember it, as he was a pretty rich businessman in London. The guy was Dalton Lockwood. Ring a bell?"

"Fucking right, I remember. A good friend of mine was the lead investigator on that, Detective Jeremy Cookston. Sadly, he took his own life with his service pistol. Helluva thing. I miss that boyo. Anyway, the murder of Lockwood was written off as a bloodbath inflicted by a gang of thugs. His body was torn apart, beheaded. The wife, Ann Lockwood, insisted he was killed by a monstrous beast, the devil, was what she had said. The department thought she was nuts, but Cookston believed her, right up to his death."

Sam thought he would be sick. He struggled to maintain his composure. The realization that Kennett was describing the same scene as his former partner, Steven Benning, and Chelsea's, was no coincidence. He fought to remain calm and asked: "What was the date of the murder, Matthew?" Sam asked.

"Don't recall exactly the day, but it was in the fall, sixteen years ago."

He dropped the phone onto his desk, momentarily paralyzed with the realization that it was also in the fall sixteen years ago, that the attack on Steven and Chelsea happened. He reached down and quickly picked up the phone, remaining as calm as he could, and asked: "Detective, was Ann Lockwood pregnant at all, around the time of the attack?"

"In fact, she was. That was the only thing I think that saved that poor woman's soul. She had conceived right around that time, or just before, because her son Michael was born exactly nine months later. The department, I remember, was overjoyed for her, the memory of her dead husband lived on with the birth of her son. Are you thinking she gave birth to her attacker's child? That would be impossible, as Ann's son is the famous kid from that rock band, Vasallus."

Detective Kennett never got a response to his last question, because the line had gone dead. Disconnected. "Overseas connection must have been wonky", he thought. "Oh well, he'll call back if he needs to."

****

Sam buried his head in his hands in the hope that they would somehow make the realization of what he had learned just go away. Rubbing his eyes, he went back up to his wall chart and added Patrick and Michael together, under Best. He focused on the Leroux kid and contacted an investigator from the Royal Canadian Mounted Police he had met at a law enforcement conference last year in Chicago. He dialed up the cell phone he had for him.

"You're talking about the famous Elizabeth Leroux from Panterra fame and now with that band everyone is going crazy about, Vasallus? She is as revered in Canada as Wayne Gretzky. What the hell do you want to know about her?" Sergeant Scott Pallin asked.

"It's a long story Scott, and I don't have time to get into it. Can you just inquire into the circumstances surrounding her birth, and her parents, and get back to me right away? I would greatly appreciate it." Sam asked.

"Alright Sam, but give me a little bit okay? You caught me at the right time, I'm working late so I'm still in the office, but I'll have to do some digging. I'll get back to you when I have something." He replied.

While he waited for Pallin to get back to him, he made the same inquiry with the Providence, R.I. city police on the death surrounding James Campbell. He also inquired with a South Dakota Bureau of Investigation buddy of his, who retired to his home state, after twenty-five plus years with the LAPD. He was making more money as an investigator with the state bureau than he was as a LAPD detective. He got back to Sam within fifteen minutes.

Investigator George Bekins was on the line: "My security clearance level with the department has its dividends Sam, and I got the information you were looking for without turning any heads as to why. Connor Asker's birth parents died tragically from a car accident on the way to the hospital to deliver Connor. The father, Brent Asker, died at the scene and the mother, Brent's fiancée, Lori Weston, lived long enough to reach the hospital to give birth to Connor. Things went crazy at the hospital. The family preacher was lying in wait for Lori to arrive and tried to stab her with a cross. A security guard got to him first with a bullet to the neck. The baby was saved and was adopted by Lori's sister, Jocelyn, and her husband Ben, from Rapid City. The rest is history as you know. The kid is more famous than Michael Jackson and a lot better singer too."

Another sound resonated in the back of his mind, the familiar *click*. He was about to ask another question, when George continued: "The other thing that came up that might be of interest to you Sam, is the attack and rape of Lori nine months before, that almost took the life of Brent. His father Bert was killed, along with his ranch hand. All of their horses were slaughtered as well. It was a bloodbath, by a ruthless gang of thugs that were never caught. Does this help at all?"

Like a gumball making its way down its planned trajectory, then finally popping through the chamber, Sam answered: "It does help, George. Thank you, and remember if you ever a have a lunatic from your neck of the woods that dares come to the city of opportunity to hideout, I promise you, I'll blow away his ass. Just for you. Thanks George!"

The news reports Sam brought up on Google regarding the attack and murder of Bert Asker indicated that they happened in August. The same as the others. It wasn't long before he heard back from Pallin, informing him that Elizabeth's birth father was a Crown Prosecutor for the province of Quebec. The mother was a Montreal city police officer. He explained the events surrounding the death of the father, Gerard Louveneau, by his wife Francoise in the hospital. He continued with the subsequent death of Francoise, months later in May of that year, sixteen years ago, by hospital security in a hail of bullets as she tried to murder her newborn child.

****

It was almost midnight when Sam had checked his watch. His entire night had been washed away in the sea of terror-filled circumstances he dug up surrounding the births of the children of Vasallus. Bethany obviously had given up any notion of having pizza with her husband. The information he had uncovered tonight left him weak. He was exhausted and physically drained. He had no idea where to go from here or who he could turn to for help. He was alone. He was about to go upstairs, wake up his wife, and try to offer up some sort of apology, when his cell phone went off, scaring the hell out of him. The number had an overseas prefix to it. He answered the phone and identified himself, thinking it was the Scotland Yard detective calling him back with more terrifying accounts. It was a woman.

"Is this Detective Sam Showenstein?"

"Yes. Who is this?" Sam quizzed.

"My name is Ann Lockwood, from London. I understand you were making inquiries tonight about events surrounding the death of my husband and the birth of my son?" She asked.

"Ms. Lockwood, I am a detective with the LAPD, I was just…" He didn't finish.

"No need to explain detective. I am calling you for a reason. It's about my son Michael. He is in grave danger, as all of the kids in Vasallus are. I need to meet with you as soon as possible, Detective. I am arranging to have my private jet take me to you in Los Angeles, immediately."

Chapter 42

The North American tour ended in Miami with much fanfare. It included three encore performances by the band, new songs from the second album, plus new solo acoustic performances by Michael, Brittany and Elizabeth which electrified the packed crowd at the American Airlines Arena. The final performance was attended by an abundance of VIPs, all wanting to get in on the incredible wave of the group's popularity. From professional athletes to politicians, including the Governor of Florida, they all wanted to get face time with the band and, of course, to be photographed with them. Giant screens were set up at two locations outside the arena in the parking lot. The screens attracted another thirty thousand fans, in addition to the twenty-one thousand inside. Radio station *Mfan*780 ran a contest where the winner and a friend received backstage passes to the show, autographed CDs, concert t-shirts and jackets plus a signed photo of them with the group. The contest created more excitement than the radio station anticipated, and the day of the concert, when they were getting ready to announce the winner at a local mall, the crowds became so large inside, that security brought in local police for crowd control. Tens of thousands of people showed up, all dreaming of winning the opportunity to meet the band in person. The disappointment after the winner was announced spilled out into the corridors of the mall, as fans, frustrated at the missed opportunity, began rioting inside the mall. Store windows were broken, looting soon followed and local police called in the National Guard to help deal with the crush of thousands of kids, bent on destruction. The uniform of authority seemed to trigger something in them, and soon the looting and rioting turned into outright violence.

National Guard troops launched canisters of tear gas into the crowds, inside the mall and out. Enraged fans attacked the troops, police, and security with anything they could get their hands on. They hurled steel clothes racks from looted stores, any items heavy enough to throw like rocks, and glass ornaments rained down on the police like hail stones. The tear gas couldn't stop the escalating violence, so the troops opened fire, hitting a particularly out of control gang of thugs, killing two of them instantly, and injuring dozens more.

It wasn't until the Governor of Florida threatened to shut down the concert that the crowds began to disperse. Hundreds were arrested and what started out as a mega promotion turned into an ugly afternoon of extreme violence. Religious leaders across the nation were outraged that the Governor allowed the concert to go on, but it was widely believed he feared an angry backlash from fans more than any remarks by the outraged Christian leaders. Plus, he also had VIP front row tickets, and the backlash from his granddaughter, if he stayed away, would have been far worse than the angry mob that earlier in the day had almost destroyed a mall.

****

The planned day of the first interview of the kids of Vasallus had arrived, and the excitement inside the mansion was palpable. The kids were pumped, talking about it non-stop all week with Bentley and Avery. They good naturedly teased Bentley, offering up their own set of interview questions for her. Connor wanted her to ask him why he cut his hair, much to the disappointment to the millions of his female fans. Elizabeth good naturedly instructed Bentley to ask her if she needed to consider dyeing her hair blond, because she felt might be losing admirers to her blond band mates. It was all in fun, and it helped take away the tension that threatened to overwhelm Bentley, as she struggled to separate her fear regarding the kids' origins from what wonderful human beings they appeared to be.

NBC 'Dateline' was once again chosen as the interview

show, as it had been four years ago after Connor Asker had won the 'America's Got Talent' contest. Film and production crews arrived at the mansion in the early afternoon to set up their cameras and build the set for the big interview that would be aired in three days on prime time TV. The interview had been promoted for weeks on *NBC* as a joint project with *Music Talks* magazine.. Billboards across the nation's cities splashed the photo of the band along with the logos of both *NBC* and *Music Talks*. People knew very little of the personal lives of the members of Vasallus, so the anticipated TV audience was expected to be the biggest audience since the Super Bowl.

'Dateline' producers and their staff prepared the kids for the interview, assisting in the selection of their clothes, hair and makeup. All of them were going casual from blue jeans to tights. Bentley, along with Avery, took a minute alone to go over what she would cover in the interview, away from the producers and staff of *NBC*, who were busy preparing the room for the interview, less than an hour away from taping.

"Have you even heard from Best today, Avery? Has he said anything about the interview to you, because he certainly hasn't mentioned anything to me about it? I thought he might ask me what direction I would be going with the interview, anything. I find that curious. I can't help but think of the interview I did with him and Watermark all those years ago. He's not going to be able to contain these kids. I've never seen them so excited, Avery."

He replied: "We might get lucky and he won't even show. I doubt it though, he won't want to miss the opportunity of a national TV audience." There was a knock on the door and both of them turned towards the door and saw Best standing in the open doorway, dressed in a dark suit, shirt and tie. He was ready to go. He looked at them both for a brief second before speaking: "You're right Avery, I won't miss this opportunity to reach out to the world. You guys look like you're ready to go. I know I am. I'll see you both in a few minutes. Excuse me for the interruption."

"Robert, I didn't mean anything by what I said. I didn't

realize you were standing there." Avery replied.

"No worries, Avery. No offense taken. Listen, I will leave you guys be and I will see you out here in a few minutes. Good luck Bentley, I'm sure you'll give Vasallus a great interview." Best stated. He closed the door behind him as he left the room.

Bentley looked at Avery and said: "That was weird. It's like he just appeared in the room. The door was closed and we would have heard it open. Let's just get this over with sweetheart."

****

The interview was set up in the large study in the mansion. A large, wooden, square coffee table was surrounded by overstuffed, chocolate brown leather sofas, on all four sides. Hand carved, ornate wooden shelves flanked the one wall, filled with leather bound and hard cover books. On the other wall was a beautiful matching hand carved table adorned with an antique lamp. The room was completed by a huge open fireplace, a stack of wood on one side, and expensive brass fireplace tools on the other. The mantel included framed photos of the kids from Vasallus, taken during the tour. *NBC* cameras were set up behind each of the four sofas, giving the producer multiple opportunities to capture the kids from every angle possible. Lighting was everywhere. The room was transformed into a studio.

The seven members of Vasallus were split into two sofas. Connor sat in the middle, with Chloë on one side and Brittany on the other. Patrick straddled the huge arm of the sofa beside Brittany. Elizabeth sat in the middle of the next sofa, flanked by Michael and Juan. Best and Avery sat on opposite ends of the third sofa, looking uncomfortable sharing the same piece of furniture. The producer had to work a little extra to get the two of them seated just to the right of Bentley, who occupied the final sofa, opposite the two sofas where the kids were all seated. Bentley had chosen to wear a loose fitting blouse that dropped off of one shoulder, her long dark hair falling over the exposed shoulder. Her stunning beauty, combined with the air of intelligence she projected, made her an intoxicating package, and the cameras would linger on her every chance they could. When everything was in place, the director rolled the cameras, and the interview began. The advantage was that it wasn't live, so the editors could do their thing before it was broadcast to millions.

Bentley started things off lightly, joking with the kids, getting them to giggle and joke with the camera. The kids were gorgeous, their beautiful smiles projected their personalities to the hilt, and the multitude of cameras in the room caught every second of it. The varying accents from the kids all added to their charm. She bounced between the two couches, responding to the comments the kids were making, and asking leading questions that would elicit a response from most of them. The producer loved it, knowing the massive fees charged to the sponsors and advertisers would be worth every penny for them.

She decided to take the interview in a completely different direction from the feel good back and forth between the kids when she turned to Avery and Best, and asked them both: "The tour was a huge success, a complete sellout in every city and the popularity of the band is through the roof. The tour has also come under fire for the outbreaks of violence that were occurring in these cities surrounding the concerts. People were getting killed at these concerts. Did you anticipate the level of violence that has been occurring, and what will you do differently if the band is to launch another tour?"

Best didn't even look at Avery for a response. He fully intended to address this question, knowing full-well it would be asked: "The magnitude of the violence certainly took all of us by surprise, and we regret deeply that it has happened. All of us associated with the tour, including the band, send our heartfelt sympathies to all of the families who have lost loved ones due to the outbreak of violence associated with the tour. It is tragic, and we will do everything we can to work with local authorities to ensure it never happens again."

Bentley continued pushing the same button: "There have

been reports that the lyrics of the band's songs encourage disobedience to authority figures, including police, and teachers, to name a few. What do you say to that?"

Best shot right back, the cameras zeroing in on him: "That's ridiculous, Bentley. I couldn't disagree more. The songs are all about hope, they encourage free will, creativity, and using one's choice to make decisions in life."

She left it at that and turned to Avery: "Avery, you have been at the top of this business for many years. Have you ever seen anything like the success Vasallus has enjoyed?"

Avery found it hard to relax and knew the cameras were focused on him, but after a brief second of fumbling, he found his voice: "I would have to say no, Bentley. The phenomena surrounding these kids could never have been anticipated. These kids are truly exceptionally talented individuals, and when you put them together on one stage, and in one studio, magic can happen, and that is exactly what has happened here."

She continued: "You have heard Robert's words describing all of the controversy surrounding the lyrics of the songs recorded by the group. I am curious to know, how you feel about that, Avery?"

She noticed that Avery glanced for a second at Patrick, who was off camera, so the viewers would not have caught it before he responded: "Patrick Bennings' song writing abilities are remarkable. He is beyond genius. The lyrics, if taken in the context they were meant to be followed when Patrick wrote them, are exactly what Robert described, uplifting and exhilarating. If there are people who disagree with that, then they are missing everything the songs have to offer them."

She turned to Patrick: "Where does the inspiration to write your music come from Patrick? You're so young, yet the lyrics reflect someone who has lived several lifetimes. Your talent is unbelievable. Share with our audience, if you will, where it comes from."

She half expected some sinister type of response from him, but he surprised her when he answered: "I have written music my whole life, for as long as I can remember. A lot of my inspiration came from being around my mother as I grew up. Watching her raise me as a single mom, her dedication and commitment to my success, her sacrifice, inspired me, more than I can say."

"Do you miss your mother, Patrick?" She asked him.

He looked away from the camera for a second before replying. She couldn't tell for sure if he was genuine or not but it sure seemed like he was when he said: "I used to. A lot. But now I have my friends in the band and I don't miss her as much anymore."

It was an unexpected tender moment in the interview that couldn't be scripted. Bentley quickly recovered and turned to Best.

"Robert, can these kids keep up to the demands their success is generating? Is it too much for them?"

Bentley watched as Best flashed the smile that would show the viewers he was a genuinely caring man as he replied: "In normal circumstances I would have to say no, but with these kids I can honestly say yes they can handle the success that has been bestowed on them. Not only are they intelligent young men and women they are also very mature and comfortable in who they are and what they are. They know they are talented and they respect the industry that has given them this opportunity. Ego is not in their vocabulary, Bentley; they are just a group of kids who get along together better than brothers and sisters do. They love and respect each other and truly enjoy each other's company. I would say they are the very best of friends, all of them. For that reason, I think they have what it takes to navigate the challenges that will confront them as they continue to move forward in their careers."

The interview switched back to the kids and Bentley focused on the kids' personal interests outside of music and discovered their favorite musical artists, TV shows, and movies. She wasn't surprised to hear Patrick describe how much he enjoyed horror films, the more violent, the better. She was pretty sure the producers of 'Dateline' would edit those remarks out of the show. She was coming to the end of the interview when she turned back to Best and Avery with: "Tell me, gentlemen, where does the band go from here?"

Best motioned for Avery to take the question. Avery responded: "Well, after a short period of taking some time off to rest, the kids are back in the studio, wrapping up the band's second album, *Next Step*, which will go on sale shortly." Looking directly at the camera, Avery finished: "Get ready music fans, the new album takes the band to a new level and we have made sure there are a few surprises in it for you." Avery offered up a wink to the camera as a playful reminder to the fans.

Bentley looked over at Best: "Robert, I will let you have the last word. What can we expect from Vasallus in the near future?"

He clasped his hands and then unclasped them as he looked at her and made the big announcement she knew was coming: "Bentley, on behalf of Avery, and Vasallus, I am very excited to announce that the band will be launching their new worldwide tour next month, starting in Madrid, Spain. The tour will include all of the songs from the first album, *New Beginnings*, of course the new album coming out, *Next Step,* and selected songs from the band's third album, out later this year. The tour will feature new choreography, with lots of surprises from the kids. It will be extremely exciting."

****

The interview was a major success for *NBC*. Ratings were through the roof when it aired on Sunday night. Bentley and Avery had Jenn Steinart, now fully in charge of Alive Records, and her date over for dinner at the mansion as guests to watch the interview, along with all of the kids. The kids squealed with delight, as they watched themselves on TV, laughing and high-fiving each other as they answered Bentley's questions.

Michael, always the serious one of them all, in a rare light moment, challenged Juan and his accent, "Bugger to hell, Juan, your voice sounds like a dog's breakfast!"

The room exploded in laughter at Michael's crack that

forced an equally funny response from Juan, "Excuse me Shepherd's Pie lover, but I must tell you Michael, women love the Latin accent way more than the offensive and arrogant lackey you speak."

After it was all over and the kids had returned to their rooms or gathered in another TV room to watch more television, Jenn told Bentley: "That was a great interview, Bentley. You looked beautiful and so composed, with all that star power sitting across from you. I can guarantee, that clothing stores across the world, will be scrambling to stock the style of clothes the kids were wearing."

"It wasn't that difficult, really Jenn. Remember, I'm here at the mansion almost every night, and I've been with the kids constantly. We're like one big family." She replied.

"I guess you're right. Are they really like that from day to day? Are they really that nice?" Jenn asked.

Bentley looked at Avery for a second before she replied: "They are Jenn. Even more so than you saw on TV. They are as genuine and real, day to day, as you just saw on TV with cameras in their faces. They are a gift from the Heavens, Jenn, I really believe that. Avery and I both feel blessed to be a part of all of this and the kids' lives."

Jenn smiled as she spoke, tears welling up in her eyes: "Watching the two of you together, on the couch, I get it now. You are so in love, it's blatantly obvious, and the love you both have for these kids is just as obvious. I am happy for the two of you and I'm happy for the kids that they have you both, during the crazy and insane journey they are on."

****

Rioting broke out in Madrid, the first stop in the worldwide *Next Step Tour*. Fans went berserk, desperate to buy tickets to the live performances. Advance ticket sales to shows in London, Paris, Moscow and Berlin were cancelled as rampaging fans, determined to be the first to get tickets, were tearing the cities apart in their quest. Concert ticket companies released a lottery system for the sale of tickets in a bid to avoid the madness.

Another disturbing trend that first started in the United States was gaining momentum, but now it was spreading around the world. Kids were beginning to stay home from school in increasing numbers. Parents were reporting that their children were so engulfed in the music, they refused to go to school, instead wanting to spend hours at a time listening to the music of Vasallus. There were also a few reports circulating that there were even some parents skipping work and calling in sick. Some were so engrossed in the music that, in some cases, they were incapable of basic functions. They were spending hours and hours on Facebook, following the band, watching videos, and following news reports of sightings of the band members in public. There was a cult-like following that was growing by leaps and bounds daily, all over the world.

Sitting in his office in New York City, Robert Best stood up and looked out over the chaos that always seemed to envelope Manhattan at night. His delight in the huge success of Vasallus was impossible to contain. He would hit the streets and inflict a swath of destruction on unsuspecting New Yorkers, just to remind them that in this city, you could never let your guard down.

"Murder and mayhem in New York. It just doesn't get any better", laughed Best as he grabbed his coat, turned off the lights to his office and headed for the bank of elevators that would transport him to the streets and to his killing fields.

Chapter 43

Sam hung up the phone with Ann Lockwood and a cold hard fear ripped through him. It was true, all of it. "Satan is among us!" His theory, including the realization that the seven members of Vasallus were the offspring of the most evil force on earth, hit him like a hard slap. The phone call by Ann Lockwood was the confirmation of it all, and now she was on her way to America.

What could he possibly do to stop any of this? He was just a cop. So many people close to him had lost their lives already. His partner, Steven Benning, sixteen years ago and then his wife, his current partner, his brother, all taken by a demon. Yet he was still alive and so was his family. He was not sure why, but it wasn't this realization that drove him out of his desk chair and up the stairs to wake up Beth. She needed to know the truth. They needed to protect their son. There would be no protection from the department. The LAPD could not stop what was coming their way. He had an aging priest from Ireland and a rich heiress from London as his only line of defense. The demon would come for him very soon, now that he knew the truth, just like Jacob. He might be waiting for him outside his office door.

****

His sword could not penetrate the thick plates of bone that covered the body of the beast before him. Every blow from his blade glanced off as if he was swinging at a steel wall, his blows made no difference; he barely had enough time to raise his shield in time to absorb the crushing blows from the massive claw of the beast's arm.

The last swing of the beast's claw crashed down on him, splitting his thick wooden shield into pieces. He mustered his remaining strength and brought the top of his sword upwards as hard as he could, knowing that in the next second he would surely die. His blade found an opening between the layers of bone plates, and he could feel the tip of the sword break through and enter the flesh of the beast. He heard it cry out, its body recoiling away from his sword. He drove the sword upwards again and again, the stabs getting deeper and deeper. The creature was dying; its cries rang of death. Like a crazed animal, he continued to swing his sword upwards into its flesh and then he twisted his blade to inflict maximum damage. The beast would no longer be a threat to his family, nor to anyone. Then he heard a sound behind him. It was like a primal scream, but it came straight from hell.

He looked over his shoulder to see the monster rushing towards him, its claws snapping like giant steel shears. Patrick Benning, now fully transformed into his true self, readied himself to deliver the death blow. Then he heard another voice. It was Seb. He was crying out to Patrick to stop, and to leave his father alone. Sam yelled at Seb to get back, to run. He wouldn't listen. He attacked Patrick, void of any fear, and his scream was muted from the roar that escaped Patrick, as he drove his claw straight through Seb's chest. Sam sobbed out the name of his son: "Seb, oh Seb, please dear God, don't let him die. He is a good kid, he doesn't deserve this. Please Lord, save him."

It was too late, he was killed instantly. No cries of help to an unhearing God would work now. Sam yanked the sword from the dead chest of the beast he had splayed and went after Patrick. He would kill this evil entity like he should have months ago and maybe his son would still be alive. He raised his sword, ready to drive it through Patrick's misshapen skull.

"Sam, wake up. Sam, for heaven's sakes, wake up. You're scaring the hell out of me. SAM!!!" Beth screamed, as she shook Sam awake.

Groggy, shaking from the nightmare, he looked up at his wife and said: "Is Seb safe? Where is he?"

"Of course he is Sam. He is in school. It's 11:00 a.m. in the morning. She will be here in twenty minutes." Beth said.

"Who will be here in twenty minutes?" He asked.

"The Lockwood woman. She called from the airport and she is on her way here." She stated.

"Jesus, that was quick. What does she own, a Concorde? Okay, give me ten minutes to shower. Will you put some coffee on? I think we're going to need it."

"It's already made." She replied.
    She continued, "I still can't believe what you told me last night when you came to bed. I kept telling myself downstairs in the kitchen, after I woke up, that all this is just a bad dream. She is coming, the woman who was raped by the devil, to our home. To tell us Patrick is also the son of the devil. We can't do this alone, Sam. We need help from someone in the Church, a rabbi with expertise. Jacob got himself killed, Sam, poking around. The same will happen to you." Beth struggled to remain calm.

"Nothing is going to happen to me, Beth. I would have been killed long ago if that were true, but I'm still alive, at least for now, and that must mean something. So is the Lockwood lady. Maybe she can shed some light on why we are still alive. When she leaves Beth, I want you to pick up Seb from school, and leave this city tonight, go to your sister's in Texas and stay there till its safe here." He instructed.

****

"I didn't expect to see you for a few days at least, and here you are the next day." Sam said. Placing her coffee cup on the kitchen table, she looked up at him and then to Beth before she said: "When I got the call from my sources in Scotland Yard regarding your inquiry surrounding the murder of my husband and the birth of my son, I knew immediately that I needed to come to Los Angeles to talk with you in person. I have means that includes having a flight crew on call twenty-four hours a day, and within thirty minutes of our phone call, I was in the air crossing the Atlantic. I hope you don't mind my intrusion, but the truth is out there, and I will no longer sit back and not do whatever it takes to protect my son. I am prepared to fight this with everything I have and everything I am." Ann explained.

She was beautiful and rich, but not in a snobbish way or with any attitude. She carried herself with class and dignity, even in the exhausted state she was in. No wonder she was so revered in her country, her kindness, and philanthropy were well documented, yet she had been nearly invisible since the attack on her husband. He now knew why. It was because of the secret she had carried since the birth of her son.

"Something tells me you haven't been sitting back." He stated.

"That applies to you and Bethany as well. I'm not surprised that you have been able to figure this out on your own. My friend in the Yard says you are a highly regarded and respected detective in the LAPD." She replied.

Sam reached over and took Bethany's hand in his and gave it a reassuring squeeze before he replied: "I just wish we would have been able to figure this out sooner. Maybe we could have done more to save Patrick's mother and my brother. Now that I know the truth, there was probably nothing we could have done. People die when they find out the truth. Why are you still alive? Why are we still alive?" Sam asked.

Ann looked at them both silently for a second, then with a deep breath she said: "There is so much you don't know, but it is imperative that you know everything. You are both part of this now. Let me begin by telling you what happened to me."

She began to tell him and Bethany an incredible story of brutality, wicked evil, and sheer bravery in spite of her adversary. She must have been scared out of her mind, but she never showed it throughout her story. The loss of her husband and her rape by the beast, the subsequent birth of her son, the brutal murder of her mother in front of her eyes and the dire warnings by the demon had to have taken their toll, but it was the attack four years ago by the beast that almost killed her that left him shaking. It was her belief that she was saved by God and that was why she still lived. She believed He spoke to her, willing her to live and fight. He needed her to fight His enemy.

He could feel Beth's hand squeeze his, the two of them looked at each other, and then it was Beth who asked: "That is an incredible story, Ann. You have been through so much. What can we possibly do to help?"

"To be perfectly honest, I have no idea what any of us can do. I hope you don't mind, but I have asked Father O'Sullivan to join us here in Los Angeles. My plane left immediately after dropping me off, to travel to Rome to pick him up. He will join us at once, arriving in the morning." She explained.

****

They talked for a while longer, then Sam excused himself to head to the office to do some more work and research. Giving her husband a kiss goodbye, Beth returned to the kitchen and offered Ann more coffee. She declined her offer, but asked: "Would you mind taking me by the mansion where they live. It's too dangerous for me to just knock on the door, but I just want to see where he is, to feel Michael's presence, to know that he is alright."

After a few minutes for the two of them to freshen up,

they were in Beth's SUV, making their way to Malibu. Ann asked: "You're a doctor, Beth?"

"I am, but I'm not a life saver, more of a life changer, I guess you could say. I'm a plastic surgeon."

"I bet you're very good at what you do. You're certainly in the right market." Ann commented.

"You must mean Hollywood. I really don't have anyone famous as a client. My partner at the clinic has a few, but I try and avoid them, if I can. There are lots of people in the Los Angeles area that aren't famous, but are loaded, and want a tuck or a lift. I would like to go to a country someday, Ann, where I could do some real good. A country with kids that have the facial birth defects, or children with shrapnel wounds from the wars. That is my dream, but now I just want to survive this and for my family to be safe." Beth stated.

"Oh I'm sorry if I implied anything by what I said, Beth. I'm sure you will have that opportunity to help those children soon. It is very noble for you to want to do that."

Soon they were entering the exclusive beachfront mansion area in Malibu. Beth glanced over and discovered that despite all of her wealth, Ann's face still had a look of wonder on it as they drove by all of the palace-like mansions on the beach front in Malibu.

"Why do people feel the need to live so lavishly? I just don't get it, really Beth. When Dalton and I married and moved into our home in London, we could have lived in a home that rivaled Buckingham Palace, but it was never about that. We had each other and that was all that mattered to the both of us." Ann explained.

"So what are you saying, Ann? That you and Dalton lived in a little row house with a white picket fence?" Beth couldn't help herself and she started to laugh after she said that. Soon Ann was roaring right along with her.

"Okay, maybe that sounded a little foolish. But seriously, these homes dwarfed our mansion. Ours would look like a guest house in the back of these." The two of them broke into further laughter as the conversation got more ridiculous. Ann continued, "This is fun Beth. It has been a very long time since I have been able to laugh like that. Thank you."

"No need to thank me, Ann. I'm just thankful that you're here." She reached over and squeezed Ann's arm. She recognized the area and knew they were approaching the home of Vasallus. She looked over at Ann, and said: "This is it. Right over there is the mansion the kids live in, rehearse, and record in. Isn't it quite something?"

Ann instantly felt the wave of fear begin to flow through her. She could feel the evilness that lived in that mansion. It was a very dangerous place. She sat frozen in her seat, quiet, looking out the window into the bright sunshine, taking in the enormous estate. She finally said: "Whose home is this? Is this the home of Robert Best?" She asked Beth.

"Not from what I know, Ann. Apparently it was a wealthy industrial tycoon from Europe somewhere who owns it. He purchased it just for the group to live and work in." She explained.

The fear and suspicion began to build and she asked: "Beth, is there any way you could call your husband and ask him if he could check with the local government to see who it was that bought this place?"

Noticing the look on her face, Beth dialed Sam. He picked up and Beth asked: "Ann and I are in Malibu. She would like you to see if you can find out who the owner is of the mansion the kids are living in."

"Beth you guys shouldn't be out there. It's not safe. Why does she want to know that?" He asked.

"Just do it, Sam, please. We're leaving here now and going home. Call me when you find out anything. Love you." She clicked off and looked over at Ann, who sat quietly staring out at the mansion, a look of sadness in her eyes. "Ann, did you want to stay any longer? Sam suggested we shouldn't be here, that it's not safe."

In a quiet voice, she replied: "We can go Beth. I'm sorry if I creeped you out. There is an evil presence in that place Beth; I can feel it in every bone in my body. I can't help but fear for

Michael. For all of them. "

Beth finally turned her SUV around to head out of the neighborhood and back onto the freeway when she slammed on her breaks. The vehicle came to a screeching halt just inches from a child, no more than ten years old. The kid was wearing long pants, and a heavy sweater with shoes covered in mud. His clothes were also smeared with mud. He was filthy and he looked like he'd been living in the bush for months. His skin was snow white, not browned from the hot, California sun. Beth screamed out: "Oh my God, I almost killed this kid." She wrenched open her car door and was about to climb out when she heard Ann yell: "Wait Beth. Get back inside the car. Now!" Beth, confused, looked over at Ann as she closed the door and was about to say something when she heard a loud bang. She looked back through the windshield and screamed.

At first glance, she didn't recognize the child, but now there was no mistake. It was Patrick. He wasn't a long haired, muscular teenager, but a child. He was slamming the corpse of a large dog onto the hood of her SUV. The look on his face was purely demonic. His lips, cracked, bleeding and festering, were shaped into a half moon of a sneer. His eyes burned a bright crimson red from within the shadows of his hoodie pulled over his head. Bang! The dog bounced off the hood again. Horrified, she put the SUV into drive and thought about slamming her foot into the accelerator. She looked over at Ann, who sat frozen in place, stunned by the evil sight. Suddenly, Ann looked over at her, and screamed: "Beth, you must get out of here now. That is no child. Move!"

She reacted in an instant by slamming the vehicle into reverse and gunned it. The tires screeched below her as they fought for traction on the warm pavement. There was a loud thump from the back of the vehicle. She was scared half to death thinking she backed over a child crossing the road. Without hesitating, she put the vehicle into park, opened the door and stepped out onto the street. As she walked towards the back of the vehicle she forgot all about the demonic child Patrick with the dead dog and she never even heard the screams coming from inside her vehicle, from Ann telling her to get back in. She needed to make sure the little child she backed over was okay.

She came around the corner of the SUV and could see the shoe of a child, a running shoe, visible on the pavement. "Oh Lord, she thought to herself, she had crushed an innocent child." Then she heard the laughter. A guttural, almost hysterical laugh. As she came fully around the rear corner of the SUV, she saw him. It was Patrick, no longer a child, but himself. There was a gaping wound on his head and blood was flowing down the side of his face and onto his shoulder. His laugh caused the blood to pour into his mouth, staining his teeth red. He held the dead dog in both of his hands out in front of him, ready to hand it over to her. She found herself reaching for the dog, mesmerized by the glowing red eyes which stared at her from within the hoodie. In a flash, the dog was gone and Patrick's hands were wrapped around her throat as he slammed her against the back of the SUV. He moved his demonic face within inches of hers and the look of death terrified her. Then he spoke: "Do I scare you, Mrs. Showenstein? I should, because you're going to die. Your Jew God will not protect you here, bitch. I'm going for Seb next. Take that with you into hell when you take your last breath."

Beth struggled to maintain consciousness as Patrick's hands continued to squeeze the life from her. She stared into his eyes and thought she could see the dark opening into hell in the distance of his eyes. He was the gatekeeper to hell and he was inviting her in. She closed her eyes and began to pray. She prayed for the God of all man to save her. She prayed for the salvation of Patrick's soul. The heat from his breath as he laughed in her face was vile, the words of prayers continued to spill from her lips.

Then she heard a primal scream that wasn't hers. She opened her eyes in time to see Ann swing the large metal tire iron at Patrick's skull. The impact to his head came with a sickening crack and she watched as Patrick slumped to the pavement, the bright red glow in his eyes diminish. Suddenly, there was a pair of hands on her shoulders, they shook her and then she heard Ann's voice yell out "Beth let's go. He's not dead, only dazed. He wants to kill you. Let's go now!"

She looked into her eyes and cried: "Ann, I killed Patrick. I killed him. Oh my God, what have I done?"

"You didn't kill him, Beth. He's not dead and besides it was me who hit him." She screamed.

She looked down to see Patrick moan and begin to thrash around. She looked up at Ann and said: "Okay, let's go."

As they sped off, Beth looked in the rearview mirror and watched Patrick stand in the middle of the street, soaked in blood, as he watched her drive away. His eyes were unmistakably, glowing red and they were looking straight into hers, even from that distance. It was an image that would be ingrained in her memory forever.

They drove on in silence, the horror of what they had just gone through, rendered them both unable to speak. Finally, Ann broke the silence, her voice was hauntingly quiet when she looked over at her and said: "I think Patrick was protecting the mansion. He senses what I have known for quite some time now. I wasn't quite sure, but now I know for sure."

Beth looked back at her as she made her way to the off ramp to the subdivision leading to her home, and asked: "Know what?"

"The love of God's mercy surrounds us Beth. He is protecting us. He is protecting us and Sam as well as Father O'Sullivan, because we are the key to stopping the demon from whatever it is he's planning."

Chapter 44

Connor, who never pulled his drapes shut, awoke to another beautiful, warm and sunny day inside the mansion. As he trudged into the ensuite bathroom of his massive bedroom, he couldn't help but feel great about today. It was his birthday, after all. He was turning seventeen and he couldn't believe how fast everything in his life was going. He didn't want to sleep, thinking he would wake one morning and he would be seventy. Time seemed to pass by like a blur. Time, he knew, was his most precious commodity, even more so than his musical abilities. He knew he was different than other people and knew he had special talents. For years he didn't know what to think about his abilities, but the minute he came together with Juan and the rest of Vasallus, he knew he was home. They were his friends and they were just as talented as he was. They had become one big happy family and with Ms. Paxton and Mr. Johnson always around, it all just felt right.

There were, of course, a couple of wrinkles, but nothing major as long as they all stuck together. Patrick was a real threat to all of them. He was a ticking time bomb waiting to explode and when he did, it would be bad, no, really bad. His brain was wired completely differently than the rest of them. He wrote hit songs like ordinary people change their socks. It was effortless for him. Whatever it is that is bouncing around in his head was unique to him and no one else.

He just wanted to play music with the others. Sitting around the mansion, spending hours and hours rehearsing was boring, and a waste of time. None of them needed to rehearse. Why didn't Avery understand that? Mr. Best certainly did. He knew we could step on stage without ever seeing the music

Patrick had written and play it like we've been playing it forever. If anything, rehearsing kept them busy as they waited to go back on tour. He just wished they could tour and perform every single day. He didn't understand exactly, but none of them ever tired physically. This is what he and the others were born to do.

"Turning seventeen was pretty cool", he thought. He was just a few years away of shedding the teenage years for adulthood. "I'd better enjoy these years while I have them", he chuckled to himself, "because when I become twenty, then I'll have to deal with all the adult responsibilities in life." As much as he tried to think what those responsibilities would be, he had no idea. He was thinking he would ask the others to join him for a day on the public beach, Malibu Beach. They could all have some fun, let loose a bit. He needed to ask Avery, of course, but it shouldn't be a problem.

He knew he would find Avery down in the studio fine tuning the new songs to their upcoming third album. As he made his way down into the studio, he said hello to Amber, the office secretary and went to the glass door leading into the mixing room. Like clockwork, there he was, hunched over the massive mixing board, twisting small little knobs all over the place, headset over his ears. He didn't bother knocking, knowing Avery wouldn't hear him anyway. He approached him from behind and reached out and tapped him on his shoulder, and watched as he launched himself off of his chair and almost propelled himself through the sound proof glass leading out into the studio.

"Jesus Christ, Connor, you scared the crap out of me."

"I'm sorry Mr. Johnson, I didn't mean to. I just wanted to come down and talk with you for a few minutes." Connor stated.

"No worries Connor, I guess I was a little too wrapped up in my work. What's on your mind bud?"

"I was wondering, if today, me and the rest of us could have the day off from the studio. It's my birthday today, and I just thought it would be fun to hang out and kick loose, you know." Connor asked.

Avery replied: "It's your birthday? Congratulations Connor! I don't see any problem with that. You guys could certainly use a break. What did you have in mind?"

"I don't know, I was thinking, maybe we could all go down to the beach, check out the girls, play some volleyball, and then maybe have some dinner." He stated.

Avery paused for a second to contemplate what Connor had in mind, then replied: "I don't know if that is such a great idea, Connor. You guys, if you remember, are a tad famous and your appearance down in such a public place would cause quite the scene."

Connor pleaded: "Come on Mr. Johnson, please. We'll be careful, I promise. If it gets out of hand, we'll take a taxi out of there immediately and come home."

"It's going to get out of hand, I promise you that. Once the thousands of kids that are down in that area find out the members of Vasallus are making sand castles, it's going to get out of control. I will agree to it Connor, if you really insist on going down to the beach, that the security team is down there with you. I'm not worried about the girls crying for an autograph, I'm worried about the jealous boyfriend watching his girlfriend fall apart when she sees you nearby. Do you know what I mean, Connor?" Avery explained.

Connor flashed the smile that guaranteed the girls would fall apart, replied: "Totally, Mr. Johnson. We'll be careful I promise, and thank you. I can't wait to tell the others!"

Avery smiled back and said: "Happy birthday, Connor, you guys have fun and be careful please."

"We will. See you soon."

Avery called out to Connor as he turned to leave and said: "Oh, and Connor, please don't call me Mr. Johnson. My name is Avery. You can call me that okay? The same goes with Ms. Paxton. Her name is Bentley, call her that. You're seventeen now, right?"

Avery watched as Connor left the studio, smiling from ear to ear, running to tell the others the great news. He couldn't help but be worried about them out on the beach. They were the most famous teenagers in the world, after all.

****

Avery gave the security team some final instructions to ensure that they gave the kids some space, but also to make sure they stayed together as a group. Once word got out that they were there, the area would swell with autograph seekers. He was able to secure Duke's Malibu restaurant down on the beach, a popular eatery, for a private party for Connor. It would be a surprise for him and he was looking forward to seeing the kids have some fun. Bentley was busy making arrangements to have the place decorated and have a special cake made. The party was taking on a life of its own and it would be a fun way to end the day for them. Hopefully, they would all still be in one piece by the time they got to Duke's.

****

Two limousines pulled up in front of the Malibu surf shack down from the world famous Malibu Pier that stretched out into the Pacific like a giant finger. The thousands of beach lovers that stretched for miles down the sandy coastline never paid them any attention. Limo service was as common as surfboards down at the beach. Taxi's wheeled down by the pier area, one after another, dropping off excited young kids anxious to get in the water and soak up the atmosphere. The limo's brought large groups of people, wedding parties, VIP's, you name it. There were a large number of celebrities living in the Malibu area, and they could often be seen down on the beach, either with their own families or with a group of friends.

One young girl was standing nearby with two of her friends, her tanned, bikini-clad body bursting with development. She took notice of the two black and long SUV limo's that came to a stop. It was her dream to someday catch a dreamy celebrity down on the beach so that she could get her friends to take a photo of her posing with him. She never in her wildest dreams ever expected to be in the vicinity and to be one of the first to even notice who was climbing out of the limousine. She was so stunned she couldn't breathe. She tried to get the attention of her friends, who were locked into a couple of young surfers wading out into the water, but her voice would not escape from her throat. She found herself moving away from her friends, towards the limos. She watched in amazement as the occupants of the first limo, a bunch of huge, muscled guys in shorts and tank tops, jogged over to the first limo to open the doors. The first person she saw climb out of the second limo almost made her lose her balance. She started to bawl, her amazement at who she was seeing only fifty feet away, overwhelmed her. Connor Asker, there was no mistake about who it was, stepped out of the car and onto the beach. The tears streamed down her face as she watched him pull off his t-shirt. He was beautiful. His perfect body, so tanned and muscled, made her so weak she had trouble standing. He was quickly followed out of the limo by none other than Juan Jimenez. Then two girls followed Juan. They both looked to be wearing bikinis underneath their long t-shirts. She recognized them both immediately. It was Elizabeth Leroux and Brittany Campbell! This was insane. Vasallus were on the beach! The only thing that stopped her from fainting was the enormity of her scream.

"OH MY GOD, IT'S CONNOR ASKER FROM VASALLUS!"

Her two friends joined in, screaming at the top of their lungs, hands over their faces as the tears poured down their cheeks, they were so excited. So it started. Kids heard the screams from afar, saw the limos, came closer to see what it was all about and realized they were in the presence of the most famous music group in the world. Kids and adults alike were running from everywhere. Connor, with a security guard right on his tail, approached the three girls who had seen him climb out of the limo. He chatted with them for a few minutes and accepted their request for a photograph. He wrapped his arms around them and the security guard snapped their picture. He then took a black marker offered up by the smiling security guard and signed each of the girls on the back of their shoulders, passing on their requests to sign their boobs.

The six man security team then enveloped the kids, and led them down to the water. The kids were awkward at first, and surprised by the hundreds of people gathering around the perimeter of the security, taking pictures, and screaming their names. Finally it was Chloë, who broke them out of their stupor by saying: "Hey guys, how long have we been playing volleyball at the mansion? Long time, right? Well let's play some beach volleyball!"

She waded out to the fans and called out a challenge to a team that wanted to play Vasallus in a game of beach volleyball. There was an instant rush of excitement as kids started looking at each other, mentally putting a team together, then everyone just broke out and ran for the volleyball nets further down the beach. The security team led Vasallus down the beach, following the hundreds of kids trying to be the first to the nets to play. When they arrived, the area around the nets was full of hundreds of kids, all wanting the chance to play against Vasallus.

Chloë looked out at the huge crowd and declared: "Who was the winning team that was playing a game before we all arrived?"

A kid, around fifteen or so, but tall, lean and tanned held up a volleyball above everyone's head and yelled back: "We were!"

Chloë yelled back: "Great, then assemble your team. It's only fair we win the right to take over your court!"

The challengers were five guys, but it didn't matter. Even though the five guys were pretty good players, the kids of Vasallus destroyed them. They were all athletic and had been playing the game virtually every day since they were at the mansion. Patrick was the least athletic of the group and Juan the most and he could leap up off of the sand into the air like he had springs underneath him. With his strength and agility, he hammered the ball so hard no one could touch it. The group rotated five through at a time and set up Juan for a spike every time he was out there. The two members of Vasallus who weren't playing, were busy signing autographs and chatting it up with the fans. The kids went through five different teams of challengers when the inevitable finally happened. A wise ass kid, not impressed about getting his lunch handed to him on the sand court, opened his mouth: "You fucking guys think you're pretty good, don't' you?"

Connor and Juan instantly stepped in front of Patrick, who was already making his move. The guy was a lot older than them, probably in his late twenties. Patrick tried pushing through them, but he was blocked by the two. He looked at them and growled: "Get out of my way, Connor. The guy deserves an ass kicking!"

Connor never even had a chance to respond as two of the huge bodyguards grabbed the mouth piece by the arms and dragged him away. The kid tried to break free, but was locked in so he shouted back at Patrick: "You're a pussy, Benning. You can't even fight your own battles!"

That was it. Patrick heard enough. With a surge, he pushed Connor and Juan away and rushed the kid, his arms still pinned behind his back by security. He snapped his hand around the kids neck and squeezed, moved his face inches away from his, and hissed: "You fucking punk, I could tear your head off and play volleyball with it. Why the hell do you think these guys are dragging you out of here?"

The kid was seconds away from blacking out from the ferocity of Patrick's grip when Connor and Juan pushed Patrick away. The hundreds of people surrounding the incident all thought the kid got what he deserved and clapped and cheered loudly for Patrick. Elizabeth knew the kid was a few seconds away from dying and thought: "then how would have the crowd reacted?" Patrick was a monster and she was no longer scared of him. She hated him. She barely heard Chloë call out to the crowd for another game. Soon everyone was enjoying themselves again, reveling in the company of Vasallus.

It wasn't long until the media caught on to the news that the kids were down at the beach, and news helicopters began to circle overhead. Cameras and reporters began to wade into the crowd of kids, interviewing the starry-eyed fans and trying to get close to the kids of Vasallus for an interview, but they were blocked by security. Eventually, the kids left the court and made their way down to the water, where they tried to cool off. Security became an issue as the kids became split up and were just one of many heads bobbing up and down in the water. It took some panic-filled effort by the security team, but they got all of the kids rounded up into one area where they could keep an eye on them. Everyone, except one. Patrick was missing.

****

Patrick kept low in the water and slowly backed away from everyone else in the water. He could see security trying to figure out what to do as everyone was split up. "Fucking idiots", he thought. When he felt that he was clear from the mob of kids thrashing around in the water, he made his break. He was going to find the fucker who challenged him. He waded out of the water and onto the beach. He kept his head low, and by himself, no one really paid him much attention. He scanned the dozens of kids lying on towels, standing in clusters, or standing in line at concession booths. "They couldn't be too far away", he thought. The kid would be bragging to anyone who would listen to him that he challenged the drummer from Vasallus. Then he heard a voice behind him.

"Hey pussy, are you lost?

Patrick turned towards the voice, and the kid with the mouth was standing with his two friends, a look of victory on his face. He sneered at them: "Actually, I went to look for you. I thought we could continue our conversation."

The punk looked at his two friends, then back at Patrick, and said: "Bring it pussy boy. You don't belong here, and we're going to make sure you never come back."

"You see that clearing over there? Right behind that line of concession stands? No one can see us in the trees, which means I can kick your ass, and not have to worry about your mamas screaming for me to stop hurting their little boys", laughed Patrick.

The kid launched himself at Patrick: "You motherfucker",

he screamed.

Patrick dodged away at the last second then turned and ran towards the clearing with the three young men right behind him. Once they were far enough away from the beach crowd, and all alone, Patrick stopped and turned towards the approaching punks. The main challenger, fighting for breath, put his hands on his knees then said: "Didn't think you were going to stop. I thought you'd keep running like a chicken shit."

Patrick studied the three of them for a second. They were all big guys, bigger than him, and at least ten years older. None of them wore a shirt, all three were in board shorts and bare feet. He checked over their shoulders to ensure that no one was coming or looking their way. They were too far away for anyone to see them, but they might hear what he was about to do to them. "Who cares?", he thought. The first guy came charging at him, his hands out in front of him, ready to take a swing. He never had a chance. Patrick grabbed his wrist, twisted it, bent the guy forwards, then yanked his arm straight backwards, breaking it instantly. The guy cried out in pain. Then he lowered him right to the ground, and in a split second, drove his foot into his inturned elbow, snapping it like a twig. The kid fell forward onto his stomach, screaming, his grotesquely twisted arm hung loosely behind his back. Then in another fast maneuver, he brought his other foot down onto his throat with tremendous force, crushing it, and the young man's life escaping him in a gasp. The primal scream from the mouth piece alerted Patrick, just in time. The kid launched himself on top of him, slamming his fists into his face. He could feel the blood spray out of his nose and make its way back down into his eyes. The other guy began kicking him in the side of his ribs.

Patrick shot his hand up to the guy's throat and pushed him off of him and onto the ground. With his other hand, he slammed into the face of the other guy, sending him to the ground in a daze. He held onto the guy's throat and lifted him straight off of the ground like he was a doll. His feet dangled freely a foot off of the ground as he struggled to get air into his lungs. He was dying. Patrick timed it so that, when he was about to gasp for the final time, he dug in his fingers deep into his throat and as he dropped the guy to the ground, he pulled back as hard as he could, tearing half of the guy's throat and his windpipe, away from him. The gaping wound on his neck spewed blood everywhere. He looked at the fist of flesh and bone in his hand and threw it to the ground beside the corpse. He turned his attention to the third guy. He was scared shitless, desperately trying to get up and run. He was whimpering like a wounded dog.

Patrick placed his foot on his back and kicked him flat to the ground. He then kicked him hard in the side of the ribs. The air escaped his lungs in a blast. The blow rolled him over onto his back. Through the blood that smeared his face from the earlier blow, he looked at Patrick with a look of terror and begged for his life: "Please, don't kill me! I won't tell anyone what happened here, I promise! Please don't kill me, man!"

"You think I give a shit asshole?" He screamed with a voice full of hatred. Then with speed the human eye could not detect, Patrick brought his fist down onto the guy's face like a sledgehammer. Bone and teeth flew everywhere. He pounded down again a second time, a third time. Again and again. The rage flowed through him like an unstoppable force. The guy's face was a blob of unrecognizable hamburger when he finally stepped away. Covered in blood, he looked out at the beach. He needed to get to the water and get himself washed off before he could rejoin the others. He took one last look at the destroyed three corpses and laughed. He then made his way to the back of the concession stands and snuck along the back until he got to the end of one of the huts and peered around the corner. He pulled back quickly. There was a group of kids just a few feet away that had almost seen him as they stood in line for hot dogs. He walked back towards the opposite end of the huts, all separated by a thin plywood wall. When he got to the other end, he carefully peered around the corner. There was another group of kids clustered together, caught up in small talk. Their backpacks were just a few feet away and one of them had a towel stuffed into the side of it. If he reached for it, they would see him. He could call them all over, slaughter them behind the concession stands, then wrap himself with a towel and head for the water. Too complicated and there were too many of them, one of them could break away and make a run for it. "For fuck sakes!", he thought. Then he saw him.

A doper was passed out against a tree not far from where the dead corpses of the three punks lay. He would have seen the whole thing but he was too stoned to even give a shit. "Well, he'd give a shit now." He made his way over to the tree where the bum sat. He looked up at Patrick and said: "You're a mean little prick, kid. I saw what you did. Yes I did. You punched that defenseless kid in the face. More than once. Yup, I saw it alright. You one mean shit."

Before another word could escape, he was dead. A strike from his powerful fists cracked his head wide open, killing him instantly. Within seconds, he had the drug addict's t-shirt and pants off. They reeked of piss and feces, but Patrick didn't care, he just needed to get to the water so he could wash himself off, peel these clothes off and wade over to where the rest of the group was. By the time they found the bodies, they would be long gone.

Chapter 45

It didn't take the paparazzi long to figure out Vasallus had reserved the entire Duke's Malibu Restaurant for some sort of celebration. They camped outside in the parking lot all evening, hoping to snap some pictures when the party ended. The owner, Jimmy Jahn, took advantage of the opportunity that fell in his lap for free publicity and made sure that the blinds were drawn to give the group complete privacy. He instructed his staff that he would fire anyone on the spot if they ogled the group, and didn't do their job. He also made sure that all of them handed over their cell phones until after the group was gone. There would be no scandal in his restaurant from a cell phone video ending up at the offices of 'TMZ'. Bentley had given him instructions for the party decorations and the special cake which she had brought in prior to the group's arrival. She promised him that she would mention the restaurant, by name, several times in the upcoming article that she was writing. With the group, security, staff and Avery, the party numbered about twenty-five.

****

Avery stood up at the end of the table, and nodded at Bentley, who quietly left for the kitchen, followed closed by Jimmy. He asked for everyone's attention, then said: "Okay guys, if I can have some quiet for a second. Thank you." He continued: "I'm glad all of you had so much fun today, out there on the beach. I'm glad you're still in one piece. Now, today is also a special day for one of you. As you know its Connor's seventeenth birthday, so we made something a little special for you Connor!"

Bentley came bursting through the swinging doors of the

kitchen, with the help of Jimmy, carrying a massive birthday cake, custom made into the likeness of Connor. The base of the cake was shaped like a stage and Connor stood about three feet high, with one hand clutching a microphone to his mouth, and the other arm raised above his shoulder, pointing to the sky. It was the coolest cake Avery ever saw. The seventeen burning candles were lighters, held by adoring fans, surrounding the stage. Jimmy placed the cake in front of Connor, with Bentley saying: "Okay, Connor, you know what comes next. You have to make a wish before you blow out the candles!"

Avery noticed the rest of the kids looked a little bewildered while Connor blew out the candles, so he said: "I would think you guys would know the words to Happy Birthday. Come on, what's with the long faces, you'll get a cake on your birthday too!"

Chloë looked up at him and said: "It is my birthday."

Avery, stunned, looked up at Bentley, who was just as surprised as he was, and blurted: "Wow, it's your birthday today, Chloë? Why didn't you tell us? We would have had a cake for you!"

"I never even gave it any thought, till now, when I saw Bentley bring out the cake. Connor never said a word today that it was his birthday", she said, ruefully.

Avery looked over at Connor, who had blown out all of the candles, and said: "Connor, I thought you wanted everyone to go out to celebrate your birthday today, and yet you didn't tell anyone that it was your birthday?"

He shrugged his shoulders before he replied, somewhat sheepishly: "Sorry, Avery. I forgot all about it actually. I was thinking about it when I spoke to you this morning, but I never thought about it again, until I saw the cake." He gazed around the table and said: "I'm sorry everyone." Then he looked over at Chloë and said: "Happy birthday, Chloë!"

Then to Avery's utter astonishment, he heard Patrick say: "Umm, it's my birthday today too."

"Mine too." It was Elizabeth this time. Avery struggled to

maintain his composure. Jimmy looked around at everyone, not quite sure what to think. Bentley looked over at him. Her face was etched in pure terror. The next voice did not surprise him, in fact he expected it. It was Michael.

"I turned seventeen today as well. At least I'm pretty sure I did."

Brittany, followed by Juan, both repeated: "It's my birthday today too."

The silence that fell over the restaurant was eerie. No one knew what to say next. The staff gathered around, thinking that they would be partaking in the singing of Happy Birthday to the famous Connor Asker, but now were witness to the most bizarre incident they would ever encounter in their lifetime. The realization that seven complete strangers, brought together from different parts of the world, were all born on the exact same day, was beyond anything any of them could imagine. It was a loud bang on the front glass entrance doors to the restaurant, which broke them all out of their numbness. Brittany let out a short, sharp, exclamation at the sudden noise.

Jimmy made his way over to the doors and unlocked them. Avery watched as four uniformed police officers stepped into the restaurant and declared to the group: "I'm afraid I have to ask everyone to leave at once. There has been a multiple murder, not half a mile away from here. The area is being closed down as a crime scene, including the restaurant. Please, give your full names, and contact information to these three officers on your way out. That is just in case we need to get a hold of you for any reason. Thank you for your cooperation, if you would please make your way out of the restaurant and to your cars."

****

Avery and Bentley readied themselves to call it a night. The revelation of the kids' birthdays and the news of the multiple murders right next door to where they were celebrating, had taken its toll on the two of them. Bentley was already under the covers when he clicked off the night lamp and crawled in beside her. He kissed her cheek and was about to roll over, when she said: "Honey, we need to talk about this. Of all the things that have happened or been revealed to us so far, none of them scared me as much as finding out about the kids' birthdays tonight."

"I know, it scared the hell out of me, too. I just don't know what to think anymore. This is just getting more and more crazy." "They were all born on the same day, for Christ's sakes. Do you know what that means?" She propped herself up on her elbows as she spoke.

"It means everything Father O'Sullivan has told us is true. These seven kids were born, or you could almost say, manufactured for a specific purpose. I just don't understand, or comprehend, what that could possibly be? They are truly exceptional kids, without flaw, I just don't get it." Avery's tone of voice conveyed his complete exasperation.

Bentley replied, somewhat tentatively: "Maybe you just answered your own question." "I did? How so?"

"You said yourself, these kids are exceptional, without flaw. Maybe that's it. They are too perfect, too talented. They are the key to whatever evil plot exists. Best has brought them together into this band for a reason. I just don't know why. The kids are doing nothing, but bringing terrific music into people's lives. They set good examples for kids, they behave themselves in public. I just don't see the connection. What is it that Best is doing with them?"

They chatted for a while longer, until the words got softer, and faded away completely, replaced by soft snores and light breathing.

****

Sam's cell phone buzzed. He didn't recognize the caller i.d., but answered anyway. It was Sgt. Pallin, from the RCMP. Sam picked up the sense of urgency in his voice.

"Sam, it's Pallin again. Listen, I did some more digging around on the Leroux kid. Her adoptive parents, Daniel and Michelle Leroux, of Rigaud, Quebec, are missing. They haven't been seen or heard from in months. Neighbors have no idea where they could be, and the closest relative we could find was a sister of the father, Daniel, who lives out west, in Vancouver. She hasn't heard from her brother in months. She just assumed he and his wife, Michelle, were busy following their daughter around on tour with Vasallus. She said they are not close, they never were and that never changed when Elizabeth became famous."

"I have a connection to Vasallus. My deceased partner's son is under my care, after the death of his mother and guess what? He is the drummer for Vasallus. So I don't think the Leroux's are down here with Elizabeth, Scott. I've never seen them around." Sam explained.

"Are you kidding me? That is quite the connection. Listen, I'll keep checking up here for them. Daniel Leroux has been retired from the government for years, but the wife still worked after accepting a consulting contract from Canada Post, upon her retirement. She just walked away one day and never came back. They just assumed she had enough and didn't need to be working anyway. The popularity of her daughter and her skyrocketing career, made everyone assume she left to follow her daughter's concert tour." Pallin explained.

"Will you keep me posted if you find them, Scott?"

"I will. What's going on down there anyway, Sam?"

"It's complicated, and I don't have the time to explain it over the phone right now, but I will when I know more. I have one more favor to ask."

"Depends, Sam. What is it?" Pallin asked.

"Can you send me the police reports of the events surrounding the birth of Elizabeth and the death of her birth mother in the delivery room? I need these sent to me on the QT, Scott." "Jesus Christ, Sam, you know I can't pull confidential files without just cause. We're not the Wild West up here."

"That's the second time I've heard that in the last day." Sam replied.

"Heard what?"

"Never mind, Scott. Tie the request into your

investigation of the missing adoptive parents. I need this report yesterday, Scott. It's important." Sam asked.

"You owe me, Sam. Get me an invite to a police convention or something down there. I'll use it to get my family down to Disneyland. You know what it's like."

"Sure. Whatever you want. Just get me the report. Okay Scott?" Sam replied before he hung up the phone.

****

"That was a strange call", thought Pallin. He'd known Sam for a long time and he's a stand-up guy and a well-respected investigator. He's working this away from the prying eyes of the department. He wondered why. His former partner, he remembered, was killed years ago in a bloodbath, where his wife was viciously attacked and raped by the thugs. Now the partner's wife was dead? Something weird was going down in Tinsel town. He decided to get what Sam needed. "Why all the tie-ins to Vasallus?", he wondered. His thirteen-year old daughter would love to meet the band or get to a concert. Yeah, screw Disney. He'd get Sam to get him backstage passes. Sometimes this job had its perks and he didn't mean free coffee at Tim Horton's.

He wasn't going to make this official, not yet. He would use his contact in records to pull the reports from the shooting surrounding the birth of Elizabeth Leroux. He grabbed his jacket on the way out the door. The brownie points he would score with his wife and daughter, from obtaining tickets to Vasallus, made him smile. Yup, sometimes this job had its perks.

He ran down the back stairwell, two at a time, to the parking lot. As he reached the last flight of stairs, he was going at a pretty good clip when he smashed into the exit door. He'd used this door a million times and it was never locked. It should never be locked. It required a security pass card to get in, but it was just a release handle to exit out into the parking lot. The impact of his body weight hitting the locked door, threw him backwards, causing him to lose his balance as he struggled to grab onto a railing to break his fall. He missed and hit the last stair hard. He heard a crack when his wrist tried to break his fall, but instead his wrist broke. Son-of-a-bitch that hurt. "Who the fuck locked this door? He was going the kill the stupid bastard. This is also a fire exit for shit sakes, it's not supposed to be locked."

He struggled to get back on his feet, the pain shooting up his forearm from the broken wrist hurt like hell. Then he heard someone laugh. It was probably the dumb prick who locked the door. "This asshole was getting his kicks watching cops fall flat on their faces. Well, he just broke his fucking arm, so this was no joke. Time to kick some ass."

He looked up the stairwell, but could see no one. He called out: "Hey, asshole, I just broke my fucking arm, so get down here and unlock this door so I can get to my car." He heard the laugh again. Jesus, it sounded awful. A hoarse, guttural type laugh. He wondered: "What's this guy's problem?" "Hey asshole, unlock this door, I've got to drive myself to the hospital."

"This prick wants to play games", he thought. "Unbelievable." Now he would bring charges against this jackass, including a lawsuit. He had started to make his way up the first flight of stairs when he heard it. A deafening sound descended down from the stairs above, a sound like a million birds flapping their wings, making their way down the stairs, towards him. "What was this all about?" He stopped on the last stair, of the first stairwell, and looked up. He wished he hadn't. What came down the stairs towards him was something out of a really bad nightmare. A grotesque creature, with a huge wingspan that filled the stairwell, wings slapping the walls as they flapped, propelling its body, with incredible speed, towards him. It had huge arms, with claws at the end of them, making it look like an eagle, diving towards earth to snatch its prey.

He screamed because that's all he could think of doing. He didn't have his pistol with him. It was stupidly tucked away in his secure locker back in his office. The claw like talons entered his skull like knives and, before everything went dark in his mind, he looked into the burning red eyes of this creature. This thing was taking him to Hell.

****

A cop from Providence was on the line. "You're looking into the birth of Brittany Campbell? Can I ask you why would you have any interest in knowing the circumstances surrounding her birth? You're a cop from L.A. How do I know you're not one of those paparazzi shitheads from 'TMZ' looking for a scoop on the kid from Vasallus."

"Listen officer, feel free to call down to LAPD Homicide and speak with my superior, Captain Rodney Bitters. I don't have time to verbally jostle with you. If you can help me out great, otherwise I'll instruct the Feds to issue a search warrant for what I want. Tell me if there was anything at all on the birth records that was unusual. Did the attending doctor or nurses make any comments that were put down on the birth records?" Sam asked.

"Actually there is and the only reason it catches my attention is because of who Brittany is."

"What do you mean?" Sam asked.

"Purely off the record and I'll deny ever having this conversation with you. The attending doctor, a Dr. Bensen, made an unusual notation. He said at first he was concerned when, after he delivered the baby, it did not cry. Not a sound. He placed the wrapped baby on her mother's chest and still no sound. He was about to take the baby back and place her into the hands of the nurses when suddenly the baby made a sound. Not a wail, or crying, but a cooing noise that sounded like angels singing. He mentioned it was surreal, one of the delivery room nurses commented that it was a miracle. Sort of fitting don't you think, Detective considering who she is and how beautiful she sings? My wife and daughter worship this young girl."

"Jesus!" Sam thought, just like the birth of Patrick.

****

Sam quickly called Pallin back to get him to take a look at the doctors' and nurses' comments in addition to the police reports on Elizabeth's birth. His phone was picked up immediately, but it wasn't Sgt. Pallin. He had heard the voice once before. The cold chills snapped through his body like lightning. His mind was spinning out of control. The voice was not of this earth. He gripped the receiver with such force, it almost cracked in two.

"You think you know what is going on here, Detective? Let it go before it's too late and there's no turning back." The voice on the other line barked into Sam's ear.

"Who the fuck is this. Where is Sgt. Pallin? Put him on the phone!" Sam yelled into the phone.

The voice on the other end of the phone boomed: "You know who this is Detective! Your Canadian friend can't come to the phone. Let's just say he has a headache." Laughter crackled through the receiver.

A thought entered his head at that instant and Sam blurted: "You don't scare me motherfucker whoever you are, or what you are. You can't get to me can you? You'd have killed me a long time ago if you could have. I'm protected by God's mercy, isn't that right?" Sam was cut off by the voice on the other end of the line. It cut right into his chest as if it had reached through the phone when it laughed it's horrible, guttural and mocking sound before it said: "You think so Detective? Then tell that story to your son Seb, why don't you?" Sam caught the thunderous laughter coming from the dropped receiver as he raced out of the office. His cell phone vibrated as he by-passed the elevators and went straight for the stairs. It was Bethany. He quickly hit the send button and raised the phone to his ear as he flew down the stairs.

"Sam! Sam! You've got to get home. It's Seb! Jesus Sam something has happened to Seb!" Beth was sobbing uncontrollably.

Sam was going to be sick. He gasped, raggedly:, "What is it Beth? What's wrong with Seb?" He braced for her answer.

"He's screaming like a wild animal in his room! Something is torturing him, Sam. We can't get through the door. It's completely sealed. Sam, please hurry! You have to hurry. His screams Sam. Oh my God!"

"I'm coming Beth, I'm coming! I'll be there in fifteen minutes. Get the axe from the garage and get through his door Beth! I'll be right there!" He hung up the phone and burst through the door and ran into the parking lot to his car, almost getting clipped by a departing squad car.

"Sweet Lord, don't let him hurt my son!"

Chapter 46

Sam tore out of the parking lot with sirens blaring and lights blazing as he streaked for his house, desperate to get home as fast as possible. His mind raced almost as fast as the squad car did, trying to make sense of what was going on. The demon had attacked Seb? "This nightmare just keeps getting worse", he thought, dodging an oncoming car after he took the opposite lane to pass another vehicle. Idiots, with their stereos cranked, couldn't even hear his sirens as he came up behind them.

He dialed the house as he careened off the interstate and into his subdivision. The phone rang four times before going to voicemail. Feeling panic settling in, he dialed again. The same thing happened, voicemail again after four rings. He dialed Beth's cell, but it went straight to voicemail with no rings. He tossed the phone onto the passenger seat, and cursed under his breath, as he gunned the car down the last few blocks towards his house. He finally reached the end of the street before it turned into his bay, his tires squealing as he barreled around the final turn and into his driveway. The siren and lights turned off when he shut the car off, climbed out and headed for the front door at a run. He went to open the front door but he found it locked. He banged as hard as he could on the door and rang the doorbell several times. He heard no movement inside the house, so he peeled around towards the back. As he made his way around the side of the house, he stopped at the window and peered inside, using his hands to shield the sun. He didn't see anyone or anything unusual. He rapped on the glass as hard as he could without breaking it. Again, there was no response from within. It was eerily quiet inside. "Too quiet", he thought. He turned the corner to the back of the house and then he heard the scream.

A blood curdling scream erupted from the front of the house. It was a scream for him. It was Beth. He pulled his pistol from his holster, clicked off the safety and ran for the front of the house. He stopped at the corner and peered around it, saw nothing, then continued to the front step and bounded through the opened front door, his sidearm out in front of him. What he saw next defied reality.

His son Seb was sitting on his mother; he had her pinned to the floor. Her face was covered in blood as Seb's fists rained down on her. Sam tried to scream, but his voice stalled completely, he was unable to voice words. He holstered his gun and launched himself at his son, tackling him off of Beth. The two of them rolled on the hardwood floor, crashing into the wall. Sam found his voice and screamed at his son: "Seb, what are you doing! Seb!"

He watched as his son quickly leapt off the floor and towered over him, his eyes blazing red, a twisted and demonic look of pure hatred etched all over his face. He didn't even see Seb's foot until it was too late. It came out of nowhere and slammed into the side of his head, sending him spiraling back into the wall. Pain shot through his brain, dazing him, and the complete ferociousness of the kick stunned him. He quickly rolled the opposite way to avoid a follow-up kick by his son, looked up at him and yelled: "Seb, stop it! What is the matter with you?" Then he watched as his son growled like a dog with the rabies virus, readying to launch himself once again. His face was the color and texture of sun-dried clay. The demon was in him. The thought scared him to his core. He tried to reason with his son: "Seb, it's not your fault. You're not in control. Let me put my handcuffs on you, so you can't hurt anybody else or yourself, until I can figure out a way to help you. Please!"

He heard Beth moan behind him and, for a split second, he took his eyes off of Seb to look back at her. Relief flooded through him, knowing she was alive. He turned to face Seb, but as he did, he realized he was gone. He reached to his belt clip, snapped his cell phone open, and dialed 911, requesting paramedics at once. He frantically turned to his wife and checked her condition. She had been badly beaten by her own son but she was alive. He could feel hot tears stinging his eyes as he looked down at his wife's bloody and swollen face. He placed his hand on her cheek and she immediately began to respond to his touch, her eyes opening, trying hard to focus through all the dried blood surrounding them. He took the sleeve of his shirt to try and remove some of the blood. She coughed, then whispered: "Sam, you have to help him. Help our son; don't let him hurt anyone else."

He looked at her, full of grief, then said: "I won't, I promise. He is not himself. This is my entire fault. I allowed this to happen. The medics are on their way sweetheart. Lay still okay. I'm going to go find Seb."

She struggled to respond: "Ann, you must help her. I think Seb might have killed her. My God, what is happening?" Tears streamed down her face as she spoke.

Shocked, he looked at his wife and said: "Where is she? Where is Ann?"

"Upstairs in the hallway, I think. Unless he moved her. The two of us used the axe to smash through the door and when we did, Seb was waiting for us. He attacked her. It was awful." She sobbed again.

He reached down, kissed his wife on her forehead, patted the side of her cheek softly with his hand, then stood up and said, shakily: "Don't move Beth, the ambulance will be here any second. I'll be right back as soon as I know what is going on upstairs. I love you."

"Please be careful. Find him before the police get here. Get him away from this. It's not his fault."

"I'm on it. Don't worry honey."

He took off up the stairs and was confronted by Seb as he made it to the top. His son had been waiting for him and he was too late to stop another vicious kick, aimed at his head. His foot caught him flush, sending him toppling backwards down the stairs. He landed with a thud against the wall. Pain shot through his back and down his legs. Slowly, he lifted his head, the dizziness making him nauseated. Then he heard a loud roar, horrible sounding, coming from upstairs and down the hall. He lifted himself off the floor, desperate to get upstairs and put a stop to this madness. He shouted up the stairs: "Seb, it's your father. Please son, I'm not going to hurt you. I'm coming up the stairs now."

There was nothing but silence as he carefully made his way to the top of the stairs and peered around the corner. The hallway was empty. He walked slowly towards Seb's room, checked the main bathroom as he did, found it empty and moved on. He had almost reached his son's bedroom, when he damn near came out of his skin, because a loud and demonic voice, which came from within the bedroom shouted out towards him: "Come inside Sam, we're having a party!"

Sam gathered himself and made his way to the doorway. He pivoted his body until he was in the bedroom. What he saw next made his heart sink. He stood, frozen, gasping in air, unable to move as he watched the carnage on the bed in front of him.

Patrick, his body half-human and half-monster, had mounted a naked Ann lying on her back on the bed and he was about to assault her. Seb was lying in a heap on the floor beside the bed, unconscious. Patrick's long hair covered most of his face as he looked over at him, a demonic smile stretched across his face. His eyes blazed red when he spoke: "Good to see you're joining the party Sam! Listen, if you don't mind, would you happen to have an extra condom lying around? Don't really want to knock this bitch up again; you know what I mean Sam?" Then he laughed again, making him sound like a lion about to devour his caught meal.

The anger rose within him to a level he had never experienced before. The thought of his injured wife downstairs took over his mind, combined with the images of Ann helpless on the bed, and his son unconscious on the floor. The monster, who was living inside of Patrick, mocked him, and laughed as if he could read his thoughts. Sam exploded off of his feet, letout a primal scream he didn't recognize, and charged the demon. He caught him flush in the chest with his shoulder, sending the two of them flying off of the bed and into the wall. Sam quickly rolled on top of the beast and pounded his fists into its face, the cracking sound of the facial bones as they crunched was louder than he would have imagined as his fists hammered away. The beast continued to laugh, and mock him, as blood leaked everywhere from his face. Then, all of a sudden, the mocking and laughing stopped and was replaced by the voice of his brother Jacob: "Sam, I'm sorry I let you down. I have failed you, brother. Please, forgive me."

Sam could only look and stare at what was once Patrick. The sound of his brother's voice sucked every last ounce of energy from his body. It was he who had failed his brother. He was the detective and he should have protected him, but he failed. He cried out: "Jacob, it was me who let you down. I failed you just like I have failed everyone else." The words came out of him in anguished sobs, his shoulders heaving with grief. Then the laughter returned.

Roaring like a caged animal, Patrick screamed: "You big dumb kike. Get off of me!" With incredible strength, Patrick heaved him over the bed, where he crashed, hard against the opposite wall. Sam struggled to get up, the pain wracked his bodyand he found it nearly impossible to get up and rush the demon beast. He tried to reach back for his pistol, when he heard the commotion of people as they came down the hallway towards the bedroom. Three uniform cops stood at the doorway, disbelief written all over their faces, as they tried to decipher what it was as they witnessed it. Before they even had a chance to draw their weapons, Patrick, who had changed completely back to himself, launched himself at the first cop with such speed, the cop never had a chance.

Sam screamed at him: "Patrick stop! Don't do it!" It didn't matter as he could only watch, helplessly, as in one fluid motion that took less than a second, Patrick twisted the cop's head completely around, and dropped him to the floor where he lay with his face on top of his back, his tongue stuck out of his mouth, and his dead eyes which stared back at Sam. The other two cops tried to fire a shot, but Patrick had the one by the throat and the other by his balls, as he lifted them both up in the air. In a flash of speed, Patrick pulled back his arms, tearing the throat of the cop clean off his neck with his one hand, and the genitals with the other. With the mangled flesh in his hands, he raised them up in triumph, and laughed once again.

Bang bang! Sam fired two shots into Patrick's chest from his lying position on the floor. The force of the bullets sent him flying backwards into Seb's dresser, and then he and the piece of furniture toppled over and onto the floor. Sam propped himself up on one elbow, and then up into a sitting position. He heard a moaning sound and he could see Seb beginning to move from his position on the floor beside the bed. He had shot and killed Patrick. The realization of what he had done as he watched Seb come around, was overwhelming to him. He called out to his son, as his tears came to the surface and threatened to spill over. "Seb stay there, don't move..." His words were cut off as he watched in horror, as Patrick had somehow risen up off of the floor and approached Seb. His eyes were on fire, the hatred burning from them had an unspeakable intensity He screamed as he approached his son: "You filthy rotten punk. I should have smashed your head against a tree like your neighbor's dog. Your big daddy can't save you now Sebastian, because I'm going to send you straight into hell!"

Sam raised his pistol to fire into Patrick and end this nightmare once and for all when he heard a booming voice from behind him. He turned to see Father Thomas O'Sullivan. He stood in the doorway, he gripped a large cross in one hand, which he thrust straight out in front of him and he clutched his bible in the other hand.

"In the name of Jesus Christ, Son of the Lord Thy God, I command you demon, to leave this home at once. You don't belong here. Leave now, before the wrath of the greatest power on earth, descends down onto you from the heavens and smashes you."

Moving towards Patrick with great purpose he continued to shout: "Your wickedness is a reflection of your cowardice, demon! You are no match for the love and grace of a powerful God!" Sam could see the eyes of the priest as he moved. They were ablaze with a light that was so amazing; Sam could feel the warmth from them hit his body. The Lord was in Father O'Sullivan. He could feel it.

Patrick, momentarily in a frozen state, snapped out of it and went berserk. Objects from all over the room came to life and flew into walls. Sam, saw his son watch in wonder, and moved to check on Ann, who lay motionless on the bed. He quickly covered her naked body with a blanket, and then checked her pulse. She had a pulse and it was strong. Father O'Sullivan pushed on: "The cleave of righteousness will impale your soulless body!"

The room suddenly went dark; the light from the late afternoon sun was no longer able to pierce the windows. The bedroom became frigid cold as if transformed into a refrigerated meat locker. A white glow of light surrounded Patrick as he once again stood motionless under the power from the word of God. Sam reached over and grabbed another blanket off of the floor and handed it to Seb, and instructed him to stay put. He watched in wonder, as Father O'Sullivan moved within a few feet of Patrick, the cross inches from Patrick's face. He continued to speak the Lord's commands into him: "You have entered this world, uninvited, through the soul of this young man. I command you in the name of God, to abandon his soul, and set him free, into the loving arms of His Son, Jesus Christ!"

Patrick let out a blood curdling scream that sent chills down his spine. It sounded horrifying, as if his soul was crying out. Father O'Sullivan moved even closer, and he continued to command and pray. Patrick did not move, but he began to arch his back towards the floor, to avoid the cross of Christ bearing down on him. Sam watched as the priest tucked the bible under his arm and reached into his pocket with his hand and produced a small, round bottle of water. He flipped off the cap, raised it in the air and declared: "Let this Holy water burn the fear that lives inside of you demon. The very fear you deny exists but the fear of Thy Lord is real!" He raised the bottle and sent shards of water onto the chest and face of Patrick. Sam watched in shock as the skin touched by the Holy water burned deep. Patrick screamed in pain. Father O'Sullivan raised the bottle, and once again, splashed Holy water onto Patrick: "Jesus Christ commands you. Leave this home at once. He commands you in the name of the Father."

Suddenly the demonic, restructured face of Patrick roared up towards Father O'Sullivan, his mouth stretched to a grotesque size, his hands poised to strike. Sam pulled his gun from the holster and took aim. He watched and waited to take his shot without fear of injuring the priest. Patrick wrapped his hands around Father O'Sullivan's throat and moved so close to his face, Sam thought he would devour it, then blared: "Fuck you to Hell, priest!" Patrick then threw Father O'Sullivan against the far wall, sending him crashing to the floor in a heap. Sam could only watch, as Patrick turned and ran towards the far window of the second floor bedroom. He launched himself through the glass and onto the ground below. Sam rushed to the window, seconds behind him, but when he looked out the window, Patrick had disappeared into thin air. He was gone.

****

Later that night in the hospital, Sam sat beside his wife's bed after checking on Seb. She was asleep, the medications had knocked her out for the night. She had suffered no serious injuries or broken bones. She was lucky. The pounding she took from Seb, or from Patrick to be precise, left her with bruising and facial lacerations that required over thirty stitches to repair the cuts above and below her eyes and around her nose and mouth. She had terrible swelling and would require lots of rest over the next several days. Ann had a concussion from a blow to the head and like Beth, suffered bruising all over her body, but she would soon recover. She was awake and alert and had just finished telling him what had happened, including what happened earlier that morning when the two of them drove out to the mansion. Seb was awake and alert and had no memory whatsoever of the entire event. He didn't even remember waking up in the bedroom with all the carnage unfolding around him. He will remember, Sam knew, he just hoped it wasn't for a while.

Father O'Sullivan, after Patrick had thrown himself out the window and disappeared, left the house without any explanation. Sam tried to get him to stay at the house, but he refused, stating he had many things that needed to be done and time was of the essence. He informed Sam that he would be in touch very soon, in the next few days, and not to worry. He reassured him that Patrick would not return to the home, he knew that it was not safe for him there. The home was now under the protection of God.

Sam's faith did not have a place for Jesus Christ, Son of God. After what he had witnessed, he prayed his own faith in Judaism would find a place in his heart for Christ, because he felt he was in His presence today.

Errol Barr

Chapter 47

Elizabeth's suspicion of Patrick grew every day. There was just something not right with him. They were all different, she knew, but he was different from the rest of them. She didn't trust him and she didn't like him, in fact, she loathed him. He had done some terrible things when he went out at night and last night must have been really bad. He had been beaten within an inch of his life by the look of him. His face was bruised and swollen. No one else had enough courage to confront him about the bruises, but she did. He didn't scare her, not one bit. He was a bully and he was capable of terrible things. She felt it, right down to her bones. He was evil. This afternoon, she was going to confront him. She would wait until everyone was around, then she would call him out. They were all about to begin their worldwide tour and she couldn't take it anymore and she wouldn't spend another minute on an airplane with him. She thought about complaining to Avery, but she knew he would only blow her off. Patrick played by his own set of rules, because he was the hotshot songwriter of the group. Big, bloody deal.

Brittany and Chloë were terrified of him, and she bet Connor, Juan and Michael were too. "Nope, enough bullshit", she thought. The other night at the birthday party for Connor, when they all discovered that they were born on the same day, it was a revelation they could barely wrap their heads around. However, when those cops came in and announced there had been a murder nearby, she knew without a shred of doubt that it was Patrick. She didn't know why, she just knew. He was a cold-blooded killer. Today, she would confront him and she didn't care if the rest of them didn't back her or believe her.

She wanted him to know that she wasn't afraid of him.

****

Captain Bitters looked at Sam across his desk. The man looked exhausted and ready to drop. Sam wasn't going to like it, but he was ordering him to take time off, before he wore himself down to the point where he could get sick. He worried that Sam would have a heart attack from all of the stress and overtime he'd had in the past few months..

"Sam, what the hell are you doing here? You should be at the hospital, not here. You understand me?" Sam shook his head at him, then replied: "I am tired Cap, but I have work I need to do. I know you think I'm crazy, but I'm getting close to figuring this all out. I need access to the database for a few hours, then I'm outta here, I promise."

Bitters narrowed his eyes as he continued: "Sam, what is it you're close to figuring out? Everyone around you is dying. The Bennings, Ryerson, your brother for Christ's sakes, Sam. Plus, countless other cops. You don't know what the hell is happening, and neither do I. Besides, it's out of our hands anyway."

He watched as Sam leaned over his desk, ready to pounce on him, before he asked: "What do you mean, Cap? Why is it out of our hands? Speak to me Rodney." He only spoke to him by his first name when he was really pissed.

"The Feds have taken over. You've been ordered on mandatory leave, starting immediately. Go to your wife and son. They need you and you need them, not this fucking job. Take two weeks, four weeks, I don't care, you've got the time, now take it. Rest up, re-charge and then come back." Bitters instructed.

Sam quickly retorted: "You sound like a fucking department shrink, Cap. Tell you what, I will disappear, now that the Feds are involved. The last thing I need right now is a feeb crawling up my ass. Let me finish up some stuff on the computer for a few hours, and then I'll take you up on the time off."

****

"Federal agents will go hog wild once they get their hands on this", Sam thought to himself as he left the Captain's office. Their sophisticated laboratories and resources won't mean a hill of beans in this investigation. They will come to the same dead end in the road that Sam hit, and when that happens, the internal head scratching will be epic. Sam had found the secret passageway at the dead end, whether he wanted it or not. The FBI won't know what hit them.

****

Elizabeth burned off some nervous energy in her bedroom, singing vocals to the music track that played in her headphones. The song, from the band's new album, was all hers. On the first album, she was relegated to a lot of the background vocals, but on the second album, she got a bigger role. It was the group's new single and she couldn't be more excited. She couldn't deny that Patrick knew how to write a great song. With her eyes closed, the headphones on and her voice ringing off the walls, she never even heard someone enter her bedroom.

****

Patrick circled behind her on the bed, watching her head bob up and down to the music in her headphones, her voice soaring. He thought of just sticking a knife into the middle of her back, killing her instantly. Quick and easy. Then wait for the shit to hit the fan.

She was suspicious of him from the very beginning and he hated her for that. She knew what he was doing. She was the only one who knew he was responsible for the Malibu Beach murders. The more he thought about it, the madder he got: "Somehow she could sense what he was doing. No one else could and the little bitch was filling Chloë's head full of crap too. Was she that stupid that she didn't realize that we were one and the same? We shared the same blood, the same father? Our mothers were worthless humans, but our father is more powerful than God? At the birthday party, when it was discovered we were all born the same day, that never clued her in? He would clue her in now. The Master would bring his

497

fury, like he did in Las Vegas, but he didn't care. He was born to kill, to wreak havoc and no one was going to stop him. Misery and mayhem was the fuel that powered his car."

He reached across the bed and grabbed her by the hair. Yanking her, hard, backwards, across the bed towards him, he put her head in a choke hold and squeezed. He moved so fast, she never had a chance to react or scream. The last thing he needed was the rest of the crybabies to come to her rescue. She was faster than he anticipated, quickly spinning her body and her head, freeing herself from his grip. Her eyes blazed with hatred at him. "This was good", he thought. Her hatred came out of her like a hiss when she seethed: "What do you think you're doing? You plan on killing me like you did those innocent kids down at the beach? I'm not scared of you, Benning. You're a raving lunatic and everybody knows it. How many people have you killed anyway?"

His rage erupted like a volcano. He launched himself at her, knocking her hard against the wall, hearing the breath escape her lungs. "He would tear her apart; discard her body in the trash, like a torn rag doll. She and the others actually thought they were making a difference in this world with their music. She was so stupid. They were all born for one reason only. To carry out the Master's plan to destroy mankind. Why was he the only one who got it? They weren't going to live this fairy tale life as rock n' roll stars for much longer. A couple more albums, a few more tours and their fans, which would be just about everyone in the world, would fall off a bridge for the Master, at his request. All of them were born for his purpose. Nothing else. For him."

In the split second he was distracted with his thoughts, she connected, hard, with a roundhouse kick to his groin that sent him to the floor, and the white hot pain resonated through his body. The pain fuelled his rage to another level. He jumped off the floor, his anger out of control now. He looked around the bedroom, but she was gone. As he prepared to go after her, he caught a glimpse of himself in the mirror above her dresser. He had already begun to change, his demonic transformation fuelled by his rage. There was no turning back now. He didn't have much time. "The Master always sensed when his rage got too out of control and he would soon be here to beat him down, temper his rage, telling him that now was not the time; there would be plenty of opportunity in the near future to let his dark side run amok. Stick to the plan. Always the plan. Well fuck the plan. He was going to kill one of his own and he knew that would change everything."

He roared like a caged lion, his hatred for the Leroux bitch taking full control of his mind.

****

Elizabeth raced from the room, desperate to get away from the crazed Patrick. She had never seen such hatred and anger in anyone's eyes as she just saw in his. They were actually glowing red and it terrified her to the core. She needed to warn the others. She knew they were all downstairs in the media room watching a movie or hanging out. She was pretty sure Avery and Bentley were in the other wing of the mansion, in the studio, working as usual. Running as fast as she could down the winding staircase to the floor below, she heard the demonic scream coming from her bedroom and the fear that ran through her body just then caused her to cry out. She knew for sure that he wasn't just a psychotic killer, but a monster and all of them were in grave danger.

Almost at the bottom of the stairs she saw Chloë, who must have been in the kitchen and heard her running down the stairs. She could see the fear in Chloë's eyes as she flew down the last few stairs.

Chloë cried out: "Elizabeth, what's going on? You look like you're being chased by a ghost? You're scaring me."

Reaching the bottom of the stairs, she stopped for a second and looked her in the eye before saying: "It's Patrick, he's out of control. He just tried to kill me in my bedroom, Chloë. None of us are safe right now. Come on we have to warn the others and get out of here."

She just stared back at her, fear registering in her eyes.

Finally, she said: "Okay, let's go, the others are down the hall, watching T.V. I don't know where Avery and Bentley are, but let's go get the others and we can all make a run for the studio, lock ourselves in there and wait for the police."

Then a voice boomed down to them from above on the staircase, an unrecognizable and demonic cackle that froze the two of them in their tracks: "The police won't help you here, you filthy sluts. It's just us and no one else. This charade we're all living is going to end tonight with your deaths." Laughter rained down on them. The realization of who Patrick was, or had become, snapped them out of their trance, and caused them to turn and run.

The two of them rushed into the media room to warn the others, but to their shock, Patrick was already sitting on the couch between Connor and Brittany. He flew off the couch at Elizabeth, pinning her against the wall before she had a chance to react. He held her head hard against the wall, his powerful hand wrapped around her neck. No one in the room moved, the fear of Patrick locking everyone in place. It was Chloë, who finally spoke: "Leave her alone, you animal. You're hurting her!"

"Don't you worry my little Irish butterfly, I'll do a lot more than hurt Elizabeth. I'm going to kill her." The sound of his laughter woke everyone else up in the room.

Connor took a step towards Patrick, and said: "Get your hands off of her Benning. You're taking this too far. Let her go. Now!"

Patrick violently threw Elizabeth to the ground, then turned his attention to Connor and said: "Or what Asker? You want to take me on? Then bring it, pretty boy. You too, Juan? Both of you. In fact I dare you both and Michael to try and stop me. Don't you guys know what is going on here? Do you know who you are?"

Michael called out: "Patrick, we are a family, remember? We need each other. We're all we have. We have to trust one another. Take it easy, please."

Elizabeth, lying on the floor, gasping for air, cried out:

"He's a killer, idiots! There is no trust. He will kill all of us eventually. He killed those kids at the beach the other night. He's killed many times, haven't you Patrick? I'm calling the police."

What happened next was so shocking and so evil, no one in the room breathed or moved. Patrick was on top of Elizabeth so rapidly; there wasn't a hint of discernible movement. His ferocious punch to her chest happened so quickly that no one could react to stop him. His fist entered her chest cavity and ripped out her heart, then blood poured down his arm, and a diabolical grin transformed his face. Elizabeth's eyes fluttered with her final breath. The genetics of the Anti-Christ were unable to save the human blood that flowed through her. She died instantly.

The reaction around the room was one of total shock at what had just happened. Chloë screamed and Brittany fainted. The boy's all stood, and they looked back and forth at each other and at Patrick, unable to speak, the gravity of what just happened sucked the air out of their lungs.

Patrick, his arm raised in triumph as his fist still clenched Elizabeth's heart, screamed: "I am what you are, you are what I am. We are all the spawn of our Master. Accept it or die like her."

Michael, in a voice so low, it was barely a whisper, broke everyone else's silence: "You killed her Patrick. You killed Elizabeth! Why, Patrick, why?" Michael fell to his knees, his head between them and began to scream uncontrollably.

Chloë rushed Patrick, a primal scream escaping her lungs as she tackled him. She wailed away with her fists onto Patrick's face, crying and sobbing at the same time. Patrick effortlessly rolled her over onto her back, pinned her wrists to the floor and let loose: "You think you're any different than me? You carry the same mark on your right thigh as I do. We all have the mark. Do you know what that means?" He screamed into her face. He then climbed off of her and turned his attention to the rest of the room: "Elizabeth, did not understand or accept who she was or who we are. We are all the children of the greatest power mankind has ever known. We have a great purpose bestowed upon us that will be revealed. You can hate me for what I have done, but it will not change who you are or why you were born. You will obey our Master or you will die, just like her."

Chloë had picked herself up off of the floor and confronted Patrick: "Who gave you the power to kill one of us? I don't believe you, Benning. I will kill you for what you have done to Elizabeth. That is my promise, to you. You will die for what you've done."

It was Juan who spoke next: "Chloë, he is right. This is our destiny. What you cannot see now, you will very soon. Elizabeth could not see and she would have exposed our true purpose. She had to die."

Connor cut in: "Don't you feel it when the Master is around? He is our God. He will rule the entire world very soon and we are his children. We have been chosen by him to carry out his plan. Don't you see how fortunate we all are, Chloë?"

The despair she felt in her heart was heavy, weighing down her soul. Did she even have a soul? Was she human at all? The sight of Elizabeth's destroyed and bleeding body made her sick. Her body suddenly doubled over, retching, then shaking. She had always known there was a deeper connection with Robert Best, but not like this. To know that she was bred for the sole purpose of, furthering evil on a global scale was something she could not live with. She would rather die than be forced to do anything like Patrick was capable of doing.

Brittany began to cry uncontrollably, then through her tears she spoke: "I don't want to live anymore. Not without Elizabeth. I don't care that we've been chosen. I'm not like you Connor or the rest of you. I cannot kill anyone, nor will I. This band was a beautiful dream and now it's my worst nightmare."

Chloë couldn't believe her eyes as she watched Patrick's body begin to change in front of them. His skin changed to ashen gray, dry and cracked. He was changing into some sort of beast. "Would she transform like him?" thought Chloë.

"Please, don't make me change into that." She thought of her mother who died giving birth to her, and how horrible an ordeal it must have been. She would trade it all, her music, everything, for a chance to have had a life with her birth mother and father.

Michael closed his eyes, and tried to block out the image of Elizabeth's mutilated corpse, just a few feet away. He thought of his mother, Ann, and how badly he wanted to see her and be with her back in London, away from all this chaos and bloodshed. "How did all of the good things he shared with the rest of them, turn out so badly?" He didn't want anything more to do with Vasallus or the other members of Vasallus. He just wanted to get away and leave this place. "Disappear from this nightmare for good."

Looking at Patrick transform into his beast self, Connor was indifferent. He had seen Patrick transform many times in the past. It never bothered him before this because he understood the bigger picture and accepted it. Seeing Elizabeth so cruelly murdered by Patrick was horrific and he struggled to keep strong. He needed to support Patrick, despite what he had done. The Master demanded it and he would obey. He watched as Juan transformed, like Patrick, but different. The room was beginning to fill with misery and fear. He wasn't scared, nor was he alarmed at the depth of the carnage, but he was worried about the girls and Michael. They were struggling with their identity.

Boom! Boom! The loud banging coming from the front door of the mansion echoed through the TV room, startling everyone. Brittany sobbed louder, spiraling deeper into further despair. Patrick and Juan tensed, expecting the Master to appear. *Boom. Boom.* It was not a loud knock or a fist banging on the door. "It was if someone was trying to knock it down with a sledgehammer" Connor thought. Chloë made a move to leave the room, but was immediately blocked by Juan. Her voice was a snarl as her eyes, glowing a menacing deep red, locked into Juan's: "Get out of my way Juan, before you join Elizabeth on the floor." Connor put his hand on Juan's shoulder and said: "Let her go Juan. There is nothing to fear. It is her destiny, give her time, she will come to understand. They all will."

Chloë bolted from the room, with Michael and Brittany on her heels. *Boom! Boom! Boom!* It sounded like a large tree was swinging like a pendulum against the door. Chloë would confront whatever was on the other side of that door. She would have no part of this evil pact that their group had become. She would escape from here somehow and never come back. The door was shaking on its hinges from whatever was slamming against it. It was close to collapsing open. A few feet from the door she heard a command call out from behind her, a terrifying, but familiar voice pierced her brain. She turned around to confront Patrick, ready to take a stand, but instead she was stunned and petrified by what she saw. Michael and Brittany were suspended in the air, their backs arched so severely that their heads almost touched the backs of their feet. They screamed in pain.

The Master levitated about six feet in the air, fully transformed into a creature so large it almost filled the expansive lobby of the mansion. It pulled the breath from her lungs and she struggled to breathe. The fear pulsated through her body like a blast of a thousand watts of electricity. He was a giant gargoyle, suspended in mid-air, its wings twenty or thirty feet across. His voice was monstrous, demonic, when it boomed: "Don't open that door! Open it and they will die!"

Brittany, her back arched at a grotesque angle, screamed in pain and terror. Michael was unconscious, the pain knocking him out. She had to do something to stop this! She cried out: Stop! Please! Put them down! You're killing them! Please!"

The voice of raw evil boomed again: "Move away from that door, NOWWW!!"

Boom! Boom! Boom! The thunderous sound of wood splitting, the door's hinges losing their hold, strained to keep the intruders out.

"Who is behind that door?" Chloë thought. "What is it that the Master desperately wants to keep out? If she made a move to open the door, then Brittany and Michael would die!"

The horror of her life flashed in front of her in a split second. She was surrounded by misery, anguish and death. She was caught in a vortex of circumstances she had been born into. She was in Hell. The other side of that door was something else but she knew it was a goodness she would never have. The door bulged from the blows and an intense light knifed into the room as cracks began to appear. The Master's massive bulk of horror shook with hatred at what was on the other side of that door. Chloë could never imagine so much hatred coming from one source. She dropped to her knees in surrender, held her hands high in the air, closed her eyes and prayed to a God, a righteous and beautiful God that was on full display in her mind. It felt like she was in heaven, a place she never knew existed, but now she knew there was such a place. With her arms in the air, reaching up to the skies above her, she dropped her head to the ground, continuing to pray, not realizing that she was praying out loud. Her voice, like an angel, called out to God: "Lord, have mercy. Save my soul. Don't let the wicked one before me claim it as his. I seek a love as great as You!"

The mansion shook so violently, it felt like it was ripping off of its foundation. The beast was screaming, its huge tongue thrashed in and out of its mouth. Chloë, born from the blood of the Anti-Christ, prayed for salvation from the human blood put there by the Mighty God. The swoosh from the monster's beating wings whipped up the air in the room like a landing helicopter. She looked up to see it hover directly above her. The look of pure enmity reflected back at her, communicating the knowledge that her imminent death was now only seconds away. She lifted her arms higher, as if they were trying to reach out beyond the clouds to His Kingdom. The beast swooped down toward her, its claws completely engaged to gorge her into pieces, when suddenly, the sound of a large boom echoed through the room like a nuclear explosion.

The massive lobby was engulfed with an intense light. Chloë struggled to look into the light, but the brightness was almost blinding. Somewhere in the back of her mind, she could hear the retreating beats of the giant wings of the beast. She continued to look into the light, despite the blinding brightness.

Coming through the light, she knew, had to be a miracle from God. A giant sword pierced the brilliant light, the tip of the blade poking through.

Vasallus

ABOUT THE AUTHOR

Errol Barr lives in Calgary, Alberta, Canada and is busy completing work on the final installment of the Superstars trilogy, *Songs For Survival.*
Release date for *Songs For Survival* is Fall 2013.
Feel free to contact Errol at info@errolbarr.com

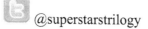 @superstarstrilogy

www.facebook.com/SuperstarsTrilogy
www.facebook.com/ErrolBarrAuthor

Blog: www.errolbarr.com

Made in the USA
Charleston, SC
24 April 2013